"A beautiful and emotionally gripping fourth novel, *Winter Kiss* is compelling and will keep readers riveted in their seats and breathing a happy sigh at the love shared between Delaney and Ginger. . . . Sizzling-hot love scenes and explosive emotions make *Winter Kiss* a must read!" —Romance Junkies

"A terrific novel!" —Romance Reviews Today

"All the *Pyr* and their mates from the previous three books in this exciting series are included in this final confrontation with Magnus and his evil Dragon's Blood Elixir. It's another stellar addition to this dynamic paranormal saga with the promise of more to come." —Fresh Fiction

Kiss of Fate

"An intense ride. Ms. Cooke has a great talent. . . . If you love paranormal romance in any way, this is a series you should be following."
—Night Owl Romance (reviewer top pick)

"Second chances are a key theme in this latest Dragonfire adventure. Cooke keeps the pace intense and the emotions raging in this powerful new read. She's top-notch, as always." —*Romantic Times*

Kiss of Fury

"This second book in Deborah Cooke's phenomenal Dragonfire series expertly sets the stage for the next thrilling episode." —Fresh Fiction

continued . . .

Kiss of Fire

"Cooke, aka bestseller Claire Delacroix, dips into the paranormal realm with her sizzling new Dragonfire series. With a self-described loner as a hero, this heroine has to adjust to her new role in the supernatural and establish bonds of trust. Efficient plotting moves the story at a brisk pace and paves the way for more exciting battles to come."
—*Romantic Times*

"Wow, what an innovative and dazzling world Ms. Cooke has built with this new Dragonfire series. Her smooth and precise writing quickly draws the reader in and has you believing it could almost be real. . . . I can't wait for the next two books."
—Fresh Fiction

"Deborah Cooke has definitely made me a fan. I am now lying in wait for the second book in this extremely exciting series."
—Romance Junkies

"Paranormal fans with a soft spot for shape shifting dragons will definitely enjoy *Kiss of Fire*, a story brimming with sexy heroes, evil villains threatening mayhem, death and world domination, ancient prophesies, and an engaging love story. . . . An intriguing mythology and various unanswered plot threads set the stage for plenty more adventure to come in future Dragonfire stories."
—BookLoons

The Dragonfire Novels

DARKFIRE KISS

A DRAGONFIRE NOVEL

DEBORAH COOKE

A SIGNET ECLIPSE BOOK

SIGNET ECLIPSE
Published by New American Library, a division of
Penguin Group (USA) Inc., 375 Hudson Street,
New York, New York 10014, USA
Penguin Group (Canada), 90 Eglinton Avenue East, Suite 700, Toronto,
Ontario M4P 2Y3, Canada (a division of Pearson Penguin Canada Inc.)
Penguin Books Ltd., 80 Strand, London WC2R 0RL, England
Penguin Ireland, 25 St. Stephen's Green, Dublin 2,
Ireland (a division of Penguin Books Ltd.)
Penguin Group (Australia), 250 Camberwell Road, Camberwell, Victoria 3124,
Australia (a division of Pearson Australia Group Pty. Ltd.)
Penguin Books India Pvt. Ltd., 11 Community Centre, Panchsheel Park,
New Delhi - 110 017, India
Penguin Group (NZ), 67 Apollo Drive, Rosedale, North Shore 0632,
New Zealand (a division of Pearson New Zealand Ltd.)
Penguin Books (South Africa) (Pty.) Ltd., 24 Sturdee Avenue,
Rosebank, Johannesburg 2196, South Africa

Penguin Books Ltd., Registered Offices:
80 Strand, London WC2R 0RL, England

First published by Signet Eclipse, an imprint of New American Library,
a division of Penguin Group (USA) Inc.

First Printing, May 2011
10 9 8 7 6 5 4 3 2 1

For all the Dragonfire fans
who wanted Rafferty to have his firestorm.
I hope you enjoy reading his story
as much as I enjoyed writing it.
Let the darkfire begin!

Prologue

The *Slayer* Chen retreated to his most secure lair. Hidden deep in the Himalayas, lost between China and Tibet, it was located in a labyrinth of switchbacks and dead ends. He disguised his scent as he descended to the deepest chamber, ensuring that no one—*Pyr*, *Slayer*, or human—could follow him.

Only there—once he had secured the perimeter of the chamber, once he was convinced he was utterly alone and knew for certain none had dared to give chase—did Chen unearth his most treasured prize.

He caught his breath at the beauty of the dark crystal, created so long ago within the earth's deepest core. It could have been an amethyst, but was so deep a purple as to be nearly black.

And deep in the stone's heart flickered a light of bluish green. It looked like a spark, an electrical spark, restless and unpredictable. Chen admired the power that had trapped the fire within the stone, so many millennia before.

Once there had been three such stones, so went the

tale. Chen didn't care. He had this one, and he had saved it for this moment.

And now, finally, it was time to set the flame free. The moment had come when he could conquer the *Pyr*, and this would ensure his triumph.

No ordinary force would break this stone.

Chen, though, was no ordinary *Slayer*. He stretched himself across the rocky floor of the chamber, remaining in darkness for days and weeks. The chill of the rocky cave permeated his body, the element of earth aiding him to calm himself and heal. The element of water gave him a connection with Gaia, granting him the ability to hear her woes. He knew an eclipse was pending; the *Pyr* would turn the energy of the eclipse to their own agenda, and the element of fire gave heat to his passion. He forgot his recent defeats and focused on the future.

Only the element of air eluded Chen's mastery, but he would conquer it yet. The finest prize was not gained readily, after all. He had waited eons, he had schemed and acted decisively, and he would do so again.

His pursuit would begin again, in this moment, in this cave.

It would start with the loosing of the spark that would so distract the *Pyr* that they would not perceive his plan until it was too late.

He exhaled, his dragonfire lighting the wicks that floated in vessels of oil, mounted upon the rocky walls of the chamber. Once his hidden chamber was flickering with the golden light of the element he knew best, he began to hum.

He sang the song of the earth. He sang a ballad to Gaia. He had heard her complaints, and he encouraged them. He lent his voice to her battle cry, urging her to greater violence than was her intent. His song gained in volume and in stridency as he coaxed her to change the surface of the world. He fed the fears within Gaia, ensuring that she thought of her own survival and not of the welfare of those who occupied her surface.

They were no better than parasites.

His would be a killing cure. Gaia would be best protected with only one resident—himself. Together, he and she would form an infinite and immortal union. The turmoil he had stirred would ensure that the *Pyr* would be busy and divided, responding to Gaia's woes.

The loosed flame would take care of the rest.

Chen turned his attention on the dark crystal two days before the eclipse. He sang to it; he chanted to it; he hummed to it. And finally, just as he began to fear that he had overlooked some critical element, the crystal cracked.

The restless spark was freed.

His lair lit with eerie blue-green light, sparks bouncing from wall to wall as the darkfire reveled in its freedom. Even Chen cowered low beneath its force. It gathered again in the middle of the cave, in midair, becoming a cluster of light so brilliant he could not look directly upon it.

And he said the word that untethered the flame from his lair. With that, the light gathered, exploded in a nova of bluish green, then disappeared. Chen felt a charge ripple through his body and into the air. He knew it slid into the water and the fire, then spread throughout Gaia. Even in the darkness, his eyes stinging, Chen could feel his body and his lair simmering.

It was done. The darkfire flame was freed. The *Pyr* would not be able to conquer it. He would be the last and the best of the Dragon Kings, and the earth would be his prize alone.

Perfect.

Thousands of miles away, in a loft in Chicago, Erik Sorensson watched the moon wax ever more full. Each night in December, he had stood on the roof of his building and stared at the moon, willing it to tell him of the future.

There would be a total lunar eclipse when this moon became full on this very night, the first total eclipse in nearly three years. Erik guessed that it would trigger a firestorm of great importance for the *Pyr* he led and for their mission. It would also be the first of three total lunar eclipses in succession, occurring at roughly six-month intervals.

The next calendar year, Erik knew in his heart, would have tremendous import for the *Pyr*.

But he felt only dread. The future, wreathed in shadows and obscured, was a mystery to him, even with his foresight. Erik couldn't change that, but he didn't have to like it.

He was standing on that roof when he felt a dark shock race through his body, one that left him shaken and disoriented. It was gone as soon as it had struck.

Erik didn't recognize it, much less understand its intent or its significance. What was even more troubling was that after that initial shock, he couldn't sense it anymore.

Had he imagined it? Or dreamed it? Was it real, or a portent of the future?

Or was he losing his grip on the realm of the *Pyr*?

*   *   *

In a bunker on the coast of the Caspian Sea, the *Slayer* Jorge was vexed.

His had been a perfect plan. He still believed himself to be the ideal candidate to lead the *Slayers* in the absence of Magnus. He had been certain he had planned for every eventuality, even stealing a store of Dragon's Blood Elixir to sustain himself. Mouthful by mouthful, syringe by syringe, Jorge had slowly and steadily filled a vial of Elixir for his own use.

He hadn't counted on his injuries.

He hadn't counted on Magnus surviving—that old serpent.

After Delaney's firestorm, Jorge's leg had been a ruin. He'd had to retreat, regroup, recover. He had needed Mallory and Balthasar then; he had needed them as his own bodyguards while he had the reconstructive surgery on his leg in a private clinic in Moscow.

He had let Balthasar have the surgeon as his reward.

Mallory, of course, had wanted another sip of the Elixir in exchange for his services. Jorge had grudgingly shared.

Then Balthasar had abandoned him, without a word of explanation, simply disappearing in the night. That had been August. Jorge might have pursued him, fully certain of who had summoned the other *Slayer*, but he'd been tricked instead. Even Mallory had been no help, having settled into the deep slow sleep that enabled *Pyr* to live for centuries with little sign of aging.

Jorge blamed them for Chen's subsequent success.

Chen, a *Slayer* Jorge vaguely recalled from Magnus's lair in Ohio, had appeared the morning after Balthasar's departure. Chen had looked haggard and told the tale of Niall's firestorm in breathless terms. He had begged for sanctuary so pitifully that Jorge let him into his own refuge.

It had been precisely what Chen had wanted. It turned out that Chen wasn't what he appeared—he was ancient, deceitful, and vicious. He had not only deceived Jorge; he had not only stolen Jorge's stash of the last of the Elixir; but he had consumed it before Jorge's eyes.

Then Chen had sealed Jorge inside his own refuge. His song was intricate and ancient; primal and powerful. Chen had departed, the Elixir in his gut, and Jorge had been trapped inside a dragonsmoke barrier, the like of which he'd never seen. It didn't simply resonate—it tinkled like thousands of little bells. And he could see it, as thick and impenetrable as the densest fog.

A wall of ice.

But this dragonsmoke burned like a corrosive acid, ten times worse than regular dragonsmoke. Jorge had thrown himself at the dragonsmoke barrier, worn it down, forced himself to take the abuse of gradually destroying it. Each time, he had to retreat to let the burns recover. Each time, the Elixir still in his body was less potent, more dilute, and the healing took longer.

It was an infuriating process. He called in old-speak to the surviving *Slayers* in the world, but they weren't interested in helping him. Not when he had nothing with which to reward them. Even Mallory continued to hibernate. Jorge had been on his own.

And so it was that he was finally down to the last increment, a thin wisp of a barrier that Jorge knew he could destroy in one last intense volley. The problem was that the Elixir was virtually gone from his body. He wasn't certain he'd survive one more assault on the smoke.

So close and yet so far.

Hatred of his kind, both *Pyr* and *Slayer*, rose within him. He felt the pending eclipse, and the dragon within him roared with a lust for vengeance.

His gaze turned to the dozing Mallory. Jorge hated that he was saddled with such an ineffective, slothful, and passive partner. When he broke free—and Jorge would—Mallory would also be freed, at no cost to himself.

It was wrong.

If only Jorge had more Elixir.

Just one more sip would do it.

Jorge's eyes narrowed as he realized there was yet one dose of Elixir within his refuge. He considered Mallory, his thoughts flying. Mallory had drunk the Elixir several times. It ran through his veins, limned his bones, slid into his muscles. It would be dilute. Its power would be fading.

Which simply meant that Jorge would need every single drop.

Jorge regretted there might be a mess.

Then he sprang on his unsuspecting prey.

Unbeknownst to Chen or Erik or Jorge, thousands of miles from any of them, the waxing moon influenced another change. Deep in his hidden lair, almost forgotten by his own kind, the Sleeper stirred.

Chapter 1

E thics were so inconvenient.

Melissa Smith had worked with many people who either had no ethics or could easily ignore them. She'd never been that way, even in pursuit of a story.

No matter how much was at stake.

She parked her car on the street, not too close to the house she'd driven past a hundred times, and took a deep breath. It didn't help. She was still freaked out. She closed her eyes and saw the wreckage of Daphne's body, as vividly as if she were still standing in the morgue.

She wondered whether it was time for a change. In a real sense, her principles were all she had left. Melissa had lost her husband, her house, her dream job, her health, and her future. Her confidence had taken a pretty big hit, too. All she had left was the chance of restarting her career, in the hope of bringing truth to light. A legacy of truth was the only thing she could hope to build.

And maybe those ethics were the only thing standing in her way.

Did she want justice for Daphne enough to bend her own rules?

Daphne, Melissa knew, would have told her to make her own luck.

Melissa frowned, unhappy with the available options. She pulled out the note from Daphne one more time. It was terse, just as Daphne had always been, and just reading it made her feel her obligation to the girl.

It was her fault. . . .

The note had come two days before, in the mail as if it were no more important than a credit card bill. Enclosed with the note had been a key—a numbered key, likely to a storage locker.

Melissa had spent the whole day trying to guess where that storage locker might be. She hadn't really believed that Daphne was dead. The girl was a consummate liar, albeit one with a good heart. She'd had to deceive to survive on the streets of Baghdad, which was where Melissa had first met the engaging, pretty, opportunistic girl. Daphne had had a charm about her, and she'd been reliable in unexpected moments.

Melissa had lost track of Daphne when she'd returned stateside again. She'd thought of the beggar girl often, worrying about her when she should have been worrying about herself.

No one had been more surprised than Melissa to encounter Daphne again three years later in the most unlikely of places—right in DC, dressed to the nines and on the arm of an affluent older man.

Magnus Montmorency.

It couldn't have been a coincidence; Melissa had

known that immediately. Montmorency had been the rumored power behind illicit arms deals in Baghdad—every trail led to his vicinity and stopped cold. Melissa had wanted to get that story more than anything. She had wanted to reveal Montmorency for the villain he was, but she'd run out of time.

In more ways than one.

Still, she would have known him anywhere. Seeing Daphne with Montmorency hadn't reassured Melissa at all. She didn't like that Daphne had become his mistress; that she had used Montmorency as her ticket to the future.

And it really didn't help that Melissa had once asked Daphne in Baghdad to find out more about Montmorency's connections. That had been before she'd realized how brutal he was.

She had a responsibility. . . .

The sight of Daphne's body flicked through her thoughts again, as if the dead girl would taunt Melissa with her obligation. Montmorency must have killed Daphne. Melissa suspected as much but couldn't prove a thing. It was the past all over again—the trail led to Montmorency's vicinity and stopped cold.

But Daphne had provided the inside intelligence Melissa needed. If she had the guts to use it. She eyed the letter and tried to summon her resolve.

Melissa had done her homework, checking all the angles before she leapt into trouble. She'd always been thorough, instead of running with half a story. She'd gone to the morgue first, halfway suspecting that Daphne had been putting her on. No one could have been more astonished than Melissa when she found Daphne there, labeled as a Jane Doe. Not just dead. Fried. Only half of her face had remained intact enough to identify her remains.

Melissa would never forget that sight.

She'd then hunted down the lock that fit the numbered key, working her way through train stations and airports. She'd found the match at Washington Dulles. There'd been a duffel bag in it, one filled with Daphne's apparent necessities. It confirmed that Daphne had been poised to run; that she'd known she was taking a big risk. She hadn't lied about that.

The stuffed puppy Melissa had first given Daphne in Baghdad was in the bag, now well loved. The sight nearly stopped Melissa's heart.

Deeper in the bag, she found Daphne's diary.

It was a riveting read. The girl was a good reporter, thorough and detailed. If she'd survived, though, her story would have created questions. She was, after all, a beggar girl saved from the streets by Montmorency— her word against his wouldn't stand a chance.

But in her diary, Daphne had documented where correlating evidence could be found against Montmorency.

It was in a small blue leather-bound book, one that was always in a certain place in the top right drawer of a desk in Montmorency's fortified DC residence. Everything—*everything*—was documented there, according to Daphne.

It was the evidence Melissa needed.

The evidence she had wanted all those years ago.

She just had to break into the house to get it.

It wouldn't be hard—Daphne had also provided the security codes to the house.

Melissa hesitated. It was a crime to break and enter. It was wrong. Even though Montmorency was suspected of being an arms dealer, even though he made sure nothing ever stuck to him and nothing could be traced to him, even though bringing him to justice would tip the balance in favor of good guys everywhere and would fulfill a personal goal of Melissa's, it was still wrong to break into his home.

Dangerous, too.

Melissa swallowed and considered the house. She could almost hear Daphne calling her bluff. That girl would never have worried about a comparatively minor infraction, especially one in the pursuit of a greater good.

She'd taught Daphne to record the evidence, follow a trail, and build a story. Maybe Daphne was teaching her to take a chance.

What, really, did she have left to lose?

Headlights swept over Melissa's car, and she instinctively hunched down in the seat. A large black armored Mercedes sedan pulled out of Montmorency's driveway, the engine gunning as it headed downtown. Where was it going at this hour?

Melissa checked her watch. Ten past midnight.

Maybe the car was going to pick up Montmorency. The windows were tinted dark, so Melissa could see only the silhouette of a driver when it passed. She was sure its departure was a sign, if not an invitation. If the house was empty, this was her chance. Who knew how soon the car would return?

Daphne deserved justice. . . .

Melissa knew a person couldn't always count on getting a second chance. She wouldn't damage anything. She wouldn't take much, just that little blue book from Montmorency's desk. It wouldn't take five minutes.

It would be easy.

It was a moral infraction that wouldn't matter in the greater scheme of things.

Melissa didn't believe that for a minute, but she got out of her car anyway. It was snowing lightly, the snow melting on contact with the pavement. There would be no mark of her footsteps—another sign.

She pulled on her leather gloves and turned up her collar. She wrapped her scarf across her face as if she were cold, even though she was perspiring in her anxiety. After all, she wasn't in the habit of breaking the law. She reminded herself of the power of the greater good. She reminded herself of her debt to a little beggar girl who deserved justice.

Then Melissa marched across the street toward Montmorency's house, as if she had every right to be there.

In a way, she did.

Daphne would have insisted as much.

Rafferty was once again stymied in his efforts to spontaneously manifest elsewhere.

His archenemy, Magnus, could perform this feat, one traditionally claimed by the Wyvern alone, which rankled. Rafferty had managed it twice, and it would have been useful on this night. He stood outside Magnus's securely barricaded home and considered his options. There were few. Although he suspected that Magnus was home, the alarms would still be armed. Magnus would not take chances with his security. Spontaneous manifestation inside the house was the only choice that would have ensured that Rafferty didn't trip any alarms.

But he couldn't do it. No matter how hard he tried, he remained lodged in the shadows of the garden.

He began to wonder why he had been unable to master the skill beyond those two instances. During his successful attempts he had wished to be in Magnus's presence, just as he did now.

But both of those times, Magnus had wanted something of Rafferty. On this night, however, Magnus would not welcome Rafferty's company.

Rafferty wondered whether he had truly moved on those occasions—or whether Magnus had summoned him. It was Magnus who had drunk the Elixir, and it seemed that only those who had consumed the Elixir could assume the Wyvern's powers.

Could he do this? Doubt gnawed at Rafferty, even as he tried again.

Rafferty's pursuit of Magnus had led the *Pyr* through dark passages and hollows, deep into the earth and under the ocean. That the old *Slayer* was wounded hadn't slowed his passage that much, apparently. That Magnus had the ability to disguise his scent, at least at intervals, meant that Rafferty had taken many wrong turns. Magnus's talent for disappearing and appearing elsewhere at will only made pursuit more challenging.

The trail ended at the most obvious location of all—Magnus's lair in Washington, DC.

Rafferty hadn't expected his enemy to be so brazen. Maybe he should have known better. Maybe it was a trap. Either way, Rafferty was tired of the unfinished business that lingered between the two of them. He and Magnus had exchanged challenge coins, which meant a fight to the death—until one was dead, the duel continued. Rafferty had thought Magnus dead several times.

This time he would be certain.

He'd guessed that Magnus had restored his own strength

from Niall's firestorm—with Chen's assistance and maybe a last hidden increment of the Dragon's Blood Elixir. He'd wanted to corner his old foe before the lunar eclipse that would occur in the wee hours of the morning, but he hadn't been sure of Magnus's location until this day.

Rafferty would have bet Magnus had planned it that way.

It hadn't helped that Rafferty had been distracted by the chaos in the earth. It hadn't helped that he'd felt compelled to halt his hunt and sing to Gaia, to calm her and try to soothe her. Recent months had seen earthquakes, tsunamis, and mud slides mar the surface of the planet. There had been blizzards, droughts, monsoons, and tornadoes. The weather had gone wild, and humans were suffering on every continent. Rafferty had tried to help, but he grew exhausted from his efforts.

He was beginning to think that it wasn't just Gaia under duress, but that she had been incited to violence by someone else.

Was it Magnus? The old *Slayer* could sing the songs of the earth, as well. Rafferty wouldn't have believed Magnus to be so strong, but his old adversary had secrets Rafferty hadn't begun to guess.

Rafferty had only one, one that had been hidden from Magnus with complete success. Each passing day made Rafferty fear that truth would be revealed and all would be lost.

It was time to finish their blood challenge, to see Magnus dead. Rafferty didn't have the gift of foresight, but he had a bad feeling about the chaotic changes in the earth. Could that awaken the Sleeper? He feared what Magnus would do if he ever learned of the existence of the hidden one.

Rafferty had come to Magnus's lair, determined to do the deed before the eclipse. He was lurking in the shadows of the garden as Balthasar left the house to start the car.

The big sedan departed, which meant that at least one of Magnus's staff was gone—probably two. Was Jorge here? Mallory? No one had sensed their presences since Delaney's firestorm, almost two years ago. Rafferty didn't like when *Slayers* were quiet—it usually meant they were scheming something.

Maybe they were terrorized by Chen.

Or controlled by him. That *Slayer* was a new variable, one impossible to predict or pursue. He was older and stronger than any had guessed, and he had drunk the Elixir. Rafferty inhaled deeply but couldn't sense any of his kind. He wasn't fooled.

Magnus's lair was in a quiet neighborhood, one with large houses and discreet entrances, beautiful landscaping, and high-tech security systems. Rafferty could see the stars overhead and smell a storm coming off the ocean. Snow. It was beginning to fall already in soft white flakes.

He felt something else, too, something nameless that resonated deep in his marrow. Was he becoming more sensitive to the eclipses as he grew older? Or was it the influence of the Dragon's Tail, the cycle of karmic retribution and the last chance for the *Pyr* to defeat the *Slayers*? Rafferty wasn't sure, but he felt tingly and agitated in a way that wasn't characteristic of him. He was the temperate member of the *Pyr*, but in this moment, he felt audacious. Impulsive.

Edgy.

Maybe that was a trick of Magnus, intended to set

him off guard—or to compel him to make a mistake. Rafferty gritted his teeth and fought the quiver deep inside himself. He would be as resolute and controlled as ever.

The house was dark, its windows gleaming squares of impenetrable darkness. Rafferty smelled malice, but he couldn't hear a dragonsmoke perimeter mark.

It made sense that Magnus would abandon that tradition, since he could cross it himself. Also, the resonance of a dragonsmoke ring might draw the attention of the *Pyr*.

Attention Magnus wouldn't want.

No, he wanted everyone to believe he wasn't at home. The absence of a dragonsmoke ring implied the house was unoccupied.

Rafferty wasn't persuaded. He couldn't sense or smell anything that told him Magnus was in the house, but he believed he was with every fiber of his being. Tonight was the night.

Rafferty turned the black and white ring on his finger one last time. This would be a fight to the death, and he wouldn't necessarily be victorious. Right didn't always prevail, unfortunately. Rafferty prepared himself for the possibility of his own death, then stepped out of the shadows of the cedar hedge.

He saw the woman then, and the sight of her stopped him cold.

Rafferty stared, but she was no illusion. She marched up the driveway, with all the force of a hurricane hurtling toward the shore. She was slender and tall, her skirt swinging as she moved, her features hidden by her scarf. Her hair was short but as dark as a raven's wing.

Ebony curls.

Her skin was golden, the hue of buckwheat honey. She had terrific legs, lean and muscled, and she walked with a purposeful femininity. Rafferty was snared by the sight of her, by the fluid way she moved. She could have been dancing.

And her perfume, so feminine, so faint, enthralled him with one whiff. His body responded to her presence with such enthusiasm that he was startled, startled enough to ease back into the shadows.

Lust at one sight? That wasn't like him. Was it the influence of the moon? He didn't know; he only felt himself harden as he watched the sweet sway of her hips.

And wanted.

How long had it been?

He forced himself to think rationally. Could Magnus have a guest? At this hour? Was she a mistress? She didn't appear to be Magnus's type—he favored flashy women, whereas this one was dressed simply in dark colors. She was older than the usual jailbait Magnus chose, as well.

A woman, not a girl.

And that perfume. Not sweet so much as seductive. Musk instead of honeysuckle. It was the perfume of a woman who knew her powers, knew her allure, and wasn't afraid of either. Confident and potent. Forthright.

Rafferty's mouth went dry. He was intrigued when she went directly to the back door. Was she visiting someone else in the house? Presumably Magnus had staff.

It couldn't be a coincidence that she came right after the big sedan's departure. Not at this hour.

Rafferty eased closer to watch her. He narrowed his eyes, his *Pyr* vision enabling him to see the silhouette

of her gloved hand. She raised her fingers to the pad
of the security system, the leather pulling to reveal an
increment of skin. Rafferty could see the bone of her
wrist, fine and delicate. He was certain it would be soft,
scented with that intriguing perfume.

When had a glimpse of a woman's skin aroused
him so?

She didn't knock or ring the bell. Instead, she cast
a furtive glance over her shoulder, then punched a se-
quence of codes into the security system. Though she
had the codes, her every gesture revealed her conviction
that she wouldn't be welcome.

Not staff, then.

Not a mistress.

But she had the codes right. The door opened, revealing a slice of deeper darkness. Rafferty was sure he saw
her hesitate for a moment before she slipped into the
shadows of the house.

Then he was horrified. He couldn't begin to imagine
how Magnus would treat an intruder in his lair.

Well, he *could* imagine—that was the problem.

The woman was either incredibly brave or stupid. Either way, she was a human who would shortly be in need
of his protection.

Rafferty was across the property in a heartbeat, refusing to think further than that. He moved quickly
enough to catch the lip of the closing door with his fingertips. That lingering perfume taunted him, teased him,
beckoned to him.

And he followed the woman into the house, wondering all the while at her audacity.

Instead of thinking about Magnus, Rafferty Powell

wanted to see the face of the woman who dared to take such a chance.

No, he wanted more than that.

Melissa had done it.

Well, she'd done the first part. She was in Montmorency's house.

Her heart was thumping so loudly, she was sure someone would hear it. The house was so quiet, so still, so dark. She had to stop for a minute, only eight or ten steps into the back hall, to let her eyes adjust. It felt as if it took an eternity.

Sweat slid down her back during those precious seconds.

She thought she heard a step behind her, but when she glanced back, there was nothing but more darkness. Could she hear someone breathing? Could she feel someone watching her?

Or was she imagining problems that didn't exist?

She forced herself to recall Daphne's description of the house and peered into the shadows. If this opening to the left was the main corridor, then Montmorency's office would be the first door on the right.

What kind of person wouldn't leave on a single light at night? It was so dark in the house that Melissa felt she was being swallowed alive. It was weird and a bit creepy. There should have been appliances with lit displays, at least. Not a lot of light but *some*.

Instead, the house was as devoid of light as a black hole. Melissa could feel the hair standing up on the back of her neck.

She couldn't sense the ceiling and guessed that it was

high. A grand interior, then. Well, Montmorency could afford it, if he was doing the business she knew he was. Crime paid well. She wouldn't consider that she might benefit financially from this theft.

No. She reminded her conscience that her choice was about Daphne and justice and the greater good. Melissa stepped with care, ensuring that she didn't make a sound.

It was hard to shake the sense that she was being watched.

Maybe just by her moral code. Were there motion detectors? Daphne had insisted that the computerized door locks were the only security. Trapped in the house's shadows, Melissa began to doubt that assertion.

Was it really plausible that a man like Montmorency, a man in his high-risk business, had such a simple security system?

Was Daphne lying? Why would she? Doubts assailed Melissa, but it was too late to turn back. She kept going. The crime was done: she might as well try to get the book.

Melissa turned the corner and guessed that she was leaving the servants' quarters for the main house. The flooring changed, becoming wood instead of practical tile. She could hear the trickle of water ahead, and it relieved her to hear something that could orient her. She recalled Daphne's description in the diary of the fountain in the foyer.

She was on the right track, then. Another step and an open doorway loomed on her right, a rectangle of obsidian that arched high overhead. What high doorways Montmorency had. Why? Maybe his ego required that much space.

Cold air seemed to emanate from the room, and there was an earthy smell that made her shiver in revulsion.

There was her conscience again.

Melissa eased into the room and pulled the flashlight from her pocket. Daphne had said the office had no windows and that it was secure in the middle of the house. If she was in the office and she was alone, no one would see Melissa's light.

She hesitated, her thumb on the button. What if she was wrong?

She took another step, put out her hand, found the corner of a piece of furniture. Her fingers quickly discovered it was a desk.

Ha. She wasn't wrong.

Relief flooded through her, and she turned on the flashlight. She had a moment to note the midcentury teak furnishings that Daphne had described before a man whispered behind her.

"Bad choice," he said.

Melissa spun in terror. She almost dropped the flashlight, and certainly it wavered in her grip.

A man stood behind her, a man unlike any man she'd ever seen before. He was tall and broad, his leather jacket doing nothing to hide his muscular build. He looked powerful—powerful enough to snap her in half, if he so chose.

Instead, he waited for her explanation. His hair was long and wavy, the kind of hair she'd love to have, a dark chestnut color filled with red glints. He wore a black and white ring that looked to be made of glass, a ring she saw when he folded his arms across his chest.

It was his eyes, though, that captivated her. They were dark, as dark as bittersweet chocolate, and filled with a

knowingness that shook her to her toes. They shone with
wisdom and disappointment, and she knew he could be
a hard judge. She had the sense that he could see right
to her heart, that he knew everything she had done and
said, everything that had brought her to this place, every
secret she'd ever ferreted away.

And he didn't approve of her choice.

It was her conscience live and in person.

But in the guise of a sexy stranger.

A *very* sexy stranger.

But who was he? Did he work for Montmorency?

Thinking fast, Melissa swallowed and struggled to
come up with a good explanation for her presence. It
was pretty much impossible, given that she was lost in
this man's incredible eyes. She opened her mouth and
closed it again, more inarticulate than she would have
believed possible. He waited, patient and motionless,
and she felt herself start to blush.

"Very bad choice," another man said, his voice not
as low as that of Mr. Conscience. He had a European
accent. Although Melissa couldn't place its origin, she
recognized that voice.

As Mr. Conscience spun, Melissa cast the light of
the flashlight over his shoulder. The light glinted on the
smile of Magnus Montmorency, who stood in the doorway of his office.

Holding a gun.

The barrel was pointed directly at Melissa's heart.

Okay, so the plan hadn't worked out as well as she'd
hoped.

Melissa didn't have time to come up with a new strategy, not before the guy with the great eyes began to
shimmer blue around his perimeter. It had to be an illu-

sion, a trick of the darkness. People didn't shimmer. But by the time she'd blinked and looked again, something even stranger had happened.

There were two dragons in the light of her flashlight, and the two men were gone. Montmorency's gun fell to the floor with a clatter as Melissa gaped at the dragons.

What had happened to Mr. Conscience and Montmorency?

And where had the dragons come from? She would have noticed them, no matter where they'd been hiding. They were huge.

She thought about that blue shimmer and wondered. Impossible.

The dragons roared at each other and started to fight.

The light of her flashlight shone on the gun on the hardwood floor. The gun was reassuringly real and lethal, something she understood.

The sight of it gave Melissa her new plan.

How could a thief look so innocent?

Maybe that was how she got away with her crimes.

All the same, Rafferty felt something melt inside him when he confronted the woman who had illegally entered Magnus's home. Her skin was a rich gold, maybe indicative of a mixed racial background.

Rafferty was entranced by her eyes. They were marvelous—thickly lashed and exotic, tipped up at the outer corners. They were a vivid shade of green.

Her lips were full and luscious, tempting him to touch them with a fingertip, to see if they were really as silky soft as they appeared. The yearning that had been nudging at him redoubled in her presence, reminding him how long he had fought alone. When she caught her breath and retreated, the end of her scarf fell at the move, revealing the sleek golden length of her neck.

Rafferty took a step closer, beguiled by that perfume, enchanted by the sight of her, wanting as he had never wanted. Something primal in him roared, demanding satisfaction, and he thought he saw an answering desire in the woman's magnificent eyes.

Her blush made him forget himself completely. It had seemed so out of character for a bold thief to blush, and he'd been transfixed by the slow spread of rosiness. He'd been so awed by her beauty that he hadn't been listening as keenly as he should have for Magnus.

And Magnus *was* home.

Rafferty pivoted to face his old foe, shifting shape in a heartbeat. He forgot about defending the woman from the sight of his transformation, more intent upon protecting her. Magnus was ahead of him, already having changed to a jade and gold dragon. His gun fell to the floor just as Magnus breathed fire at Rafferty.

Rafferty was astonished to see how Magnus had healed since their last encounter, and he wondered again whether the old *Slayer* had a hidden stash of Dragon's Blood Elixir. Or had he learned some new secret from Chen? There was no doubt that the *Slayer* was in fine form once again.

But he was as vicious as ever. Magnus was immediately on the offensive, slashing toward Rafferty with one claw and catching him across the jaw just before he completed his shift. Rafferty stumbled backward at the sting of the blow, then leapt at Magnus. Magnus retreated to the foyer, Rafferty bounding after him, and the pair locked claws to grapple for supremacy.

Did the woman work for Magnus?

Had she been sent to distract Rafferty on purpose?

Or was she being manipulated by Magnus, as well? Rafferty had no time to think about it. Thief or pawn, she wasn't a woman he should trust.

Much less one he should want.

The old *Slayer* was strong, stronger than he had been. He bent Rafferty's talons back and exhaled a stinging torrent of dragonfire. His eyes glittered dangerously, and Rafferty wondered what new tricks his enemy had learned.

"Always good to see you again," Magnus murmured in old-speak. *"Although I would have expected you to knock."*

"The door was open," Rafferty replied in kind.

Magnus laughed. *"You thought the house was empty."*

"I chose to accept your lure." Rafferty smiled with confidence, letting Magnus think he might not be alone.

Magnus moved like lightning to strike Rafferty again, sending the *Pyr* into one wall. That wall vibrated hard, but Rafferty barely felt the blow. He leapt after Magnus, locking his talons around his throat. Magnus shook free, the pair exchanging blow after blow as they moved down the corridor.

"You didn't know," Magnus scoffed. *"You couldn't sense me."*

"No," Rafferty insisted, *"but I know you. I can anticipate you."* He proved it by ducking a blow, feinting, and driving his head up hard beneath Magnus's ribs.

Magnus hissed in pain, then kicked Rafferty. *"So, you stepped willingly into the trap. How . . . valiant."* Magnus emitted another mocking laugh, one that was cut short.

Rafferty had quickly locked his tail around Magnus's tail. He entwined their two tails, holding Magnus captive, then tugged hard. Magnus lost his balance and stumbled closer, just as Rafferty slashed at the *Slayer*'s gut with one back claw. Rafferty's golden talons cut deep, leaving four parallel wounds across Magnus's gut—cuts that oozed black blood. The blood pooled on the floor, gleaming and slick. Rafferty slammed Magnus into the wall, and the entire house shook.

Where was the woman?

Rafferty strained his ears, trying to hear some sound that would indicate her presence. Nothing. He didn't dare to glance away from Magnus to look for her.

If she'd chosen to run, she wouldn't get far.

What if she was on Magnus's side? What if she was preparing a trap? He struggled to hear some hint of her presence, alarmed when he could detect none.

At the same time, he held fast to Magnus.

He squeezed, letting his talons dig into the old *Slayer*'s hide. Magnus cried out in pain and struggled for release. Rafferty held him, loosing dragonfire on his enemy.

An elegant runner, rich with pattern, ran the length of the hall floor, and Rafferty regretted when the carpet ignited. It had been stained, probably irreparably, with the *Slayer*'s blood, anyway. It burned quickly, and the light of the hungry flames danced high, illuminating the pale walls with orange.

Rafferty spared a glance toward Magnus's office, but there was no sign of the woman.

The gun was gone, too. Interesting. Had she taken anything else? He suspected then that she wasn't in league with Magnus at all.

Maybe this thief was smarter than he'd thought.

Magnus twisted in Rafferty's grip, appearing to be more injured than Rafferty expected. He coughed and writhed, then moaned feebly. Rafferty held fast, declining to be fooled by this old serpent. He thrashed his opponent, then aimed his dragonfire at the scarred skin where Magnus was missing a scale.

He would finish this now.

Magnus cried out in pain, arched his back, then froze.

He began to breathe slowly and deeply, his eyes narrowed to shining slits of malice. Rafferty had a moment to feel dread before Magnus's dragonsmoke unfurled.

Chapter 2

Rafferty saw the tongue of dragonsmoke winding toward him before he felt it. He knew the silvery ribbon of smoke would make a conduit if it touched him, allowing Magnus to steal his strength.

The dragonsmoke coiled, beginning to spiral around Rafferty. He had the sudden thought that it would strangle him, catch him around the throat, and milk him dry. He decked Magnus one last time and backed away, his blow making no difference to Magnus's breathing.

In fact, the old *Slayer*'s eyes glinted brighter, shining like jewels even as his blood pooled on the floor and his carpet burned. The fire burned high, surrounding the old *Slayer* and illuminating his jade scales.

His dragonsmoke wound ever closer.

Rafferty struggled to evade it, even as Magnus breathed a longer and longer tendril of unbroken dragonsmoke. Rafferty ducked and weaved, aiming dragonfire at Magnus all the while, but the old *Slayer* had focus. He never broke that stream of dragonsmoke; ultimately, Rafferty had to retreat to escape its touch.

He backed down the hallway, the silvery dragon-smoke still targeting him. It wound through the air toward him, relentless in its quest. Rafferty backed away as quickly as he could, but the dragonsmoke kept pace.

He saw that Magnus had straightened and that he was holding his injured gut with one claw while bracing himself against the wall. He continued to breathe slowly and deeply. He was grinning, well aware of Rafferty's predicament, but his pleasure in his deed didn't interfere with his performance.

The tendril was impressive in its length. It was thick and robust, too.

"Why don't you come closer?" Magnus taunted in old-speak. *"Why don't we just end it now?"* His smile broadened. *"Or are you hoping to negotiate for a sip of the Elixir?"*

He flicked his tongue then, catching the last tendril of dragonsmoke. His eyes brightened as he deftly wove that last end together with the one he had started to breathe, breaching the interruption with startling ease.

Rafferty kept backing away. *"The source is destroyed. If you have any left, and I doubt you do, you'll never share it."*

"Then maybe you want an old secret or two."

"You have no secrets I wish to know."

"How can you be sure? Kill me and so much knowledge will be lost forever."

"We'll be well rid of it."

Magnus laughed in disbelief, breathing smoke all the while. The smoke came after Rafferty, shimmering in the light of the fire, but moving with steady determination. Magnus breathed with more power, and Rafferty wished he had the *Slayer's* ability to cut smoke.

Without it, he had to retreat into the servants' corridor, shifting back to human form to fit into the working spaces. There was no sign of the thief anywhere. He suspected she was smart enough to have fled the house. He could see Magnus in the foyer, his dragon form silhouetted by the flames that consumed his carpet. He was so fixated on breathing dragonsmoke that he didn't seem to care about any damage to himself from the fire.

Rafferty hastened for the back door, the smoke right behind him. It wound through the air, at shoulder level, relentless and persistent. As soon as Rafferty stepped out of the house, the smoke halted, much to his surprise. It was as if Magnus had wanted only to drive them apart.

To give himself time to recover.

That meant this was Rafferty's chance to finish their duel to the death. Magnus was weaker than he'd believed.

Rafferty made to step back into the house, but the dragonsmoke had spun itself into a wall of glittering white. It was impenetrable, like a barricade of ice, one that would burn him if he touched it. It defended Magnus better than his security system, blocking Rafferty's access completely.

"The disadvantage of a long acquaintanceship such as ours," Magnus said in melodic old-speak, his words sliding into Rafferty's thoughts, *"is that we each can anticipate the other."*

Rafferty felt frustration that Magnus knew he couldn't cut the smoke. *"This isn't over. We exchanged challenge coins. . . ."*

"Of course it's not over. But you're concerned for the human. As always." Magnus sighed with forbearance.

That Magnus believed humans to be disposable was

key to his perspective as a *Slayer*, but that didn't mean Rafferty didn't find it annoying. *"It is our mission as* Pyr *to defend the treasure of the earth, including humans. . . ."*

"Yes, yes. But you and I define treasure *rather differently."* Magnus paused, and Rafferty heard laughter in his tone when he continued. *"I wonder which of us will find her first."*

Rafferty heard a car engine start. It sounded as if it were down the street. He could have guessed whose car it was, especially when the tires squealed in the driver's haste to get away.

Magnus chuckled darkly, as if in anticipation of a tasty meal.

The woman's perfume teased Rafferty's nostrils, kindling that very male awareness of her. Rafferty knew she was a fool if she imagined she could break into Magnus's home wearing that scent and get away with it. The *Slayer* would be able to track her anywhere.

Rafferty knew he'd need to do that first.

Just as Magnus anticipated.

Maybe the woman didn't know Magnus's truth. Maybe she didn't realize how keen his senses were.

Why hadn't she been driven mad by the sight of them both shifting shape in unison? It was a puzzle he had no time to solve.

Because Rafferty felt the first tingle of the pending eclipse. In that moment, he knew he had lost this opportunity to finish Magnus. The next time he met Magnus, the *Slayer* would be stronger.

All the same, he had to find the woman first.

Magnus laughed when Rafferty turned away— evidence that he had come to the same conclusion. Maybe the spark of a new firestorm would draw the

Slayer from his smoke-defended lair. Rafferty could only hope. He strode into the garden, deaf for once to Gaia's complaints, and shifted shape. He was just about to take flight when Magnus shouted.

"My book!" Magnus's fury was clear. "The bitch has taken my book! *Find her!*"

This last utterance was broadcast in old-speak, a command from Magnus to his minions, whoever they were and wherever they might be. Rafferty felt a stab of fear for the woman's safety.

The thief's safety.

The thief whose crime he had enabled by fighting Magnus. She had probably entered the house with the intent of stealing from Magnus, and he had facilitated her crime by keeping Magnus busy while she got away.

And now, Magnus and his *Slayers* would hunt her.

Rafferty bounded into the sky. He quickly soared high and turned slowly over the neighborhood.

It was easy to spot the woman's car—an older model moving too quickly out of the quiet neighborhood. It was the only car on the roads in the area, and the driver was in a hurry. It also emanated the scent of that perfume. Rafferty followed it, scanning the roads for a big black sedan.

Magnus's Benz had to be somewhere, coming closer. In a trio of heartbeats, he spied the car.

Rafferty had been right. He raced toward the woman's car, hoping he could reach her before Balthasar did.

Dragons!

Who would have believed it?

Melissa wasn't sure she *did* believe it. Maybe she had imagined the dragons she thought she had seen. She certainly hadn't seen the men shift shape, even though it

was the logical conclusion. Where else could the dragons have come from? And where could Mr. Conscience
and Montmorency have disappeared, as quickly as that?

Melissa didn't know. She reviewed the facts as she
drove. She hadn't imagined the fire, because she could
smell the smoke on her coat. And she wasn't imagining
the blue leather-bound book on the seat beside her. She
touched it again with her fingertips. It was real and she
had it in her possession.

Daphne had been right about that. She hoped
Daphne had also been right about the book's contents.

Melissa wasn't imagining the gun that she'd dropped
on the floor in front of the passenger seat, either. It
gleamed in the darkness there, looking evil. She hated
guns. Why on earth had she taken the gun? And what
was she going to do with it now? It was probably stolen
or linked to some other crime.

She wished she'd taken her camera into Montmorency's house. She would have had evidence then, evidence
she could review later, as to what she had actually seen.

Dragons? Probably not.

But what if there were? That would be a story!

Melissa was driving erratically, her palms damp and
her hands shaking on the wheel. So much for being a
smooth intruder, getting in and getting out without a
hair of bother. James Bond she was not.

She was okay with that. She never needed to break
the rules again.

Because she had the book. When she got home and
had a good look at it, she'd figure out how best to proceed. She hoped that Daphne hadn't been lying about
its contents and that it really did include the evidence
needed to condemn Montmorency.

She hoped she hadn't taken a stupid chance for nothing.

Melissa checked the rearview mirror again, not in the slightest bit reassured that no one was following her. It was hard to believe she could have gotten away with this.

Of course, if she had, it had been because of Mr. Conscience. She recalled his dark eyes, the understanding in his expression, and felt something a little different from terror. When was the last time a man had looked at her, *really* looked at her, like that? Why couldn't she have met him under other circumstances?

Maybe when she would have made a better impression.

She certainly couldn't complain that she felt isolated from life anymore. She wouldn't be able to tell her brother when they next talked that she still felt insulated from the world, wrapped up in quilt batting and unable to feel anything real. Her heart was pounding, and her breath was still coming in anxious gasps. Running to the car had made her aware of her muscles and the power of her body in a forgotten way. It felt good to push her body, to *do* something, to take a chance.

As if she'd awakened from a long sleep.

Melissa hoped a lack of practice had not led her to take a stupid chance instead of a calculated risk.

She'd know when she read the book.

There was still no one behind her. Melissa forced herself to relax her grip on the wheel, schooled herself to take a long slow breath, and lifted her foot slightly off the gas pedal. The car slowed just as she saw the lights of a busier thoroughfare ahead. She found herself reassured by the prospect of the presence of other normal people.

People who presumably hadn't broken the law.

Why had Mr. Conscience followed her into the house? Didn't that make him complicit? Or had he been hidden in the house all along?

Was he friends with Montmorency?

No. Friends wouldn't have fought like that. He must have followed her into the house. Why? What had been his plan?

Not that she was going to have the chance to ask him.

Melissa reached over, grabbed the book, and put it in the pocket of her winter coat. No point in losing it now. Then she opened the glove box, keeping her gaze fixed on the road, and felt around for her digital camera. When she had it in her other coat pocket, she felt more composed.

Ready for anything.

With luck, the evening would proceed without any more excitement.

Dragons. Right. What *had* she seen? Even the morphine hadn't given her that kind of delusion. Feeling guilty was one thing; losing touch with reality was quite another.

Get a grip. That was what the cameraman, Bill, had said to all the new arrivals who lost their nerve. Panic didn't fix anything, after all, and adrenaline was best used sparingly. She could see Bill, lighting a cigarette with that nonchalant attitude, rolling his eyes, and advising the new kid on the team—the freaked-out one—to get a grip.

Usually while bombs were detonating close by.

Melissa smiled.

She had just wiggled her shoulders, easing the tension away, when a sedan rocketed out of a side street and T-boned her car.

*   *   *

Melissa's car was slammed hard to the left, skidding across the pavement. There was a crash of metal on metal, the tinkle of breaking glass, the squeal of her tires sliding crosswise over the pavement, all before she could make sense of it.

Melissa's head snapped hard to one side as her car hit the curb. Her left front tire leapt over the concrete, and the car lurched to a halt, its tires sinking into the muck of the boulevard. She exhaled shakily, incredulous at her misfortune.

What crappy timing.

What kind of rotten luck set her up for an accident right now?

Then she got mad. She knew all about rotten luck—this was about bad choices. What kind of loser wouldn't stop at a stop sign? Was the other driver drunk? Melissa glanced over the damage as she got ready to give the driver a piece of her mind.

And get his insurance information. She wasn't going to pay for this.

A large black sedan was slammed into the right side of her car, its hood having pushed in the doors and broken both windows of Melissa's car. Melissa ground her teeth. Her right mirror was gone, too. It was going to be miserable to get her car fixed, given its age and the rarity of parts, and the hassle was the last thing she needed. On the other hand, she wasn't going to be buying a new car anytime soon.

What an idiot!

She realized suddenly that the big sedan hadn't had its lights on. That was why she hadn't seen it. The car was dark and the windows were tinted, and it had come out of the darkness. She couldn't see the driver even now.

Why hadn't the driver had his headlights on?

He or she certainly wasn't getting out of the car to apologize.

Melissa had a moment to hope he or she wasn't hurt, and to reach for the door handle to get out and check, before she saw the silver Mercedes hood ornament. It was gleaming right where her passenger door window should have been.

The anger slipped out of her, only to be replaced by a very bad feeling. She'd been hit by a big black Mercedes. Montmorency owned just such a car.

It hadn't been an accident.

Her theory was proved when the driver of the Mercedes put his car abruptly into reverse. The tires squealed as the vehicle sped back into the street, then halted abruptly enough to rock on its shocks. It was about twenty feet away, its front fender rumpled, its lights still extinguished. The street was empty.

To Melissa's left was a gully, a darkened valley of a park that fell away from this side of the road.

She had a sudden intuitive understanding of what the other driver was going to do, and it terrified her.

Melissa hit the gas, slamming the pedal into the floor. She flooded the engine with that quick move, and her car choked once before it stalled. She couldn't start it again. The engine of the Mercedes revved loudly as she tried.

Shit!

Melissa reached for the door handle in the same instant that her door was ripped open from the outside.

"Hurry!" Mr. Conscience said. She gaped at him, astounded to find him right by her side again. How had he gotten all this way so fast? Where was his car?

He didn't seem inclined to chat. He grabbed her hand and hauled her out of the car. His hand was warm, and he moved with decisive power. Melissa could like that in a man, along with a conscience. She stumbled after him, her heels sinking in the soft winter lawn, even as she heard the Mercedes's engine roar.

She looked to see the car racing toward her own once more.

"You can't outrun him," she managed to say; then Mr. Conscience did that shimmering thing.

Melissa closed her eyes against the pale blue light that surrounded him, then felt a claw holding her hand.

Not a dragon claw. It couldn't be.

That would have been impossible.

But it sure felt like one. Melissa might have recoiled, but she didn't have a chance. She felt herself scooped from the ground as the dragon caught her up and took flight. She kept her eyes closed, even as she felt the wind on her face and heard the sound of leathery wings.

Maybe she *had* seen what she thought she had seen.

Now was the time to be sure.

She would have looked, but the crash from below drew her attention instead.

Melissa glanced down to see the big sedan perched on the boulevard, all four tires over the curb. Her car was rolling down into the gully, in slow motion. It came to a halt on its roof, looking crumpled and wrong.

An instant later her car exploded, sending a plume of fire and smoke into the sky. The driver of the Mercedes got out of the vehicle, looked up at them, then leapt into the sky in pursuit.

Melissa knew she shouldn't have been surprised to see him turn into a dragon, as well. He did it quickly, a man one minute and a dragon the next, but there could be no mistaking what he'd done. There had been a bit of that shimmery blue, too. This dragon looked as if he could have been carved of agate, his scales all in shades of gold and russet with a bit of green. He looked both jeweled and fierce.

She guessed that his plan wasn't to make friends when her dragon accelerated, soaring toward the clouds with purpose. The dragon who held her—was it really Mr. Conscience?—had scales that looked more like opals edged in gold.

It could have been exciting, if she hadn't been pretty sure these dragons fought for keeps.

She could die.

But then, she'd spit in the eye of Death before.

The fact was that Melissa couldn't do much in her current situation, at least not to help herself get out of trouble. The outcome was out of her hands. She was hundreds of feet up—if the dragon dropped her, she'd be a goner. Her best bet was to hang on and not distract him—and hope he landed somewhere solid soon.

In the interim, Melissa did what came naturally—she tugged her camera out of her pocket and documented what was happening around her.

Even though it was a dragon fight.

Rafferty couldn't believe he had gotten himself into such a mess. It was his nature to think twice and act once, and his inclination to always be on the side of good. Yet, here he was, protecting a human thief.

And lusting for her all the while. That perfume wound into his nostrils, stirring a desire that had slumbered deep for centuries. Rafferty was distracted all over again, keenly aware of the press of her breasts against his chest, of the softness of her hair against his scales, just when he needed to focus. He could have done without Balthasar hot on his tail, undoubtedly at Magnus's command.

She'd get them both killed.

Did she get away with her crimes because she was so beautiful? Rafferty didn't believe he was the first to be enchanted by her beauty.

That realization didn't temper his response. Not one bit.

This woman was dangerous in oh so many ways.

He was exhausted. He didn't know when he'd last slept well. He was injured—it wasn't a huge cut on his forearm, but it needed tending.

Worse, he was rattled in a way that was utterly uncharacteristic of him. Rafferty had other things to do, priorities to resolve, blood duels to finish . . . Yet he was saving a human he wasn't entirely sure was as much of a treasure as many other humans—at least not in the truth of her heart. In so doing, he was unable to help all the others who were tormented by the earth's current violence.

He felt disheveled, as far from his usual composed self as possible, and not in the least bit in charge of his choices. That was an unfamiliar and unwelcome sense.

Yet he defended her still.

What spell did this woman weave around him?

Rafferty shot skyward, trying to break through the cloud cover before he and Balthasar began to fight. The last thing he needed was to attract human attention. He could do without the legwork of persuading countless humans that they hadn't seen dragons in the sky overhead.

The eclipse was just two hours away. Already he could sense its impending shadow—maybe that was why he felt edgy. He was always the calm *Pyr*, the bedrock of the group led by Erik—not the impulsive one who got himself into awkward situations. That was usually Thorolf's territory.

No doubt about it—this woman, with her eyes and her perfume, was affecting him, and not in a good way.

Rafferty was within a talon's breadth of the clouds when Balthasar slashed at his tail. The *Slayer* breathed dragonfire, the flames licking at Rafferty's scales. They weren't through the clouds yet, but Rafferty had to defend himself. He hoped the falling snow would obscure them. He passed the woman to his back claw, using his body to disguise his move from Balthasar.

Then he suddenly pivoted in the air, raged at Balthasar, and locked claws in the traditional fighting pose. The pair breathed fire at each other, tumbling end over end as they struggled for ascendancy. Something flashed, and Rafferty assumed it was lightning. The weather had been so strange of late, after all. Balthasar bared his teeth and raged flames at Rafferty.

The woman, to Rafferty's surprise, didn't make a sound, not even as he thumped and slashed at Balthasar. Theirs was a quick and vicious fight.

Wasn't she afraid?

Maybe she had passed out. That would be consistent

with the *Pyr* conviction that humans couldn't accommodate their truth very easily.

"Tired of running already?" Balthasar taunted in old-speak. *"Or am I just faster than you?"*

"Maybe I just chose the place of battle." Rafferty slugged Balthasar with his tail, sending the *Slayer* spinning through the falling snow. Balthasar swooped and turned abruptly, turning on Rafferty with talons bared again.

He snorted. *"Hardly! The* Pyr *are cowards."*

Rafferty laughed at that ridiculous notion. *"It's not fear, but a protectiveness of humans that brought me this high in the sky."*

"A misguided plan," Balthasar retorted. *"Or maybe just an excuse, to explain your cowardice."*

"I'll show you cowardice," Rafferty roared, and the battle turned more violent. He slashed at Balthasar, holding fast to one claw to keep the *Slayer* close. His talons dug into the *Slayer*'s chest, and Balthasar cried out in pain. Black *Slayer* blood gushed from the wound, dripping like black rain, as Balthasar tore free. Rafferty lunged after him, pursuing his advantage.

When he saw the second flash, he spared a glance to the clouds. There was no lightning. He heard an electronic whir from close proximity, then saw a third flash.

The woman was taking pictures of them! Rafferty was so astounded by her choice that Balthasar nearly ripped his wing off.

Then he was furious that this thief, this temptress, should attempt to compromise the privacy of the *Pyr*. For what purpose? It couldn't be a good one. Rafferty would ensure she never had the chance to profit from this sight.

But first, he had to defeat Balthasar.

Rafferty didn't miss the irony that so doing would ensure the woman's safety.

The shots were great.

Melissa focused on the challenge of taking good photographs while hurtling through the sky. It was better than thinking about being in the middle of a dragon battle.

She'd played this mind trick before, in Iraq, when the crew had been embedded and besieged. Bill had taught her then to focus on the story, on the documentation, instead of worrying about her own survival. The idea was to focus on what you could control and not worry about the rest. It wasn't always easy. As distraction techniques went, having something to do worked pretty well.

Even when the fire breathed by the dragons singed the hem of Melissa's coat. She slapped out the flames, pretending it was perfectly reasonable for that to happen when she was taking pictures. As Bill had said, there'd be time for nightmares later. The immediate goal was always survival.

Fortunately, the dragon that Melissa knew best seemed determined to defend her. She wasn't going to think about why, much less what he might want in return. After all, Mr. Conscience had made his disapproval of her clear with one look, and she was pretty sure this dragon *was* Mr. Conscience.

If so, she couldn't really blame him for his conclusions.

Even if she did want a chance to explain.

Through the camera viewfinder, she had a good look at him. It gave her a bit of emotional distance, as if the large opalescent dragon were an illusion and not part of her current reality.

Her dragon was large, larger even than the other dragon, and powerfully muscled. His scales were the color of opals, all mysterious shadings of gold and blues and mauves. Gorgeous. Each scale was tipped with gold, like a piece of jewelry, and his talons were gold. His belly could have been covered with golden chain mail, the scales there overlapping one another in beautiful rhythm.

Was he Mr. Conscience? Her dragon moved with the same deliberation as the man in Montmorency's house, as if holding huge power in check. His eyes had the same shimmer of gold around the pupils, although the dragon's pupils were vertical slits.

What clinched his identity was that the black and white ring, the swirled one that Mr. Conscience had worn on his finger, was on her dragon's talon. It *was* him. His talon was massive compared to his finger, and Melissa wondered how that had worked. Did the ring stretch? It looked solid, like glass, but there was no mistaking that its diameter had changed.

A lot.

Then Melissa wondered what else he had in common between the two forms. His dragon form was generously endowed, and once she'd looked, she couldn't *not* look. He was impressive, all muscled strength. She couldn't decide whether he was better looking as a man or a dragon.

The driver of the Mercedes, the one who was now bleeding black from his wounds, was a seriously flashy dragon. His scales reminded Melissa of an agate chess set she'd bought in Mexico for her brother. There was a swirled pattern on the scales, just like agate, and they were the color of gold and russet, even with a few veins of dark green. His eyes were so dark as to be black, and he seemed more inclined to breathe fire at his opponent. He was slimmer and moved faster, more impulsively. She had a sense he might be younger, like a kid just coming into his chops.

Melissa got a shot of the flames erupting from his mouth, brilliant against the overcast night sky. She checked it on the camera's display and knew it was a keeper.

The pair locked claws again, and Melissa heard a rumble. It sounded like thunder, very close at hand, but there were no storm clouds overhead. She'd heard it at the house, too, and had assumed it was thunder. It couldn't be.

Meanwhile, the dragons tumbled end over end, making her dizzy with their combat. A drop of the black blood landed on her sleeve. It burned right through the cloth, leaving a smoking hole. Melissa shook her sleeve, trying to ensure it didn't burn her skin. Fat snowflakes fell against it and sizzled. The hit just increased her sense of being in a war zone and her disassociation from her circumstances.

She framed a shot of the opal dragon taking a strike, and the flow of his red blood on his gleaming gold chest. Another keeper.

Wait. Why was their blood different colors?

It seemed a bad time to ask.

Her dragon rallied and raged after the agate dragon, slashing at his opponent's face. The agate dragon seemed to choke on the fire he'd started to breathe, and his neck made a ferocious crack.

So, they had bones. Melissa clicked and clicked.

Even after that, the slimmer dragon didn't give it up.

He launched at Melissa's defender, who swung his tail and smacked the other dragon down. It was like being in a cloud of pure testosterone, and Melissa was taking pictures as quickly as she could. She was glad she'd invested in a new memory card.

Another heavy blow and the agate dragon lost the rhythm of his wings. Her dragon cast him aside and he plummeted toward the earth. He looked limp and broken, but Melissa heard that thunder again.

Her dragon charged after the agate one, breathing fire on his descent. Had they been communicating? They were over the Lincoln Memorial, and the fight was reflected in the pool. The National Mall was deserted, which was probably a good thing.

Her dragon swooped down and set Melissa on her feet.

"If you will excuse me," he said with a slight inclination of his head.

"Sure," Melissa said, loving the rich sound of his voice. He had an accent, as well, a more subtle one, but she couldn't place it, either. He sounded like Mr. Conscience, too, which just confirmed her conclusion.

As bizarre as it was.

Her dragon inclined his head slightly, then leapt back into battle, finishing off his opponent with a prolonged thrashing. He seemed to be more vicious now that she wasn't in his grasp, and she guessed that he had been ensuring her safety.

There was more black blood and more fire; then the agate one evidently decided he'd had enough. He started to retreat, flying somewhat less gracefully than he had earlier. The opal dragon hovered over the Reflecting Pool, watching him retreat, as if guarding a threshold.

Or her. Melissa shivered with pleasure at the thought and focused on her camera. The reflections made for a fantastic series of shots.

Especially when the opal dragon—her defender— fired one last long plume of flame after his opponent. It flared orange against the night, a gorgeous vivid tongue of fire, accented by the falling snow.

Gorgeous.

He then began to breathe long and slow, as if exhaling something Melissa couldn't see. The agate dragon kept flying away, but he sped up, apparently desperate to put distance between them.

Soon he was lost in the distance, and even the zoom couldn't catch a good shot of him.

But she had lots. She checked the memory and was relieved that she hadn't run out. This was pure gold.

Melissa glanced up from the camera to find Mr. Conscience on the other side of the pool, watching her. She cursed herself for missing his transformation, even as her heart skipped. His gaze was locked upon her, and she could feel his disapproval across the distance.

She had a feeling he would have something to say about her taking the pictures.

She was pretty sure he wouldn't want souvenir copies.

In fact, she knew he'd want them destroyed.

Fat chance. Melissa also had some pretty strong ideas about what she wanted. She had every right to document what she witnessed.

Her grip tightened on the camera even as she stared back at him. She studied him, liking the fit of his jeans and the span of his shoulders. Dragon or not, he would have caught her eye anyplace, anytime. Her heart skipped a beat at the certainty she'd caught his, as well, and she wondered what he'd say to her.

How he'd want to negotiate.

Her mouth went dry at the possibilities.

Mr. Conscience glanced between her and the Washington Monument, looked unhappy, then turned away. Melissa's lips parted; then she realized his destination. He strode toward the monument and the sentries posted there, purpose in his every step. They were watching him openly.

Melissa was curious. Did he intend to try to convince them that they hadn't seen what they must have seen?

It didn't much matter. She had the photographs, which meant she had not only a great story, but the proof of it.

And she had a chance to ensure that she got to keep those pictures.

Melissa eased away from the pool, not knowing how closely Mr. Conscience was monitoring her. He didn't seem to notice, so she backed away more quickly. She could see him talking to the one guard, his intensity palpable even from here. When she reached the shadows, she looked around with care, her heart thumping.

There was no sign of the dragon working for Montmorency, and she knew Montmorency himself was injured. This might be her only chance to escape from dragons.

Her gaze clung to the figure of Mr. Conscience, and she hesitated. Didn't it just figure that he was the most interesting man she'd met in years? She wasn't sure what to make of the dragon thing, but well, he was easy on the eyes either way. And he was living so definitely in the moment. She liked that he was so *alive*.

That was exciting, especially after the places she had been.

But it wasn't meant to be.

Melissa took one last look, regretted again that they hadn't met under other circumstances, then ran as quickly as she could.

Chapter 3

Rafferty knew the woman would run. He told himself not to be surprised that she was gone when he looked back.

She had to be the kind of person who looked for easy solutions, at least those solutions that were easy on herself.

And which yielded a profit.

He had no doubt of what she'd do or try to do with those photographs.

He also had no doubt he would stop her. He didn't much care how he did so, or what it took to change her mind.

Rafferty knew he could have solved his dilemma by beguiling the woman before approaching the guards, but he hadn't been able to bring himself to do it. Why not? He couldn't explain his resistance and hadn't wanted to explore it, not when time was of the essence. Now, away from the distraction of her perfume and her eyes, he had to wonder at his own choice.

Why did she have this power to confuse him?

How?

Rafferty beguiled the two guards, easily convincing them they hadn't witnessed anything unusual at all. In moments, he was striding away from the monument, feeling their gazes track his movements. They remained puzzled by his presence, but that was fine. He resented the lost time and the trouble of needing to track the woman.

His senses were more keen in dragon form, but he didn't dare shift until he was well out of the sight of the guards. No point in undoing what he had achieved.

Balthasar, Rafferty was certain, had returned to Magnus's lair. Or maybe he'd retrieved the car first. Rafferty wouldn't have wanted to be in that *Slayer's* scales when Magnus heard he had failed on all accounts.

He still had to find the woman first.

Although it felt as if it took ages to walk into the side streets adjacent to the National Mall, it couldn't have been more than a minute. Impatience chafed at Rafferty, another unfamiliar mood. There was no sign of the woman, but the scent of her perfume drew Rafferty onward.

It occurred to him that she wasn't a very experienced thief to leave such a clear sign of her presence. That scent would linger for hours, and it was sufficiently distinctive that it would identify her to anyone with a sharp nose.

Never mind a *Slayer*.

Was it possible that she wasn't what she seemed?

Or was that wishful thinking on his part? He didn't like the idea that he had helped a felon escape the repercussions of her crime. Should he have left her to Magnus? Rafferty couldn't imagine that any human deserved that fate.

What was the book Magnus said she'd stolen? *Had* she stolen it? If so, why had it been worth the risk? Maybe she didn't understand the danger in such a choice.

She'd know now, after Balthasar had tried to kill her.

How many other *Slayers* were in alliance with Magnus these days?

Rafferty quickened his pace.

The woman had known the security codes—did Magnus know her? Maybe they'd been allies but had had a disagreement. If so, she and Rafferty were in the same company—he'd once been friends with Magnus, although those days were long behind them. He knew what it was to be tricked by Magnus. Did he and the woman have something in common?

He wouldn't think of the price of learning Magnus's true nature.

Instead, he thought about the woman. Just who was she, anyway?

The scent of her perfume never wavered and never disappeared. She couldn't have taken public transit or hailed a cab, because it remained consistent. She must have just kept walking. This choice intrigued Rafferty— and told him that her destination couldn't be far.

And it wasn't. He turned onto a cul-de-sac, about a fifteen-minute walk from the National Mall. The scent led into the curved street.

The street was a dead end, curling back on itself. The outer curve was lined with town houses, built in a Georgian style. Rafferty guessed, however, that their exteriors were stucco, not cut stone. There was no resonance of rock from the buildings.

Stucco on Styrofoam, then. Why humans persisted

in this kind of artifice was a mystery to Rafferty. It was cheaper but not worth the price. He disliked the lack of authenticity.

Maybe he was just getting old.

In this moment, though, he felt vigorous and vital. It was because she was close, and Rafferty knew it. He'd fought and he'd won. He'd defended a human, saved her from certain death, and there was a certain part of him that demanded such triumph be celebrated.

In a very physical way. He surveyed the street, and his pulse increased with the certainty that she was close.

The front yard of each town house was neatly fenced off and landscaped with formal austerity. The town houses all faced a small green space on the circle in their midst. The green space's landscaping was in the same flavor as that of the houses. Rafferty saw that there were laneways at intervals, going between the houses to an alley behind. That must be where residents parked their cars.

It was quiet, strangely still, and the windows facing the street were mostly dark. The snow fell in fat lazy flakes, spinning out of the sky as if time stood still. It was peaceful, even as the pending eclipse nudged at the edge of his awareness.

The streetlights ensured that anyone who entered the crescent would be visible. Rafferty had no doubt that he was being watched from at least one house, and he fought the sense of walking into a trap.

He strolled down the street, the snow stirring as he walked, his boots quiet on the pavement.

Was she watching for him?

From which house?

Her scent provoked him, leading him on and promising more than he thought she would deliver. It tantalized him and made his blood pump with unruly desire. Rafferty couldn't do anything other than follow that trail to her. He thought of sirens, singing their alluring songs and enchanting sailors to shatter their ships on hidden rocks.

Rafferty recalled her fine bones, the exotic tilt of her eyes, the intelligence and certainty in her gaze. He thought of the way she'd lifted her chin in determination, the way she looked both delicate and world-weary. He thought of how slim she was, and yet she was tall. Statuesque even. Resilient, and feminine. He recalled how she walked, how the hem of her skirt swayed with the grace of every step, and knew he was not nearly as indifferent to her physical charms as would have been ideal.

He needed to destroy her camera. That was all. He needed nothing else from her, and he would not linger.

Nevertheless, his blood was pounding and his heart was pumping. Desire surged through his veins. He told himself it was the natural reaction to having fought in dragon form, and that the pending eclipse only strengthened that reaction.

It sounded perfectly rational, but Rafferty knew something had changed.

He knew this woman had a mysterious and potent effect upon him.

A dangerous influence.

Rafferty wanted to explore it, consequences be damned.

That alone should have warned him.

The woman's perfume led Rafferty to a town house just to the right of the middle, a unit indistinguishable from its fellows. The windows were dark, but he knew she was home. He sensed her presence. Rafferty strode up the walkway and noted the number, in case he ever had to return.

Eighteen.

The door was glossy black, a stone urn to the left holding a holly bush carefully trimmed into a perfect globe. The red berries shone in the light from the street-lights, glistening as if they were artificial.

But the plant was real. He appreciated its authenticity in this street of illusion and touched the berries with a fingertip.

There was a brass knocker on the door. Rafferty hesitated for a moment, confirming that he was correct about her presence. It was an hour when humans normally slept. He glanced back at the silent street, inhaled, then knocked with conviction.

To her credit, she didn't play games. She opened the door immediately, her expression wary and her lips tight. He liked that she was direct.

She was still wearing her coat, although she'd removed the scarf and gloves and unfastened the front buttons. "What do you want?"

"The camera."

She almost smiled. "Forget it," she said flatly, and made to close the door. Rafferty wedged his boot into the gap and saw the slight flare of her nostrils when she noted the obstruction.

Then she met his gaze, unafraid.

Her boldness made him yearn.

And burn. He didn't doubt that his gaze brightened, that the hunger she awakened was clear.

"I'll scream," she said softly. "We have a very active

residents' association. I'm sure there are half a dozen people already wondering who you are and why you're here."

Rafferty smiled and braced his hand on the doorframe. He leaned closer, taking a breath of her scent and watching her eyes darken ever so slightly.

"I'll shift," he replied quietly. "Then you'll have even more to explain."

Her eyes widened an increment. "You wouldn't."

Rafferty let his smile broaden. The eclipse was close, close enough that it was easy to let the shimmer slide through his body. He knew he started to shine blue around his perimeter, a sure sign of a pending shift.

Evidently she also understood what it meant.

Unfortunately, giving rein to the dragon within only increased his desire to a fever pitch. He wanted her enough to do anything to possess her.

Where was his temperance on this night?

"All right." She spoke tersely and turned back to the foyer. "I'll get it."

He made to step after her, but she held up a hand.

"Be serious. You're not coming in." Her glance was fierce, an interesting fact given that she knew what he was.

What he could become.

What kind of a woman defied a dragon of unknown intentions? No. She *knew* his intentions. She'd read them in his eyes. And she knew exactly what he was. Rafferty was intrigued again by her confidence, just when he didn't want to be.

"So inhospitable, after I saved your hide," he whispered.

She eyed him for an endless moment, then stepped back, letting him into the foyer. "That's fair. But not one step farther."

Rafferty smiled but played by her rules. He knew he could destroy the house if necessary, follow her any-where, hunt down the camera himself, if she tried to trick him.

He was content—more or less—to wait.

And simmer. He heard her catch her breath, felt her heart leap, and knew she was as aware of him as he was of her.

Even knowing what he was.

Interesting.

She returned almost instantly and handed him a digital camera. Rafferty turned it on and saw that the memory card was full. Something was wrong, though. Her mood and her scent didn't match up. He considered her again, but she held his regard steadily.

"You're giving this up pretty easily," he noted, letting his gaze slide over her.

She blushed a little, much to his surprise, then shrugged. "I know when to not push my luck." Rafferty arched a brow and she continued. "Seeing what I'm up against here."

"And you still have what you wanted in the first place, anyway," Rafferty guessed. "His book."

Her gaze hardened instantly. "Are you friends with Montmorency?"

"No!" Rafferty couldn't hide his disgust at the idea, even though he was aware that she was watching him closely. "We have been adversaries longer than we ever were allies." He met her gaze. "I have no interest in de-fending Magnus or his property."

"But you're both dragons, deep down inside." She folded her arms across her chest. "You must be the same."

She wasn't convinced. She wanted to hear his explanation.

"No. We are as different as two souls can be. In my kind, there is good and bad, just as in all kinds."

"You bleed red."

Rafferty was startled that she'd noticed. He was wary then, concerned that she would learn too much about him and the *Pyr*.

She was observant. He stepped back and inclined his head slightly. "That is none of your concern." He held up the camera. "I thank you for not making this more difficult than it needed to be."

As she watched, he popped out the memory card and crushed it to oblivion in his hand. He opened his fist, and the pieces fell to the floor, no more than a handful of black glittering dust.

She blinked in surprise. "You shouldn't be able to do that."

"I do many things I shouldn't be able to do," Rafferty murmured. She caught her breath and eyed him warily, his desire sparking at the look in her eyes.

Was it admiration?

Was it an answering heat?

Or did he see the invitation he wanted to see?

Rafferty handed the camera back to her, letting their fingers brush in the transaction. Her skin was soft, and she didn't recoil from his touch. He was certain that he let her fingers linger against his. "With our business completed, I bid you good evening."

"That's it?" she said, a challenge in her tone.

Or was it disappointment?

Rafferty met her gaze, and she lifted her chin.

Then she smiled a smile that could only have been

called seductive. Her perfume seemed stronger then, as if it would ensnare him completely. Rafferty's blood roared right on cue, and he found himself lifting his hand from the doorknob.

He could not resist. "Is that an invitation?"

Her smile warmed. "Don't make me ask twice."

His heart leapt at the welcome in her eyes.

She pivoted then and strolled into the house, shedding her coat on the way. Rafferty watched avidly. She put the camera down on a table in the foyer and glanced toward him.

He'd been right—it was a dare. He could tell by the light in her eyes. And the curve of her lips was an invitation he wasn't inclined to refuse. He surveyed her, letting his appreciation of her beauty show, and his smile broadened when she flushed slightly.

She didn't flinch.

Even though she knew his truth.

A bold beauty, then. Forthright. Decisive. Attractive and intelligent. Not averse to risk. Rafferty liked that, liked that it was a different tendency than his own. Desire stirred deep within him one more time, more vigorous and demanding than it had been in a long, long time.

This was a rare and possibly treacherous impulse. He wasn't entirely certain that they adhered to the same moral code, that they would draw the line between good and evil in the same place. His attraction to a woman he knew so little—and about whom he had so many questions—had to be due to the pending eclipse. He didn't know her name. He didn't know her allegiances. He didn't know her intent.

And Rafferty didn't care.

He wanted her, and that was all that mattered. He surrendered to his desire, despite the danger.

He'd take this risk, and take it willingly.

"Maybe that's not quite it, then," he murmured, and stepped into the house. He flicked the door shut with his fingertips, then closed the distance between them. The dragon within roared in anticipation, and his heart skipped a beat.

She held her ground as she watched his approach, a choice that excited him even more. He heard her catch her breath, saw the anticipation light her eyes. That she could want him, even knowing what he was, and that she would lift her hand to his shoulder and part her lips in welcome were more than he expected.

It was all he needed. Rafferty bent his head and caught those full soft lips beneath his own, his heart pounding when she touched her tongue to his.

Then he caught her against him, spreading his hand across the small of her back, and lost himself in the passion of her kiss.

Unbelievable.

He kissed like a god. Melissa knew she shouldn't have been surprised. He was both tender and demanding, an intoxicating combination that left her hungry for more. She hadn't kissed a man in half of forever, but this man's kiss had definitely been worth the wait.

His mouth closed over hers with a surety; yet at the same time, Melissa knew she could have pushed him aside with a fingertip. He was so powerful, so confident—so *sexy*—but she instinctively understood that he wouldn't take more than she offered.

That made her want to offer him everything.

Immediately.

It made her want to shake him, stir him, drive him wild, and wring him dry. He was vibrant and alive, whereas she had been marking time, going through the motions. If this was a dream, she wanted to experience every facet of its splendor before she woke up.

Melissa locked her fingers into his hair, loving the luxuriant thickness of it, and hauled him closer. This was no time to be shy, or coy. She wanted him, and she wanted him to know it.

She closed her eyes, slipped her tongue between his teeth, and felt the jolt of his surprise. His pulse pounded beneath her palm, evidence that he was flesh and blood, just like her, independent of his other powers. She felt bold and daring, and his kiss awakened that impetuousness she thought she'd lost forever.

She was alive, and he was here. What else did she need?

Not one thing. Melissa angled her head and tugged him closer, feasting on his mouth. His one hand was spread across the small of her back, under her shirt. His fingers were fanned out, his hand warm and still against her flesh. They were pressed together, the heat of his erection between them, her nipples taut against his chest.

Melissa liked that he was as aroused as she was. He slipped his other hand around her nape, a possessive move that made her feel feminine and fragile; one that made her keenly aware of his power and heat.

Her blood simmered.

Other parts of her hummed.

Then he made a little growl, deep in his throat, and lifted her off the floor, trapping her between his hips and the wall. He felt good—hard and ready—and Melissa purred in response to his ardor. She stole a glimpse of him through her lashes as she wound one leg around his thigh. She'd never been so bold, but he seemed to like it. His eyes glimmered, dark and dangerous; then he pinned her there, both of his hands in her hair. He deepened his kiss until Melissa thought he'd taste her very soul.

He slid his hands down her throat, pushing her crisp white shirt over her shoulders with impatience. It caught against the wall, behind her waist, but Melissa didn't care. His fingers wandered over her curves, caressing her breast, sliding over the indent of her waist, all without breaking his feverish kiss.

He lifted his head, then, and looked her in the eye, almost willing her to deny him as his hands slid around her collarbone. His fingertips traced eight lines, then halted at the top button of her blouse. He surveyed her, looking very pleased with what he saw, and smiled. Melissa's heart leapt at his intensity, and her mouth went dry.

"No questions?" he asked, his breath as soft as a summer wind.

There was that knowingness in his eyes, along with the challenge in his words, and Melissa understood what he was asking. The very fact that he asked told her she had nothing to worry about.

At least not immediately.

But still. "Do you ever change without choosing to?"

He shook his head once, so resolute that she knew there was no chance.

She had to know for sure. "During sex?"

Again, he shook his head. "It's a fighting posture." He turned his hand and slid his knuckles up her throat, the proprietary gesture and the heat in his dark eyes making Melissa tremble with desire. "We change to defend what matters to us."

"There are even more of you?"

He smiled, looking a little more dangerous than he had before. "It's not important now," he murmured, and Melissa understood.

He was claiming her, for a night at least. If any others chose to attack, he would defend her.

It was more than she had expected him to tell her.

And it pleased her more than she could have anticipated. She wasn't a woman who needed someone to protect her on a regular basis, but when there were dragons around, it wouldn't be all bad to have one on her side.

She let her hands dance over his shoulders, then opened his jacket to her own scrutiny. "Maybe I imagined the fights," she whispered.

"You don't seem the type to be uncertain of what you've witnessed," he purred.

Melissa slipped her hands into the heat under his jacket and slid them over the hardness of his muscles. She met his gaze and smiled as she caressed him. "No dragons here."

"Maybe just one," he said softly.

"Maybe I have to see more to be sure," Melissa replied.

His eyes glittered; then he smiled. There was a hint of dragon in that look, but then it was gone. She didn't care—she wanted him anyway. He must have seen as much in her eyes, because he kissed her again. This kiss was rougher, more demanding, more exciting.

More vital. How could there be half measures with a

dragon? Melissa closed her eyes and arched her back, catching her breath when the warmth of his hand closed over her breast.

He slid his thumb over one nipple, urging it to a peak, then bent to take the nipple in his mouth, nudging the edge of her lace bra aside. Melissa gasped in pleasure, feeling the constraint of the lace and the persistence of his seductive tongue. She locked her fingers into his hair and heard herself moan.

She didn't even know his name.

She didn't care.

She'd never been impulsive about sex, had never had a one-night stand, but she knew that if she turned him away now, she'd regret the choice for the rest of her life. This was her celebration of survival, and she would take it, without reservation. She would let loose, for the first time ever, and doubted she'd regret it.

Her lover seemed to understand as much. He pushed her shirt away, then flicked the front clasp of her bra. She saw his smile before his hands closed over her breasts. His thumb teased the first nipple while he kissed the other. Melissa closed her eyes and savored his touch.

She squirmed against him, and he inhaled sharply. Before Melissa could blink, he lifted her into his arms and headed for the living room. He laid her on the leather couch with reverence, stepping back to look at her as he peeled off his jacket.

She watched him, unashamed of her attraction. His dark gaze locked with hers as he shed his jacket and put it on the opposite chair. He crossed his arms before himself and pulled his long-sleeved amber T-shirt over his head, revealing a tight white undershirt.

And one heck of a six-pack. Melissa propped herself

up on one elbow to watch. The light from the streetlamps filtered through the blinds on her living room window, painting his form in alternating stripes of light and shadow. Had she ever seen such a powerful male specimen? His shoulders were so wide, every muscle pumped, and his skin an evenly tanned gold all over.

The white T-shirt was removed with similar methodical haste; then he bent to unfasten his boots. His attention was fixed upon her all the while, and again she had the sense that he would stop with a single gesture from her.

Melissa's mouth was dry, but she had no intention of making that gesture. This was a night for second chances, for making up for lost time, and for fresh starts. She knew she wasn't going to regret whatever happened in this room in the next hour.

He set his boots, socks tucked inside, neatly at the foot of that chair and faced her again, his hands on the waistband of his jeans.

Melissa smiled encouragement.

His slow, responding smile made her heart thump against her ribs. He unzipped the fly of his jeans and eased them over his hips, utterly confident in his own body. The sight of him made Melissa's heart gallop in anticipation. He paused, and she took advantage of that instant to rise to her feet.

Aware of his hungry gaze upon her, she shed her clothes, many of which were already unfastened. She didn't have his grace and patience, and certainly wasn't as neat. Melissa peeled the garments off and cast them aside, unafraid if he knew just how much she wanted him.

And how soon.

She hesitated when she was wearing only her panties.

His eyes were bright in the darkness, his gaze locked on her. That this man could find her appealing was all the aphrodisiac Melissa needed. She knew she wasn't unattractive—she also knew that her body had been through the proverbial war. It had been years since a man had looked at her with anything but pity.

Melissa crooked one finger in invitation and didn't manage to complete the gesture before he was right in front of her. "Beautiful," he whispered, that smile putting a lump in her throat; then his arms were around her again.

One minute, they were kissing and she was running her hands over his strength; the next, she was on the couch, his hands locked around her waist and his kiss on the inside of her thigh. His hands slid over her hips, taking her underwear with them.

Melissa saw those panties fly across the room, then closed her eyes and moaned at his caress. She could find underwear later. She wasn't going to miss one second of this interlude worrying about such details.

Then his tongue touched her hidden softness with gentle persuasion, and she parted her thighs, wanting only more. Melissa surrendered to the moment, to passion, and to the man with the amazing eyes.

She almost dissolved beneath his touch, lost to more pleasure than she'd felt in years. Her body tingled in places that had slept for too long, places she'd forgotten she possessed.

And it felt so good. In a trio of heartbeats, Melissa forgot everything except the seductive power of this man.

A man with at least one dangerous secret.

But he made it worth her while.

Rafferty awakened with an effort. He wanted to sleep, to lose himself in the softness of this woman's embrace, but he knew it would be foolish to do so.

In fact, his lingering in her home only endangered her. Now that his desire had been partly satisfied, he was thinking with slightly more clarity.

And he was alarmed by the risk he had taken. Would Magnus and Balthasar come after him? Rafferty expected at least Magnus would—the challenge between them still stood.

But the woman's perfume, now mingled with the distinctive scent of her own body and her pleasure, seemed to surround him, making it difficult to leave the warmth of her embrace. She had met him touch for touch, unafraid of either him or her own passion.

She was a woman unlike any other he'd met.

He knew so little about her, except that she had evidently stolen a book from Magnus.

That recollection galvanized Rafferty. Magnus had no sense of humor about the loss of his property. He'd come after that book, and the only way to defend this woman from the *Slayer*'s vengeance was to give the book back to Magnus.

Even then, Magnus might demand retribution from her.

Rafferty would finish his own blood feud with the *Slayer* instead. If that went well, maybe he'd bring back the book the woman wanted and find out then what it was about. For the moment, he had to ensure that Magnus had no reason to pursue her.

Where had she put the book? The bookshelf at the far end of the room was loaded with volumes, but Rafferty suspected it wasn't a published book. What did Magnus's book look like?

Rafferty checked the pockets of her coat and smiled at the weight in one pocket. It proved to be a book bound in blue leather, like a Day-Timer or a diary. He opened it at a random page and found a list of appointments. They meant nothing to him, and he didn't recognize the handwriting—had he ever seen Magnus's handwriting?—so he scanned the text to be sure he had the right book.

Find Jorge ASAP was one note from several weeks before.

Mention of the *Slayer* who had been Magnus's most loyal henchman was all the confirmation Rafferty had time to seek. There was no time to linger. He could feel the eclipse beginning and shivered at the chill of the moon as it slid into shadow. The darkness of the night seemed to become deeper and more filled with threats.

But eclipses had become increasingly more treacherous for the *Pyr*. It seemed that they were all more sensitive, or maybe that the dragons hidden within each of them were more stirred by an eclipse's shadow.

Rafferty would have to ask Sloane whether his impressions were correct.

There would be a firestorm linked to this one, one presaged by the total eclipse. That much was certain, as was the fact that Magnus would try to use the energy of the firestorm to his own advantage.

Rafferty had to go.

He glanced back at his lover, sleeping on the couch. She was all golden perfection, her lips parted as she slept, her lashes like dark feathers on her cheeks. Her hair was short and wavy, fine like that of a baby. There was one mark on her stomach, an incision healed over, but the scar didn't make her less ideal in his eyes.

Rafferty wished he could have lingered. He wished he could have learned more about her, discovered the root of her extraordinary confidence, unfurled her secrets, defined the line of her moral code.

Hungry for details of her, he surveyed the living room of the town house but found no clue to her nature. It had no more character than his hotel room. Did she deliberately hide her nature from sight? Or did she—unlike Rafferty—have no need for a home and a haven? He wanted to know more about her with a ferocity that astounded him.

But his presence here was a lure for Magnus.

Rafferty dressed in haste, the dragon roaring for another taste of her. His lust had never been so strong, even beneath the light of an eclipse. On one level, he marveled at the change.

On another, he simply wanted.

He crossed the room, unable to leave without one last caress of her silken skin. He slid his fingertips across her breast and her nipple tightened immediately, as if it had already learned his touch. He smiled at his own whimsy, then stared at the blue light that danced over her body.

That light appeared to emanate from his fingertips, to spark at the point of contact, then dance over her body in a flash of electric blue. It slid, more like liquid than flame, and Rafferty blinked in confusion.

It was gone.

If it had ever been. Was Rafferty seeing things that weren't there? Who ever heard of a liquid blue flame?

He *was* tired. He must have imagined it. His fingers hovered an inch above her skin as he hesitated.

An old portent echoed in his thoughts, but it was one that had no credence. He was twelve hundred years old. There had never been darkfire in that time.

There never would be darkfire.

Even if darkfire was said to burn with a strange blue flame.

Besides, darkfire was a kind of firestorm, and Rafferty felt no tingle of heat, no sizzle in his veins beyond the one she had already lit. He made to reach for her one more time, to check, then knew he couldn't possibly have seen what he'd thought he'd seen.

No. It couldn't be darkfire.

He was wasting time by considering pure folly. Myth. Superstition. Nonsense.

Rafferty stepped away, tucked the blue leather-bound book into his jacket, and turned away from his ardent lover. He glanced back at the threshold of her doorway, drinking in one last glimpse of her. He paused, thinking about that light.

Impossible.

Rafferty turned and strode into the night, shuddering at the sense of the eclipse. He left the cul-de-sac, aware that her neighbors could be watchful, and didn't shift until he found an alley connected to the street beyond.

"*I have your book*," he taunted in old-speak, broadcasting the message to Magnus. "*Come get it—alone.*"

"*In your dreams*," Magnus snarled, his old-speak carrying from everywhere and nowhere.

Rafferty smiled, his thoughts flooded with memories of what he and the woman had done together. "*My dreams are otherwise occupied*," he replied, knowing that she'd have command of them for a while.

Maybe when this business with Magnus was resolved, he'd seek her out.

Assuming that he was triumphant. It wouldn't pay to be too confident too soon. Magnus had tricked Rafferty before.

But not this time.

Not this time.

Chapter 4

Melissa rolled over and stretched, feeling as languid as a cat in the sun. The rosy light of morning came through the window blinds in stripes, light alternating with shadow. She felt good, remarkably good, and couldn't remember when she'd last awakened with a smile like this one.

It was amazing what a few orgasms could do for a woman's perspective.

Great sex was the cure for insomnia; that was for sure.

She listened and was disappointed to find herself alone. She knew she shouldn't truly be surprised. Although Melissa wasn't much for one-nighters, she'd heard enough about them from friends and coworkers. Only those men committed to the duration—or those giving that possibility due consideration—stayed for breakfast.

She told herself not to be disappointed in Mr. Conscience. She wasn't entirely convinced, but got a robe from the bathroom and made a pot of coffee for herself. As the coffee perked, filling the town house with its delicious smell, she opened the top right drawer in the antique desk she used for the computer.

It had a false bottom, one she'd discovered while cleaning a century of muck from the wood.

And nestled in that hidden niche was the other memory chip for her camera.

The one with the dragon pictures.

It was too bad she'd had to sacrifice her old chip, the one filled with pictures of her brother's kids and their last vacation together. The best of those pictures had already been copied and sent to California, at least.

Melissa had guessed Mr. Conscience would come after the photographs of him in dragon form, and she'd known he wouldn't leave without them. She hadn't had long to hide them, and exchanging the chips had been her only chance.

It had worked.

When she had a hot cup of coffee, she started to import the files to her computer. She put a watermark—a copyright symbol followed by her name, Melissa Smith—across the middle of each one. Then she started to compose them on her blog, queuing up a series of draft posts that she could schedule to appear hourly throughout the day. The whole world would know about the dragons by midafternoon, and she didn't doubt the images would cause a sensation.

And probably a controversy. She'd be accused of doctoring them, which would only lead to more hits and more publicity.

The increased traffic to her blog would mean that more people would be watching it when she broke the real story, the story of Montmorency and his crimes.

It was exactly what Daphne would have wanted. A

big finish and public denunciation of Montmorency.
There would be an inquiry and charges laid and lots of
drama of the kind that made for good journalism. Melissa might even get that real job again and that second
chance.

Funny how it didn't feel like the right thing to do.
Melissa kept the posts private, considering her options.
Showing the dragons to the world was certainly not
what Mr. Conscience wanted.

Was it really fair to reveal his secret?

He'd defended her, after all. And he'd been a heck of
a lover. He'd treated her with courtesy. The idea of re-
paying that with the public revelation of his true nature
made Melissa uneasy. There were those ethics again,
whispering in her thoughts.

The right thing to do would be to destroy the pictures.

Even if they were the truth. She had a right to her
own experience of witnessing the dragon fight, but sharing that with the world might have repercussions for Mr.
Conscience.

On the other hand, was Melissa really the first to
know that these dragons existed? How many people
had seen them fight the night before? They hadn't been
that far from a busy street when the one working for
Montmorency had trashed her car. The honor guard at
the monument must have seen the fight. She was sure
she'd seen them staring, and she couldn't imagine that
Mr. Conscience could have said anything to change
their memory of the truth. If they'd had cameras, they
would have snapped shots, as well.

They could steal her story.

Lots of people could reveal the same story as Melissa.

But still. It just seemed wrong.

She had to be sure.

Melissa drained her cup of coffee and got up to check Montmorency's book. Her coat was still on the floor where she'd tossed it the night before. She should be sure that she had *something* before she made such a choice. What if Montmorency's book didn't include the information that Daphne had insisted it did? Melissa knew already that the girl could—and would—lie to defend her own interests.

She checked the left pocket of her coat, but it was empty.

She checked the right pocket.

It was empty, as well.

Melissa's eyes widened. She patted down the coat and shook it out. No book. Had she removed it from her pocket? She didn't think so. The camera was on the table in the foyer, just where she'd left it. Her other clothes were scattered across the floor. She went through them like a whirlwind, her dismay growing with every second. There was no sign of the book.

It couldn't have disappeared!

Her gaze fell on the spot where Mr. Conscience had left his clothes so carefully folded. She knew then, she knew with utter conviction what had happened to the book.

He'd taken it.

He'd *stolen* it.

That settled everything. That she could take a huge risk and end up with nothing at all was a familiar tune, and one she'd never dance to again.

Furious, Melissa tossed her discarded shirt back onto the floor and strode back to the computer. She didn't know his name. She didn't know where to find him, or even where to begin a search. She wasn't going back to Montmorency to ask directions.

No, she'd bring Mr. Conscience straight to her.

She set her lips as she posted the first set of dragon pictures to her blog. She queued up the other posts, scheduling them for hourly postings.

She doubted it would take him long.

She was ready.

The old-speak shook Rafferty out of a sound sleep. It wound into his ear, slid through his brain, and rang in his thoughts with all the subtlety of a cobra's strike.

"*Who is Melissa Smith?*" Erik demanded, his question a low, hostile hiss that had Rafferty immediately on his feet.

Rafferty was naked in his hotel suite, his gaze darting from one side to the other as he sought Erik. He'd been sleeping deeply, more deeply than was his tendency, and was rattled by both that and the interruption. His heart pounded, even though he knew Erik likely wasn't very close. The leader of the *Pyr* could cast his old-speak much farther than anyone Rafferty knew.

Melissa Smith?

Rafferty had a funny feeling he knew who that might be. Melissa Smith might have green eyes with an exotic tilt to the outer corners, golden skin and a penchant for wearing seductive perfume.

The very perfume that still clung to his own skin.

But how did Erik know her name when Rafferty didn't? He wasn't entirely sure he wanted to know, given the force of Erik's anger.

This wasn't going to be pretty.

"*I might know*," Rafferty replied with his customary

caution, a caution that might have served him well the night before. *"Why?"*

"You might *know,"* Erik echoed, his disgust clear. *"Perhaps you* might *know how she has pictures of you and Balthasar?"*

Rafferty's eyes widened. *"She doesn't."* He clearly remembered destroying the memory chip from her camera.

"Think again," Erik snarled. Rafferty's cell phone chirped that it had received a text message, and Rafferty had a good idea what it was.

A hot link.

To Melissa Smith's blog, which exhibited a picture of Rafferty in dragon form.

He sat down hard, scrolling down the blog and blinking in astonishment at the number of images.

On one hand, he was impressed. The colors were rich, and the images captured the action of the fight beautifully. They were well-framed shots, each one in perfect focus. Melissa knew what she was doing with a camera.

Melissa.

On the other hand, he understood why Erik was so angry. The *Pyr* weren't supposed to reveal themselves to humans, beyond a select complicit few, and when accidents happened, it was incumbent upon the individual *Pyr* to beguile the humans into dismissing their own observations—or forgetting them. He'd done that to the honor guard on the mall. It was true he hadn't beguiled her, and he felt a stab of guilt at the oversight.

He *had* been somewhat distracted.

But how had Melissa done this? Rafferty had destroyed the chip.

Unless it had been the wrong one.

Rafferty felt sick. He realized suddenly why she had surrendered it to him as easily as she had. *It had been the wrong chip.*

He reviewed the images, horrified by what he had inadvertently done.

Rafferty didn't bother to apologize to the leader of the *Pyr*. Apologies were just words; that would be Erik's reply, and it was true.

What Rafferty had to do was repair his mistake.

Somehow.

"*I'll fix it,*" he said to Erik, who snorted in disdain and didn't reply.

Melissa. Her name was Melissa.

Rafferty was going to see his temptress again.

Rafferty suspected, however, that this exchange would not end so amiably as the one the night before. He showered and dressed in haste, trying to think of an acceptable solution—one that he could demand and she might accept. He was pulling on his jacket just as there was a knock at the door. Rafferty sensed the presence of another *Pyr*, checked the arrival's scent, and knew who stood there before he opened the door.

"Hey, dude!"

Thorolf was grinning from ear to ear as he removed his aviator sunglasses. He was dressed with his usual outlaw flair, his black leather jacket ornamented with crests from motorcycle companies and his jeans both worn and torn. He wore a bright blue T-shirt emblazoned with the name of an obscure band, and the color made his eyes look more vivid. He was an imposing figure, given his height and obvious fitness, even without his many tattoos visible. Thorolf evidently had decided to have his long dark blond hair woven into dreadlocks since Rafferty had last seen him.

He looked hungover, which wasn't a surprise early in the day. It seemed to Rafferty that Thorolf spent most mornings regretting his indulgences of the night before, and most nights repeating those indulgences. Thorolf had no restraint in enjoying earthy passions, and Rafferty had little doubt of how the other *Pyr* had spent the night of the eclipse. He didn't want to hear the details, given that they had probably indulged in similar activity.

Rafferty was usually kind about the other *Pyr*'s weaknesses, but on this day, irritated with his own failures, Rafferty didn't feel kind. He didn't want to have anything in common with Thorolf.

In fact, he was insulted by Thorolf's presence and didn't bother to hide it. "What are you doing here?"

"Come to save you from yourself, or something like that." Thorolf shrugged and grinned, amiable as ever.

"I can take care of this on my own."

"Hey, no offense." Thorolf held up his hands. "Erik told me to get my butt here pronto and help you out, and I'm here. He's not someone I want to piss off." Thorolf's grin widened. "Kind of a treat that someone else is in his bad books, that's for sure. Never would have guessed you'd steal the honors from me."

Rafferty pushed past the other *Pyr*, more annoyed than he'd been in as long as he could remember.

Help him. Ha. No, Thorolf had been sent to ensure Rafferty didn't screw up again. To *spy* on him. Even though he could respect that he had made several mistakes in rapid succession and that Erik was justified in his concern, the decision to monitor his activities still infuriated Rafferty.

That his guard was *Thorolf* was just salt in the wound.

Thorolf was easygoing, old, but undeveloped in his abilities. He was a good fighter, had an impressive appetite, and was often the one who earned Erik's anger— usually for his irresponsibility.

Any other *Pyr* would have been more tactful and more welcome.

Any other *Pyr* might have had useful ideas to contribute.

Thorolf fell into step beside a disgruntled Rafferty, apparently unconcerned that he wasn't particularly welcome. If nothing else, he wasn't the sensitive sort.

Rafferty poked at the elevator button, annoyed that it always took so long in this hotel. He was feeling volatile and edgy, as unlike his usual self as was possible. There could have been a thousand needles beneath his skin, irking and irritating him.

It didn't help that he couldn't think of a solution to the issue of the images being public.

"So, she must be really hot, huh?" Thorolf asked with undisguised interest. "I mean, for you to forget yourself like this, *va va va voom.*" He chuckled and dug his elbow into Rafferty's side.

"Leave it," Rafferty said tightly. Thorolf blinked at his bluntness. Rafferty ignored the other *Pyr*'s surprise and jabbed at the button for the elevator again. He lost patience and headed for the stairs.

"Hold it. Didn't you get any?"

"I don't want to talk about it!"

"No need to take your frustration out on me," Thorolf said, loping down the stairs behind Rafferty. "That's incredible. I mean, usually the women are all over you. What did you say to her?"

"I don't want to talk about it."

"But really, if you struck out . . ."

"Leave it!" Rafferty roared.

"Touchy, touchy," Thorolf said with a low whistle. "She *has* got your number." At Rafferty's warning glance, he held up his hands. "Okay, okay. Consider it left. What's the plan for the pics?"

"I don't know. And even if I did, I wouldn't tell you."

"Why not? I'm on the make-it-right team today." Thorolf began to whistle, clearly proud of his changed status.

Rafferty pivoted so quickly that Thorolf almost ran into him. "Aren't you supposed to tell Erik every single thing I intend to do?"

Thorolf averted his gaze, looking discomfited. Fortunately, he wasn't much of a liar. "Well, it's not my fault. Orders, you know."

"I can't stop you from following me, I can't stop you from telling Erik what I do, but I don't have to tell you what I'm thinking," Rafferty said. When Thorolf didn't reply, he turned and marched down the stairs, each step falling with force.

This eclipse had really rattled him. He felt out of touch with his usual serenity, more easily roused than was his tendency.

Was there a *Pyr* having a firestorm somewhere in close proximity? He was sure he could feel the sizzle of a firestorm's heat.

Were there any *Pyr* in DC other than the two of them? No! It couldn't be!

Rafferty spun again, but Thorolf was keeping a wary

distance. "It's not your firestorm, is it?" Bitterness welled within Rafferty at the prospect.

If Thorolf, who did not care at all for romance or love or long-term relationships, should have a firestorm before Rafferty, then the Great Wyvern truly had no place in Her heart for him, even after all these centuries.

It occurred to him, not for the first time, that perhaps She didn't. Perhaps he was reaping what he had sown. Perhaps the delay in the arrival of Rafferty's own firestorm was retribution for what he had done.

"Me?" Thorolf looked as horrified by the prospect as Rafferty. "Wouldn't I be, like, the first to know?"

"Can't you feel it?" Rafferty couldn't keep the anger from his tone. If Thorolf was having a firestorm, it wouldn't be unreasonable that he, of all *Pyr*, wouldn't have a clue. Rafferty had never met a *Pyr* so disinclined to use his abilities. "*Someone* in our vicinity is having one." He switched to old-speak. *"Feel it!"*

Thorolf stared at Rafferty, then started to chuckle. "Dude, I can't feel anything except the pounding in my head. That's no firestorm—that's plain old beer. Lots of it. With vodka shooters." He leaned closer, eyes dancing. "If you can feel a firestorm burning, and you and I are the only *Pyr* in DC, then do the math yourself."

Rafferty gaped in horror at the other *Pyr*.

No.

No!

Rafferty pivoted and raced down the stairs, needing to know for certain.

"Whoa, I gotta meet this chick." Thorolf galloped down the remaining stairs, passing Rafferty as he swung around a corner on the railing. "She must be really something to have thrown your game so much."

"I am not having a firestorm," Rafferty insisted hotly. "Not with that woman . . ."

Thorolf leapt to land at the steel door ahead of Rafferty. He looked back, his expression confident. "Is that so? I didn't realize we got to pick and choose."

"We don't, but it's, it's *impossible*," Rafferty sputtered.

Thorolf shook his head, his expression pitying. "Maybe we ought to go see her and find out for sure." He hauled open the door, pushing it wide with his fingertips. "After you."

"It can't be her."

"Hey, if you say so." But Thorolf grinned.

Rafferty strode into the street, his heart heavy. He couldn't have a firestorm with a woman who had betrayed him and his kind to the world. No. That was even a greater sign of disapproval from the Great Wyvern.

Could it not be what he deserved?

Suddenly he recalled that blue flicker dancing over Melissa's skin, and his mouth went dry.

Not *darkfire*.

Not with her.

The Great Wyvern couldn't mess with him that much.

But he knew She could.

"So, like, maybe we could score something to eat on the way," Thorolf said cheerfully. "I'm dying after that flight from New York—not even peanuts! How lame is that?—and I'm guessing there's going to be some *Slayer* butt to kick before the end of the day. Whaddaya say? Steak and eggs? Maybe chased with a couple of slices of pie. There has to be a diner someplace. . . ."

"I'm not stopping to eat," Rafferty said tightly. "Not when there is such a major issue to be resolved."

"But we need to keep our strength up. . . ."

"You're welcome to suit yourself." Rafferty hailed a cab and climbed in the back, feeling the lump of Magnus's little blue book in his pocket when he sat down.

The book Melissa had stolen.

The one she undoubtedly wanted back.

How badly would she want it?

Either way, it reassured Rafferty to find something with which he could negotiate. Not commenting when Thorolf flung himself into the cab beside him, he simply gave the address to the driver. He ignored the other *Pyr*'s sigh of forbearance and even the loud rumbling of his stomach.

All Rafferty could think about was the night before. Was it truly possible that this would be his firestorm, and Melissa his destined mate?

Could there truly be darkfire?

Everything certainly was being turned upside down, which wasn't the most reassuring realization Rafferty could have had. He decided in favor of caution and used the time in the cab to send Donovan a message. He didn't dare use old-speak, not with Magnus at large, and he didn't want his words to be audible at all.

He used his phone to send a text message.

Melissa's phone rang. She picked it up without thinking, her attention fixed on the images she was editing. She was proud of herself for getting such good shots in the midst of the fight. "Hello?"

"Melissa? Doug Cameron here."

With four words, her former producer had Melissa's undivided attention. "Doug! It's great to hear from you." She spun in her chair, wondering why he'd called.

She hardly dared to hope.

She crossed her fingers.

Doug, being Doug, didn't beat around the bush. "Those are some images on your blog. Are they real?"

Melissa smiled. "Actually, yes, they are."

"Do you have more?"

"Well, yes, I. . . ."

Doug interrupted her. "Daylight shots?"

"No. They're all of the same incident, last night on the mall."

"Hmm." Even in that one sound, Doug's disappointment was clear. "I like the one with the moon in the background. Atmospheric."

"Thanks."

"Too bad you didn't get one with the eclipse."

There'd been an eclipse the night before? If it had been after the dragon fight, Melissa had missed it for a good reason. "Um, they were gone by then." Her grip tightened on the phone, her heart sinking that he didn't immediately say anything more.

Why had he called? Just to ask for more pictures?

"Look, Melissa, this story of yours is striking a chord," Doug said suddenly, his words falling quickly as they did when he had an agenda. He'd made up his mind about something; Melissa heard it in his voice, and she straightened with interest. "I don't know if you're aware how much it's been picked up."

"I have an idea," she admitted. In fact, she'd been tracking her blog hits, track backs, and incoming links with devotion all morning. She knew her images had been slurped and posted to news services all over the world. It was kind of exciting how many people had been taken with it. The story was going viral, and she felt as if she stood at the middle of a maelstrom.

"Of course, the first assumption anyone has is that the images are bogus. It would be great to have more shots, shots that proved that assumption wrong."

Melissa held her breath. "Yes," she managed to say.

"I'll pay you for exclusive rights to daylight images, if you can get them." Doug named a price that nearly made Melissa drop the phone. "Can you?"

"I think so," she said.

"Good!"

It was tempting to simply leave it there. Melissa could have used a whack of cash in that moment. She had lots of medical bills to pay, but there was one thing she wanted more than a lump sum payment.

She wanted a chance.

Melissa braced her elbow on her desk and dared to ask for what she wanted. This was what she had done all the time, back in the day—pledged to get a story that she hadn't been positive she could get. It was exciting. It made her feel alive again. Tingly.

She was even perspiring. Was the thermostat out of whack, or was it just her?

She kept her voice level. "Actually, Doug, I don't want money."

"Excuse me?"

"I want a job." She swallowed the lump in her throat and spoke more clearly. "I want back on camera."

Doug's silence wasn't encouraging. Melissa waited, her heart thumping, and wondered what to say to persuade him. They'd worked computer for years. She shouldn't have to remind him of her skills, but she would, if necessary. She heard him drumming his fingers and pulled up her résumé on her computer so she wouldn't miss any salient points in her own defense.

Before she could speak, Doug did. "I suppose you want back on the national news." His indecision was obvious. "Foreign affairs?"

"That would be ideal. No worries about travel. I'm good to go."

"What about your husband?"

"What husband?" It was easier to say it now, but Melissa appreciated that Doug responded quickly, covering a potentially awkward moment.

"Right. No houseplants?" Doug asked lightly. It was an old joke between them, and Melissa was glad to hear it. Doug preferred foreign correspondents with no ties. He'd guess that she had no kids, because he'd know her story. Gossip was good for that.

"Not so much as a goldfish," she said with confidence. "And you know that hot zones don't trouble me."

"You were always good in the tight spots," he mused. "Composed under fire. And you dug deeper than most, no half-researched stories. You were really good, Melissa."

"Thanks." His use of the past tense didn't feed her confidence at all.

But he hadn't said no yet. She scanned her résumé, picking the best point to make first, choosing which one she'd make last.

Doug cleared his throat. "You know, I haven't seen you in three years." He spoke with care, and Melissa knew what he was asking. She was accustomed to having her appearance bluntly discussed—it came with the territory of television news.

"Give me your e-mail address," she said, her tone decisive. She thanked her lucky stars that she'd not only taken a chance to shower, but that she'd tugged on her favorite cashmere sweater. The deep purple hue was a good one for her. That she'd put on the freshwater pearl earrings her brother and his wife had given her for Christmas was a bonus.

She could thank Mr. Conscience for making her feel good enough to make the effort.

Or the prospect of his return making her want to look her best.

Melissa used her computer's camera to take a shot of herself, cropped and resized it, and e-mailed it to Doug with a click of the mouse.

"No makeup," she said into the silence. "That's as bad as it gets."

"You look good," Doug said, his relief clear. "A bit thinner, but good. The camera loves thin, anyway. How are you feeling?"

Melissa ensured that her tone was firm, leaving no room for doubt. "I'm all clear and ready to get back in the game. I just need my chance."

There was one beat of hesitation before Doug spoke. "Get me the pictures. In the meantime, I'll talk to some people, see what I can do. You were damn good. I could use more good reporters."

Doug could make this happen, and Melissa knew it. He had an instinct for news and a talent for timely production that gave him cachet at the network. The ratings of the broadcast he produced were consistently higher than those of any other show. If he argued for her to have a job, she'd probably get one.

"Worst case, the lump sum," he said, his tone growing warmer with every word. He'd made up his mind. "But I'll throw my weight behind the job idea."

There was a solid knock at Melissa's door, a knock so

resolute that she had a pretty good idea who was on her porch. Her heart leapt.

He'd come back.

"So, do we have a deal?" Doug asked.

Melissa was staring at the door. Her mouth went dry as she rose to her feet. There was another knock, a more impatient one. A bead of sweat rose on her upper lip, and she licked it away, tasting salt, just as the third heavy knock fell.

Before she could end the call, wood tore and steel bent. She gasped as her door was kicked into the foyer in pieces. It fell heavily, leaving a cloud of dust.

"You can get the pictures, can't you?" Doug asked, obviously misunderstanding the reason for her hesitation.

Mr. Conscience had come, just as she'd expected. He stepped over the threshold of Melissa's house into the debris of the foyer, looking every bit as delicious as he had the night before—an ethics cop with a mission. His gaze flicked over the living room.

And locked on her. His eyes brightened, and he took a step closer, his anger and determination making Melissa's knees weaken.

"Oh no," Melissa whispered.

He glared at her, emanating hostility, and all she could think of was the way he had pleasured her the night before. There were better things they could do with all that passion than fight. For the second time in short order, she was glad to be looking her best.

"What do you mean? Can't you get more dragon pictures?" Doug demanded.

Montmorency's blue leather book was in her lover's left hand. Melissa clutched the phone more tightly, anticipating that he wouldn't give up the book without a fight.

Or a negotiation. He glared at her, although she didn't know what might have put him in a worse mood in the last five seconds.

"Of course I can," she said to Doug with new confidence. "Maybe even today."

"I look forward to it," Doug said; then he was gone, the dial tone echoing in Melissa's ear.

Her uninvited guest stared at her, seeming not even to blink, but she already knew that he wasn't inclined to hurt her. She had to hope that she didn't change his mind. There was a shadow behind him, another guy with blond dreadlocks, but Melissa didn't care if he'd brought a friend.

Her business was with him, and that book.

"I was hoping you'd come back," she said, crossing the living room and stretching out one hand. She spoke with cool composure, as if her heart weren't thundering in her chest. "Thanks for bringing back the book you took from my coat pocket."

"How dare you post those pictures?" he said, moving so quickly toward her that Melissa was astounded. One instant he was in the foyer, and the next he was right before her.

"How did you do that?" she demanded.

"How could you do *that*? How could you betray me and my kind?" he retorted.

"I have no problem betraying Montmorency."

"But you didn't! You betrayed me!" He dropped the book and snatched her up by her shoulders, his gaze boring into hers as he held her off the floor and shook her. "Do you have any understanding what you have done? Do you realize what you have put at risk?" His eyes were snapping, and his grip was resolute.

But he didn't hurt her. He was restraining himself.

"I've done what reporters always do," Melissa retorted, not in the least bit convinced that she was in the right. "We tell the world about news, and if that wasn't news, I don't know what is."

Even as she spoke, she felt a strange heat sliding through her, as if she stood close to a bonfire. No, it was more than a heat against her skin; it was one inside her. It hummed along her veins and warmed her muscles from within. It was a heat that awakened a languorous fire inside her own body. That flame swept through her veins and left her blushing like a schoolgirl.

It was a hungry inferno that reawakened parts of Melissa that he'd caressed the night before.

That tide of heat left her taut. It left her tingling. It made her want him all over again, immediately, if not sooner. He had his hands on her shoulders, his gaze locked upon hers with a passion other than desire, and all she could think about was doing the wild thing with him all over again. She wanted the weight of his hands on her, the caress of his fingertips across her skin, the strength of him inside her. She wanted to feel his breath mingling with hers.

She wanted to feel vibrantly alive again.

She swallowed and looked at him, tormented by an itch he'd yet to satisfy. His eyes darkened, looking like molten chocolate, and when she licked her lips, he caught his breath. She watched him inhale, knew their thoughts were as one, and wished his friend hadn't been in her foyer.

Or, to be fair, that her front door could still be closed.

"Do you recognize what you have put in peril?" he demanded, his words softer than they had been.

Why *were* his hands so hot? It was as if the heat were surging from his body into hers, an electrical current flowing along a conduit. But that made no sense.

Melissa tore her gaze from his and looked down at his hands. He held her in his powerful grip, ensuring that she couldn't escape but not hurting her. That alone might have been worthy of interest, never mind his intensity, but it was the dancing flicker of blue flames across her skin that confused her. It seemed to emanate from the points where they touched, then slither across her skin before it disappeared.

"What's going on?" she asked. "What are these flames?"

He looked away, and she knew he could see them, as well.

"How did you make them, and what do they mean?"

"Darkfire!" he whispered, his tone carrying mingled awe and dread.

"What's darkfire?" she demanded. The way he closed his eyes told her that he knew and that he didn't intend to share the story.

He put her down, turned away, and strode across the room. He shoved a hand through his hair, his agitation clear, and turned his glare on the view out the window. "It doesn't matter," he said tightly. "What matters are those pictures."

His reaction told her exactly the opposite of his words.

The heat was fading, leaving Melissa inclined to shiver. It had something to do with his touch, something he didn't want her to know.

That just meant she was even more determined to find out.

"Bullshit," she said. "You wouldn't be hiding the truth from me if it didn't matter. What's darkfire?"

He cast a glance over his shoulder, leveling a cool look at her. "Nothing I need to tell you about."

"Why not?" There was nothing more infuriating to Melissa than a man saying she didn't need to know some aspect of reality. She could take whatever truth he dished out. She pursued him across the room and touched his elbow. A green-blue flame leapt between them at the point of contact.

His friend swore and took a step backward, his shock clear.

Melissa looked between the two of them. "It seems to affect me. Looks like I have a right to know!"

Mr. Conscience turned then, his eyes narrowed. "But I don't trust you."

Melissa smiled. "Why not?"

"Because you've already told the world too much." Anger thrummed beneath the rich depths of his voice. "I see no reason to tell you anything more. I see no reason to give you the power to destroy us."

Oh, that was interesting. This flame was big, big stuff. There was a story behind it, and realizing as much only made Melissa more determined to learn what it was.

His lip curled. "Particularly not so you can get a job."

That he could dismiss her objectives without understanding anything about her, that he could judge her and find her wanting without two crumbs of the truth, just made Melissa mad.

"Not even to make a deal?" she challenged, then took a step back as his eyes flashed with answering fury.

Chapter 5

Outrageous! That she thought she could negotiate after her willful exposure of the *Pyr* pushed Rafferty over the edge. This woman had put all of his fellows at risk, for no other reason than to share what she knew. He had no doubt that any other secrets she worked free of him would end up on that blog, as well.

As determined as he was to not shift in her presence, her defiance provoked him almost beyond reason.

Maybe that was her plan. Hadn't she pledged to the man on the phone that she'd get daylight pictures of the *Pyr*? Rafferty was glad of the sharp hearing that was characteristic of his kind—although he didn't welcome the news, he was glad to know her intent.

That this woman, this *opportunist*, was the mate chosen for him by destiny and the Great Wyvern was a disappointment beyond Rafferty's current comprehension.

He'd mourn that fact later.

He'd atone for his crime later.

First things first.

"You tricked me about the camera," he said.

Melissa smiled a little, that smile feeding Rafferty's libido in a dangerous way. Her lips had such a ripe fullness to them, and were tempting enough—when she smiled, just a little, he had a hard time thinking of doing anything other than kissing her. "I guessed what you'd want. I thought you might follow me to get it." She shrugged. "So I prepared for that eventuality."

"Your planning could have been a little more complete," Rafferty said. "Did you plan for Magnus to surprise you in his home?"

Her alarm showed for only a heartbeat, just a glimmer in her eyes, before bravado dismissed it. She *had* been surprised, then. "I thought he might be home or come home. I didn't realize what he might become." She lifted her shoulders. "Could I really have prepared for that?"

"You could have avoided breaking into his house, maybe not stolen from him." Rafferty scooped up the book from the floor. She reached for it, but he held it beyond her grasp.

"You're not his friend," she charged, pursuing him. "What difference to you?"

"You entered his house, and you stole from him. You call yourself a journalist, but I don't think that's responsible pursuit of a story." He shook the book before her, his heart pounding that they were toe to toe. "Is that why you have to *negotiate* to get a job?"

She slapped him hard, right across the cheek.

It didn't hurt Rafferty, but it astounded him. Did she have no fear?

"I am a good journalist," she said through her teeth, her eyes flashing. "I am one of the best. I have been at the top of my profession. . . ."

"Yet you apparently aren't there now. Did you bend the rules too much in pursuit of your ambition?"

"No!" She was livid, furious as he'd never yet seen her, and Rafferty was fascinated by the heat of her response. She composed herself with an effort, hiding all that passion away. Then she continued with a control that he knew was hard won. "Something interfered, but it's done now, and I'm going back to work."

"Something?" Rafferty echoed.

"Something." She spoke firmly, that fire lingering in her eyes. It was almost as if she had been a victim of some injustice, but Rafferty wouldn't give her that much credence. She folded her arms across her chest, looking formidable and self-assured, then smiled. "But I don't have to confide in you any more than you have to confide in me."

"Something," Rafferty repeated, his gaze slipping over her. What on earth could have interfered with this woman's pursuit of her goal, whatever it was? He couldn't begin to imagine. She was so determined, so resolute, and—he had to admit—enticingly sexy when she spoke with such ambition and resolve.

She wasn't one for half measures; that was for sure.

And she wasn't afraid of him.

Or if she was, she hid it well.

She put out her hand, her manner imperious. "Give me the book, please."

Rafferty fanned through it. "Why did you want it? Didn't you understand that he wouldn't let anything in his possession go without a fight?"

Her smile was rueful, and her tone was hard. "Oh, I knew that about Montmorency. That's why I took the chance."

"Excuse me?"

"The potential reward was worth the risk." Her gaze was unflinching; the set of her lips hard.

"He won't pay you a ransom."

"I don't want one."

"What do you want?"

"Justice." The word erupted from her lips with such force that Rafferty knew it was the truth. He was intrigued. Had he misjudged her? Justice for whom? Over what? "Give me the book, please."

"It's just a date book," Rafferty said, fanning through it again, as that seemed to annoy her.

Her eyes flashed on cue. "Well, I happen to think it's important where Magnus Montmorency has been and when, not to mention who his friends are."

What did she know about Magnus? Rafferty watched her as concern replaced his anger. Magnus knew who Melissa was, and he could probably follow her scent to wherever she hid. She obviously had some scheme against him.

And Rafferty knew Magnus well enough to know that his old foe wouldn't let a mere human interfere with his plans.

Rafferty's mate was toast.

He might not want her to be his mate, but he certainly didn't want her to be destroyed by Magnus. No one deserved that.

Rafferty toyed with the book, the firestorm messing with his ability to think straight. "If you know anything about Magnus Montmorency, you have to understand how dangerous it is to plot against him."

"And if you know anything about the world, you have to know that the truth will come out and justice will prevail. Particularly if there are people who have the guts to do something about it."

"That would be journalists?"

"Some of us." Melissa tried to grab the book, but Rafferty deftly moved it out of the way. "How can you be so fast?" she said with irritation.

"Montmorency's just as fast," Rafferty murmured.

She flushed, but her lips set in a firm line. "I don't care. I know what he does, and he has to be stopped."

"Even if the price you pay is your own life?"

Melissa paused, then leaned back, her arms folded across her chest and her head tilted as she watched him. "You didn't come here to bring back the book. What do *you* want?"

"I want you to say that the pictures are a hoax, and remove them from your blog."

She smiled. "And I want that book."

"Stalemate," Thorolf said from the foyer. It wasn't the most helpful comment he could have made. Rafferty gave him a poisonous look.

"Friend of yours?" Melissa asked.

"Sometimes," Rafferty admitted, and her smile broadened.

"I've had friends like that," she murmured. Their gazes locked, and Rafferty felt a tenuous sense of common purpose with her. It was as seductive as her perfume.

Or was that just his own ideas about the firestorm at work?

Thorolf cleared his throat, seeming to see Melissa's words as an opening. "I don't suppose you've got anything in the fridge that needs eating?" he said, his manner cajoling. "You know, a roast chicken or, maybe, a ham?"

The prospect that Melissa, who was so slim, might have such a quantity of cooked meat in her fridge amused Rafferty. He found an answering humor in Melissa's eyes, one that made his heart skip a beat.

"I think there's some chickpea salad," Melissa said, her tone all innocence. Rafferty nearly laughed out loud at Thorolf's disappointed expression.

"Come *on*," Thorolf said, a plea in his voice.

"The salad is pretty much it. Some antipasto. Half a head of romaine. Please, help yourself," Melissa said, her smile fading as she faced Rafferty again. "I think we've got a bit more to discuss here."

"I don't think we have anything more to discuss," Rafferty replied, but Melissa planted her hand on his chest. The surge of heat from her palm made him stagger. The power of the firestorm—and the desire it awakened in him—pushed the thought of everything except claiming his mate from his thoughts.

Claiming her again and again and again.

It was too easy to remember the softness of her skin beneath his hands. To remember how she sighed and shivered when he ran his tongue over her tight nipple. To remember the taste of her and the smell of her, and the way she tightened just before she came.

He could almost feel the tug of her fingers in his hair, the way her teeth had grazed his skin, the scratch of her fingernails in his shoulders, and he stepped closer to seduce her all over again. The darkfire flickered blue with green lights, consuming him, tantalizing him, dazzling him.

"You haven't told me what this is," Melissa said, her words falling on a breathless note. Her eyes were wide and clear, her lips parted, and Rafferty could smell the sweet perfume of her desire. She knew exactly what she had to negotiate with, which should have worried Rafferty more than it did.

As it was, all he could think about was her smooth heat around him, her softness urging him closer, her perfume ensnaring him.

"Darkfire," she prompted when he didn't answer. "What's darkfire?"

"It's a special kind of firestorm, one that has been foretold for millennia."

Her eyes widened, and he saw the golden flickers in her irises. He took another step closer, his hands rising to her shoulders again. She felt small and fragile in his grip, feminine, delicate.

Delicious. She was staring at his mouth, and she licked her own lips as she let him draw her even closer. The heat roiled through him, pushing every thought but one from his mind.

"What's a firestorm?" she whispered, just as her breasts collided with his chest.

"This," Rafferty said with satisfaction, and claimed her mouth with his own.

Melissa closed her eyes as he kissed her again. She'd provoked him, and she was only glad that it worked. She'd been sure that her memory of his kiss must have been overrated, had known that she needed to taste him once more to be sure, had pushed him until he kissed her again. She had a fleeting realization that she still didn't know his name, followed by the recognition that in this instant she didn't care. Then his kiss obliterated all conscious thought.

There was only feeling and sensation.

There was only heat, like molten glass flowing through her body. It incinerated her defenses, melted her resolve, destroyed any inhibitions she might have thought she had. She caught him close, those blue flames snapping and crackling between them. They rolled over her skin, sexy and seductive, making her feel vital.

They were like a visual clue to the desire that raged between them. Every place she touched him, sparks danced. Every place they fell upon her own skin simmered with an answering heat. Then they slid, moving more like liquid than flame, slipping across her skin and leaving a trail of lust. She was burning up with desire for him.

He was moving more quickly than he had the night before, and she knew that he was feeling the same incredible desire. He unfastened her jeans with impatience, and she loved the smooth heat of his broad palms sliding over her skin. The fact that he couldn't control himself, that he couldn't wait to have her, fired her blood as surely as his touch. She wasn't—or had never been—the kind of woman who made men lose control. It was dizzying to be so desired. His hands were strong and capable, deft and utterly distracting. She felt his fingers slide beneath the elastic of her underwear, and she sighed in contentment.

She hadn't imagined his powerful tenderness.

His touch was, in fact, even better than she recalled.

His fingers made her moan; that spark leaping against her skin left her dizzy. She locked her arms around his neck and hung on, rolling her hips against him. He had a massive erection, straining at the front of his jeans, and she remembered the sweet fullness of having him inside her.

He wasn't the only one who was impatient.

She thought of his friend in her kitchen but heard the persistent rattle of dishes. He was busy.

And there was something exciting about the need to be quick and quiet. She met the intense gaze of Mr. Conscience, so determined to please her, and her pulse fluttered.

Then it thundered.

His fingers moved with greater demand, and she thought she might just faint with pleasure. Was that possible? She wanted to find out. She reached for the front of his jeans and unfastened them, sliding her hand inside. He inhaled sharply, cast aside her jeans, then cupped her buttock with one hand. He touched her again, and she squirmed with impatience.

"Now," she whispered. "Here."

Melissa slid one bare foot up the muscled strength of his calf, and, once again, he was holding her above the floor. She freed him from his jeans, pushing them down over his hips, then met his gaze.

His gaze was simmering, a heat that echoed the fire in her own veins. He slid two fingers inside her, easing his thumb across her clitoris as he did so, and Melissa trembled. He smiled, then repeated the gesture, driving her higher and higher with each sweep of his thumb.

Melissa thought she couldn't stand it any longer just as sparks exploded through her body. She cried out in her sudden release, arching against him. The orgasm was amazing, potent enough to leave her shaking.

She was ready for him, but he dropped her on the couch suddenly. Melissa bounced slightly, right where they had made love repeatedly the night before, and watched him stalk across the room. What had changed? What was wrong? Was his friend returning?

No. The fridge opened again, as if the friend was optimistic that its contents might have changed while he wasn't looking. She heard Mr. Conscience refasten his jeans. He had his back to her, but she could see from the set of his shoulders that he was as taut as a bowstring.

However taut that might be. Melissa wasn't sure she'd ever seen one.

She caught her breath and straightened her panties, trying to pull her thoughts together. This guy really shook her. "Is there a problem?" she asked.

He pivoted then, his eyes flashing. "The pictures. You have to remove them."

"Well, I won't." Melissa got to her feet, pretending to be more composed than she was. She was chilled to the bone with the absence of his touch.

No. It had been his rejection that had left her so cold. She pulled on her jeans and shoved her feet into her sheepskin boots. "And no matter how many times you do that, you won't change my mind."

If she'd thought he'd been angry before, Melissa learned otherwise right then. He pivoted, eyes blazing. "I did not do *that* to win your acquiescence. I am not manipulative!"

He did have a tendency to speak formally. Melissa had noticed it before. Where was he from? Where did dragon men come from? He had a slight accent, as if music underlay his words. His voice was so rich and deep. A radio voice.

She folded her arms across her chest again, knowing they wouldn't keep him away if he chose to come after her. "You were doing some good manipulation just then."

He swore under his breath, then approached her, shaking a finger. "I will *not* be seduced." His voice rose with anger, resonating more loudly with every syllable. "I will not be charmed into abandoning my principles and the defense of my kind, firestorm be damned! I have principles, and they cannot be cast aside so readily as that. Do we understand each other?"

"No," Melissa said just before a knock sounded on the frame of her front door. "I don't have any idea what you're talking about."

He faltered then, glancing toward the door in frustration. Then he straightened, looking daggers at the porch.

"Bad time?" Montmorency asked sweetly, smiling so broadly that Melissa could readily recall him in dragon form. He was dressed in his usual conservative style, looking like a successful European businessman.

He held his side with one hand, as if a bit stiff. Melissa realized that the injuries these guys sustained in their dragon form carried to their human form.

Interesting.

"Not at all," she said. She crossed the room, pushing her lover back behind her. "My house," she muttered to him.

"Your battle," he replied, and he was right.

That was a bit daunting.

"I just wanted to stop by and pick up my book," Montmorency said smoothly. His eyes glittered. "Assuming that it *slipped* into your possession last night."

"I don't have it," Melissa said with a shrug. She wasn't lying, although she couldn't see what Mr. Conscience had done with it. There was no sign of the book in her living room. No doubt, he'd moved just as quickly in hiding it as he had in flashing it in the first place.

"Come, let's not play games," Montmorency said, his manner oily. "I'm prepared to make its return worth your while."

Mr. Conscience began to protest, but Melissa held up a hand to silence him. "How so?" she asked, and he snorted disdain. She glanced back to see him settle into her computer chair. He looked disgruntled, irritable, and unpredictable.

Sexy as hell.

She would have loved to have had the time to explain to him that their ethical standards were exactly the same. As it was, she found it irresistible that he had no troubles pointing out her moral infractions, a choice that could interfere with their being intimate again.

That was a different choice than many men made.

Of course, she hadn't exactly been playing hard to get. Maybe he knew that she found him irresistible.

Montmorency spoke, and Melissa glanced back toward him. "Perhaps it would be better to discuss this on the porch, away from the surly stare of my old friend, Rafferty. He seems to look askance on our discussion, and I wouldn't want him to dissuade you from accepting very good terms."

Rafferty.

The name suited him better than Mr. Conscience.

"Don't," Rafferty warned. She heard the squeak of the chair as he rose to his feet.

Melissa respected his concern, but she knew what she was doing. She didn't trust Montmorency any farther than she could throw him, either. But taking two steps onto the porch didn't put her appreciably out of range—

should Rafferty decide again to defend her. She already knew he could move at the speed of light.

Although he *had* warned her that Montmorency could, as well.

Melissa stepped into the foyer, even so. "What do you offer in exchange for the book?" she asked Montmorency. "Assuming I could lay hands on it again."

Montmorency smiled, and this time he resembled nothing more than a hungry crocodile. Melissa didn't flinch or show her fear. She held his gaze, letting him become overconfident. He said something, very quietly, and she couldn't hear him.

"I beg your pardon?"

"Melissa!" Rafferty cried. "Don't look at him!"

What a ridiculous thing to say. It was critical to hold his gaze to persuade him of her own integrity. She knew a thing or two about making a deal. Melissa looked.

"Pictures," Montmorency said, just an increment more loudly. His eyes gleamed. "I offer you pictures of *Pyr* in daylight. Just come closer to see."

"I don't have my camera."

"You don't need it. You can use mine."

"You don't have one."

"Oh, yes, I do." Montmorency held her gaze. "Just come with me."

There were flames in his eyes. It was so strange. It couldn't be. Melissa took a step closer to see them better.

"There's dragonsmoke!" Rafferty roared, but Melissa had already taken the last two steps, over the threshold. She stood on the porch beside her foe, staring into his eyes.

Montmorency began to laugh.

Rafferty lunged after her, and Melissa glanced back. To

her shock, he seemed to collide with an invisible barrier right where her door had been. She saw him grimace in pain and throw himself at the invisible barrier once more. It repelled him again, and she smelled flesh burning.

The smell was horrible. She turned back to Montmorency, even clutching his sleeve. "What are you doing to him? Make it stop!"

"Oh, don't tell me that it's love," Montmorency said with a chortle. "Not just a firestorm, but true love, too." He turned to a very frustrated Rafferty. "My friend, you have waited so very long for such a prize. Too bad I am going to steal it from you."

"No one is stealing me," Melissa said hotly. "I'm going right back in there. . . ." She pointed through the doorway, and, when her hand crossed the line that should have been marked by the door, Rafferty seized it.

Green and blue sparks flew, like the light of a sparkler on the Fourth of July, and Melissa had to close her eyes against the brightness. His hand was warm, his touch soothing, and she wanted more than anything to be back at his side.

"Oh yes, I am," Montmorency said, his voice strangely low. "Darkfire, too. Oh my."

Melissa glanced his way, intending to argue with him. Those flames were dancing in the depths of his eyes again. Surely she was wrong. No one had flames in their eyes. She looked more closely, and she was snared.

"Melissa!" Rafferty shouted.

She released his hand, pulling her own hand away from him, and stared at Montmorency's eyes. So strange. So fascinating.

"In fact," Montmorency said with quiet intensity, "you're going to come willingly with me."

"Willingly," Melissa echoed, unable to look away from the brilliance in his eyes.

"We'll take a ride, together."

"A ride together." Melissa hated how she repeated his words, like some kind of zombie, but she couldn't stop herself. What was going on?

"See the sights." His words slipped into her mind, mingling with her thoughts until she couldn't distinguish the two. She fought against whatever spell he was casting, but he opened his eyes wider and spoke more slowly.

Drawing her into his web.

The flames flickered and danced, and Melissa watched them hungrily.

"Come with me, Melissa," Montmorency said, then smiled. "Mine is an offer you can't refuse."

"Can't refuse," she echoed, and put her hand into Montmorency's elbow.

She vaguely heard Rafferty's bellow of rage, but it didn't seem to have much to do with her, not so long as Montmorency kept talking to her. He patted her hand and guided her off the porch.

She heard the steady chop of the blades of a helicopter, guessed that it was on the circle in the center of the cul-de-sac, but couldn't look away from Montmorency's eyes.

Not until he looked away from her.

And by then, they were five thousand feet above the ground.

She was horrified as she saw her town house far far below. There was no sign of Rafferty.

What had she done?

Rafferty was infuriated. It wasn't like him to lose his temper—to even have a temper—but the firestorm seethed beneath his skin, feeding the beast and turning his nature more passionate. It was the darkfire, he knew it, but that only made him more furious. It was like the power of the eclipsed moon, but a thousand times more potent.

Inescapable.

Now his mate had been captured by Magnus, his own anger persuading her that that villain's company was a better choice than his own. Whether Melissa believed as much for the long term or not, she'd believed it long enough to step through the dragonsmoke barrier that Rafferty couldn't cross, and to be beguiled by that old snake.

The reality of his situation—of her situation—and his own responsibility for it made Rafferty want to shred something.

Magnus would have been the ideal candidate.

"Good choice," Thorolf said, shoveling back chickpea salad as if he might never have the chance to eat again. "Gotta say, I wouldn't have expected you to be the one to screw up a firestorm." He shrugged. "Although it's not like there's much we can do about it now."

"The dragonsmoke perimeter ring is complete," Rafferty said through gritted teeth.

"Yup," Thorolf agreed easily. "Even I can hear its resonant ping. Magnus is one sneaky dude and breathes smoke fast. What now? We call Erik in old-speak?"

Rafferty ignored him. He didn't need any help to consummate his firestorm. He didn't need any advice to secure the safety of his mate. Magnus had just raised the stakes of their duel. Rafferty would not see his destined mate endangered as a result of his choices—whether he and she successfully negotiated their firestorm or not.

She was human. She was one of the treasures of the earth he was charged to defend.

Not only that, but his firestorm was the fabled darkfire. He had another responsibility, one that Magnus didn't suspect existed but would be determined to derail if that *Slayer* learned the truth. The Sleeper would awaken, according to Rafferty's grandfather's ancient charm, because the darkfire burned and Rafferty was bound to defend the Sleeper until the darkfire was extinguished.

That he had never believed this day would come was irrelevant. This was not the moment for regrets.

He had to save Melissa.

Yet Rafferty was trapped. He couldn't cross the dragonsmoke barrier without Magnus's permission, not without being singed to cinders and surrendering all of his life force to his foe. He couldn't leave the town house through the door or the windows, or even the roof.

But there was another way out.

Through the earth. He just had to open a path.

Indeed, he had no choice but to do so.

Regardless of the cost.

Rafferty clenched his fists, closed his eyes, and began to sing the song of the earth. Such was the force of his anger that the earth was quick to respond, a ripple running immediately beneath the foundation of the town house.

Rafferty sang louder, and the building began to dance. He felt the earth begin to crack deep beneath its footings, and he sang louder, pouring his heart and his soul into his song. He sang with all the force he could muster; he sang every song with a vehemence he'd never experienced before.

And the earth responded in kind.

There would be an earthquake, and this house would be its epicenter, because Rafferty sang from its foyer. And when the crack in the surface was wide enough, he would walk through the earth to save his mate.

"Oh shit," Thorolf said, putting the bowl of salad down on the counter. "What are you doing?"

Rafferty ignored him and sang. The floor jumped, a jagged crack opening above the doorway as the house split. Bricks began to fall and plaster crumbled. The dragonsmoke roiled through the gap, unseen but toxic, and Rafferty sang louder. They had to escape before the smoke burned them, before it could create a conduit to Magnus and cheat them of their life force.

Rafferty sang with renewed vigor.

A mighty crack sounded, and the foundation of the town house split like an egg. The earth yawned open, a crevasse bisecting the cul-de-sac. It was wide and deep, opening like a great rift before Rafferty's eyes.

He sang even louder.

The earth rumbled and the pavement tore, the crack yawning ever wider. Rafferty didn't know how long it would hold. He jumped down into the gap, singing all the while. Then he ran down the length of the crack toward freedom.

The dragonsmoke gave chase. He could feel its chill seeking him.

"Erik is going to be pissed!" Thorolf shouted, but Rafferty didn't care. Both Erik and Thorolf could take care of themselves.

His mate could not.

Two hundred yards farther, just before the cul-de-sac connected with the main road, the earthquake ruptured a water main. Water spurted upward like the plume from a whale, and Rafferty took advantage of its cover to leap into the air. He shifted shape in the mist of the spraying water and soared into the clear midday sky.

He heard the crowd of observers behind him, but it was too late to care about that detail.

He had more important things to do in the immediate future.

He had to save his mate.

He had to defend the Sleeper.

He had to destroy Magnus before both were lost forever.

Chapter 6

Erik could have done without Rafferty screwing up, especially at this point. As much as he would have liked to aid his old friend, Erik had too important a mission to just abandon it and go to Rafferty's side. He'd dispatched only Thorolf to the ancient *Pyr*'s firestorm. He hoped Rafferty would see that choice as a sign of Erik's faith that Rafferty didn't need any help to have a successful firestorm.

Erik wished he felt a little more sure of that outcome himself.

Thorolf, though, was more inclined to empty refrigerators than be of real help. He was a good fighter, but charming a mate was a different kind of battle.

But if Erik had sent all the *Pyr*, Rafferty would have taken that as a sign that Erik expected him to fail. Sloane would have been a good choice, but Erik needed him right where he was.

He kissed Eileen and Zoë farewell without another word. So much had been said already. He met Sloane's gaze and shook his hand, knowing the other *Pyr* would do whatever was necessary to protect Erik's mate and child, should it come to that.

"*With my life*," Sloane vowed in old-speak.

A *Pyr* couldn't ask more than that.

"Be careful," Eileen said, and Erik cast her a rueful smile.

If he'd been careful, Erik wouldn't have been beguiled in the first place. And he wouldn't be heading out to confront the wily *Pyr* who had managed to beguile him. He had no idea what to expect from Lorenzo.

But times demanded that he had to ask this powerful *Pyr* for his aid in the battle against the *Slayers*.

Even if he expected to be denied.

Even if he feared for his own health.

He glanced to his daughter, Zoë, wondering whether she would cast some useful old-speak into his thoughts. She held his gaze unblinkingly, her eyes wide, her lashes thick and dark. He could feel nothing from her and it frightened him. Was he simply expecting too much too soon? The evidence that she would be the next Wyvern was thin. He'd been convinced of it, as was Rafferty, but several of the other *Pyr* had their doubts.

There was nothing he could do to hasten her development.

Erik left the hotel suite, welcoming the heat of the Nevada sun. It was early, but the air was hot already, unseasonably hot for this time of year. His sunglasses only slightly diminished the sun's glare. He got into his Maserati sedan and wished yet again for his Lamborghini, which was safely back in Chicago. As much as he liked this car—and the room it had to carry his family—the Lamborghini was closer to his heart. The throb of its engine would have soothed him in a way this car never could.

But that was just a detail. He started the Maserati's engine and let it idle until the air-conditioning started to work. Erik had no reason to hesitate. He knew the way to Lorenzo's private compound in the desert, he had a full tank of gas, and he knew he was expected.

Still . . .

He put the car into gear with some impatience and backed out of the parking spot. There was no point in delaying the inevitable.

He wouldn't think about jumping from the fat into the fire.

Not an hour later, Erik stood in a large room in the house within Lorenzo's gated estate and awaited the other *Pyr*'s presence.

Actually, he wasn't sure of the dimensions of the room. It seemed large, but that could have been an illusion. Its walls were covered with faceted mirrors, reflecting images from one another. Those reflections should have stayed at the perimeter of the room, but they didn't.

There was something odd about the mirrors, or their positioning, something Erik couldn't quite figure out. In this hall of mirrors, he could have been standing in the middle of a crowd of men who looked exactly like him. They were on his every side, some appearing to be close enough to touch, others a hundred yards away.

The visual effect disoriented him, even though he knew it was a trick. It made him doubt his perceptions. It was a telling reminder of Lorenzo's current occupation as a stage magician, and it irritated Erik that the illusion worked so well, even on him.

One instant, he was alone in the midst of a crowd of his own reflections.

The next, there were two kinds of men in the room—
he and Lorenzo, replicated over and over again.

How had Lorenzo entered the room?

"Good morning," Lorenzo said, his voice as smooth
and rich as ever. He smiled and stepped closer with leisurely confidence.

At least, Erik thought he stepped closer. Which was
the real Lorenzo?

Erik chose an image of Lorenzo and spoke to it.
"Good morning. You're looking well."

Lorenzo did look well. He was as tall and lithe as Erik
recalled, his hair dark and curly. His eyes were hazel,
a brownish green with a flick of gold, just as they had
always been. The smile Erik remembered so well still
curved Lorenzo's lips. He'd never been able to decide
whether Lorenzo was on the verge of laughter or not,
much less what exactly was the source of his amusement. Lorenzo had his mother's irreverence, as well as
her lust for life and her fondness for luxury.

"This life suits me," Lorenzo said easily. "I like the
desert and the heat, especially after all those years in
damp chill. I suppose it's less congenial to you."

His old friend's easy manner made Erik more wary of
his intent. He found himself standing stiffly, answering
more curtly than had been his intention. "I like the turn
of the seasons."

"Ah yes. Traditional as always." Lorenzo's smile
broadened. "Some things never do change."

They eyed each other, the fact of Lorenzo's beguiling
of Erik hanging between them. It had been wrong—a
violation of every rule or expectation of the *Pyr*—yet
if Erik made an issue of it, he might not be able to persuade Lorenzo to aid him in the battle against the *Slay-*

ers. He tried to assess the other *Pyr*'s mood, but Lorenzo only smiled, his thoughts hidden.

He seemed to enjoy Erik's indecision.

"I came to ask for your help," Erik said finally, but Lorenzo swept aside his words.

"I know why you came, what you will say, and what you want to say. We can cut this whole matter short. I won't help you. I won't join you. I won't follow you."

"But why not? This battle against the *Slayers* is key. . . ."

"If so, it's not important in the way that you think," Lorenzo argued.

"What are you talking about? They want to destroy humans to save the earth. We need to defend the humans and stop the *Slayers*."

"By destroying the *Slayers*?" Lorenzo asked.

"Yes. If need be."

"And how exactly is that different from the *Slayers*' quest to destroy the *Pyr*?"

"They are wrong! Their hearts are stained with darkness. . . ."

Lorenzo lifted a hand, and Erik's protest fell silent. "War does not create peace. It never does. Violence breeds only more violence."

Erik appealed to him again. "They are close to being eradicated. We are on the cusp of success, and if I can muster every *Pyr* . . ."

Lorenzo laughed. "And what happens when they are eradicated?"

"Then we live in peace."

"No. We are by nature adversarial. If we have no foe, we will invent one."

"I don't believe that for an instant."

"We will become our own worst enemies." Lorenzo shrugged. "Or maybe humans will hunt us again, and, this time, succeed in exterminating us."

"I don't believe that," Erik argued, although he had his doubts. It had happened before, after all. And there was that blog post from Melissa Smith. He knew there would be repercussions from that, and they might not be positive for the *Pyr*.

"Doubts?" Lorenzo asked. "I'm not surprised. We can't exist in this world in the old way any longer, Erik. We have to adapt."

"Adapt?" Erik eyed his old friend. "By becoming conjurors? You use your powers as a parlor trick, to beguile humans into believing the illusions you create."

"It works beautifully, and to our mutual benefit. They are entertained, and I live in the style to which I have been accustomed. I find it much more congenial than warfare."

"But each of us can be a target. . . ."

"No. I won't be targeted. They don't realize where I am or what I am."

"It could still happen. I found you."

"My lair is not undefended." He smiled again. "Do you really imagine you could attack me here and live to tell about it?"

Erik snatched at the reflection he'd been addressing, just to prove his point, only to have his hand slip through nothing.

"There is an advantage to living in a house of smoke and mirrors," Lorenzo commented.

Erik pivoted, choosing another version of Lorenzo to address. Which one was real? Were any of them real? "What if you have a firestorm?"

He saw the glint of desire in Lorenzo's eyes, flashing in a thousand eyes around him, before it was hidden. "I'll call you if I need help."

"But I need your help," Erik appealed one last time. "I need every *Pyr* at my side. . . ."

"Not so," Lorenzo argued. "You let Quinn slip away for centuries."

"I have to balance the needs of the individual against the needs of the group," Erik said gruffly, feeling very much on the spot. There was something about Lorenzo's voice, something melodic and persuasive about it, something that made Erik say more than would ever have been his own intent. "He needed time to grieve and to learn, so that he could become the Smith of the *Pyr*. I couldn't have forced that role upon him sooner, and we had the time—at least I believed as much. I didn't expect him to be able to disguise himself."

"You didn't expect to lose him."

"No." Erik was embarrassed that he had confessed so much. He knew that on some level, Lorenzo was beguiling him again. He turned his back on the other *Pyr*, only to be confronted by another knowing reflection of him.

"And what of Drake and his fellows?" Lorenzo asked. "Where are they?"

Erik was shocked to realize that he did not know. He couldn't sense Drake or any of the Dragon's Tooth Warriors. Not anymore. His eyes widened and Lorenzo chuckled.

"Some kind of leader, to lose an entire batallion."

"You have no right . . ." Erik began, only to have the other *Pyr* interrupt him

"And what of Brandt?" Lorenzo asked softly.

"I owe you no explanation."

"I think you do."

Erik gritted his teeth, trying to hold back the words and failing to do so. "I know exactly where he is," he said with impatience.

"Yet you do not collect him."

"Not yet. It is too soon." Erik frowned, and another confession slid over his lips. "I fear it will always be too soon for Brandt, although I hope for the day I have something to offer him in exchange." He pivoted and chose another reflection, one that looked brighter than the others. "Stop this! You cannot force me to betray the *Pyr*!"

"Oh, but it seems that I can," Lorenzo said with a thread of laughter in his tone.

"This is no joke! If I say too much, they will be in danger."

"They are in danger anyway, given your record of leadership."

"No!" It was a horrific implication, one Erik found dangerously compelling. Was he failing the *Pyr*?

"It's the darkfire, you know," Lorenzo said with confidence.

"There is no darkfire!"

"And you're the one with foresight." Lorenzo chuckled. "See? Darkfire challenges every expectation, just as foretold." His voice dropped low. "What about the Cantor's last charm? What will you do, Erik Sorensson, when the Sleeper awakens and demands his rightful due?"

What was the Cantor's last charm? Who was the Sleeper? What was his due? Or was Lorenzo simply toying with him? "You are only entertaining yourself in disorienting me," Erik charged. "Think of the others!"

Lorenzo laughed at the notion. "No more parlor tricks, then?"

"No!"

Lorenzo snapped his fingers and disappeared.

As cleanly as that.

There was no sign of him in the room. Erik turned in place, wondering how he had disappeared so quickly, and the lights subtly changed.

He was standing in a room, a room with walls covered in mirrors. They reflected him precisely as he would have expected, the images remaining around the perimeter, and leaving him alone in the center of the space. It was no trick.

But Lorenzo was gone.

"Did you summon the darkfire?" Erik shouted to the room.

There was no answer, although he thought he discerned a low laugh. Why? Because Lorenzo *had* summoned it? Or because he thought it funny that Erik could imagine his power to be so great?

A door opened behind Erik, the mirror latched to its back angling as it opened into the room. A servant stood there, his hand on the knob. "Mr. di Fiore asked me to show you out, sir."

No illusions. Lorenzo was gone, and his answer was clear.

So be it.

Erik marched out of the room, through the foyer, and into the midday sun's heat. He got into the car and glanced back once at the house. "*I ask you as a friend*," he said in old-speak, making one last plea.

"*And I decline you as one*," Lorenzo replied immediately.

Erik started the car and squealed the tires as he drove away. The gates opened automatically for him and closed behind his car with a resolute clang.

All he could see in his rearview mirror, though, was the cloud of dust raised by his departure.

And within that dust, he saw the dead, crowded behind his vehicle, himself in their midst.

Was the vision real?

Or another illusion of Lorenzo's?

Erik was already shaken, but that vision had him pushing the car to its limit in his haste to get back to his family.

Alex rushed home at Donovan's mysterious summons. Just the fact that he'd called her at work and asked her to come home quickly, with no further explanation, meant something was up. There had been an eclipse the night before, so Alex had an idea what it was.

Donovan wasn't visible when she entered the house, but she heard movement in the kitchen. She smiled at the sound of their son, Nick, chattering to his father.

Her smile faded when she glimpsed the packed suitcases in the doorway of the bedroom. She'd been right.

"Where to?" she asked, noting that the kitchen was perfectly clean and organized.

"Flight at three," Donovan said, his manner terse. "Chicago first. Then London, then Cardiff. After that, we'll drive."

Wales. They were going to Wales. Alex guessed whose firestorm it was and couldn't hide her smile. "Commercial flights?" she asked.

"It's too far for me to fly us all."

Alex understood that the truth was he didn't know

what to expect when they arrived. He wanted to be well-rested. Alex's hand slid over her still-flat stomach.

Donovan's gaze followed her gesture and his lips tightened. "I'm sorry. Centuries ago, I made a promise, and today is the day it must be kept."

"What kind of promise?"

"To defend the Sleeper, if and when he awakened." He winked at her. "Although I still need to protect you. That's why we're *all* going." Donovan checked his watch, then scooped up Nick. "I think I got all the essentials. Could you check? The cab will be here in ten."

"But who's the Sleeper? Whom did you promise? And why does this Sleeper need to be defended? I thought this was about a firestorm!"

"It is. I'll tell you more on the way."

Alex stepped into his path. She'd had a rough first trimester and wasn't up for puking in strange places if it wasn't entirely necessary. "Tell me something now."

Donovan flicked a glance between Alex and Nick. "The Sleeper is under Rafferty's care. I promised Rafferty to help if the Sleeper ever awakened, but that's only supposed to happen when there's darkfire. I never thought the darkfire would burn."

"Darkfire?"

He grimaced. "A really ominous kind of firestorm. And it's Rafferty's firestorm." He met her gaze steadily. "He needs our help."

"Not fair!" Alex protested, that explanation completely committing her to the cause. "Rafferty gets the rotten kind of firestorm? How unreasonable is that?"

"He might be the only one who can turn darkfire to good," Donovan said softly. "We have to have faith in the wisdom of the Great Wyvern, Alex."

Right. Alex had never been much for religion, and she didn't share the *Pyr*'s admiration of their deity. But she knew when to shut up. And she knew when to hurry. It was entirely possible that she'd be able to help Rafferty, too.

"Okay," Alex agreed with a nod. "Nine minutes to departure."

She was ready to go in seven point five.

Just as the cab pulled up in front of the house.

Sloane felt the prickle of heat from a distant firestorm. When he closed his eyes and let himself sense the firestorm, he could see it was tinged with a strange blue-green light.

Like a chemical reaction.

And in a way, darkfire was just that. The blue flames indicated a mythic firestorm, one that changed everything before it was subdued. Surrendering to the sexual demand of the firestorm was less important than accepting the transformation it wrought. Sloane had heard a great deal about this possibility from his mentor, but he had never expected to see it in his lifetime.

Tynan—Sloane's mentor, father, and the Apothecary before Sloane—had yearned to see darkfire all his long life. He never had. Sloane shared his father's awe, but not his expectation.

Yet the darkfire had come.

And it had come for Rafferty. It was fitting, in a way, that the member of the *Pyr* most interested in firestorms should have this special one. On the other hand, darkfire posed a challenge that could break a *Pyr*. Sloane hoped it wouldn't destroy Rafferty with its demands.

Sloane remained at his assigned post, defending the

mate and child of the leader of the *Pyr*. He had breathed dragonsmoke, thick and deep, around the hotel. He had piled it against the door and windows, in the vents, in every access he could find.

It felt inadequate, given that he knew some *Slayers* could cut smoke and pass through its barrier.

The old ways weren't as effective anymore. Would the darkfire change that, too?

Either way, there wasn't much else he could do. He remained alert, his keen senses attuned to the world beyond the suite, and he hovered on the cusp of change. The tickle of the firestorm already fed the power of his dragon side, making him feel both vulnerable and powerful. It was worse than the sensation of the eclipse; worse than the call of the moon.

It must be the darkfire. What else would it change?

Eileen stood at the window of the hotel suite, watching the parking lot. There was nothing Sloane could say to console her, nothing that would relieve her other than Erik's safe return. Without the gift of foresight, Sloane couldn't even predict that.

Zoë played on the floor, happily stacking brightly colored plastic cylinders. When the pile was knee-high, she cheerfully hit the bottom one, laughing as the cylinders scattered.

It was hard, in times like this, to believe that she truly was the new Wyvern—as Erik believed—and not simply a cute child. How could she be so indifferent to the burn of darkfire and the tingle of a firestorm? How could she not be troubled by the uproar in the earth? Sloane was vexed enough to prod her.

"*Do you feel it?*" he asked her in old-speak.

Zoë gave no indication that she had heard him. She

crawled after the last red cylinder, then offered it to Eileen. "Mama?" she said, her voice rising in a question.

Eileen smiled, her thoughts clearly elsewhere, and bent down. "Biggest on the bottom," she said. "What's next?"

"Orge," Zoë said, dragging out the soft *g* sound. She picked up the orange cylinder and placed it on top, her smile triumphant.

"*What do you know of darkfire?*" Sloane asked, just as she was putting the orange cylinder on top of the red one. Did she waver for a second before putting it in place? Sloane wasn't sure. He would have tried again, but found Eileen's gaze upon him.

"You're talking to her in old-speak, aren't you?" Eileen asked. Her disapproval was more than clear, and Sloane felt chided. Most humans disliked the notion of a conversation they couldn't quite discern. Old-speak sounded like distant thunder to humans. "You needn't bother."

"What do you mean?"

"Erik has been complaining that since Zoë started to talk, she doesn't respond to his old-speak." Eileen shrugged, and Sloane knew she wasn't entirely displeased about this. "He's not sure whether she can't hear him or she doesn't want to."

"When did she start to talk?"

"Just a couple of days ago. She's late with it, but maybe she didn't have anything important to say."

"Mamamamamamamama," Zoë supplied, intent upon her toys.

"And here I thought you were your daddy's girl," Eileen said. "Her eyes have changed color too. They were blue when she was born."

Sloane had another look. Eileen was right: Zoë's eyes had become green. Like Erik's. "Maybe she's not responding to old-speak because she's not the Wyvern, after all," he dared to suggest. Maybe she wasn't the Wyvern *anymore*.

Had Zoë changed? Or was this another price of the darkfire?

Eileen met his gaze, her own steely. "Maybe being a smart little girl is good enough."

"What do you mean?"

"I mean that it's too much of a burden upon a child to have everyone waiting for her to become the next Wyvern. She needs to just be a child, and if it is her destiny to become the next Wyvern, that will happen of its own accord. Having all of you watch her like hawks doesn't help. It's not healthy for any child to bear such pressure and expectation." Eileen exhaled after her impromptu lecture and visibly composed herself. "Not that *my* opinion has anything to do with it."

Sloane caught a whiff of an old battle, undoubtedly one between Erik and Eileen. Eileen might not be *Pyr*, but she had a ferocity and determination—particularly when it came to defending her daughter—that Sloane wouldn't want to face.

She averted her gaze with care, perhaps sensing that she had said too much. "What did you say to her, anyway?"

"I asked her what she knows about darkfire."

Eileen glanced up, her confusion clear. "What's that?"

"It's a special kind of firestorm. It's characterized by a bluish green flame and is said to change everything before it's done. It's supposed to come in a period of great trial for the *Pyr*."

"Why doesn't that sound like fun," Eileen murmured, bending to put the lime green cylinder in place on the stack. Zoë scattered the blocks again, unconcerned. Oblivious.

Had darkfire stolen her fledgling gifts?

Even Sloane could sense Erik's agitation, and he was no Wyvern.

He heard the tires of the Maserati only seconds before Eileen did. She was at the door in a heartbeat and opened it as Erik strode closer.

The leader of the *Pyr* looked grim.

Sloane understood that his meeting hadn't gone well.

"Lorenzo refused to join you," Eileen said, no question in her voice.

"Worse," Erik said with a nod of agreement. "He compelled me to speak of things I had vowed never to reveal." His intent gaze landed on Sloane. "You must go to Brandt."

"Brandt?" Sloane took a step back in his shock. "But I promised him. . . ."

"As did I." Erik spoke tersely. "You will go."

"No." Sloane frowned, aware that he was defying the leader of the *Pyr*, but knowing he had no choice. His honor was at stake. "I gave my word to leave him be."

"As did I."

"But I swore it in blood!"

"I have inadvertently revealed him," Erik acknowledged, every line of his body taut. Sloane could see that Erik was angry that Lorenzo had worked this information from his lips. He was even shimmering blue, on the cusp of change, so great was his agitation. "I fear Lorenzo's intent, for I do not understand him." Erik's lips tightened into a hard line. "*He* hides his thoughts very well."

"He beguiled you again?" Eileen asked.

"I don't know what he did. I only know that I couldn't keep from answering his every question." He flicked an imperious glance at Sloane. "Go, now."

Sloane didn't. "Why me? Why can't another *Pyr* go, one who hasn't sworn an oath to leave Brandt in peace?"

"Because he is your cousin," Erik said with heat. "Because he will receive you."

"I'm not certain of that!" Sloane flung out his hands. "In his place, I wouldn't receive an oath breaker!"

Erik's voice dropped to a low hiss, and he stepped closer, eyes blazing. "Would you have Brandt die for that? Or worse, be turned to Lorenzo's will—whatever that is?"

"I promised," Sloane insisted. In some part of his mind, he was incredulous that he was defying the leader of the *Pyr*.

In another, he believed Erik should have known better than to ask this of him.

Erik inhaled sharply; then his words softened. "Recognize that I understand what I am asking you to do. I ask it because I fear for Brandt's safety." He sighed, his frustration clear. "I wish with all my heart that it might have remained unnecessary, but whether he follows me or not, Brandt is still *Pyr*, and that makes his welfare my responsibility." He swallowed visibly. "Since I cannot command you to follow my order, then I *ask* you to go to him. For his own safety."

Sloane shoved a hand through his hair, seeing Erik's point, but not looking forward to the exchange. "You're really afraid."

"I am." Erik's lips were a tight line. "I saw something in the future, something I would avoid at all costs."

"What?" Eileen asked.

"I will not speak of it. I have already said too much on this day." Erik eyed Sloane. "Please go."

"And if I am too late?"

Erik averted his gaze, his throat working. "Then his son may need you more than I do." He met Sloane's gaze steadily. "Go," he urged softly. "And may the Great Wyvern be at your back."

With those words, Sloane knew Erik wasn't sure what he might find when he reached Brandt, much less what Lorenzo might be able to do. To see uncertainty in the eyes of the *Pyr* he had revered for so long shook Sloane to his marrow.

And it had him on his way to his cousin's side.

As he left, Sloane recognized that this was the work of the darkfire, changing everything, challenging assumptions, reassigning precedence—not just for Rafferty, but for all of the *Pyr*.

Where would its influence stop?

What would be left of them afterward?

Niall was on the phone in his office in New York City, getting help to his tour groups. Heavy rains had caused flooding and mud slides in Bhutan, the like of which no one had ever seen. A violent snowstorm in Mongolia had those on his Silk Road trip trapped in a rustic caravansary. Mud slides in Peru imperiled the group at Machu Picchu. The Galápagos group was facing tsunamis, caused by the earthquake in the South Pacific. Iceland's volcano was erupting, and there was sudden new violence along the border of Morocco and Algeria. Ocean levels were rising fast, and the sea was roiling. In London, they had shut the Thames Barrier and were hoping it would hold against the deluge.

It seemed Niall had trips everywhere that natural disaster had struck.

"Everything goes to hell at once," Barry muttered, managing the incoming calls while Niall solved problems. Niall had to get his people out of all these hot zones, and it was impossible to prioritize. He was juggling three calls at any given time, and had been doing so all day.

To top it all off, Niall felt the burn of the firestorm. It was reasonably close, down toward or in DC, and it burned with a strange cold light. Awareness of it made the hair stand up on the back of Niall's neck. It made him fidgety, as if he stood on the verge of disaster.

It was darkfire.

The only good thing was that it was Rafferty's firestorm, but what a mixed blessing. The older *Pyr* had the firestorm he'd yearned for, but it was of a mythic, unpredictable kind. With any other *Pyr*, Niall would have worried more about the outcome, but Rafferty was as consistent and steady as the earth he could command.

On the other hand, there'd been that earthquake in DC this morning. Niall wasn't sure what to make of that, and he didn't have time to ponder its import.

Thank goodness he had Barry. The kid was a natural at customer relations and a whiz with computers. He'd calmly and cheerfully stayed on top of phone calls and e-mail all day. He'd even ensured that they got something to eat in the middle of it all.

Niall had just secured a military helicopter and guarantee of fuel in Burma for the Bhutan trip—at a hefty premium—when Barry shouted from the front office.

"Holy shit!" he cried. Niall leapt up from his desk, fearful that something else had gone wrong. There was an edge in the air, a shadow of dark possibilities that seemed to have been awakened with the eclipse early that morning. Niall could smell danger in the wind, unpredictability, and he didn't like it one bit.

It made him jumpy.

"What?" he demanded.

Barry turned from his computer. "My friend just sent me the link to this YouTube video. Isn't this Rox's friend T?"

Niall's heart sank. "Is it? What's he up to this time?"

Barry shook his head, his amazement clear. "He changes into a dragon, right on camera."

"What?" Niall was across the room in a flash.

"I mean, it's kind of shaky, like someone took it with a cell phone, but still."

Niall wasn't listening to his employee. He was staring at the video, the bottom dropping out of his world as he watched. Thorolf emerged in human form from a large crack in the pavement. A crowd had gathered when the ground had split, and Thorolf seemed to be alarmed by its presence. Then he started to jump, as if being stung by something invisible.

It had to be dragonsmoke. Niall's lips thinned. Thorolf leapt from the crevasse, jerking with pain as he tried to outrun the smoke. The crowd of people gathered closer, and he seemed to suddenly recall that he was being watched.

Thorolf looked around himself with dawning horror, then leapt into the air and shifted shape. He soared into the sky in dragon form, the moonstone and silver of his scales soon disappearing against the overcast sky.

A trio of lightning bolts lit the scene in rapid succession. The crowd gasped and backed away from the flashes of light, just as the thunder rumbled in three loud booms. The video blurred, then focused on a burning tree. Evidently it had been struck by the lightning—Niall could see the black singe mark on its bark. A light standard had also been hit, as had the peak of a building. The shingles there had started to burn.

What was in Thorolf's head?

Niall pinched the bridge of his nose. In a way, it figured Thorolf would be the first to lose it under the influence of darkfire. In another, the last thing he needed was another item on his To Do list.

"It's totally viral," Barry said with excitement. "Look at the hits, and it was only posted fifteen minutes ago. They're going to crash a server someplace. Maybe two."

Servers were the last of Niall's concerns.

"Wait until I tell everyone I know this guy!" Barry said, leaning over the keyboard.

Niall dropped a hand to his shoulder and tried to sound indifferent. "It's not as though it's real," he said with a shrug. He had the tempting thought that he could beguile his employee but resisted the urge. It wouldn't matter in the long term, and it would be a betrayal of trust. Instead, he was dismissive. "I mean, you know T. He'd do anything for twenty bucks, or even for a beer. They can do some incredible stuff with CGI these days."

Barry's excitement evaporated immediately. "Yeah, you're right. Mr. Pragmatism." He smiled at Niall. "But still, it's cool."

"Tricks usually are." Niall winked. "Don't get suckered."

"Right."

"I've got the fuel lined up in Burma and the rescue chopper," Niall said, his tone brisk. "There's a coast guard ship within minutes of the Galápagos team. I'm expecting a confirmation from Reykjavik on arrangements there, and a guarantee of protection from my contact in Marrakech."

"Mongolia?"

"Nothing we can do but pray for them. No communication in or out, and no one's heading out in that storm."

Barry nodded. "Greg's sensible, though. He'll have them holed up and safe."

Niall nodded, agreeing with this assessment of that tour leader. He had already checked on Greg once, and would do so again that night. His newfound ability as the DreamWalker was proving to be quite useful—in navigating the dreams of humans, he could discover truths otherwise hidden to him. "I have to take care of something else, though. Are you good here?"

"Something *else*?" Barry grimaced. "What else could go wrong?"

Niall leaned down to whisper, hating that he was going to mislead his employee. "Surprise for Rox. I forget and I'm a dead man." Barry grinned. "If she calls, tell her I'm backed up, will be home by eight, and would love that vegetarian pizza for dinner."

Barry gave Niall a thumbs-up. "I'm all over it. You two have a good time tonight. Looks like everything's calmed down here."

"You know where I am if not." Niall patted his cell phone and headed out the door, leaping down the stairs to the basement. Rox's surprise wouldn't be as romantic as Barry envisioned. In fact, Niall hoped he could find Thorolf and sneak him into the apartment. That *Pyr* looked overwhelmed, but he had to be hidden for the short term for the safety of the other *Pyr*.

"Where are you?" Niall asked in old-speak, urging the wind to take his message to Thorolf. *"Meet me at the dock, the usual one."*

"Deal," Thorolf said, his fear and relief both clear.

Niall could get the rest of the story later, once he had Thorolf hidden. The dock he'd used for landings before was abandoned and routinely deserted. They could walk from there and slip into the underground network below the city. Niall had explored it enough to be able to find Rox's building easily.

Thorolf wasn't fond of the underground passageways, but using them was the only way to get him safely hidden away. Then Niall would figure out what to do next. It was a case of prioritizing, something he was learning to do better all the time.

Sara Keegan returned to her bookshop in Traverse City, having mailed the last of the orders that had to ship before Christmas. She did a turn around the shop, checking the doors and windows, lowering the thermostat, backing up the computer files. She was taking a couple of weeks off and wasn't planning to open again until the fourth of January.

Business was slow in the winter anyhow, and she was exhausted by her second pregnancy. She just couldn't get warm and was sleeping poorly.

Sara needed a break.

She flipped off the lights and did one last scan, then stepped out into the street. She was locking the door when she noticed the door knocker.

It was the mermaid that Quinn had made, the piece she had bought from him when they first met. During their firestorm, it had heated when she was in danger, but ever since she'd moved the shop, the mermaid had been completely normal.

But on this day, as the snow began to fall, the mermaid sparkled with a strange blue light. The knocker could have been made of blue glass, and glittered oddly. Sara touched the mermaid's tail, but it was stone cold.

Its chill launched a shiver that went right to Sara's toes.

What was going on?

On impulse, she returned to the shop and removed an old book from a locked case. It was Sigmund's book, *The Habits and Habitats of Dragons: a Compleat Guide for Slayers*, and it was the closest thing to a guidebook to the world of the *Pyr*. She looked up "blue flames" which referred her to "darkfire."

> Darkfire—a fire that burns with a blue or blue-green flame, frequently referenced in *Pyr* mythology, always with a dire tone, but never in very clear terms. Darkfire is predicted to occur during a firestorm when the *Pyr* are in the midst of a major struggle.
>
> Among its effects, darkfire is said to cause all or some of the following: secrets revealed; clear paths obscured; converse with the dead; the conception of prophets; the development of mystical powers among those who have never shown such tendencies; the loss of prophetic powers among those who have been seers in the past; the emergence of affinities; the loss of affinities; the gathering of outcast *Pyr*; the division of loyalties within those *Pyr* who were allied; etc., etc. Even this brief list exhibits the legendary and disruptive nature of darkfire.

There is no record of darkfire ever having occurred
or even a clear story of how it was created in the
first place, although (as always) it must be acknowledged that *Pyr* records are notoriously scant.

Sara shut the book with dissatisfaction. It wasn't much
of an answer. She considered the door, even though she
couldn't see the mermaid, and recalled when Quinn had
given her the knocker.

In her old shop, the one that had been her aunt Magda's shop.

At that time, she'd been helped by the ghost of Aunt
Magda. Could she do that again? If darkfire could allow
contact with the dead, maybe Aunt Magda would help
her now.

She retrieved her aunt's tarot cards and unwrapped
them carefully from the silk that covered them. She held
the deck in her hands and closed her eyes, asking her
aunt for guidance.

"Are you even here, Magda?" she whispered before
cutting the deck.

The air conditioner in the store came on, even though
it was winter and the circuit breaker was switched off. It
ran one cycle, then cut out, sputtering to silence.

Then it did it again.

Sara smiled, recognizing the calling card of her aunt's
ghost. She shuffled the cards with new confidence.
"What's the greatest threat to the *Pyr*?" she asked, then
chose a card. Sara was shocked by the card she drew,
and its dire implications.

It was number thirteen of the higher arcana—Death.

That card meant, at the very least, profound change.

Maybe worse. Sara put the cards away and packed up

quickly, feeling even more chilled than she had before. The mermaid twinkled coldly at her as she locked the door, but she didn't touch the knocker again.

Instead, she shuddered and pulled her coat closed, then turned to find Quinn waiting for her. He was leaning against the front fender of his black pickup, arms folded across his chest as he watched her. Their son, Garrett, was still in his car seat, driving his toy truck across the dashboard.

"Have you had a vision?" Quinn asked as he came and took her elbow in his hand. The warmth of his touch almost banished the cold that plagued her.

But not quite.

Sara wasn't sure how much to tell him. "Why? Is there a firestorm?"

"There was an eclipse on Monday night." Quinn's lips tightened as he helped her into the truck. "We will not be going."

Sara was shocked by this, for Quinn was the Smith who repaired the armor of the *Pyr*. They had attended every firestorm since she'd met him. "But whose is it?"

"Rafferty's." Quinn was terse, and Sara saw that this hadn't been an easy choice for him. "He'll make it work." He shut the door before striding around the front of the truck, then getting into the driver's seat. He pulled into traffic with care.

Sara worried. Had she foreseen Rafferty's death? "But what if he loses a scale?"

"He'll make it work," Quinn insisted.

"But . . ."

"But this firestorm is marked by darkfire, Sara." Quinn stopped at a red light and turned to face her, his gaze intense. "I have lived without the *Pyr*, and they have lived without me. Darkfire is about risk, and it is about loss. I will not risk losing you, and I will not leave you behind, undefended, when darkfire burns. We will not go."

Sara saw his determination and was uncertain she could change his mind. Should she try? Sara was fond of Rafferty, but more than that, she knew that Quinn would blame himself for any bad results of his choice. On the other hand, she trusted his instincts. What should she do?

What kind of death did Magda anticipate?

A literal one or a symbolic one?

Unfortunately, she didn't receive a vision to answer that.

In a coffee shop in Manhattan, Viv Jason froze in the act of making her eightieth soy latte of the day. Her hand shook as she felt the tingle of darkfire. She'd felt the firestorm in the night, during the eclipse, just as she'd been cursed to feel the firestorms of the *Pyr* for centuries. She'd barely dared to hope.

She closed her eyes and inhaled deeply, smiling at the unmistakable tingle of the blue-green flames. It was an electric tongue of energy, flicking at her skin, charged more strongly than a usual firestorm. There was only one firestorm she awaited. The blue flame was unmistakable for what it was.

Darkfire.

The end of the era she despised, and the beginning of the one she anticipated. She would no longer be a victim. No, she would define the rules from this point.

Viv put down the paper cup and stepped away from the coffee machine, knowing what she had to do. It had nothing whatsoever to do with making soy lattes.

"Hey, Viv. Aren't you going to finish that one?" Mandy asked sharply. "Customer's waiting!"

Viv ignored her. She had no use for these humans anymore, no need of this petty income. Humans had served their purpose. She had survived, and her moment for vengeance had arrived. That was the only thing of importance.

Viv untied her apron and tossed it on the stainless steel counter, walking briskly to the back of the shop. She ditched her hairnet in the trash on the way past, grabbed her jacket and purse, then marched right out the door of the coffee shop where she'd worked for three years.

"Hey!" Mandy shouted, but Viv didn't care what she had to say.

Darkfire.

Viv tipped her face to the sky, closed her eyes, and inhaled deeply. The crowd of pedestrians on the busy sidewalk surged around her, but she didn't care about them. Darkfire's spark tingled all the way through to her toes, the unmistakable sensation making her grin like an idiot.

Finally!

Viv let herself be moved by the crowd on the sidewalk, ignoring the slow tumble of snowflakes and the chill in the air. She listened, intent on discovering the location of the one who had loosed the darkfire's flame.

Viv beckoned to the darkfire. She let it awaken all the old words that had lain dormant; she let it flick its tongue against the locked corners of her mind. She let it draw her to its current master.

All the while, she recognized that she would have to watch her back. Darkfire was unpredictable, never fully controlled, always ready to leap in an unanticipated direction. It was unfurled, and there was no telling what would happen. It was fickle, and would abandon the intent of he who commanded it now.

Viv was counting on that.

He was in Asia somewhere. She'd refine the location once she drew closer and was better able to sense the source of the darkfire.

Right here and right now, she had to catch a plane.

Secure in his hidden lair, the Sleeper yawned for the first time in centuries. His eyelids flickered, he stretched, he rolled to his other side, and then he dozed again.

He was content, at least for the moment, to dream.

Chapter 7

*G*et a grip.

Melissa was in big trouble and struggling not to panic. Being captive in the private helicopter of an arms dealer who could also turn into a dragon was not an ideal situation, not by any accounting.

The pilot, she was pretty sure, was the same guy who had driven the big Mercedes into her car the night before. He wasn't likely to be inclined to help her escape.

Judging by Montmorency's smug manner, this particular story wouldn't end well for her. Rafferty had the little blue leather-bound book, so she had nothing with which to negotiate. Melissa had a feeling Montmorency wouldn't be tempted by her freshwater pearl earrings. The helicopter rotors were loud enough that she couldn't ask him any damning questions.

But the worst part was that she didn't have her camera.

Or even her cell phone. Both were on her desk beside her computer, waaaaaaay down in her town house.

She checked the view, saw that they were soaring

over the Potomac, and wondered at their destination. Where did Montmorency like to barbecue his victims? She tried not to think of being on adjacent slabs at the morgue with Daphne, but she shuddered all the same.

Montmorency watched her so closely that even when she wasn't looking at him, the hairs prickled on the back of her neck.

What exactly did he want from her? Besides her disappearance?

What could she do to save herself?

One thing was for sure—Melissa wasn't going to look at him again, though, not if she could help it. Those flames in his eyes had been weird, and they had somehow been part of her losing her ability to resist him. They had been responsible for her going with him so meekly in the first place, and were utterly untrustworthy.

How had that happened? What had those flames been about? It must have been some kind of hypnosis. Did Rafferty have that power? If he did, she was pretty sure he hadn't used it on her. In fact, it was interesting that he hadn't done so, but had argued with her instead.

Now that she thought about it, he *had* warned her not to look into Montmorency's eyes. So, he'd known what to expect, but she'd ignored him.

If she had the chance to do it again, she'd listen to Rafferty.

Were there different kinds of dragon dudes? Rafferty had said he and Montmorency weren't friends. Did that make them enemies? Rivals? Or just mutually indifferent? They didn't seem to be that indifferent to each other.

Not that their relationship mattered right here and right now. The better question probably was how she was going to get out of this alive.

Too bad she didn't have the answer.

A headset appeared in her peripheral vision, and Melissa glanced toward it, seeing that Montmorency was offering it to her. She kept her gaze on his hands. He pointed upward to the rotor, and Melissa had to admit it was a good idea to shelter her ears from the noise.

She took the headset and tugged it on, acting as if she had every right to protect herself against potential hearing loss, as if she had every reason to expect to live to a ripe old age.

Melissa easily recalled being captured with her crew by some fringe group with automatic weapons; she remembered the duct tape and the blindfolds that smelled of dust and the commands shouted in Arabic. She'd kept her cool then and had survived to tell about it. She could do it again.

Maybe.

"You were in my house," Montmorency said, his words making her jump. He could have had his lips against her ear. There must have been a transmitter in the headset.

Melissa refused to look at him. She stared at the ground beyond the window. They were heading over the river. Arlington, maybe. "Yes," she admitted.

"You took my book," he added. His voice was low, not as melodic as it had been, now filled with threat. His tone made Melissa fear for her life, and she supposed that was the point.

It seemed ridiculous to lie, since he knew the truth. Maybe cooperation would make him more amiable.

Maybe not. "Yes," she agreed.

Montmorency sighed. "So, you know its contents. And that means you must know I can't simply forget the transgression."

It wasn't hard to see where this discussion was headed. Melissa wished she'd had time to read the book. It would have been nice to know precisely why she was doomed, rather than simply suspecting as much.

On the other hand, there wasn't much about her time with Rafferty she was inclined to forget. If she was going to die, it was good to have made love so wonderfully one last time.

She didn't want to die, though.

Melissa swallowed and stared out the window. She could see something zooming toward them from the ground, something that shone iridescent beneath the overcast skies.

Like opals.

Edged with gold.

Rafferty! She deliberately hid her reaction, waiting for Montmorency to fill the silence. His hand landed on her wrist at that moment, making it perfectly credible that her pulse would leap in terror.

Still, he spoke in that even tone. "What I need to know is how you even knew of the book's existence. And its location."

Melissa shrugged and kept her gaze averted. She could almost feel him willing her to look into his eyes again, but she wasn't going there. A trickle of perspiration slid down her spine. "Most people keep appointment books," she said, her tone carefully neutral.

"I am not most people," Montmorency hissed, so close that she felt his breath on her cheek. "But perhaps you've noticed as much."

She almost glanced his way, almost slipped, but caught herself in time. "No," she said quietly, "I guess you're not."

"Who told you the security codes?" His voice dropped to a low thrum as his hand tightened on her wrist. "You didn't break into the house, per se. Someone told you how to unlock the door."

"A lucky guess?"

Montmorency was unpersuaded. "Name the one who betrayed me."

Something pointed dug into her flesh, and Melissa glanced down at the stab of pain. His hand had changed to a claw, a dragon claw, the long talons piercing her skin.

As she watched, the transformation spread slowly up his arm, his skin shifting from tanned flesh to hide encrusted with jade green scales.

"Tell me!" he commanded, and Melissa glanced up.

She caught herself when her gaze landed on his mouth, on his smile, on the teeth that were changing before her very eyes to sharp predatory dragon teeth.

She snapped her head to look out the window, telling herself that this wasn't happening, that she wasn't seeing what she thought she was seeing, that he wasn't going to eat her alive.

There was no sign of Rafferty.

Had he abandoned her to her fate?

"Tell me!" Montmorency commanded again, his voice louder. His grip tightened, and she felt the talons dig deeper.

"I guessed!" she declared, just as something slammed the helicopter sideways. The force of impact nearly gave Melissa whiplash, and it threw Montmorency across the cabin.

Served him right for not fastening his seat belt.

Melissa peered out the window, heart hammering with hope. She saw Rafferty, hanging on to the skids far below her in dragon form. The helicopter tilted with his weight, and his opalescent tail swung through the air, scales catching the light. She saw his tail fall, then heard the crack as he struck the boom of the helicopter tail. The helicopter dropped and swerved.

The pilot swore and tried to correct the flight path. The helicopter dipped, not entirely under his control.

Montmorency roared in frustration and shifted shape, which didn't help. He lunged across the cabin, and the helicopter dipped lower from his sudden move. The pilot muttered a curse as Melissa saw Rafferty's tail swing high again.

This time, the boom broke. Melissa glimpsed it falling toward the ground as the helicopter began to spin wildly. It also dropped toward the earth, the plunge sickening in its speed. She tucked her head between her knees to keep from puking and crossed her fingers.

She heard the glass shatter as the window beside her was broken from the outside, almost certainly by a massive dragon fist. *Yes!* Melissa wanted to cheer. Shards scattered over her back and she felt the heat of flames about her back.

It seemed a good time to pray, so she went with her impulse.

Montmorency's presence was suddenly gone from beside her. One instant he was there, looming large in dragon form and filling the cabin—the next she felt alone behind the pilot.

It was enough to make her look.

In the same instant, the helicopter lurched upward with dizzying speed. It was still spinning. Melissa found the space beside her empty. In fact, she was alone in the cabin, alone with the pilot. But where had Montmo-

rency gone? The opposite window wasn't broken, and
Rafferty filled the one beside her. His weight made the
helicopter tip in that direction.

There was a sudden flicker of motion on the floor,
and Melissa saw a small jade salamander there. It contrasted with the black carpet, looking like a piece of jewelry. Melissa blinked and it was gone, as surely as if it
had never been there.

Then she was snatched from her seat and hauled into
the open sky. She panicked and screamed, fearing she
knew then where Montmorency had gone.

But that strange blue-green fire danced over her
skin. Melissa dared to be relieved. She looked up at the
dragon holding her captive in one claw, and smiled.

At least until she saw the fury in Rafferty's eyes.

"Darkfire!" the pilot breathed, his amazement clear.
Melissa guessed that the blue fire was almost as unusual
for the dragon men as it was for her.

Rafferty swung his tail and cracked the front window
of the helicopter. The pilot shouted as Rafferty breathed
a stream of fire that ignited the upholstery inside the
helicopter. The pilot might have shifted shape, too—
Melissa couldn't be sure, because Rafferty flung the dis-
abled machine across the sky like a discarded toy.

All the while, he held Melissa fast against his chest,
one arm protectively curled around her. That seductive
heat rolled through her from the point of contact, making her recall everything they had done together.

And some things they hadn't tried yet.

The possibilities made her forget Montmorency and
his pilot.

Melissa saw the gleaming leather of Rafferty's wings,
and was amazed at how leisurely their beat was, even

as he kept them both aloft. She saw the light glimmer on his scales, an armor that might have been made of gemstones. She saw the ferocious edge of his talons and knew he could shred anyone and anything with ease.

But he held her with tenderness.

And this was the second time he had saved her from Montmorency's rage. She hadn't even done much to earn his protection.

Melissa decided it was time she learned what motivated him.

Rafferty clearly didn't agree with her choices, and he didn't seem to always like her much. But he wasn't the kind of person who did things for show. No, he'd risked his hide to save her. She'd guess there was a principle at work, and she wanted to know what it was.

It was time to get to the root of this particular story.

Rafferty landed in a park past the cemetery, one that was thick with pine trees and far out of range of other humans. His blood was pumping, and he was enraged with his mate. She had ignored his counsel and put herself in danger. He was even more angry with Magnus for having beguiled her.

He was most furious, however, with himself. Now both Magnus and Balthasar knew not only about the firestorm but also about the darkfire. And it was his own fault. Rafferty had a bad feeling. Where had Magnus gone? It was no good thing that the wily *Slayer* could spontaneously manifest anywhere at will.

Rafferty had to find him, soon.

He shifted shape quickly within the shelter of those trees, landing on his feet before putting Melissa on the ground. He didn't know what to say to her, how to begin, how to control the frustration raging inside him. He'd never felt so besieged in his life, so ferocious, so unpredictable. This firestorm was certainly messing with his game.

He saw Melissa shiver and realized the temperature. She wasn't dressed for it, not in the least. He tugged off his leather jacket and handed it to her, casting a glance at the snowflakes beginning to fall. They were different from the snowflakes of the night before, smaller and harder. There would be a storm—he realized as much from the smell of the wind—and it would be a blizzard of epic proportions.

Better they leave DC now.

Rafferty knew exactly where they'd go.

He could imagine what his mate would say about that.

Maybe it was time for an increment of charm.

Melissa smiled as she tugged his jacket more tightly around her shoulders, clearly surprised by his gesture. "Always a gentleman?" she teased.

"Clearly not," Rafferty said, his mood easing against the odds. "I try to make up for lost time."

She laughed. It wasn't a long laugh and it was a bit high-pitched, but, after what had just happened, she laughed. Rafferty looked at his mate and realized once again there was more to her than met the eye.

"Never let them see you sweat," she said, a wary twinkle in her eye. "First rule you learn in a hot zone." She exhaled heavily and shuddered, then nestled into his jacket. "Thanks."

He extended his hand, palm up, and she looked at it.

"The camera's on my desk, beside my computer. With my cell phone." She shrugged, not looking entirely disappointed.

Rafferty remembered as much. "What about Magnus's camera?"

"He lied. Big surprise."

She didn't seem very disappointed in this fact, which intrigued Rafferty. "Not upset you missed your chance to document us further?"

She eyed him for a second, looking vulnerable, then abruptly disguised her thoughts. "What I missed was my chance to get a job."

She turned away from him, glancing in each direction before she chose the one Rafferty knew would take her most quickly to a road. She was more observant than most. She began to walk, and he followed her. He sensed from her manner that the job wasn't her real objective.

Then what was?

What had prompted her to take such a risk? He really wanted to know.

"What kind of a job?" he asked, keeping his tone light.

"Reporting. International news." She kept her gaze averted. "What I used to do."

"Melissa Smith," Rafferty mused, realizing only now why she looked familiar. It had been years since she'd been on the news broadcast. "I remember you. You did special reports from Jerusalem and Damascus."

"Beirut and Baghdad," she agreed with a nod. "Once upon a time." She seemed thoughtful.

He remembered also that she had disappeared suddenly from the newscast. He'd assumed she'd fallen in love, gotten married, started a family. She was young and attractive, after all. He suspected now, though, that that wasn't her story. He'd seen her home. If she didn't live there alone, then he was a *Slayer*.

Rafferty kept his tone neutral, the persistent niggle of the firestorm turning his thoughts in predictable directions. He was aware of the curve of Melissa's neck, the delicacy of her ears, the femininity of her small hands clutching his coat closed. He was taunted by that damn perfume, his body responding readily to its promise.

He fought to stay on the track of their conversation. "If you wanted to keep doing that, why didn't you just keep the job you had?"

She shrugged, and he knew she wouldn't tell him the truth. "Life happened. Things changed." Her tone turned fierce. "I just want them to change back."

Rafferty decided to push her a bit. That this woman, with her poise and protective barriers, was so obviously trying to evade his questions, was a hint that he was getting close to an important detail. "So, you broke into Magnus Montmorency's house and stole from him."

To his surprise, she smiled easily at him. "I didn't notice him inviting you in for a coffee."

"That's different."

"How so? You still entered his house without his consent. Looks the same to me. Probably would to a lawyer, too."

"I didn't steal anything, though."

"No, you just trashed his foyer, beat him up, and burned his rug." She regarded him with humor in her eyes. "You're not looking so innocent yourself, Mr. Conscience."

"Rafferty," he said, realizing his omission. "Rafferty Powell."

She murmured his name, and Rafferty was stunned by how much he enjoyed hearing her say it.

Then she gave him a hard look. "How is it different, Mr. Powell?"

"Rafferty," he corrected. "It's different because Magnus and I have a blood feud."

She halted in the middle of a group of pines and turned to face him, the scent of the trees tickling Rafferty's nose. "A blood feud? How medieval is that?" She eyed him when he didn't answer her. "What exactly does that mean? Are you going to kill him?"

"Unless he kills me first."

"But that's murder. You'll go to jail!"

Rafferty smiled. "And what jail would hold me?"

She frowned, her gaze dancing over him, then pivoted and started to walk quickly in the direction she'd already chosen. They cleared the trees, and there was only frozen ground between them and a busy street. "What about my house?" she asked. "You couldn't leave it. I saw you try."

Rafferty hesitated. He was telling her far more than he had intended, but he sensed they might somehow become allies in this. It was his firestorm. There had to be at least a chance of their making a permanent relationship.

He wouldn't be that skeptical of the Great Wyvern's intent.

He wouldn't even consider that darkfire could change that much.

He dared to hope.

Rafferty spoke with care. "Your house had been surrounded by dragonsmoke, breathed by Magnus and his minion."

"Dragonsmoke?"

"It's a boundary mark, one that traditionally could be crossed only by the one who breathed it and/or any other *Pyr* explicitly granted permission to do so. We've used it to protect hoards and treasures for millennia.

Humans cannot see it and are not affected by its presence. Particularly sensitive humans may feel a slight chill in stepping through it, but that's it."

"Traditionally?" she echoed, glancing at him again. "What's changed?"

He didn't tell her that everything had changed; that the darkfire between them was foretold to completely turn the world of the *Pyr* upside down. That could wait. "Magnus and his fellows can cut dragonsmoke and move through it, even without permission. It offers no obstacle to them."

"So, you couldn't even keep him in jail with dragonsmoke."

"No." Why was she interested in Magnus going to jail? She trudged onward, and Rafferty thought about what she'd said. "Is this your goal, then? To see Magnus in jail?"

Her eyes were filled with conviction. "I want to see justice prevail. I want to see him punished for what he's done."

"And what are his crimes?"

"Don't you know?" She turned to face him on the sidewalk, a steady stream of cars moving past them on the roadway. There was a cluster of shops about two blocks away, but they were the only pedestrians. "I mean, you must have a reason to have a blood feud with him. Or do you dragon men do that all the time?"

"*Pyr*," Rafferty supplied. "We call ourselves the *Pyr*."

"Why?"

"That's ancient Greek for fire."

She surveyed him, clearly thinking about his words. "Because you can breathe fire?"

Rafferty nodded. "But we don't have blood feuds all the time. Or at least, I don't."

"What did he do to you?"

That list was long and complicated. "I'd like to hear your list first," Rafferty said, then smiled. "It's probably shorter."

"You're right. It is." She tipped her head back and held his gaze, as if she would dare him to believe her. "He killed a friend of mine. So far, he's gotten away with it, but she wasn't the first and she won't be the last. I want to ensure that he's caught."

"And the book?"

"She said it was a record of his arms deals, of his appointments, of his contacts." Melissa grimaced. "She said it would condemn him, and she gave me the security codes to go get it."

"Why didn't she get it?"

"She tried. She wrote to me in advance, as insurance. She said I'd hear from her before the letter came, if she succeeded." Melissa's eyes were filled with a conviction Rafferty respected. "I never did."

He voiced the possibility that she had been deceived. "She could have run away instead."

Melissa shook her head, a shadow claiming her features. "I found her at the morgue, yesterday." She swallowed and blinked back tears; then her expression closed. "A Jane Doe." Her words were tight, her composure tenuous. She had cared about this woman. "Burned to death."

Rafferty grimaced and walked beside her, wishing she hadn't seen that. No one should see such a sight.

No one should suffer such a fate.

Her voice dropped, filling with passion, and her words almost perfectly echoed his own thoughts. "That's not nearly good enough, not for anyone."

"How did you know her?"

She smiled a little then, kicking the ground as she walked. "She was a street kid in Baghdad. Pretty but living in a tough world. Inquisitive and stubborn. She found things out. She was more reliable than most."

"But not entirely so."

Melissa shrugged. "No one would have believed her story, even if it was true."

"But how'd she get here?"

She sighed. "I think she was Montmorency's mistress. I couldn't believe it when I saw her here, all turned out in Dolce and Gabbana." She met his gaze. "Daphne was pretty, she was cunning and self-motivated, but she wasn't all bad. And no one but no one deserves to die like that."

Rafferty was struck by her passion, and found himself responding to it. "So, you broke into his house."

She heaved a shaking breath. "So, I tried to make my own luck. I tried to get the evidence that would see Daphne avenged."

"Which might get you a job again."

"Yes. Although it wasn't all about the job." She looked at him. "The thing is, that's what reporters do. We ferret out the truth and tell it to the world. I used to be good at that."

Rafferty suspected she was still good at it. "And that's important?"

She sighed. "It's the only legacy that counts, isn't it? Truth and justice are the things that stand the test of time, that make the world a better place. I want to be a part of that solution."

"There are other ways."

"This is the one I'm good at." She spoke with fervor, with such conviction that Rafferty knew she was right.

He'd have to watch those old broadcasts again. They must be archived somewhere. He wanted very much to see her in action.

"I still have the book," he admitted softly.

She looked at him, her eyes alight. "I'm guessing you won't just give it to me."

Rafferty shook his head. "I still need the blog pictures to disappear."

She winced. "I still want that job."

They eyed each other, still on opposite sides.

Rafferty had a feeling, though, that they could find a mutually beneficial solution. "Maybe there's another way to get it, a way that doesn't involve betraying me and my kind." He arched a brow. "Maybe you need to make a gesture of good faith."

She laughed again, a sound all the more enchanting for being unexpected. "Is that supposed to be the proverbial offer I can't refuse?"

Rafferty found himself smiling in turn. "Maybe." Her expression warmed as she surveyed him.

"You should smile more," she said, her words falling breathless.

Rafferty took a step closer but never managed to raise his hand to her cheek.

"*What madness is this?*" Erik roared, his old-speak echoing so loud in Rafferty's mind that Rafferty staggered.

"What's the matter?" Melissa asked, her concern clear as Rafferty turned away.

"*What has happened?*" he asked Erik, barely daring to guess.

His cell phone rang, and he suspected it was more bad news. With some trepidation, Rafferty answered it. He was right—Erik had sent him a hot link.

To a YouTube video.

Which he wouldn't have believed if he hadn't seen it with his own eyes. Now what?

No matter how bad it was, there was nothing to be gained by avoiding the truth. Rafferty played the video, Melissa watching him so avidly that he found his face heating.

"What is it?" she asked. "Something really bad?"

He couldn't see any harm in her knowing the truth. He gave her the phone, and she replayed the video. He watched her disappointment dawn; then she handed him back the phone.

"So much for my job," she said, unable to completely keep the despondency from her voice.

It wasn't the reaction he'd expected. "Why do you say that?"

There was no joy in her half smile. "There is no second place in my business. There are winners and there are losers. First in wins, every time, and all other deals are moot."

"So, you were beaten to the story." Rafferty watched her with care, seeing her put her disappointment away, square her shoulders, and look forward again. She was resilient, his mate—impressively so. There was even an optimistic glint in her eye when she met his gaze again.

"Pretty much," she acknowledged, her tone already less rueful. "But it's not as if I had an exclusive negotiated with you *Pyr*, is it?"

"If it's meant to be, you'll find another way to get that job," Rafferty said. He wanted to console her but wasn't sure how to do it.

She forced a smile. "Maybe." She turned her bright gaze on him so suddenly that he knew she'd thought of something. "But wait a minute. You winced before the phone rang. What happened there?" She glanced around. "It sounded like thunder, or a freight train, but that can't have been what it was."

"Old-speak," Rafferty acknowledged, watching the video of Thorolf again, confirming that it was as bad as he'd feared. "We can communicate with one another at lower frequencies than humans can clearly understand."

"Someone yelled at you?"

"Not just someone. The leader of our kind."

"Ticked off the boss, huh?" She smiled, and he had a strange sense of camaraderie with her. "I do it all the time."

Rafferty fumbled with his phone, awkward with his growing admiration of his mate. "You probably recognized the guy in the video."

"That was your friend. The one who wanted to empty my fridge. Nice silvery color in his dragon form." She watched Rafferty, and he guessed that she saw his chagrin. "You left him behind."

"He's not as adept with his abilities as would be ideal."

Melissa smiled. "Yes, he looked a bit overwhelmed. He did bail, though."

Rafferty shook his head. "But he shouldn't have left

without beguiling those who had seen him." He sighed. "And I should have been with him, to ensure that he didn't make such a mistake. I should not have lost my temper." He met her gaze steadily. "I have failed my fellows."

There was no condemnation in her eyes. "Because you chose to save me instead."

There was no arguing with that. "You are my destined mate and thus my responsibility."

"Mate?" she repeated, biting off the word. "That's a bit presumptuous, don't you think? I mean, last night was one thing, but starting a family is quite another. Unless that's not what you mean."

"It is what I mean. But what's more important is that defending you is my responsibility...."

"Sex isn't destined," Melissa argued. "I don't believe in fate, and I'm not sure I believe in happily ever after...."

"That's fine." Rafferty knew he'd already told her too much and feared he'd only alienate her with more explanation. He tried to prioritize the challenges before him, but she was waiting, hands on her hips. "It's not entirely about family," he admitted.

"But partly so?"

Rafferty sighed and nodded.

"You don't think you should have mentioned that last night?"

"The firestorm hadn't ignited yet. It wasn't an issue."

"What was?"

"You." Rafferty looked straight into her eyes, unable to deny the power of his desire. "I could think only of you," he added softly.

She swallowed but didn't look away. "I wasn't thinking about much other than you, either." Time stood still as the heat built between them, the air seeming to sizzle in the small gap that separated them.

Melissa reached out a hand, fearless and confident, and Rafferty's desire burned even hotter. The blue flames cavorted between her fingertips and his chest, licking and flicking against his clothes and driving him to distraction. "Is the firestorm what these flames are about?"

Rafferty swallowed. He was so hard and thick and ready that he could only nod.

Melissa pulled her hand back abruptly, then clicked her tongue. Her eyes sparkled, and he recognized that she was going to make a joke to lighten the moment. "So, you abandoned a rookie in the hot zone, and your boss is ticked."

"That's an understatement. We are supposed to remain unseen, to work for the good of humanity and the planet while mankind remains ignorant of our presence." Rafferty frowned, well aware of the magnitude of his error. He had summoned an earthquake, without regard for the consequences. Had any humans been injured?

How could he have forgotten his responsibilities?

How much more would the darkfire make him forget?

Rafferty fought his rising tide of fear. He had to satisfy this firestorm and soon.

"Big mistake, then," she said lightly, arching a brow. "And I've blown my chance for a job. Looks like we're both in a corner."

Rafferty nodded, wondering where she'd go with this. He knew where he wanted to go—back to his hotel room to sate the firestorm. Darkfire was causing chaos, just as foretold, and the only way to stop it was for him to impregnate Melissa. He had to change the order of his priorities, assigning Magnus second place.

Maybe third.

Rafferty didn't need a lot of imagination to guess what this forthright and independent woman would think of such a plan.

Oblivious to his worries, Melissa squared her shoulders. "Look. I want Montmorency to go down, more than anything in the world, even more than I wanted that job. So, we might as well work together."

"How so?"

"I'll help you however I can to bring down Montmorency, even if it comes to killing him. And I won't tattle to the police."

"And you will do as I bid you to do, for your own safety."

She smiled then, her amusement taking him off guard. "Is it smart for a damsel in distress to trust a dragon dude who calls her his *mate*?" Before he could reply, she answered her own question. "Maybe it's smart to make allies, even in unexpected places." She stuck out her right hand. "Deal, Powell."

As soon as his hand closed over hers, Rafferty knew that a handshake wasn't going to be enough to seal their bargain. The sizzling flames turned his thoughts in other directions, feeding more earthy impulses and reminding him of his mate's allure. Was it possible the Great Wyvern had not chosen wrongly for him? Rafferty desperately wanted to believe it.

Either way, he had to answer the call of the flames. He wanted to try to make his firestorm work, even if the odds were long.

Maybe because the odds were long.

Rafferty closed the last step between them, watched Melissa's eyes widen, and smiled at her as his fingers wrapped more tightly around her hand. He knew the instant their thoughts were as one. It was clear in the way she glanced at his lips, the gleam that lit her eyes, the blush that touched her cheeks. It was in her sharp intake of breath, the leap of her pulse, the increase in adrenaline. It was in the way his body matched its rhythms to hers.

She stepped closer, fearless—or maybe refusing to let him see her sweat—and put her other hand on his shoulder.

"Doesn't hurt one bit that you're irresistible," she murmured. "I like that in a partner." Then she stretched up and touched her lips to his.

Rafferty might have agreed, but their kiss was rudely interrupted.

A jade salamander spontaneously manifested between them. Rafferty felt it against his chest, then recoiled in horror from its slithering form.

"So, it *was* Daphne!" Magnus bellowed, his anger more than clear.

Melissa gasped as the salamander slid down Rafferty's chest.

He yelled when it bit him, hard, in the chest.

Then Rafferty, intent on defending both himself and his mate, shifted shape. He shifted right beside the road in broad daylight and did not care. He'd wounded Magnus the night before—it was time to finish the old snake forever.

Then sate the firestorm.

For the moment, other consequences could be damned.

Chapter 8

One minute, Melissa's blood had been heating in anticipation of the kiss she was going to share with Rafferty. Those blue-green flames seemed to be dancing in slow motion, sliding over her skin, outlining his shoulders in vivid light. They had a seductive rhythm of their own, those weird flames, but she liked them. She was starting to associate them with pleasure of the best kind.

The next minute, there was a green salamander slithering between them, one that shouted in Montmorency's voice.

It said something for recent events in her life that Melissa was less startled than she might have been.

She had time to gasp before Rafferty shouted. His eyes blazed, and he shimmered a lighter blue around his perimeter. It wasn't the same blue-green hue as the flames that lit where he touched her, and was more of a glow than a burning flame. She saw red blood on his chest, probably where the newt had chomped him.

One blink later, there were two dragons grappling for supremacy on the boulevard of frozen grass. Melissa stepped back and wished—one more time—for her camera. Car tires squealed, and there was a fender bender beside them as drivers were distracted by the sight of a dragon fight.

She couldn't blame them for that. She, too, was riveted.

It was clear to her that Montmorency had made a mistake in initiating this fight. Even he appeared to be surprised by the vigor of Rafferty's reaction. The sight of the four long scabs on his belly reminded Melissa that he had been wounded the night before, as well.

Why had he struck when he was weakened? What did he know that they didn't?

The opal and gold dragon who had been her dream lover was vicious in his fury. Rafferty didn't hesitate. He simply battled his foe with incredible strength.

Of course, there was still red blood running from a small bite mark on his chest. It looked deep, and Melissa could imagine it hurt.

Rafferty struck at Montmorency, opening the scabs on those wounds with four more deep cuts. Montmorency, a glittering jade green dragon with gold edging on his scales, fell backward in pain. Black blood flowed over the gilded splendor of his stomach.

Again she wondered why their blood was different colors.

Melissa thought Montmorency might be faking his pain. Rafferty pursued him hotly, breathing dragonfire until the orange flames completely obscured Montmorency's form.

It didn't hide his screams of pain, though.

Rafferty snatched at Montmorency, hauling him upward. He bit into the other dragon's chest, ripping

Montmorency open so that his chest was a raw mass of bleeding flesh. He slammed him into one of the cars damaged in the fender bender, denting its roof deeply.

The people were already out of the car, and they backed away in shock. Rafferty leapt on top of the vehicle, planted one foot on Montmorency's neck, and shredded the wings from his opponent's back. He flung them aside, the massive leathery appendages falling close to Melissa. A bystander reached out to touch the tip of one, his amazement clear.

Montmorency began to beg for mercy. Rafferty spit in his eye. Melissa heard that thunder again and knew they were speaking in their dragon way. Rafferty held the other dragon down, staring into his eyes as he lifted one sharp talon.

"This is for Maximilian's son," he said out loud, his words so resonant that Melissa's bones vibrated along with the words.

"His *son*?" Montmorency echoed, his shock clear. "But Maximilian has no son!"

Rafferty smiled. It was a cold smile, a dragon smile, a knowing smile. It showed a great many sharp teeth.

Melissa saw Montmorency's shock, and enjoyed watching his dismay. She didn't know who Maximilian was, much less who his son was—never mind what the two of them had witnessed at Montmorency's hand— but she really liked that Montmorency was discovering a detail left unattended in his last moment.

It was justice of a most basic kind.

"Now to ensure that you are gone forevermore." Rafferty slowly glanced over the fallen dragon, even as Montmorency's breath heaved. Montmorency tried to move away, but he was too broken to make much progress.

Melissa saw a little shimmer of gold, like a newt, appearing quickly beside Montmorency. By the time she'd looked again, it was gone and she thought she'd imagined it.

She watched Rafferty again. Melissa knew when he found what he sought on the other dragon's body, because his eyes glittered with satisfaction. "Where's that missing scale?" he mused. "Aha! Although it's hard to believe there was ever anyone you loved, Magnus."

"No!" Montmorency protested as Rafferty lifted his sharp talon high. "No. We can negotiate. We can find a solution. We can . . ."

"We will finally end this," Rafferty said. "Did you love yourself best of all?"

The jade dragon hissed and breathed a feeble stream of fire. Rafferty decked him, and Montmorency's head cracked against the ground. His eyes closed and didn't open again.

Rafferty raised his claw to strike the telling blow, and she was ready to cheer. This was it! Justice, dragon-style. Melissa found it worked for her in a big way.

Those in the crowd behind her were silent and transfixed. She could feel their tension.

"And so it ends," Rafferty whispered, then struck at his opponent with vicious force. The crowd gasped, but Melissa couldn't look away. She wouldn't even blink. She didn't want to miss the killing blow.

Except there wasn't one.

Before Rafferty's blow could connect, there was a brilliant flash of gold. Melissa saw that salamander reappear, but it quickly became another dragon, a blindingly gold one. This dragon's scales could have been made with topaz and edged with gold. He was so bright that he could have been the sun touching the earth.

He appeared suddenly, right between the two opponents.

Rafferty was clearly shocked, and the new arrival blocked his strike.

"Sorry to intervene," he said, his accent Russian, "but this prize is mine."

He raged fire at the surprised Rafferty, making him step backward. Then he snatched up the unconscious Montmorency and fled into the sky.

He flew so quickly that Melissa was astounded. Then suddenly, fifty feet above the ground, both the gold and the jade dragons disappeared.

As if they had never been.

"No!" Melissa shouted.

"Yes!" one of the onlookers roared. "He was saved from *murder*!" Those in the crowd began to mutter in agreement, their mood turning hostile.

"Vicious beast," a woman cried, then spat at Rafferty. "You are *wicked*. No creature should kill its own so violently."

Someone threw a soda can at Rafferty. It bounced off his back, presumably not hurting him in the least, but he looked up in surprise.

"No!" Melissa argued. "The other one was the bad one."

"And what would you know about it?" bellowed the woman.

"A lot more than you do, clearly."

"So, was the gold one good or bad?" taunted the woman. Melissa didn't know, and her lack of reply made the woman smile.

Rafferty surveyed the crowd, clearly perplexed by the reaction. But when his jewel-bright gaze landed upon her, Melissa smiled at him. He was pumped and gorgeous, virile—and he would have been a triumphant champion if the gold dragon hadn't cheated him of victory. She liked that he had pursued justice against Montmorency. The weight of his glance made her heart leap, made her desire burn, made her think of celebrating victory in a most basic way. She didn't care what anybody else thought.

She lifted her arms toward him, in the same instant that he bounded toward her. Eyes flashing and wings beating, he scooped her up from the boulevard and soared into the sky. The crowd shouted in consternation, but Melissa didn't care. She was right where she wanted to be.

The snow began to fall in earnest, icy pellets slashing against her face as they ascended, but Melissa savored the moment. She was flying and free—well, so long as Rafferty held her tightly. She felt the wind on her body, the strength of Rafferty at her back, and knew he'd never drop her. That flickering flame of blue danced over her skin, seemingly invigorated by Rafferty's battle.

It certainly invigorated Melissa. She closed her eyes and enjoyed the sensation of flying, not knowing whether she'd ever feel it again.

She was alive.

Montmorency was seriously wounded.

And she was leaving the scene with the sexiest man

she'd ever known. Melissa had a good idea what would happen next.

It didn't get much better than this.

Rafferty was appalled by his own behavior.

He had become a monster. He had forgotten every single thing he had ever been taught about coexisting quietly in human society. He had abandoned the core principles of his kind and had endangered humans with his deeds. He had done so carelessly and recklessly, without regard for the consequences. He had been violent and vicious with Magnus, but had failed to complete their challenge.

Again.

The realization made him feel sick.

Plus, he had revealed the survival of Maximilian's son to Magnus, thereby putting the Sleeper in peril. He had *gloated*, a choice as out of character as possible. Rafferty could not have been any more irresponsible to everyone who relied upon him.

The darkfire was changing him, making him into something he didn't want to be. It was driving him farther and farther from his grandfather's ideal of how a *Pyr* should live.

Had he erred all those centuries ago, in refusing to learn the songs of the Cantor from his grandfather? He had been sure that spell casting was wrong in its very essence, and that had been the only argument he'd ever had with Pwyll.

That argument had also been the last time he'd seen his grandfather alive.

Had that denial been the decision that had driven Rafferty from the true path? His grandfather would have said so. Was the darkfire feeding upon his mistake, or was it simply creating its own disorder?

It was terrifying to acknowledge how much he had enjoyed doing injury to Magnus. It had been more than a wager to be won, or justice to be meted out. He had reveled in the violence of it. The dragon within him had been ascendant as never before, deaf to any notion of temperance or fair play. He had wanted Magnus dead—wanted him dead at any price. He wanted him to suffer. He wanted to be vicious, regardless of who witnessed his deed.

Even his mate.

How much difference was there between him and his old adversary? Less than Rafferty would have liked.

His heightened reaction had probably been because of the presence of his mate and because she had been threatened by Magnus, but still . . .

Rafferty wasn't proud of himself. He had spent his entire existence honoring others, particularly humans, safeguarding the secrets of the *Pyr*, facilitating firestorms, being the voice of reason and temperance.

In a day, he had utterly lost himself in the darkfire.

In a day, he had seen the shadow within himself, and the sight of his own truth appalled him.

Rafferty's bloodlust had overwhelmed him, blinding him to simple practicalities. He should have anticipated that Jorge would be drawn to the firestorm, that the *Slayers* who had been given the Elixir from Magnus's own hand might rally to that villain's defense.

Worse, he had retaliated against Magnus in daylight, beside a busy thoroughfare. There would be another human record of the *Pyr*. Worse again, it would show his kind in an act of savagery. In *his* savagery. It was another mistake for which he would have to atone with Erik. He couldn't blame Erik for being angry, but at the same time, the firestorm's erratic burn convoluted his thinking, twisting his impulses in unexpected ways.

Rafferty had to retreat.

He had to seek out a refuge.

And he knew the only one that would do.

Maybe secured in his London lair, he could recover his senses.

Maybe secured in his London lair, he could seduce his mate and end the chaotic influence of this darkfire firestorm. It was the only way to regain his equilibrium. He'd already told Melissa far too much.

At least Rafferty knew that Donovan was keeping his old pledge and traveling to the hoard where the Sleeper was secured. Something had gone right. Was the Sleeper fully awake yet? Rafferty hoped it took time for him to return to consciousness, at least long enough for Donovan to arrive. He didn't need another mistake to his credit. Rafferty did not dare to go to the Sleeper himself, not with Magnus still alive, lest he lead the old snake to a prize beyond all expectation.

"Where are we going?" Melissa asked as he flew over the ocean. Rafferty wasn't fooled by the casual tone of her question.

"Home."

As anticipated, she had no quibble setting him straight. "No. My home isn't this way. It's back down there."

Rafferty was feeling somewhat less than his usual diplomatic self. He saw no reason to gloss the truth. "No. Your home is gone."

"What?" She eyed him with consternation. "What do you mean, 'gone'?"

"It is destroyed," Rafferty said flatly, trying to keep the emotion out of his voice. That had been another failure on his part. He would add it to the ever-growing list. He would atone for her loss before all was done between them.

Melissa faltered for a moment. It was something for her to be even momentarily speechless. "But, but, *how*?"

"I summoned an earthquake, in order to pass beneath the dragonsmoke and rescue you." Rafferty knew he sounded stern, but he was irritated that he hadn't thought beyond that moment to the consequences. "Your house was the epicenter. It was the only way out."

"You trashed my house? On purpose?"

"It was a casualty of my actions, yes." He spared himself any comment about flimsy new construction. He also refrained from noting that her home's decor had less character than that of his hotel room. He had sensed that the town house was no more than a placeholder, an address to which she had mail sent, but he had no business accusing her of not having a true home.

He could imagine where that discussion would lead. Still, he wondered. Was Melissa as rootless as that? Was she disinterested in having a refuge or a home? He could barely imagine being without the comfort of his lair, even when he wasn't in it.

Melissa looked away, then back to him. "You could say you were sorry." Her tone was accusatory, and rightly so.

Whether her home had been decorated to his taste or not, it had been her property. He looked down at her, knowing his appearance was formidable. She didn't flinch.

"I am sorry for the destruction of your home," he said tightly. She sniffed, unimpressed. Rafferty continued, because he couldn't regret his choice. "Are you sorry I pursued you?"

She swallowed and blinked. "Okay, I'm not. It was good that you came after the helicopter, and I didn't thank you for that. Thanks."

"You need not thank me. It was my duty."

"Why?"

"Because you are my mate, and I am pledged to your defense." Rafferty concentrated on charting his course.

"I'd like to know more about this mate business, and what it entails," she said, her tone making it clear that she had already made up her mind.

And not in Rafferty's favor.

He didn't have it in him to battle verbally at the moment, so he changed the subject—even if it did feel like a trick. "Actually, I am committed to the defense of the entire human species. We all are."

"Be serious. How did summoning an earthquake do that?" Melissa certainly wasn't one to avoid the tough questions. At least she'd accepted his redirection of the conversation. "I mean, *somebody* must have gotten hurt. There are a lot of people living around there."

Rafferty felt his anger rise. The firestorm tickled at him, and he had a long flight ahead of him. He could have done without a challenge from his mate. "I made a choice, one in your favor. I would not expect you to be the one to question its merit."

"There you go, talking like a history book again. You sound as if you're a thousand years old or something."

"Somewhat more than that."

"What?"

But Rafferty had had enough. "I would appreciate your cooperation at this time. We have a long flight, and I must be wary of human observance."

Melissa laughed. "I think that one's out of the bag."

Rafferty declined to answer, his entire gut tightening at his responsibility for that.

And hers. As much as he didn't want to argue with her, he resented that she had posted those pictures. What would it mean for the *Pyr* to be revealed?

Nothing good.

Just as nothing good would come of a discussion on that subject in this moment. He was tired and would likely lose his temper.

Rafferty gritted his teeth and said nothing. They were over the Atlantic now, the coast fading behind them. The snow had settled into a pounding icy rhythm, one that didn't please Rafferty; he would be more sore for flying in its chill. On the other hand, the weather did diminish visibility, and he could do without needing to perform any beguiling of observers.

He hated beguiling anyone.

"So, who was the gold dragon? And how did he turn up so fast?" Melissa's voice was slightly higher than it had been, and Rafferty wondered whether she was afraid of heights. Or water.

"His name is Jorge. He's a *Slayer*—"

"A what?"

Rafferty saw no reason to be coy about such basics. And, maybe, his talking to Melissa would distract her from her fears. "We are of two kinds," he said, and felt her relax slightly at his calm tone. "The true *Pyr*, of which I am one, are the guardians of the earth. We defend the treasure that is the planet, and we include humans among those treasures. *Slayers*, in contrast, declare that they would defend the earth and that humans must be eradicated in order to protect the planet."

"I'm sensing some skepticism with the official explanation."

"In reality, *Slayers* act in their own interests, with indifference to anything else."

"So, they're the ones who bleed black?"

"Because of this selfishness, the Great Wyvern extinguishes Her spark within each of them. Their blood runs black, indicative of their turning away from the light, and they do not have firestorms."

"Seems you wouldn't mind being without one yourself."

"I don't see much to be gained in discussing the matter right now." Rafferty felt her expectant gaze upon him but continued with his original point. "Magnus is a *Slayer* and has led them at times. Jorge is one of his more loyal followers."

"So, that's why he saved him? Honor among thieves?"

"Maybe. It's also possible that Jorge sees something to his own advantage in saving Magnus."

"Like what?"

"Magnus had control of something called the Dragon's Blood Elixir. It conferred immortality but was addictive, like a drug, requiring a constant supply. He shared it with his favored *Slayers*, omitting the detail that they would have to come to him for more."

"A prince among dragons," Melissa said, her opinion of that strategy clear. "It's the classic ploy used by drug pushers to build their customer base. Free samples."

Rafferty nodded, relieved to find them in agreement in their disgust. "The source of the Elixir is destroyed, and most of those who drank of it have been destroyed, as well. I wasn't sure what had happened to Jorge—he disappeared quite suddenly and has been quiet for a long time."

"Maybe he was looking for a hit." Melissa snapped her fingers. "Hey, maybe he thinks Montmorency has a stash. Capturing him in a weak moment might let him persuade Montmorency to part with it."

"Maybe. At any rate, Magnus will be harder to hunt while he's in Jorge's company."

"Jorge didn't look like a nice guy."

"He is completely immoral, even among *Slayers*."

Rafferty could almost hear the gears of Melissa's mind turning before she spoke. "He's not blond in his human form, is he? Kind of an iceman look? Pale eyes, brush cut, super buff? Like a homicidal Viking?"

Rafferty was startled. "How do you know this?"

She nodded matter-of-factly. "I was watching Montmorency in the Middle East. He was suspected of being an arms dealer, a big one, but no one could ever get anything on him. It drove me crazy."

"It was a story you intended to get," Rafferty said.

"It was a truth I wanted more than any other."

"To ensure justice," Rafferty guessed.

Melissa nodded with that familiar resolve, and he felt some satisfaction at understanding her. "I tried. But the thing is, Montmorency had this bodyguard, who was scary-mercenary. Blond. I called him the Homicidal Viking."

"That would be Jorge."

"The phrase started out as a joke, but one day I was

trailing Montmorency to a meeting. It ended fast, and I saw the blond guy take out the man he'd met. He was rumored to have cheated Montmorency." She swallowed. "This Jorge pulled a knife on the guy, right in the market, slit him from gullet to groin. And then he looked around with those cold blue eyes, as if daring anyone to challenge him. Every witness melted away, and Montmorency was long gone." She shivered, and Rafferty was amazed that she had lived in such an environment by choice.

"And yet you watched?"

"He didn't see me. I made sure of that."

Rafferty wasn't as certain as Melissa. She hadn't known then about the heightened senses of *Pyr* and *Slayers*. His gut tightened at the prospect of Jorge's hunting her.

"That was the day I knew I had to nail Montmorency."

Rafferty said nothing.

Melissa clearly thought his silence was a condemnation, because she continued with resolve. "Listen, evil happens in the dark. It happens in the corners, when no one is looking, when no one is brave enough to look. And that's how it spreads, by all of us collectively pretending we don't see it."

"You think people should have challenged him?"

"If everyone had turned on him, he wouldn't have had a chance. He couldn't have single-handedly killed everyone. If I'd had a camera, I would have shown the evidence right then and there."

"Are you so sure he couldn't have killed everyone in the marketplace?" Rafferty asked softly. "Now that you know his abilities?"

Melissa frowned. "Okay. If he'd been a man, he couldn't have taken out everyone, no matter how homicidal he was." She tapped on his chest. "My point is that people are cynical about journalism, viewing it as a kind of ambulance chasing. But what news does, what news can do, is shine a light on evil. News can show it, can spread the word about it, can empower justice systems, and fuel public outrage. News makes change."

"So, we're back to justice."

"You'd better believe it." Melissa's voice was hard, filled with conviction. "And being part of that process, being key to it, is worth any price. If I had the evidence against Montmorency and I took it public, it wouldn't matter what he did to me or what he said. Justice would prevail because of the record I had made."

Rafferty was awed, both by the vigor of her argument and her impassioned sense of justice. "You're an idealist," he said, amazed by the realization.

"No. Idealists are dreamers. I'm a realist." She grinned up at him. "I'm not afraid to get my hands dirty, not if it makes the world a better place."

"You're not afraid to break the law."

She grimaced. "I had a hard time with that one—still do." Her lashes closed. "If I hadn't seen Daphne in the morgue, I don't think I could have done it."

"Why? I don't understand the connection."

She looked up, her gaze filled with vulnerability. "Because I asked her, years ago, to get evidence against Montmorency. She died because she tried to do what I asked of her. I owe her for that."

"You owe her justice."

"If not a whole lot more."

Rafferty felt relieved to understand his mate's motivation. "So you're not afraid to die, if you get a story that stops evil in its tracks."

Her smile was brilliant. "Guilty as charged. Now you know the secret of my life." She cast a glance over him, her eyes dancing with unexpected mischief. "And I'm thinking I know yours."

Rafferty eyed the distance ahead, fighting his inclination to be charmed by his mate. It occurred to him that she might be trying to manipulate him to get her story on the *Pyr*. The leaping blue flames of darkfire didn't do much to clarify his thinking. He said nothing, admitted nothing more, and kept flying.

He was well aware that she was watching him avidly.

He thought she might have fallen asleep, when she finally spoke again. "So, where exactly is it that we're going?"

"My lair. It is the only place we'll be safe."

"Safe being a relative term." That thread of humor was in her tone again, a hint of how she dealt with stressful situations.

"You don't like not being in control."

"Not one bit," she admitted easily. "My house is trashed. I don't have my cell phone. I've lost my chance at a job. A dragon is carrying me across the ocean to points unknown. Bad dragons apparently abound, and there's something weird going on called darkfire. The combination of all of the above is not really working for me."

"Knowing your destination won't change much."

"What can I say? I like information. Maybe knowledge is power." She laughed, then sobered. "Or maybe I really, *really* hate uncertainty."

Rafferty fought against an answering smile. "You must know by now that I won't injure you."

"I know that. You're pledged to the defense of your

mate." She repeated his words with care, quoting him perfectly. "Which brings up another uncertainty. What does this *mate* business mean?"

"What do you think it means?"

"Don't be coy. If I knew, I wouldn't be asking," she replied, an edge to her tone. Then she sighed. "Okay, look. We don't need to fight. I'm already involved here. We're in this together, whatever it is. You, me, and the firestorm against the bad dragons, however many there are. I have that much, so I guess I'll have to go with it. How long will this flight take?"

"Hours," Rafferty admitted.

She surveyed their surroundings, her expression telling him all he needed to know. It was less than hospitable this far out to sea, especially with the snow falling heavily against them. In every direction, there were only dark skies, dark seas, or snow.

She nestled closer to him, curling into his embrace, and Rafferty felt a warm glow in the vicinity of his heart. It wasn't entirely due to the firestorm. No, he was giving shelter to a human, to his mate, protecting her from these particular elements. It was a step back to where he belonged, and it felt good.

"You know, in my biz, in the field, you catch your z's when you can. It's not as if I can actually do anything useful right now, anyway. You have any problem with my grabbing a few right now?"

"None whatsoever," Rafferty said, liking that she was such a practical and pragmatic person. She might have cried. She might have complained. Instead, she demanded information, and she made her peace with what he told her. Rafferty admired her resilience. "In fact, it would be preferable to me."

"How so?"

"I expect that when you sleep, the darkfire flames will ebb slightly."

"And it'll be easier for you to concentrate," she concluded. "It *is* distracting, isn't it? I can't remember when I've thought so obsessively about sex before."

Rafferty found himself smiling. "It's the firestorm."

"I don't know," she said lightly. "It could be you. You'll be hard to forget, you know."

Rafferty's gut tightened. He had never anticipated that his destined mate would be interested in forgetting him— but then, Melissa had seen him at his worst. He couldn't find it within himself to argue for the side of permanence.

She sighed. "And there's that mate stuff. Let's save that for tomorrow, shall we? I'm approaching information overload right now."

"That's fair."

She eyed him closely, and he wondered how much of his thinking she discerned. He already knew she was more observant than most. "So, I'll leave you to the navigation, then."

"Sleep well, Melissa."

She watched him, but Rafferty avoided her gaze studiously. He attended to the wind and the pull of the earth's magnetic field, charting his course and remaining alert to any possible observers. He was using his favored route, the one less likely to be used by commercial airlines. It was longer and lower, but he just wanted something to be easy for a few hours.

As if she understood as much, Melissa fell asleep, curled against his chest. He could feel the moment that sleep claimed her, and her inquisitive mind finally slipped into rest.

The flames of the darkfire did abate somewhat, letting him think more clearly than he had in hours. He could think about strategy, as well as sex.

All Rafferty had to do was seduce his mate, satisfy the firestorm, ensure the defense of the Sleeper when he awakened, destroy Magnus, and get the world of the *Pyr* back to normal.

Or as normal as it could be after these events.

It wasn't going to be easy.

He was looking forward to the reassurance of home.

Chapter 9

Melissa awakened in a comfortable bed. It was such an unexpected difference from the warm embrace of an opal and gold dragon that she sat up abruptly and looked around. The sheet fell away, cool air touching her bare skin, and she realized she was naked.

She blushed, imagining who had undressed her, then took stock of her surroundings.

Melissa was in an old house, on an upper floor. She could hear the distant hum and honk of traffic, and the steady pounding of rain on the roof. Rain tinkled against the panes of the window, too, sounding icy and cold. There was a damp chill in the air, and it was light outside the windows.

Was it morning or afternoon?

The room was cozy, if not as cozy as a dragon's embrace. The floor was hardwood, the planks wide and the wood stained dark. The floor was worn and not entirely level, and Melissa found its visible history reassuring in a way. The walls were painted a honeyed beige, which was both warm and bright. She could see by the uneven surface that they were plaster.

There was a crown molding, probably also plaster, around the perimeter of the high ceiling, and a simple brass chandelier hung from the middle of the ceiling. Its shades were art glass. Melissa stretched to look at the shadings of mauve and amber and blue in their swirled surface. Their beauty had no competition, the white ceiling showing them to advantage.

The rest of the room was the same, furnished with minimal clutter. The furniture itself was so well crafted and solid that it needed no ornamentation—the grain of the wood and the rich patina were enough. The bed had a headboard in arts and crafts style, solid quarter sawn oak that reminded Melissa of the mission style furniture her brother loved so much. The house he and his wife shared in California was filled with it, and Melissa always found its clean lines attractive.

There was a quilt on the bed, pieced of brilliant cotton paisley prints. Melissa found the words *Liberty of London* carefully framed in more than one piece. Its colors echoed the mauve and gold of the art glass and gave the room a coherence that she liked a lot. The rug on the floor was hooked by hand, cut from wool in various shades of purple and blue. At a glance, it looked to be all one color, but closer inspection revealed myriad hues mingled together.

Melissa thought of William Morris's injunction to have nothing in one's home that was not beautiful or useful. She'd bet Rafferty had that stitched on a sampler somewhere.

She had no trouble believing she was in Rafferty's

house. Even this one room had an integrity, a solidity and warmth, that she already associated with him. There were no blue flames, and she felt only a distant tingle of heat.

Had Rafferty abandoned her?

Melissa couldn't hear anything beyond the rain and the traffic, but she didn't feel alone, either. She went to the door, and the heat of the firestorm increased slightly. She watched in fascination as the blue-green flames danced around the hand she placed on the door. They seemed mercurial, there and not there, more fluid than fire usually was.

That desire filled her again, her thoughts turning to the pleasure she and Rafferty had shared. She had a sudden and vivid idea of how best to spend a rainy morning in his company.

He had called her "mate," after all. Melissa grimaced, well aware that if his expectation of a partner was as basic as it sounded, she wouldn't be able to deliver.

Literally.

Maybe she'd just go with the moment and worry about the implications (and her limitations) later.

The light flared around her hand, as if to endorse the notion, and Melissa caught her breath at the way her knees weakened. A particularly bright flame dropped from her hand to the floor. She snatched at it, fearing the carpet would burn. Instead, the flame rolled through the gap beneath the door and disappeared.

Melissa opened the door in time to see the cluster of flame slip and skip across a foyer, then slide down the stairs.

In pursuit of Rafferty.

Or maybe guiding her to him.

Either way, he was here.

Melissa's heart leapt, and she knew she had to go to him. She used the compact cream and black bathroom adjacent to her room, admiring the antique wall tiles even as she hurried. She really liked his house. It was authentic and original in a way she found appealing.

But then Rafferty couldn't be mistaken for anyone other than who he was. His confidence was very sexy. He was proud of his *Pyr* nature, sure of his objectives. He'd implied that he was more than a thousand years old, which she supposed gave someone time to refine likes and dislikes. She tugged on the fluffy white robe hanging on the back of the door, then set out to find her host.

It was easy. She lifted her hand in front of her and watched for the blue flames. They flared and leapt; then the tips of the flames bent toward the top of the stairs. Melissa descended the stairs, her bare feet sinking into the thick Persian runner, her other hand trailing down the carved wooden banister.

Melissa studied Rafferty's home, wanting to know every detail about him that could be discerned from his residence. She had no doubt that everything had been chosen with deliberation.

There was a magnificent newel post at the end of the banister, one that looked as if it had been carved out of the trunk of an ancient tree. It certainly seemed rooted to the foyer, which had the same dark wood floors and thick carpets. The colors of choice here were red and gold, a deep oxblood red and a gold that approached bronze.

There was an old fireplace in the foyer, with a tiled surround in that same red and gold, and with an elaborate metal grate. A fire burned low there, casting a welcome heat into the foyer. It burned a little higher and hotter as she passed, as if the flames there were responding to the blue heat that danced from her fingertips.

The front door was solid and substantial, at least three feet wide, with stained glass sidelights and a transom. Melissa noted that the glass had been sandwiched between sheets of modern glass, probably to protect it and to provide better security. The lock on the door had been refitted with a modern lock, one that was set into the antique brass of the original.

Melissa smiled. It made sense to her that Rafferty would do sensitive restoration and modernization. He would be the kind of person to respect the past but look to the future.

He wasn't afraid to experience the moment fully. She could take a lesson from that.

Rafferty's house felt like a haven. Melissa wasn't sure she'd ever want to leave it.

She couldn't help but compare this to her own home, which was infinitely forgettable. She'd made her town house easy to leave, by conscious choice, so that she could answer the call of her profession and go wherever was necessary without a backward glance. It had never held the same promise as the house she and Zach had bought together, and when that had been sold, she hadn't wanted to invest emotionally in bricks and mortar.

She'd done the same with relationships since her marriage had ended, never investing the increment that would make another person a cornerstone of her life. She'd always been sure that was the sensible choice. Now, in Rafferty's home, Melissa realized she had denied herself a kind of solace and comfort that would have been very welcome in recent years.

No wonder she had gone to her brother's house to convalesce. Her town house hadn't been much more personal or welcoming than the hospital. Even then, she'd stayed in California for only a week, telling herself she didn't want to impose.

No. She'd been afraid of not ever being able to leave, of being drawn in so tightly that she'd want only to stay.

Cool as a cucumber her brother called her.

Ice queen Zach had called her.

Chicken shit was what Melissa decided to call herself. Was she ever going to invest in herself? In a personal relationship she wanted? In living instead of simply marking time—or working all the time?

Maybe the moment to change was right now.

Melissa stood in the central foyer and held up her hand for directions. The flames indicated that Rafferty was at the rear of the house, in the room directly beneath the bedroom where she had awakened. That heavy wood door was closed, but the hungry lick of the blue flames when she touched the doorknob told her all she needed to know.

Not just about Rafferty, but about herself and her choices.

It was time to live in the moment.

It was time to want something more than survival.

It was time to do something about getting what she wanted.

Melissa rapped once, then opened the door.

"I will make you a wager," Magnus said, even as Jorge was thrashing the old *Slayer*. He was within a heartbeat of death, badly wounded, and Jorge wasn't surprised that Magnus would use his last breath to try to negotiate.

"You have nothing I want," Jorge retorted. "Except the Elixir in your veins."

"Which is diluted," Magnus replied. "Look at me! If the Elixir ran strong within me, would I be so sorely wounded?"

Jorge hesitated. That argument did make some sense.

"I have more," Magnus said. "I have only to get to it. If you release me, I would share."

"Eighty-twenty," Jorge said.

Magnus laughed, coughing blood. "Twenty-eighty was more my thinking"—Jorge drove a talon into the old *Slayer*'s chest, and his next words required more effort—"but it appears you have the upper talon."

"Take me there," Jorge insisted. "Show it to me." He knew better than to trust Magnus Montmorency.

"I can't when you clutch so tightly." Magnus closed his eyes, his breath rasping. "I can barely breathe," he whispered, his strength apparently fading.

Jorge studied him. Magnus could be lying. But if Magnus wasn't lying, if he died, Jorge would never find that stash of Elixir. He eased his grip ever so slightly on the old *Slayer*, on his guard for treachery.

Jorge wasn't quite quick enough. Magnus twitched and shifted shape, becoming a green salamander. Jorge snatched after him, but no sooner had his hand closed around the reptile than Magnus disappeared before his eyes.

"Better luck next time." The old-speak resonated in Jorge's own thoughts. Then Magnus laughed.

Jorge's eyes narrowed. If there was a next time, he knew who would trick whom.

Next time, Jorge would triumph.

*   *   *

The door opened before Melissa to reveal a library, paneled completely in carved dark oak. The fire was built up to burn more vehemently, its flames painting the room with flickering orange light. The burgundy velvet drapes were closed against the morning; the walls were lined with books, old leather-bound books with gold lettering on the spines; and a massive desk reposed in one corner. There was a pair of armchairs before the fire, their caramel leather worn to wrinkles and shine.

Rafferty sat in the one facing the doorway. He wore only his jeans, his bare feet stretched out before the fire. His dark hair glinted; his eyes glittered. He looked both thoughtful and formidable. He was utterly still, except for his thumb, which worried that black and white ring. In his other hand was a large quartz crystal, and there were many mineral samples on the bookshelves. They made earthy and interesting bookends.

Melissa understood he had been waiting for her.

She halted in the doorway, heart in her throat. "You knew I was coming."

"Our senses are more keen than those of humans." His words were softly uttered but seemed to resonate in the room. "I heard your breathing change when you awakened. I thought your curiosity would bring you downstairs." He looked into the fire, and she had the sense he was trying to make a decision about something.

Maybe about her.

Melissa stepped into the room, closed the door, and leaned back against it. She felt as if she had entered a refuge—one of the most secure kind. "Can they follow us here?"

"Magnus and Jorge can follow us anywhere." Rafferty pushed to his feet, bending to tend the fire that didn't need tending. The golden light slid over his muscles exactly as Melissa would have liked to slide her hands over him. "When a *Slayer* can spontaneously manifest wherever he chooses, there can be no barriers to hold him out."

"Not even dragonsmoke?"

"No."

"Can you manifest like that?"

"I did not drink the Elixir." His reply was emphatic, just like his gesture as he shoved the poker into the fire. Sparks scattered and danced.

"That doesn't exactly answer my question."

Rafferty pursed his lips and frowned. "I believe only those who have drunk the Elixir have the power to spontaneously manifest in alternate locations."

Again, Melissa sensed this was only half of the story. What wasn't he telling her? "So, you've never done it?"

He frowned. "I did. Twice." His gaze flicked to hers. "Although both times I was trying to do it, I'm not sure I was ultimately responsible for my deed."

"What does that mean?"

"I wanted to find Magnus. I wanted to be with Magnus. I spontaneously manifested in Magnus's presence. But both times, Magnus wanted something from me." Rafferty shook his head thoughtfully. "I have come to think I did not make the choice to move, but he summoned me."

"Because he had drunk the Elixir, and he needed your help."

Rafferty nodded, that frown still furrowing his brow.

"Did you try again? To make sure?"

"I have failed to repeat the deed." He flicked her a look. "I was trying again, on the night we met."

Melissa had to respect his conclusion, given that. Desire couldn't have much to do with it—she knew he had wanted to destroy Magnus that night in DC.

As the Elixir—and those who had consumed it—was a topic that clearly troubled Rafferty, Melissa didn't want to talk about it. She wanted Rafferty to be in a different mood.

An amorous one.

The silence stretched between them, the fact that he kept his back to her less than encouraging. But it would take more than mere body language to daunt Melissa Smith when she was on a mission. She stepped into the room and took the chair opposite the one Rafferty had occupied. The leather was worn soft and smooth, and the fire was warm against her legs.

"So, about this mate thing," she said.

Rafferty spun suddenly to face her, his move deft and elegant. Once again, he had moved more quickly than she had anticipated. What else could he do? "What about it?"

"It has something to do with the firestorm, with these flames, right?" She lifted her hand, and the blue-green fire danced predictably from her fingertips, angling toward Rafferty as if burning in a stiff breeze. Or yearning for a connection. Melissa's mouth went dry, and she felt a yearning of her own as Rafferty's gaze brightened.

"The firestorm and its flames are a sign that a *Pyr* has found his destined mate."

"I don't believe in destiny," Melissa said. "Do you?"

"Then believe in biology," he said, avoiding her question and her gaze. This conversation made him uncomfortable, which was interesting. "The destined mate is the one woman who can conceive that *Pyr*'s son."

There was no chance of that happening, but Melissa saw no reason to tell all of her secrets just yet. "So the flames are a sign?"

"And the firestorm's heat mounts, until it is sated." Rafferty arched a brow. "It becomes increasingly difficult to deny."

Melissa leaned toward him, knowing that the white robe would gape at the neck. Rafferty's eyes shone and his fist clenched, but he didn't move closer. It seemed his entire body had become taut, which only fed Melissa's urge to touch him.

Everywhere.

"So, the firestorm is about making more dragons?"

Rafferty frowned and glanced away. He was turning that ring again but seemed unaware of what he was doing. "There are those who believe as much. There are others who think the firestorm is a chance for a deeper partnership, one that endures after the firestorm is sated."

Melissa could guess which perspective was Rafferty's. She respected his sense of tradition and longevity. She wished she'd met him sooner, when she had still believed in the future, in love lasting forever, and in the possibility of happily ever after.

Her short marriage had destroyed that particular illusion.

Rafferty flicked a potent look in her direction, and she glimpsed how important this notion was to him. "There are those who believe the most successful firestorms are those that become permanent partnerships. A union that is more than the sum of the parts."

Melissa didn't want to talk about how she couldn't be that mate for him. She didn't want to talk about the future or the past—she wanted to talk about the present.

She wanted to savor the attraction between them.

So she changed the subject ever so slightly. "And the firestorm is sated when the mate conceives?"

"It's sated when they consummate their relationship. Our understanding is that the moment is concurrent, that it takes only once for the mate to conceive the destined child."

Melissa smiled. She couldn't help it. "But we already did it once."

Rafferty didn't smile. If anything, he was more intent. "That was before the firestorm began to burn."

"I don't understand."

"Important firestorms are launched by the light of a total lunar eclipse. It is common that the destined pair meet after that eclipse, so feel their firestorm in that first encounter." He frowned and shrugged, then glanced at her. "We met sooner."

"So it doesn't count that we did it?"

Rafferty smiled warmly. "Do you think it didn't count?"

"I mean in terms of making more dragons."

"In those terms, no. Evidently it didn't count, because the firestorm is still burning."

Saved by a technicality.

Melissa didn't believe in forever anymore, but she believed in the moment. This moment. She believed in doing what felt right, and in asking for what she wanted.

If she told him everything about her personal history, this moment would be lost. She feared that he would turn against her, once he knew the truth.

Just one more taste of him. That was all she wanted before he left her and she was alone again. It seemed such a small thing to ask.

Melissa stood up and crossed the short distance between them. She caught Rafferty's face in her hands and stretched up to brush her lips across his. She heard his intake of breath, felt him tense, saw the hardness of his erection in his jeans. He wanted her just as she was, and that was the best aphrodisiac imaginable.

"Let's sate the firestorm," she whispered. "Right here, right now." She savored the flash of pleasure in his eyes, then kissed him with conviction.

A gift unexpected!

Rafferty wasn't inclined to despair, although he had felt since the eclipse that every force was allied against him. He had been brooding about his situation, uncertain how to proceed, even as he'd listened to Melissa sleeping. He had been dreading their next conversation, her inevitable questions, the airing of his uncertainties.

He'd told her about the firestorm, fully anticipating that such an independent woman would refuse the burden of bearing his child. He'd been certain that his firestorm was doomed and that the darkfire would burn long and vigorously.

Wreaking havoc for the *Pyr*.

On the other hand, he appreciated that Melissa was forthright and that she didn't shirk from hard truths. He'd known he could tell her the full story and she would rationally decide how to proceed. Even if he guessed what her answer might be, he owed her that explanation.

To have his mate consent to sating the firestorm, even knowing its import, was far more than he could have anticipated.

It was a sign that he had only to have faith and that

the Great Wyvern was indeed on his side. It changed everything for Rafferty. It gave him hope. It restored his ability to trust that all would end well, no matter how long the odds.

That was something to celebrate.

And he knew exactly how best to celebrate.

Rafferty caught Melissa around the waist and pulled her up against him, angling his head to deepen their kiss. She was as sweet and responsive as he remembered, although he sensed a new hunger in her. Was it because of the firestorm? Or was it because they already had some familiarity with each other?

Rafferty didn't care. The dragon roared within him, as the flames of the darkfire blazed with sapphire light. He wanted everything she had to give. Holding her captive to his kiss with one hand locked around her nape, he used the other hand to unfasten the belt of her bathrobe. She wriggled like a fish in his grasp, shaking the robe over her shoulders, then locking her fingers into his hair once more.

When her bare breasts collided with his chest, Rafferty started at the sparks that flew from that point, then pressed her more tightly against him. He wanted to merge their bodies in a more intimate embrace than the one they'd already shared—he wanted the consummation of his firestorm to be more than memorable.

He'd waited so long.

He wanted their mating to be perfect in every way.

He wanted this permanent bond rooted in a potent memory.

Melissa met him more than halfway, her eyes closed as she echoed the ardor of his kiss. She kissed him deeply, her teeth grazing his lips, her tongue teasing and tempting. She seemed to be starving for him, desperate for his touch, as determined as he was to push their lovemaking to the next level of passion. He could smell her wet heat, mixing with the faint lingering aura of her perfume. The combination tantalized him.

He was shocked when she broke her kiss.

He was even more shocked when Melissa unzipped his jeans, pushed them over his hips, and closed her mouth over his erection.

Forthright.

That was all he had time to think before sensation claimed him completely. Rafferty was dizzy with the unexpected pleasure of her touch, and he clutched the back of one chair to ensure that he remained standing.

He didn't evade her, though. Melissa wove a spell with her caress that drove every sensible thought from his mind, ensnaring Rafferty in a web of pleasure and sensation. He closed his eyes against the growing heat of the firestorm, against the assault of the vivid blue flames, against the sure touch of his lover.

Did he dare to imagine that they might make an enduring partnership? Did he dare to hope that in agreeing to have his child, this independent woman with her clear gaze might put her hand in his for the duration? He suspected he could spend a lifetime unraveling her secrets, and he was ready to volunteer.

As she touched him, kindling his passion so deftly that she might have shared his every thought, so sure of what would rouse him that she might have loved him for decades, Rafferty dared to imagine as much. He dared to believe that this firestorm truly could bring him his heart's desire.

When he was so hard and thick that he couldn't stand

temptation any longer, when he knew he would explode at any time, he knew it would be an abomination to spill his seed recklessly.

He caught Melissa by the shoulders just before he came. He lifted her into his arms, then set her in the caramel leather armchair he had vacated.

She gasped at his move, her eyes widening in surprise, but he braced her buttocks in his hands, dropped to his knees, and licked at her sweetness. She caught her breath in pleasure, then seemed to swoon, those lips softening as she surrendered to his touch in turn.

She put her feet on his shoulders, the smooth curve of her arches sliding over his skin as she pointed her toes. Her trust fed Rafferty's desire, making the flame within him burn higher and hotter.

Melissa leaned her head back and reveled in his touch, moaning and bucking her hips. He felt the golden heat of the fire against his skin, while the azure heat of the darkfire danced between them, illuminating every place their bodies touched. It wasn't Rafferty's imagination that the blue flames leapt higher as Melissa's passion rose.

He heard the beat of her heart and felt his own match pace to it. Their hearts pounded as one, the sound of hers echoing in his ears, the resonance of his own multiplying the sensation, overwhelming him with a sense of communion.

He heard the flutter of her breath and heard it deepen as she became more aroused. He felt his own breath synchronize in pace, increasing the sensation that they were not two meeting as one, but one that had been separated, its halves now coming together in glorious union once again. He took her to within a heartbeat of release, then paused, building her desire to the cusp of satisfaction over and over again. He denied her the final rush of pleasure each time, knowing the result would be greater for it. She moaned and writhed, gasped at his touch, begged him not to stop.

He felt the flush sliding over her skin as surely as the heat kindled beneath his own flesh, and he knew this time he would push her to the point of release. He felt her clitoris tighten and grow hard, just as he hardened at the sweet taste of her pleasure.

He nipped that taut bud, a quick and hard touch that sent Melissa over the edge.

She shouted, clutched his head, and rocked against him. Her pulse raced with new vigor as the orgasm claimed her. Her knees locked around his shoulders, and she bucked as he still refused to stop his caress, driving her on and on and on. Her release seemed to last forever, and he loved every second of it.

When Melissa slumped limp and exhausted back into the chair, Rafferty thought she might fall asleep again.

But she looked at him, her eyes blazing with demand.

"All of you," she whispered, then beckoned with one finger. "All of you, *now*."

Rafferty smiled slowly as he eased himself over her. She smiled in return as she wrapped her legs around his waist, her ankles hooking together behind his back. She inhaled as he slid his strength into her wet heat, drawing him deeper and deeper. He felt welcomed, as if they were destined to fit together so perfectly, as if there could be no other woman to hold him just so.

"More," she whispered, rolling her hips so that he was more completely buried within her. Rafferty closed his eyes and caught his breath, struggling for control. Melissa dug her nails into the back of his shoulders. "All of you," she demanded again, twining against him and kissing him beneath the ear.

Rafferty shivered and pressed into her more deeply. Melissa licked his ear and blew against the wet flesh. He shuddered. She moved her hips and he was lost in her spell again. The sapphire flames leapt and danced around them, sliding over their skin and between their bodies, heating, illuminating, exciting.

Rafferty could even see the blue haze when he closed his eyes. As he moved within Melissa, as she provoked him much as he had provoked her, he felt the heat burn brighter. It became whiter and hotter, burning more vigorously in place. Its demand increased, mingled with Melissa's scent, tickled the dragon to wakefulness, and utterly enchanted Rafferty.

He cupped her buttocks and stood up, easily carrying her weight with him. She locked her legs around his waist and her arms around his neck. He met her simmering gaze as he slid his hand between them. He felt her clitoris harden again and saw her eyes sparkle in anticipation. Feeling that she was on the cusp once more, he moved his fingers with surety, knowing already what she liked.

He dared to imagine how powerful their lovemaking would become over time, as they each learned how best to drive the other wild. The notion excited him as little else could have done.

Rafferty deliberately drove Melissa to climax, holding his own reaction back with an effort. Melissa convulsed as she reached her orgasm, her legs tightening around him, her nails digging into his shoulders, her cry rippling across his cheek. He watched her, loving how the blue flames of the darkfire touched her skin, surrounded her, and made her seem to glow like a rare treasure.

His prize.

His mate.

His treasure.

She opened her eyes and smiled at him, reaching to pull him closer. Her hungry kiss drove Rafferty to the precipice. He let loose and roared, fit to rattle the rafters. He came in a raging torrent, his seed spilling in a release so shattering that it shook him to his core.

Rafferty's orgasm both lasted forever and was over in a flash.

It left him staggering in his library, Melissa curled against his chest with a contented smile. He leaned one shoulder against the mantel to catch his breath, liking the stability of the massive slab of old oak. Melissa sighed in contentment and lifted her head to consider him, her own gaze drowsy in the aftermath of pleasure. She trailed her fingertips through his hair, down his cheek, through the day's growth on his jaw.

"What a perfect way to spend a rainy morning," she said softly, tracing a line across his mouth with one silken fingertip. To Rafferty's astonishment, he felt a prickle of the heat trail her touch.

He blinked and looked, knowing his thoughts were muddled and the angle was bad. Melissa swept her hand over his shoulder, then down his arm, as if she would memorize the shape of him.

There were unmistakable blue sparks leaping and dancing in the wake of her caress. He could see them. He could feel them. They made a burning line across his skin, one that fed his desire all over again and sent that familiar urge through his veins. They were that same elusive blue-green as the darkfire had been just moments before.

How could this be?

"Oh," Melissa said quietly as she noted the direction of his gaze. "Looks like the *Pyr* mythos has it wrong."

Rafferty stared into her eyes, unable to summon a word to his lips. How could the firestorm not be sated?

Then his heart clenched in fear. Was there something different about darkfire? Something he didn't know? Something he should fear?

"Wow," Melissa said abruptly. "What kind of rocks are these, anyway?"

Rafferty followed her gaze to his bookshelves, only to discover that each sample in his mineral collection had a strange blue flame dancing at its core. The light flickered through the stones, taking on the color of their crystals, and painted the walls in strange dancing light.

Darkfire.

The large quartz crystal he'd been holding earlier was the brightest of all, the blue flame at its heart burning with new vigor.

Rafferty was awed and horrified.

Melissa cast him an impish glance through her lashes, one that made his heart skip. "Do you need to rest up before we try again? Maybe have some breakfast?"

"This cannot be," he said. He gently put her down, shoving his hand through his hair in consternation. He reached out to touch her shoulder, catching his breath as the blue flame danced again between them.

It seemed to be burning even brighter.

His body certainly was responding to it with greater vehemence.

This made no sense.

Melissa tugged on the robe again, almost as if avoiding his gaze. "I could use a coffee before round two." She spoke lightly, which was strange since she'd been so sensitive to his moods thus far. Rafferty dismissed the idea that she could be hiding anything from him, telling himself that paranoia had no place in a firestorm.

"I'll make some coffee," he said, heading for the kitchen with purpose. Maybe the caffeine would clear his thoughts.

"Maybe it would be a good time for you to explain this darkfire to me," Melissa suggested.

Again, Rafferty heard something in her tone, a wariness that awakened his own. He considered her, and her gaze danced away from his. He was right. She wasn't surprised that the darkfire still burned between them.

Why not?

"Maybe there is more than that we need to discuss," Rafferty suggested, and knew he didn't imagine that she caught her breath. Then she walked quickly toward the kitchen, once again giving him the impression that she was hiding her thoughts.

Melissa had not conceived his son on the consummation of their relationship, and Rafferty had a feeling she knew why.

He was going to learn the truth, before the coffee was gone.

Chapter 10

Deep in the mountains of Tibet, Chen ceased his song. He felt the distinctive heat of the darkfire. He sensed the power of the firestorm. He tasted the spark of the darkfire. He heard the Sleeper stir. Chen recognized that his decision to let the darkfire loose had had unexpected repercussions, and he was intrigued.

He wasn't truly surprised. Unpredictability was darkfire's hallmark.

The sound that interested Chen the most was a quieter sound, one of a *Pyr* finding his affinity. Chen heard three quick bolts of lightning strike in succession, and he knew that particular lightning was not caused by the weather. He smiled when he realized which *Pyr* had created it, for control over lightning was a mark of an affinity with air.

Not that this *Pyr*, so new to his affinity of air, had actual control over the lightning. He drew it, without even knowing why or how.

Air was the only element missing from Chen's mastery of the four.

He suspected this *Pyr* would be easier prey than the others with similar affinities. He stirred his brand in the ashes of the fire he had kindled, checking the status of its repair. The seven pieces were beginning to soften, but it was still too soon to forge even the two smallest together.

He coaxed the flame high. He urged it to burn hotter.

Then, while it fulfilled his command, Chen laid the first trap for the prize he intended to claim.

Sara awakened suddenly, heart pounding. She'd been dozing on the couch, and the fire on the hearth had burned low. As had become typical, she was freezing cold.

But she was also shaken by the vision that lingered in her thoughts. She had seen a little girl, a little girl with long chestnut curls and beautiful dark eyes. She was a pretty child, maybe five years of age, although there was a mysterious tilt to her smile.

Something about the little girl's expression made Sara think she knew more than most people, or saw more than most.

Something about that little girl's smile reminded Sara of Sophie, the lost Wyvern.

Sara's dream had been short, just the little girl turning to smile at her. No more. Who was this child? Sara stroked her belly and wondered. Had she seen the child she would bear to Quinn? But how could the baby growing in her womb be a girl? The *Pyr* always had sons, with the exception of the Wyvern. The Wyvern was the only female *Pyr* at any given time, and Erik and Eileen had already had Zoë.

Was something going to happen to Zoë?

Was it possible that Zoë was not the new Wyvern?

Or that there might be two Wyverns, for the first time ever? Sara rose to get Sigmund's book, even though she'd already been through it six hundred times. There were no real answers there about darkfire, nothing more than what Quinn had told her, but there was nowhere else to look.

How much could darkfire change their world?

Sara had a terrible feeling that all she could do was wait to find out.

Thorolf dreamed of an enormous bar. It was his kind of place. It was smoky and dark, the music was loud, and the women were gorgeous. The drinks were free, and there was food as he'd never seen in a bar before. Everywhere he looked there was another buffet, another bartender pouring generous drinks, another hot half-naked woman giving him a come-hither look.

Paradise.

He went from one sensory pleasure to the next, his pace slowing only when he realized he was never going to run out of anything in this place.

Heaven.

He didn't know how long he was there, how far he had walked into its depths, how many women he'd kissed or drinks he'd swallowed, when he staggered into a room entirely upholstered in purple velvet. It was round and lit with sconces mounted at intervals around the perimeter. The floor seemed to be made of stars, but the effect was probably from fairy lights under Lucite.

In the center was a round couch or bed covered in purple leather. There was nothing else in the room, except the smell of incense.

And a woman. She was sitting on the far side of the bed, her back to him. Her hair was dark and straight, and he guessed that she was Asian. She was slim. When she stood up, he saw that she was taller than he'd expected.

She rolled her shoulders, slipping off her robe. It slid down her back to pool on the bed. He caught a glimpse of her nails, which were long and red. The light from the sconces danced over her bare skin, and Thorolf found himself responding to the promise she hadn't yet uttered.

He took a step closer, forgetting the free drinks. He heard the door close behind him, but he didn't care. A little privacy would be all right for whatever she had in mind.

She strolled around the bed, her head tilted down and her hair hiding her face. She was more buxom than he would have expected, but smooth and sleek. She was wearing only a pair of purple stiletto boots.

Then she flicked back her hair and smiled at him, her lips painted a glossy red. She raised one finger and beckoned to him.

But Thorolf retreated in horror. Chen could take the form of an alluring woman, *this* form. He knew precisely who confronted him. Who invited him. He heard a bolt slide home before he could get to the door; then the woman who was Chen laughed.

It was a throaty laugh.

A wicked laugh.

A laugh that didn't foretell anything good for Thorolf. He flung himself at the locked door, but it made no difference. He couldn't tear it open. And he couldn't change shape. He tried. He heard Chen coming closer, heard the click of those heels on the floor coming steadily closer. He knew he was doomed.

Chen was going to finish what he had started. He was going to claim Thorolf, just as he had tried with that tiger brand, and there was no escape.

Thorolf awakened in a panic, clutching the sheets, taking a good long time to realize that he was safe in Rox and Niall's apartment. He was panting in terror, and his skin was cold with sweat.

Bastard. Resolve grew cold and hard within Thorolf. Chen wasn't going to mess with his mind. Chen wasn't going to stalk him or torment him. Chen sure as hell wasn't going to capture or claim him. No way. Somehow, Thorolf was going to finish that old *Slayer* first.

He could guess what Niall would think of that plan. Thorolf's lips set with resolve. This was one time that he wouldn't confer with the others, when he would follow his own gut. He was right and he knew it; plus, he wasn't afraid to solve his own problem by himself. He wasn't going to endanger Niall or risk what that *Pyr* had with Rox.

He'd go alone.

Soon.

What was Melissa going to do?

She had understood the basic idea of the firestorm and had known there was no risk of her being the woman who carried Rafferty's child. She didn't understand why he would even have a firestorm with her, given her personal history.

What she hadn't recognized, though, was how important that child was to Rafferty. She'd known he wanted the child, of course, but had thought he had wanted sex more. But the sight of his dismay when the darkfire flames continued to dance between them, after the firestorm should have been satisfied, had torn at her heart.

She couldn't give him what he wanted.

She'd thought that sex would be enough, that physical expression would satisfy the desires between them. But this darkfire played for keeps. Instead of being just a physical act, intimacy had forged a stronger emotional bond between them.

Melissa herself was yearning for the permanence that Rafferty found so appealing. She admired him, his strong ethics and his patience. She knew he would be a good parent. She wanted to give him that son, more than she'd wanted anything in a long time.

And he would make a great partner. She wished again that they had met sooner, before so much had been stolen from her, but there was no point in wishing that her life had turned out differently.

She was resolved to tell him the truth as soon as possible. She liked to have all the facts before she made a decision. It was only fair that Rafferty knew her history before deciding whether they would pursue a relationship or not.

The reciprocal agreement was that she wanted to know everything there was to know about the firestorm and Rafferty's argument with Magnus. It wouldn't be an easy exchange for either of them, but there was no point shirking what had to be discussed.

Melissa had no chance to initiate that conversation, though.

Rafferty pushed open the swing door to the kitchen for her—more of a gentleman than he gave himself credit for—and Melissa was startled to find a man already sitting at the kitchen table.

The stranger's hair was mostly dark, silver at the temples with a bit of salt and pepper throughout. He wore a dark sweater and had slung a black leather jacket over the back of his chair. His gaze was simmering.

Melissa was startled by his presence, but Rafferty was not. "Good morning," he said, as if he found men in his kitchen all the time. "Where's Eileen?"

Melissa suspected he wasn't that excited to see the other man.

"She took Zoë to the park." The stranger spoke in clipped tones, his accent more emphatically British than Rafferty's. What was Rafferty's accent? It seemed more musical. "It's possible that some exercise will encourage her to take a nap."

Rafferty made no comment upon that. Eileen must be this man's partner, and Zoë a child. Melissa went with the obvious conclusion that Zoë must be the daughter of this man and Eileen.

"You might have made the coffee," Rafferty commented.

"I didn't want to be presumptuous," the stranger said.

Rafferty raised a brow, said nothing, and made a pot of coffee.

The stranger's gaze locked upon her, his disapproval clear, and Melissa found herself blushing. She *had* been a bit noisy during her climax, and the library was only a dozen feet away.

Had Rafferty known the other man was here?

If not, how had he gotten into the house?

There was silence in the kitchen except for the sound of Rafferty's preparations. Rafferty didn't rush, but then, Melissa didn't imagine that he often hurried. There was an attractive leisure to his gestures, even doing something so mundane as making a pot of coffee. It was as if he enjoyed every moment for itself.

Melissa liked that. Living in the present made a lot of sense to her, and once again, she felt a sense of common purpose with Rafferty. She wanted to live like this. She wouldn't think about the fate of their relationship—she guessed it would end soon, although the prospect saddened her.

Why did all the rotten luck in the world find her?

Soon the kitchen was filled with the welcome scent of a good dark brew. Melissa chose to take pleasure in the moment, in the smell of the coffee and the thickness of her borrowed bathrobe, in the gleam of Rafferty's eyes, and the pleasure that had left her body humming.

It was surprisingly easy to do.

"Cream and sugar?" Rafferty asked.

"Both, please." Melissa tightened the knot on the belt of her bathrobe.

Rafferty handed her a mug of steaming coffee, his smile not quite reaching his eyes. Melissa took it from him, their fingers brushing on the handle. A blue flame leapt high at the point of contact, burning so bright and hot that Melissa caught her breath. Her knees went weak, her mind filled with memories of Rafferty's sure touch, her gaze locked on his strong and tender hands.

The stranger's words came in a low hiss. "How can you leave the firestorm unsated?" His voice rose. "How can you, of all *Pyr*, be so irresponsible?"

Rafferty turned on the other man. "I am not irresponsible. . . ."

"No? What about this?" The new arrival pulled a newspaper out of his laptop bag and tossed it on the kitchen table. The headline was enormous.

DRAGON KIDNAPS JOURNALIST BYSTANDER.

Melissa's eyes widened at the grainy image of Rafferty soaring into the sky with her in his grasp.

Oops.

"The media is full of this story," the stranger continued with irritation. "It's everywhere you turn." He flicked a hot look at Rafferty. "You may be interested to know that you have been cast in the role of evil dragon, while Jorge plays a hero."

"That's not true!" Melissa said, but Rafferty held up a hand. She understood that this was his fight and sipped her coffee, burning her tongue.

Rafferty pointed at the other man. "Magnus assaulted me in the street, in the presence of my mate. What was I supposed to do? We have sworn a blood feud."

"You should have remained out of sight!" The stranger flung out his hands in frustration. "Or beguiled the crowd."

So, he knew about the *Pyr*.

Maybe he was a *Pyr*. Melissa could see a little shimmer of blue around him, as if he were annoyed enough to be on the cusp of change. And Rafferty certainly seemed to think he had to answer this man's charges.

Melissa picked up the newspaper and studied the image, hoping a closer look would reassure her. It didn't. It was from one of the wire services, so any number of newspapers and Web sites would have picked it up. It was unmistakably her—she was even identified by name in the accompanying article. There was a reference to her blog posts, featuring this same dragon, and an old photo of her, reporting from Baghdad.

As soon as she saw that, Melissa lost her interest in coffee.

Her brother, Matthew, would be worried sick.

"I have to make a phone call," she said, turning to Rafferty. "Where's your phone?"

"There is one in the library," he said, his gaze dancing over her. "What's wrong?"

"My brother. He'll be crazy with worry."

"You will not reveal us further!" the stranger protested, but Rafferty put his hand on Melissa's shoulder. She liked his protective gesture; she liked the implication that he understood her concern and meant to help her solve it.

"I will not see Melissa's family worried unnecessarily." Rafferty spoke with both defiance and resolve. Melissa saw that the other man didn't like it one bit.

But he sat down, lips tight, and said nothing more.

Melissa understood that her dragon had defended her once again. It was hard not to appreciate that kind of gallantry.

Back in the library, she immediately spotted the phone she hadn't noticed earlier. It was on that big oak desk. She picked up the receiver and punched in her brother's number, wincing at the time change but knowing Matt wouldn't care what time she called if she was safe.

He might be awake, waiting.

Rafferty hovered outside the doorway, his back turned to her as if to give her some privacy. He didn't leave her alone, though, and Melissa wondered why. Did he want to hear what she said? She recalled that his senses were sharper than human senses, and she figured he'd be able to hear her conversation from anywhere in the house.

He shimmered slightly with that blue glow. Was he aware of some threat she couldn't detect?

"What's wrong?" she asked as the line connected.

Rafferty gave her a smoldering look. "We are all drawn to the unsatisfied firestorm. Moths to the flame."

Melissa thought about Jorge and Magnus and spontaneous manifestation and swallowed. She nodded in understanding.

He was defending her again.

Matt answered on the second ring. "Hello?" There was a twinge of anxiety in his voice, making Melissa glad she'd called.

"It's me. I'm okay. I knew you'd want to know."

Melissa heard her brother exhale shakily; she knew he had been hoping for news. She felt guilty that she hadn't realized the story had spread and that she'd been making love to Rafferty while her brother worried about her.

"I suppose that's all you can tell me," Matt said. He kept his tone light, but Melissa could hear the undercurrent of fear.

She knew exactly what she had to do.

"Don't worry about me," she said. "I'm fine."

"Really?"

"The only thing missing is a piece of Mom's apple pie." Melissa deliberately used the code they'd worked out when she'd been sent overseas. It had been Matt who had suggested that they needed two phrases that seemed innocuous, but which would tell him whether she was safe or not. This was the "safe" one.

She heard his sigh of relief. "Okay," he said, his voice falling lower. "Okay, Mel. Okay. You know where I am."

"I do. Sorry. I would have called sooner, but I didn't realize the story had been picked up until just now."

"It's huge," Matt said, his tone easier. "Your ISP even

crashed for a while last night, overwhelmed by the traffic to your blog."

Those pictures. Melissa swallowed, her gaze flicking to Rafferty. There'd be no rescinding them now. Had his shoulders stiffened slightly? The blue shimmer was a bit brighter; there was no doubt of that.

"I thought people would have decided it was a hoax."

"Well, there is some of that. It seems as if the world is waiting for your update." Melissa heard the smile in her brother's voice. "Just like old times, Mel. The world is hanging on the line, waiting for the latest news from our favorite intrepid reporter."

"Not exactly like old times," she said, her heart skipping. Did she want her career back at this price? The answer was less clear than it had been.

"So," Matt mused, his tone revealing that he was going to change the subject, "this Rafferty Powell whose phone you're using . . ."

"What?"

"Come on, Mel. You know I have caller I.D."

Melissa sputtered for a second, having forgotten that detail. Rafferty turned, his steady gaze locking with hers.

He'd heard.

"Is he related to Rafferty Powell, the antiquities dealer?"

"Who?"

Matt laughed. "There's a dealer with a huge reputation in London, only takes potential clients by appointment. His warehouse is supposed to be an Aladdin's cave. Geoff's been going on and on about him."

"Geoff Davenport," Rafferty said softly, leaning in the doorway. The casual posture did exactly nothing to make him look relaxed. "Interior designer in California, impressive vision."

He *could* hear both sides of the conversation.

"Anyway, if you could get me an invitation in the course of your adventures . . ."

"Now that you know I'm safe you can talk about *work*?" Melissa teased.

Her brother laughed. "You know how it is."

"I know exactly how it is, Mr. Obsessed Architect."

"Family trait to love our work, isn't it?" Matt laughed again, untroubled by his enthusiasm for his work. "Keep me updated, Mel, when you can. Don't worry about the time."

"Okay."

"And thanks for calling. Joanna will be relieved, too."

"Kiss the kids for me," Melissa said, then hung up the phone. She had a lump in her throat, one that seemed to grow larger as Rafferty watched her.

"Not that alone, after all," he noted quietly.

"What?"

"You told the one who offered you a job that you had no commitments. Not even a houseplant. But you're not that alone in the world."

Melissa looked down at her hands, trying to avoid his intent gaze. "He's my big brother," she said lightly. "He worries about me. Thanks for letting me use the phone."

"He loves you," Rafferty insisted softly.

Melissa shrugged, that lump in her throat bigger by the second. "Isn't that what big brothers are supposed to do?"

Rafferty didn't answer that. "Your solitude, then, is more by your choice than by that of anyone else."

Those dark eyes did see too much. Once again, Rafferty seemed to be able to perceive the secrets of her heart. She wouldn't show him her fears.

"Maybe. Maybe not." She lifted her chin and saw him arch a brow.

It was a bit scary how readily this man could coax her confessions. All of her barriers just dissolved with one look from those eyes.

"It's for Matt's own protection," she insisted. "If we were closer, it would be harder for him."

"How so?"

"If . . . If the worst should happen."

Rafferty's eyes narrowed. That seemed to make him only more perceptive. "And why would a woman of your age be so worried about death? Even if your job was that dangerous, you don't have it anymore."

"Anyone can die at any time. There are no guarantees." Melissa spoke more fiercely than she intended. Her tears rose unbidden, and she pushed past Rafferty. "I really need that coffee."

"I don't think that's what you really need," Rafferty said quietly as she passed him. Melissa didn't look up; she didn't dare, because she knew he'd see straight into her heart.

Talking to Matt and hearing his relief had thrown her game. It made her think of what wasn't possible, of what she had lost, of all the dreams that had been sacrificed by her illness. She needed to get her shields back in place. She needed to remind herself how cruelly and how quickly dreams could be shattered.

ASAP.

Rafferty let Melissa return to the kitchen ahead of him. He was intrigued both by what she had said and by what she hadn't said. She had needed to update her brother and reassure him, but she didn't want to become too emotionally entwined, even with him.

For his own protection.

Was that the truth, or an excuse? Rafferty wasn't sure. What he did know was that his mate's armor was more robust than his own. She had built barriers against others, and defended them vigorously.

He understood that she had been hurt.

Badly.

Even without knowing what her injuries had been, Rafferty recognized that he wanted to help her to heal. Was that something that the darkfire would change? Would it give Melissa a new faith in the future? What had stolen that confidence in the first place?

She certainly wasn't going to tell him. She sipped her coffee and deliberately avoided his gaze.

Erik, meanwhile, was seething. Rafferty wished the other *Pyr* would just leave. Doubtless he had overheard that her brother knew Rafferty's name.

Rafferty was comfortable with that information passing to Matt, for it would reassure him. Rafferty had no fear of humans, and every passing moment only increased his determination to create a future with Melissa.

"This story is a disaster," Erik said, picking up where he had left off. "The speculation about us and our role is unbelievable. Some say the Apocalypse is come. Some say we are the Devil incarnate." He stopped pacing to glare at Rafferty. "Most say we should be hunted and exterminated."

"It's not my fault," Rafferty insisted, trying to keep his voice calm. "It's the darkfire, turning all on its head, just as the prophecy declares."

"Yet even aware of the power of darkfire, you have not

sated the firestorm and extinguished the darkfire's burn," Erik snapped. "It is not like you to be so cavalier, Rafferty Powell. Has the darkfire changed your very nature?"

Rafferty took a big gulp of coffee, feeling that the conversation was turning in a more intimate direction than would be ideal. He didn't want to embarrass Melissa.

She eyed the newspapers and looked guilty.

Of course, the pictures had originally been posted by her. In essence, she had revealed the *Pyr*.

Erik cast out his hands. "Don't you owe me an answer? Jorge is returned. We are on the front page of every newspaper and news site. Magnus is alive. Gaia thrashes and heaves, seemingly intent upon destroying the humans we are sworn to defend. We *Pyr* are divided, each torn between our responsibilities."

"And the Sleeper stirs," Rafferty added, his words low and tight.

Erik and Melissa both stared at him.

"Who's the Sleeper?" Melissa asked.

"Is that it, then?" Erik demanded. "You also feel torn between your obligations?" His tone softened. "I will aid you however I can, Rafferty. You must know that." He leaned closer. "You must sate the firestorm, though. Is that so much to ask from one who has yearned so long for this moment?"

"I have tried!" Rafferty insisted.

"*Tried?*" Erik echoed.

"It should be satisfied. We have done what should be done!"

"But . . . ?"

Even now, there was a shimmer of blue-green between Rafferty and Melissa.

"But it still burns!" Rafferty retorted, biting out the

words as his frustration rose. "I have *not* been irresponsible, but the darkfire yet burns." He put down his empty mug on the counter with force. "The evidence is before our eyes; yet it is inexplicable."

The tension slid from Erik's shoulders, as his gaze flicked restlessly between the two of them. He sat down heavily. "Darkfire," he said quietly. "So it changes even this." He rubbed his forehead. Rafferty poured himself another coffee, one he didn't really want.

Melissa cleared her throat. "There's something you should know," she said. Rafferty turned to his mate, expecting she might surprise him.

What she confessed, though, astounded him.

Chapter 11

It was time to share the truth.

This wasn't the way Melissa had intended to tell Rafferty about her history, but she didn't have a choice. It looked as if her past was important, and the *Pyr* needed to know the facts to make a plan.

"Perhaps it's time we were introduced." She stuck out her hand toward Erik. "I'm Melissa Smith."

The stranger glanced up, his expression unwelcoming. "I know who you are. I am Erik Sorensson, leader of the *Pyr*." His tone wasn't very friendly, but Melissa refused to be deterred.

She pulled out the chair opposite him and sat down with every sign of confidence. She suspected that if he was a guest in Rafferty's home, he wouldn't harm her—as frustrated as he might be with her. The fact that Rafferty stood back, evidently certain of the same thing, fed Melissa's confidence. She knew she could count on Rafferty to defend her.

"Don't look as if you'd be glad to be rid of me just

yet," she said lightly. "After all, I think I know why the firestorm is still burning."

"Why?" Rafferty asked, his hand landing on the back of her chair.

Melissa looked up at him, forgetting Erik for a moment. "Let me just make sure I've got this straight. You said the firestorm means a *Pyr* has met his destined mate; that he has found the human woman who can bear his child."

"Yes. Yes."

"And that the first time they're intimate, she conceives his son."

"Yes. That is the essence of the firestorm."

Melissa smiled, knowing her expression was rueful. "But I can't have your child. . . ."

"It is not a matter of choice," Erik said irritably. "Not if you surrender to intimacy."

Melissa continued as if he hadn't spoken. "I can't have *anyone's* child. It's not physically possible."

Rafferty seemed to be aware of the nuances of what she said, for his expression softened. He bent down, crouching beside her, his gaze searching hers. "What do you mean, Melissa?"

His kindness made her words fall less gracefully than she would have liked. "I had cancer. Uterine cancer." She caught her breath. "They took everything out." The words stuck in her throat, charged with losses well in excess of her feminine plumbing. "I can't ever have children, even if I want to."

"Melissa!" Rafferty's voice was filled with tenderness, and she felt the force of his compassion. He might have pulled her into his embrace, but Melissa raised a hand between them.

She wasn't going to go soft now.

She'd melt into a puddle if she did. Tears wouldn't solve anything.

"It's in the past," she said with resolve. "I don't want to talk about it anymore, but I thought you should know."

Rafferty's eyes looked darker, warmer, more compassionate. Melissa couldn't look away from him. "Thank you," he whispered, then kissed her fingertips. That blue flame traveled from his lips to her hand, sizzling and simmering and giving her ideas about trying again.

She pulled her hand away and put it in her lap. This man certainly had an ability to get under her defenses. "It's not his fault," she said to Erik. "He's not been irresponsible."

"But—" Erik began to argue.

"We will not discuss this further," Rafferty said, hard and fast. "Melissa has endured enough and shows great trust in offering this information now."

He even defended her emotionally.

Melissa decided she could love this man.

To what point, though? She couldn't give him the one thing he wanted. It was only a matter of time until he abandoned her. Love didn't survive shattered dreams, Melissa knew that. Zach hadn't been able to stay once it had become clear she couldn't give him a family. Those tears pricked at her eyelids, and she wanted to cry even more.

She wouldn't, though. Tears were for the weak.

There was no future for her in making families. There was only the quest for the truth.

"But why would you have a destined mate who could not physically bear your son?" Erik asked.

Rafferty sat down heavily beside Melissa, his knee only inches from hers. She sensed that they two were allied against Erik. As Melissa covertly watched the blue-green flames lick against her leg, she wondered whether he had moved so close on purpose.

She moved her leg away from his. She didn't dare rely on anyone.

"Because there is a greater promise in our alliance than the birth of a child," he said with a conviction that startled her.

And gave her unexpected hope.

"But think of what damage if the darkfire burns in perpetuity," Erik protested.

"What kind of damage?" Melissa asked. The only downside she saw was perpetual desire for Rafferty, which wasn't all bad.

"The firestorm's heat is a lure to our kind," Erik said. "We all feel it and are drawn to its heat." He stopped then, his gaze flicking to Rafferty.

That was what Rafferty had said when she'd been calling Matt.

Moths to the flame.

"You're saying that Jorge and Montmorency could use its heat to target us," Melissa guessed. "The way camera lights can draw fire."

Both men nodded. "So there must be another way to sate it," Rafferty said. His voice grew even more determined. "The Great Wyvern gives no burden we cannot shoulder."

"The Great Wyvern?" Melissa asked.

He smiled. "It is our name for the divine force that animates all of us."

"And God's a woman." Melissa nodded. She'd never

been much for religion, and her illness had destroyed any vestigial notion that there was anyone looking out for her.

In a way, though, she found Rafferty's faith both touching and powerful. Maybe faith sustained him. She was more empowered by the facts. Maybe there was something they could accomplish together. Maybe that was the point.

She looked him in the eye. "Maybe it's time you tell me everything you do know about darkfire."

"So you can put it on your blog and imperil us further?" Erik asked, his words hard.

"No," Melissa said, aware that even Rafferty was watching her closely. "I made a mistake. I'm sorry, but I didn't know what I was doing when I posted those pictures. I should have asked your permission."

"You were sharing your experience with the world, making others aware of the truth," Rafferty said quietly. "It's what reporters do, as I understand it."

Melissa stared at him, and he smiled. His approval was unexpected, and it made her mouth go dry. She decided not to tell him that she'd posted the pictures only to bring him back to her.

"Exactly," she agreed. "And I am sorry. But you know, maybe there's a reason for it. Maybe your Great Wyvern has some kind of plan that requires you to be revealed to humans. Maybe there's more to be achieved than if you're hidden."

"How so?" Rafferty asked, his gaze brightening.

"Well, you're the guardians of the earth, right?" Melissa said, and he nodded. "And how many of you are there?"

"Not enough," Rafferty and Erik said in unison. Melissa looked between them. This was evidently an old joke, but no one was going to explain it to her.

"Well, there are ten billion of us, give or take," she said. "Even a small percentage of us joining ranks with you could make a huge difference to your efforts."

Rafferty frowned as he considered this notion. Melissa liked that he didn't just dismiss her idea.

Erik, though, got up to pace again. This was clearly not a popular concept with him. Melissa knew when an idea wasn't going to fly, or even be discussed, so she changed tactics.

"Okay, let's forget for the moment about any divine plan," she said quickly. "We still need to make a *mortal* plan. We can start with what we know, identify what we can change, and go from there."

"Sensible," Rafferty said. "I like action plans." Erik, still clearly displeased, seemed to recognize that he had been outvoted. He sat down again, folding his arms across his chest.

Melissa smiled at him. She'd take any progress she could get, especially with him. "It sounds as if darkfire is about shaking up the status quo, so we should figure out exactly where we stand before we do anything more. It'll minimize the chances of making another mistake."

She looked between the two *Pyr*, finding a grudging respect even in Erik's gaze. Rafferty smiled at her warmly, and she wondered what she had done to earn his favor, even as her heart skipped a beat.

She picked up the pad of paper on the counter and a pen. "Go on. Tell me about darkfire. Don't leave anything out, even if you think I won't like it."

*   *   *

His mate was a marvel.

Rafferty was proud of Melissa's resilience and her determination. He admired that she had survived her battle and that, even in its wake, she had a zest for living. He knew her confession was only the tip of the iceberg in terms of what she had borne, but he guessed that she wouldn't confide the rest easily.

Or soon.

He respected that she didn't flinch from realities or challenges, but met them head-on. "Survivor" didn't begin to describe her fortitude and guts.

And he particularly liked that Melissa saw the firestorm as an opportunity for them to work together. That meshed perfectly with Rafferty's standing conviction that a successful firestorm brought *Pyr* and mate together in a relationship that was more than the sum of the parts.

He was intrigued by her idea. Imagine, humans working alongside the *Pyr*! He found it an exciting possibility. That Melissa had made the suggestion bolstered his confidence and fed his own resolve to see his firestorm successfully negotiated.

Or was he simply tempted by the heat of the firestorm to agree with his mate?

Erik was unpersuaded—so far. There would be repercussions, so it made sense to proceed with caution.

By the time Rafferty had put bread in the toaster and taken some fruit and jam out of the fridge, he was decided. He chose to trust Melissa with the tale of the darkfire, even knowing that Erik would have preferred otherwise.

"There is an ancient prophecy about darkfire, one I learned long ago." Rafferty heard Erik inhale but ignored him.

"Who taught it to you?" Melissa asked.

"My grandfather. He knew all the tales and legends."

"He was a storyteller?"

"No. He was the Cantor."

"That sounds important."

Rafferty looked away, uncomfortable still with this facet of his grandfather's abilities. It smacked of sorcery to him, and deceit, even after all these years. "He believed it was. I did not."

"You argued," she guessed. How much of his thoughts could she perceive? She was so much more observant than most humans.

"It was a long time ago." Rafferty smiled to soften his refusal to confide that detail. "For the moment, let me tell you the prophecy."

Erik harumphed, then rose to his feet. The toaster popped an instant later, but he was already there. He gave Melissa two slices and put two more in to toast. Rafferty knew Erik was listening closely.

He spoke carefully, giving the old verse a new cadence.

> *"Darkfire's flame burns bright as ice;*
> *No hint of compromise will suffice.*
> *Darkfire's heat will not fade*
> *Until much that is has been unmade.*
> *Until all that is hidden has been revealed,*
> *Until all that was clear becomes concealed.*
> *Until the Sleeper wakes to his fate,*
> *Until the Cantor's legacy is claimed.*
> *But out of ruin rises new growth;*
> *The flames of mercury know this truth."*

Melissa wrote quickly, using a kind of shorthand. She didn't ask Rafferty to repeat anything. He watched her read her own notes again, then tap her pencil against the paper.

He felt Erik turn, felt the weight of the other *Pyr*'s gaze, and wondered at his avid interest.

"*What* was *Pwyll's legacy? Didn't you claim it?*" Erik asked in old-speak. "*And who's the Sleeper?*"

Rafferty focused on his mate. Melissa stared out the window and frowned before speaking. Clearly she had heard the rumble of the old-speak. "Who's the Sleeper?" she asked.

In another place and time, Rafferty might have been amused that they asked such a similar question.

"I can't tell you that," Rafferty said, aware of Erik's watchfulness.

"Then what's the Sleeper's fate?"

"Who can say?" Rafferty accepted toast from Erik and made a task of buttering it. He felt Melissa watching him all the while.

"I'll guess you aren't going to tell me the Cantor's legacy."

Rafferty smiled at her. "I don't know what it was."

"Okay," Melissa said finally. "So, darkfire is a kind of firestorm, one that indicates huge change for the *Pyr*. What makes it happen?"

Rafferty shrugged. "It's random."

"Are you sure?" Melissa asked.

Rafferty drummed his fingers on the table. "It's possible that Pwyll knew more, but I don't."

Melissa made a note. "I'll consider it a random variable, until we know more. What's changed so far?"

"I see no reason to itemize our weaknesses," Erik protested.

Melissa glanced at him. "Well, we know one thing that's

been revealed. All of you. What's been concealed?" Erik didn't answer her, his lips tight. She scanned her notes. "So, the obvious Plan A would be to determine whether the Sleeper has awakened, but you won't tell me about the Sleeper. Plan B would be to itemize what's changed, but you won't tell me that either. What's Plan C?"

Rafferty sighed. He had no taste for his toast. How could he make a success of his firestorm without betraying the *Pyr*? What was the Great Wyvern's plan for him? What should he do? He yearned for a sign of how to proceed, to save him from being responsible for disaster.

Again.

To his astonishment, that sign came.

The door to the garden opened then, and Eileen stepped into the kitchen, looking tired. Zoë charged across the tiled floor, full of energy, and made a beeline for Rafferty. She climbed into his lap, as charming and demanding as always, and locked her chubby fingers around the black and white ring he wore. He dared to hope she would provide guidance to him, as she had before.

Instead, she turned to sit on his lap and considered Melissa with her clear gaze.

"You must be the new mate," Eileen said, shedding her coat. She tried to cover her yawn without success. "I'm feeling like an ancient mate this morning. Word to the wise—think twice before taking a two-year-old on a night flight from Chicago to London. On such an adventure, the last thing she'll do is sleep." She smiled and winked at Melissa, yawning once again before she offered her hand. "Eileen Grosvenor. Miss Energy there is our daughter, Zoë. I'm hoping she slides into a deep sleep any minute now, but chances appear to be slim."

"Melissa Smith." Melissa stood and shook Eileen's hand.

"Oh, you're the blogger," Eileen said, and feigned consternation. Erik, still grim faced, poured her a coffee, and she blew him a kiss as she accepted it. His attitude wasn't visibly affected by her gesture, so Rafferty knew he was deeply troubled.

Eileen sipped and closed her eyes in rapture. "You always have such good coffee, Rafferty," she murmured, then smiled at Melissa, her eyes widening. "I've heard lots about you."

"Do you want toast?" Erik asked gruffly.

"Yes, please." Eileen took Erik's place and smiled across the table at Melissa. "Don't let them intimidate you. So long as we're human and mates—neither of which is likely to change soon—they're pledged to defend us, even if they do get grumpy." She picked an orange out of the fruit bowl and peeled it, handing the segments to Zoë. The little girl hung on to Rafferty's ring, smiled, and ate with obvious pleasure.

Rafferty was less pleased. He waited with some impatience for a vision that never arrived.

The last time Zoë had grasped his ring, she'd given him a vision. He'd hoped that she'd seized it now to give him some indication of how to proceed. But there was nothing, not a glimmer of a dream, not a hint of a vision.

"Orge," she said firmly to Melissa.

Melissa smiled at the toddler. "She likes your ring."

"She adores Rafferty," Eileen supplied.

"It's only fitting that she likes the ring," Rafferty said, realizing at Erik's sigh that he'd said too much again. There was no chance Melissa would let that reaction slide.

"Why? What's the deal with that ring, anyway? How does it change size to fit when you're a dragon?"

"It seems to have some magical powers," Rafferty said, contenting himself with that response. He was keenly aware of Erik's presence and his view that nothing more should be told to Melissa. Rafferty himself was torn. He couldn't see a way forward without confiding in Melissa, but he didn't want to rile Erik even more.

He'd have to pick and choose. For the moment, he wouldn't explain that the ring had been formed of the bodies of Sophie, the last Wyvern, and her lover, Nikolas, the Dragon's Teeth Warrior. The pair had sacrificed themselves in ensuring the destruction of Magnus's academy, and all that remained was this ring. It looked like black glass spun with white, a perfect reminder of the white perfection of Sophie's dragon form and the fierce black of Nikolas's dragon form.

Ice and anthracite, forever entwined in the ring as they could not have been while alive.

"Like what?" Melissa asked.

"Let's focus on darkfire, shall we?" Erik interjected.

In the same moment, Melissa frowned. "Wait a minute." Melissa indicated Eileen. "If you're a mate, and this is your child, is she a *Pyr*, too? Are there female dragons? I've seen only men."

Silence reigned for a moment, filling the kitchen and Rafferty's ears.

"You ask too many questions," Erik said tightly.

"That's what happens when you hunt the truth," Melissa replied smoothly.

Erik leaned closer. "You will put our very survival in jeopardy. It's happened before."

"It looks to me like our goals can be combined," she countered.

"How so?"

Rafferty admired that Melissa was undaunted. She spoke in a calm tone. "I met Rafferty because I was determined to expose Montmorency as the arms dealer he is, and to bring him to justice."

"He killed a friend of Melissa's," Rafferty supplied, and Erik nodded.

Melissa tapped her pen, obviously thinking. "But Rafferty is right—no jail would hold him, given his ability to shift into a salamander and to spontaneously manifest wherever he wants. On the other hand, Rafferty's attempt to finish their duel by killing Montmorency was caught on video."

Erik passed a hand over his brow. "So we are not just revealed but reviled. Again."

"Not necessarily," Melissa and Rafferty said in unison.

"You have an idea," Eileen said, her eyes bright.

"I'm getting to it," Melissa agreed. "The thing is that the fight between Rafferty and Montmorency didn't just attract human attention. It brought this topaz guy out of the woodwork."

"Jorge," Erik supplied. "Another *Slayer*."

"And minion of Magnus," Rafferty supplied.

Melissa scribbled all of that down before she continued. "But they came off looking like heroes." She pointed her pen at Rafferty. "While you were cast as the bad guy."

Rafferty grimaced. "It is not familiar territory for me."

Melissa's lips set. "I think the immediate problem is Montmorency. We don't know where he is, but we do know he is sworn to kill Rafferty."

"Or be killed himself," Rafferty confirmed.

Melissa sat back, pushing her notes across the table. "So what would draw him out? What would make him come to you, the way Jorge came to him?"

Rafferty stared at her in horror. Eileen dropped a spoon, and Erik's eyes glittered.

"You want to lure him to us?" Rafferty asked.

"He's injured, isn't he? Doesn't that make him weaker? It only makes sense that time will let him heal, which will make him tougher to kill." Melissa frowned. "He was already hurt after the helicopter. Why did he attack you after you saved me? You would have finished him there, if not for Jorge."

"Maybe he knew Jorge was coming to his rescue," Eileen suggested.

Rafferty shook his head. "No. He was shocked by Jorge's appearance, and I sensed that he was not certain of Jorge's objectives." His frown deepened. "I'm not certain myself why Jorge would come to Magnus's aid. I had always thought his own ambition was to become leader of the *Slayers*."

"Why not let you do the dirty work?" Erik mused.

"So, there's another variable," Melissa said, adding a question mark beside Jorge's name on her list. "We have to anticipate that Jorge will follow if we manage to coax Magnus out of hiding."

Erik rubbed his chin. "So, your scheme is to lure Magnus closer, then let Rafferty fulfill his blood challenge."

"Yes. One less opponent in the world can't be all bad, and we'll be sure Rafferty isn't directly targeted."

Eileen leaned forward. "And if darkfire really does require that everything change, then eliminating the leader of the *Slayers* could be part of fulfilling its prophecy."

Erik flicked a stern look at Melissa. "If it happens, it must occur without human observation."

Melissa winced. "Actually, I was thinking just the opposite. You guys have really bad PR right now, but the truth is a great story. Guardians of the elements, safeguarding the treasures of the earth, which include humanity. It's a fabulous green story and would really resonate for people."

"No." Erik pushed to his feet. "It's out of the question."

Melissa stood up herself. "Is it? What if the change required by the darkfire is having humans not only know you're in their midst but also help you with your mission? What if the way for you to succeed in saving the planet lies in having a couple billion of us on your side?"

"It makes sense," Rafferty said softly, and Melissa flashed him a smile.

Erik paced, his disapproval clear. "No. It makes no sense. We will be hunted again. We have been driven to the cusp of extinction before, and I will not lead us there again."

"But you don't have a choice," Melissa retorted. "The story's already out there. You can't make it disappear. All you can do is add to it in your own defense."

"I don't like it!" Erik protested, his eyes flashing.

"Tell us your idea before any decisions are made," Eileen said to Melissa, her hand landing on her partner's arm.

"It's the book that will do it," Melissa said excitedly.

"What book?" Eileen asked.

"Montmorency kept a book documenting his activities and appointments as an arms dealer," Melissa said.

"We have it," Rafferty said.

"We can use his own records against him, show him

for the sinister force he is, review his crimes, then destroy him and make the world safe for humanity." She flung up her hands. "You guys will be heroes, fighters for justice, and probably superstars."

"The book will draw him, as will the threat of being revealed," Rafferty mused. "It drew him before."

"Never mind the firestorm," Eileen added. She wagged a finger at Melissa. "Your plan could work. Magnus would be destroyed, Rafferty would be safe, with the blood duel satisfied, the *Slayers* would be short a leader, and the *Pyr* would look good in the public eye. That's got to make some progress in satisfying darkfire's demand to turn everything topsy-turvy."

"I have seen the repercussions from our being revealed," Erik insisted, his arms folded across his chest. "I have survived the mania among humans for hunting and slaughtering our kind once before, and I will not let it happen again." Erik pointed at Rafferty. "You will tell her nothing more!"

"But that's the whole point of darkfire, isn't it?" Melissa replied, her tone cool. "What's the biggest upset that could happen? That you could be revealed. And it's happened already. Okay, that can't be changed. What can be made of it? What advantage can you gain from it?" She leaned across the table to confront Erik. "If you tell the truth to the world, they'll be on your side."

"Erik, that hunting happened a long time ago," Eileen suggested softly. "The world is a different place."

"It is less different from what you imagine," he retorted. "Surely you do not take this view, as well?"

Eileen also held his gaze without apology. Rafferty saw how much this shook Erik, and he recognized that his old friend was under tremendous duress.

What else had occurred?

"I have said I will tell Melissa about the darkfire," Rafferty reminded Erik quietly. "I will keep my word."

"Regardless of the cost?"

Rafferty nodded. Erik pivoted and leveled a look at Rafferty that was all-glittering dragon fury.

"*Because she might be right*," Rafferty added in old-speak.

Erik's nostrils flared ever so slightly, and Rafferty thought he saw a puff of smoke. Then the leader of the *Pyr* excused himself and left the kitchen, marching up the stairs to the bedroom he always occupied when he was visiting.

"*I will not participate in such folly*," Erik said in old-speak just before slamming the door of that room.

Rafferty knew that Erik would be able to hear their conversation even at that distance; he was merely making a point.

"Well." Eileen cleared her throat, her gaze falling on Zoë. "I don't see any harm in answering your question about Zoë. There should be only one female *Pyr* at any given time, and she should be a prophetess."

"Among other things," Rafferty added.

"Should be?" Melissa asked, once again homing in on the most important words. Rafferty once again admired his mate's intellect and perceptiveness.

Eileen shrugged. "The thing is that Zoë is just a little girl."

"She hasn't come into her powers yet?" Melissa asked.

"Or maybe she doesn't have any," Eileen replied. "Maybe the prophecy is wrong, and she's just a little girl." She calmly ate her toast even as Rafferty stared at her in shock.

Zoë had given him a dream before. Were those fledgling powers gone before they had fully blossomed? How could this be?

He guessed the answer immediately.

"Since she began to talk, she doesn't respond to old-speak," Erik confided in old-speak. *"And I have sensed no dreams coming from her these past two months."* He sighed, and Rafferty heard his old friend's exhaustion. *"All goes awry, Rafferty. Mind you don't join the tide."*

Rafferty looked down at the toddler, who was on the verge of sleep. She leaned against him, snuggling close as her hand fell to the tabletop. The orange segment in her grasp dropped, and Rafferty let it fall to the floor rather than disturb her. Her lids were drooping, and Eileen held up a pair of crossed fingers.

Zoë's grip loosened on his ring, the ring she had always liked, and she put her fist in her mouth as she fell asleep. His hope died as she slumbered, and he knew she would provide no guidance to him in this moment.

Worse, Rafferty had a terrible sense that Zoë's burgeoning abilities were another sacrifice to the darkfire. That was the variable that made his choice. He had to stop the darkfire before the *Pyr* lost everything they held dear.

And that meant confiding fully in Melissa, whatever the cost might ultimately be. The darkfire would accept no half measures until it was satisfied.

Rafferty knew what he had to do.

Eileen yawned and stood up. She smiled at Melissa. "I'm sorry, but I'm dead on my feet. I think Erik has the right idea. We'll all make more sense after some sleep." She came around the table, reaching to lift Zoë from Rafferty's lap. The toddler yawned and fussed a bit at the transition, then nestled against Eileen's shoulder and slept again. "You're not getting any lighter, are you?" Eileen murmured, then waved her fingertips at Rafferty and Melissa.

In a way, Rafferty was glad to be alone with his mate. He studied her, noting the curiosity and intelligence in her eyes, then acknowledged that it felt right to make this confidence. "Let me tell you a story," he said, and was rewarded by her smile.

Eileen pivoted in the doorway and stared at him. Rafferty saw her awareness that he was openly defying Erik, and he had no doubt that Erik, too, had heard as much.

"Ooo, a story. I'm not missing this," Eileen said, and abruptly sat down at the table again, Zoë in her lap. "Is there more coffee?"

Chapter 12

Erik stretched out on the bed without getting un-dressed. He closed his eyes and welcomed what-ever vision the world would bring to him. It took a moment to still his thoughts and slow his pulse. He was exhausted. He was frazzled. He felt pulled in a hundred directions, and he didn't know the right choice to make.

He wasn't sure there *was* a right choice.

Erik reached out to the *Pyr*.

He found Delaney, watchful at home in Ohio. That *Pyr* stood guard over his mate and son, vigilant at the farm he had chosen to make his home. Erik understood that Delaney would not come to the firestorm. He had a confidence that Rafferty would not need any aid in satisfactorily concluding his firestorm.

Erik believed and feared the same thing. Rafferty, of all of them, would surrender the most to the lure of the firestorm. Would he betray them all in pursuit of his mate's affection?

That Delaney didn't imagine his presence being necessary was a change. Did that strange blue-green fire-storm give the *Pyr* unwarranted confidence?

Did it threaten their chances of success? Erik was coming to fear as much, but he sought the other *Pyr*.

He found Donovan, somewhere in the west of England. That he was traveling west surprised Erik, although Donovan's purpose was hidden to him. He still could sense that *Pyr*'s resolve, knew that Alex and Nick were with him, and wondered at Donovan's destination. At least Donovan was close. He could be summoned if Rafferty needed him.

But would Donovan come? Erik wasn't as sure as he once would have been.

He found Quinn, still and determined. The fire burned bright on the hearth of the home in Michigan that Quinn and Sara shared, and Sara was curled in Quinn's lap. Their fingers were knotted together over her belly as she dozed in Quinn's embrace, and Erik felt her shiver despite the blaze of the fire.

Erik understood. The Seer was pregnant and she was cold. Perhaps she felt the influence of the darkfire. The Smith, though, respected the darkfire enough to be wary of it, especially when his mate carried his second son. Again, Quinn had faith that Rafferty would not need his services to successfully navigate the challenge of the firestorm—and he was determined to not bring Sara close to the darkfire.

Quinn had chosen, and he would not come to Rafferty's firestorm. Erik was not reassured, although he understood what it was to be torn between one's priorities. If Rafferty lost a scale over his mate, would it condemn him? The Smith would not be present to repair Rafferty's armor, which was a troubling prospect.

Erik found Niall, annoyed yet again with Thorolf. At least that was familiar. Erik could understand Niall's reaction well enough, and he trusted Niall to both guard Rox, his mate, and shelter the inexperienced *Pyr*.

Erik found Thorolf snoring in the spare bedroom of the apartment Niall and Rox shared. Erik was relieved not to have to worry about that member of his group. The firestorm could spare Niall and Thorolf, if Niall kept Thorolf hidden in the short term.

Erik found Sloane and winced at the heat of the argument that had already erupted between Sloane and Brandt, his cousin. They had fought and injured each other; although both had bled, they had also survived. Erik knew he could have gone himself. He had thought it better to come to Rafferty.

Now Erik wasn't sure.

At least he'd been right that Brandt wouldn't injure Sloane.

He felt Brandt's progress, in his own direction, and he knew his vision of the future had had some merit.

Erik could not find Lorenzo, which was undoubtedly exactly what the other *Pyr* wished. Irritation grew in Erik, but he dismissed it, trying to maintain the state in which he could see beyond his own circumstance. If ever he had needed his gift of foresight, this was the moment.

Of Drake and the Dragon's Tooth Warriors, there was no sign. Not so much as a shadow. Erik shivered, for he could not explain their disappearance.

Darkfire burned, tickling at the edge of Erik's thoughts, incessant and seemingly eternal. It unraveled everything, putting his convictions of how matters should be—and would be—in doubt. The *Pyr* were scattered and divided, torn between their obligations. They were revealed. They were in peril. Even loyal Rafferty was defying Erik's council. Erik and Rafferty had disagreed before, but this went deeper.

And it had only begun. Where would it stop?

Why had it started? Erik feared that Lorenzo knew far more secrets than even Erik had imagined, just days before.

That wasn't good.

Erik had failed as leader of the *Pyr*. He effectively led them no longer. With that realization, he guessed one more change the darkfire would make. He had believed he could defeat Brandt, if Brandt chose to fight over the broken blood oath, but now, now Erik gave credence to the vision he'd had in the desert.

He'd seen himself in the company of the dead.

In his mind's eye, the ghost of Sigmund, his lost son, appeared. Erik grimaced at the reminder of yet another of his failures. He'd failed as a father the first time, for Sigmund had turned *Slayer*. Was Zoë losing her fledgling powers because he was failing her as a father, as well?

He did not want to join his son in any kind of afterlife. He didn't want to die. But Erik recalled that he had spoken to his dead son once before in a dream. He dared to hope that Sigmund brought him council.

Or tidings.

"*The Sleeper stirs*," Sigmund murmured, his oldspeak soft.

"*I never knew of him before Lorenzo. I thought it was another trick.*"

"*Not a trick but a spell. The spell is the reason you need to find the crystals.*" Sigmund had once collected old secrets and myths. He had an intimate understand-

ing of the lore of the *Pyr* and had gathered more of it
than any other.

Erik trusted his son's knowledge, but he wanted
more. He sat up, casting old-speak at his son, hearing his
own urgency. *"What crystals?"*

*"The Cantor's crystals. Once there were three, a legacy
passed from Cantor to Cantor. One created the Sleeper.
One held the darkfire. Who has the third?"*

"But what power does the third crystal possess?"

Sigmund smiled and shook his head. His figure began
to fade away. *"Old secrets are the best kind, don't you
think?"*

"No!" Erik cried aloud. "You can't leave yet!"

Sigmund continued to fade, quickly becoming no
more substantial than a wisp of fog. *"But who* is *the
Sleeper?"* Erik demanded, feeling that the rules had
changed without warning.

Sigmund didn't answer.

He simply disappeared.

When Sigmund had completely vanished, Erik threw
himself back on the bed in dismay. Then he overheard
Rafferty's words from the kitchen.

"Let me tell you a story," Rafferty said in the kitchen
below, and Erik's heart sank.

"No," he whispered to himself. "Don't tell her more."

"Rafferty promised to keep the Sleeper's secret," Sigmund whispered. Erik couldn't see him anymore, but his
words could have been uttered against Erik's ear. *"But
darkfire breaks all vows."*

"But he's never told me!"

There was no reply. Erik opened his eyes and stared
at the ceiling, knowing that Sigmund had left him to his

fate knowing that a sea change was in progress. He listened to Rafferty.

There was little else he could do.

Did Rafferty know about the three crystals, too?

Where was the third one?

And why did it matter?

Melissa sat with pencil poised, waiting for Rafferty to begin. She hadn't missed that Rafferty was breaking rank with Erik in telling her anything more. She was pleased and excited that he intended to confide in her.

But Rafferty had fallen silent, a frown between his brows. "Well?" she prompted, fearing he was changing his mind.

"I'm trying to decide where to start," he said with a small smile.

"At the beginning," Eileen suggested. "And soon, before I fall asleep." She grinned. "Not to be pushy or anything."

Rafferty nodded. "Yes. I need something to tell this best." He left then, leaving the women blinking at each other. Melissa heard him go to the library.

He returned a moment later, holding the same large quartz crystal he'd had in his hand when Melissa had first found him in the library. It was six inches long and a good three inches wide, precisely formed and clear. One end came to a point while the other was ragged, as if it had been broken free of a rocky mooring. It fit perfectly in Rafferty's hand.

When Rafferty displayed it on his palm, Melissa saw the blue light still flickering in its core.

It looked like a spark, a crackling electrical fire, no

more than half an inch across. Now, it burned steadily, never dying, and never flaring brighter.

Why had it blazed so brightly before?

"Is that darkfire, too?" Eileen breathed.

Rafferty nodded. "As guardian of the Sleeper, I was entrusted not only with his defense, but with this stone that reflects his state," he explained. "For centuries, it has shone only a single dot of blue light." He inclined his head toward Melissa. "This flare first appeared this morning, while you were sleeping."

"That's what you were worried about."

He stared at the crystal. "It's even brighter now."

"Because the firestorm still burns?" Eileen asked.

"I don't know," Rafferty admitted. "I do know that it means the Sleeper stirs. It means the rate of his pulse and his breath has changed." He pursed his lips, pausing for a moment before continuing. "It means he is closer to wakefulness than he has been in centuries, if not wide awake." His voice dropped low. "My grandfather called him Cysgwr."

"Is that his name?" Melissa asked.

Rafferty shook his head. "It's his state or maybe his role. It means Sleeper in Welsh, the only language my grandfather spoke."

He turned the crystal in his hands, frowning as if lost in memories. Melissa had seen that expression on his face before and guessed the direction of his thoughts. She'd glimpsed before that he was fond of his grandfather. Maybe that made the story hard to tell.

"Your grandfather gave you the crystal, didn't he? He entrusted you with the role of guardian of the Sleeper."

"No," Rafferty said, to her surprise. "He tried to give

me that task, but I refused him. It was the only argument we ever had, and those words of anger were the last words we exchanged." He put the crystal down on the table, as if unable to hold it any longer.

Melissa could understand the burden of having parted badly. She'd been there and done that. She stretched out a finger to touch the crystal and found its surface slightly warm. Eileen was thoughtful as she sipped her coffee and rocked Zoë.

Rafferty swallowed. "I fear this is the root of everything. It is a keepsake of my pride and my error, and that argument is perhaps the reason the darkfire found me."

"What do you mean?" Melissa asked.

Rafferty impaled her with a glance. "You cannot bear a son to me. The firestorm, which I have awaited for so long, is bereft of its purpose, which means that the darkfire cannot be halted by conventional means. I have to wonder whether this is reparation for my mistake."

Melissa wasn't going to let him blame himself. "Maybe it means you're the one who can think outside of the box."

Eileen smiled. "Who better than the greatest romantic of the *Pyr*?"

Melissa was startled by this bit of information about Rafferty. "Really? A romantic?" That Rafferty appeared to be discomfited just added credence to Eileen's claim.

Here she'd thought they had a lot in common.

Including a very basic pragmatism.

Was it possible that Rafferty wanted more than a sexual relationship? Melissa had assumed their interaction was all about instant gratification.

But had she only assumed that he shared her view?

"Absolutely." Eileen put down her coffee mug. "Rafferty is the one who persuades each of the *Pyr* to make a permanent relationship with his mate, to go for the long term and to create a rewarding union. Rafferty is our forever *Pyr*."

Melissa pushed back from the table and tried to make a joke. She'd been here and done this, and she wasn't planning to live it again. Strange to have something in common with Erik.

She tried to keep her tone light. "Well, then it's too bad I don't believe in forever anymore." She felt flustered beneath Rafferty's warm gaze.

"Why not?" he asked quietly.

"There's only now. The present is what counts. The future can be torn away in a heartbeat, leaving you with nothing at all."

"And the only legacy of merit is the truth?" Rafferty asked with a piercing gaze.

Melissa nodded. "Absolutely."

Rafferty reached over and took Melissa's hand in his. His grip was warm, his hand large enough to envelop hers. "Firestorms are often about healing," he said with quiet intensity. "Maybe your view of the future is one more thing the darkfire intends to change."

"Amen," Eileen said.

Melissa stared at Rafferty in shock, the heat of desire pulsing through her body from their entwined hands. She could lose herself in his eyes, in his conviction, and in his faith that the world was a good place.

Or that he could make it better.

She could love this man.

That was perhaps the most terrifying prospect of all.

Rafferty watched her, seeming to read every single one of her thoughts, then turned back to Eileen without releasing Melissa's hand. "I know where to begin," he said with conviction. "I will begin with the firestorm. With a story of destiny and love that endured long after that firestorm was sated."

"Goody," Eileen said, settling into her chair.

Melissa understood that Rafferty was going to try to persuade her to his view. With his hand locked around hers, and his attention bent upon her, she had a feeling he might just manage the deed. The darkfire danced around their locked hands, its blue light leaping high, apparently echoing Rafferty's intensity. It also warmed her right to her core and made her want him all over again.

And yes, for the duration.

Melissa and her protective barriers were in deep trouble.

"Once upon a time," Rafferty began in that melodic voice.

What he had to do was perfectly clear to Rafferty. Melissa had been wounded, and that wound shaped her view. Rafferty knew it as well as he knew his own name, just as he knew that he was the one to persuade her to believe in forever again.

Her healing would be the gift of the darkfire.

Giving her hope in the future, helping her to dare to believe in forever, might extinguish those flames of chaos. It might be the whole point. He would begin by entrusting his story to her, by baring his own truth to this woman who would pursue truth anywhere.

It felt absolutely right.

"Once upon a time, there was a land populated by both dragons and men. While beautiful, it was a hard location for any creature to live, given the meager wealth of the soil and the length of the winter. Those who lived there loved their homeland beyond all expectation. They fought brutal wars in its defense, they survived the reigns of all conquerors, and they created marvelous epic poetry. That part of the world eventually became known as Wales, and it is my birthplace."

"Big source of dragon stories," Eileen said with approval.

"You were one of the dragons?" Melissa asked.

"My entire family hailed from Wales. But by the time I was born some twelve hundred years ago, our numbers were vastly diminished."

"Twelve hundred years?"

Rafferty smiled and nodded.

Melissa frowned at her notes. "How many firestorms have you had in that time?"

"The *Pyr* get only one," Eileen said. "Usually."

"This is the first." Rafferty spoke with conviction, for it was the truth, and saw that Melissa believed him. "By the time I was born, the exploits of my family had become legends. But they were real, as real as I am, though perhaps not so fortunate." He glanced into the darkfire, watching the blue flames leap and seeing another fire, one fed by peat, in a lost place and time. He recalled his grandfather's voice, his stories, and his poetic gift, and Rafferty smiled at the memory.

"My grandfather was named Pwyll. I never knew any other name for him, and I didn't realize as a child that he was as powerful as he was. I met him when I was eight summers of age. We *Pyr* come into our abilities at puberty—until that point, I was indistinguishable from any other child. I didn't know I was anything but a human child. I had been raised by my mother, who did not speak of my father. It was my understanding that he was dead, although no one ever said as much."

Rafferty paused, and he appreciated that Melissa watched him with care. "You might imagine my surprise when a spry older man came to me. I was sowing seeds in our garden. He knelt down beside me, told me he was my grandfather, and said he had come to teach me of my truth. I thought he was crazy, but I do remember how wonderful his eyes were. They glittered like jewels and were unlike the eyes of any person I'd ever seen. Like a dutiful child, though truly I was frightened, I insisted upon asking my mother. She took one look at him, and even I saw her relief."

"She knew what you were, then."

"She knew. And with one look, she recognized him. When he told her his name, she said, 'Owen hoped you would come.' Then she kissed me, made me put on my best coat and boots, and gave me a bundle with bread and cheese and apples. She looked into my face and told me to be good, to listen to my grandfather, and to let her know once in a while that I was well. She did not cry, not until we were gone. I heard her weep when we left the village. I would have gone back, but Pwyll put his hand on my shoulder. 'Men cannot hear women's tears at such a distance,' he said. 'Here is proof that you are different, that you are *Pyr*, and that you have need of what I can teach you. Trust your mother's wisdom in this.' And so I did."

"It must have been hard for her."

Rafferty nodded. "Yes and no. It was hard for her to lose me, but on the other hand, she had less burden without me."

"One fewer mouth to feed," Eileen said.

Rafferty nodded. "She worried less about the future, and that brightened her countenance. She stopped thinking of what she had lost—for she saw Owen each time she looked at me. The first time I went back, I was as astonished by the change in her as she was in the change in me. I had grown up, while she had fallen in love again and married."

"She was happy," Melissa said.

"She was. Pwyll knew the gift he was giving her."

"Could he see the future?" Eileen asked.

"Not exactly. He understood people, almost as well as he understood *Pyr*, and he was better than most at seeing the shadow cast by choices made. At any rate, he became my mentor and my guardian. He lived in a cave high in the hills, hidden from the sight of men. It extended far down into the earth. I never did travel the whole length of it. He liked to light a peat fire near the mouth of the cave each evening and talk. He told stories, wonderful stories about the *Pyr* and our kin and the past, and I wish I could remember them all."

"How old was he?" Melissa asked.

"I never knew. In human form, he looked like an older man. His hair was silver, but he was still strong and agile. Dates were not in such common use then as now. He said he was an infant when the Romans invaded."

"But he had a firestorm?" Melissa asked. Rafferty liked that she needed to clarify all the details and that she kept making notes in that shorthand of hers. He doubted anyone could interpret it other than his mate.

"He did. That was why his hair had turned silver. We age very slowly until our firestorms, until we create an heir. It has always been thus. Even so, we can long outlive our mates. My grandfather found purpose in passing his knowledge to the young, although I know he missed my grandmother a great deal. He had a lock of her hair that he treasured beyond any other prize in his hoard."

"Where did they meet?" Eileen asked while Melissa scribbled.

"They met because of the firestorm. He followed its heat, only to find that she had retreated from the world to a community of women. We would call such a place a convent, although it was not quite the same as our convents."

"Why not?" Melissa asked.

Eileen spoke up, sounding like the academic she was. "Most of the women would have been illiterate. No study of the scriptures. As aristocrats, they brought wealth to the establishment. In the early medieval era, cloistered women lived much as secular women, involved in needlework and music and contemplation, but in the absence of men other than a visiting priest."

Melissa nodded, then frowned. "But how could she have been your grandmother if she was in a convent? Did she leave?"

Rafferty smiled. "No. My grandfather slipped into the convent at night, went to her, and introduced himself. He said they talked that first night, as well as the second and the third. I expect he told her some of his stories, but it doesn't matter—she surrendered to him on the fourth night and conceived his son."

"Did anyone know he was there?" Eileen asked.

"Apparently not, for there was a great uproar when her pregnancy was revealed. It was deemed miraculous, or the work of a demon."

The women laughed together. "Was she tossed out?" Melissa asked.

"I'll bet not," Eileen said. "If she'd left, whatever wealth she'd brought would have left with her."

"Exactly," Rafferty agreed. "She stayed, and her son was raised within the walls."

"And your grandfather?"

"Went back. Repeatedly, from what he admitted to me. He had fallen in love with his mate and could not stay away. No wall could keep him from her; that was his claim, for his love was too potent to be denied."

"So you come by your romantic inclinations honestly," Eileen said with satisfaction.

"My grandmother conceived again, but on that occasion, the priests tried to exorcise the demon that haunted her. My grandfather wasn't so easily deterred, my father remained resolute in her womb, and so she was evicted. The convent wanted nothing to do with a woman so attractive to demons."

"Even with her money." Eileen raised her eyebrows.

"Where did she go?" Melissa asked.

"She did not want to live with my grandfather, in his cave in the hills. I think he was surprised by her independence. She remained in town, in Carmarthen, and he regularly visited, taking gifts to her from his hoard. She never married another man, and her neighbors claimed her sons were fatherless."

"Then they never saw your grandfather, either," Melissa said.

Rafferty frowned, never having considered this. "Apparently not. At any rate, my grandfather was quite taken with his sons and visited them often. He told them the stories he later told to me."

"But he didn't follow that same course with you," Melissa noted. "Why not?"

"Because it all went awry. I never knew my uncle, but he was said to have special gifts. My grandfather was the Cantor of the *Pyr*—he could cast spells with his songs—and his firstborn had the same gifts but multiplied a hundred times. My uncle had a phenomenal memory, he was a poet, and he had foresight. He also had talent with spells. He was the one conceived during the firestorm, the glint in my grandfather's eye, a bright light that burned out fast."

"What happened?" Melissa asked.

"There was much war in that time, and there came a party of men to the town. My uncle was playing with his friends while my father was on some errand. There was a dispute in the game between my uncle and another boy, and that boy became scornful, insisting that no one could take the cause of a fatherless boy. The visiting men overheard this. It turned out that they were on a quest, in search of a fatherless boy, and had feared they would never succeed."

Eileen sat straighter. "I recognize this story," she murmured, but Rafferty ignored her.

"The men took my uncle and my mother to Dinas Emrys. Here, a man named Vortigern was having a stronghold built, but the foundation was destroyed each night. His masons had instructed him to mingle the blood of a fatherless boy in the mortar to ensure that the foundation stones remained."

"And so the quest." Melissa's lips twisted. "They probably didn't know what was wrong and didn't think this solution could ever be found."

Eileen's eyes were shining, her expression rapt.

Rafferty kept his gaze fixed upon his mate. "Quite likely. My uncle knew exactly what was wrong, because he recognized the hill from my grandfather's stories. He knew Dinas Emrys was the hill under which two fighting dragons had been secured, in order to spare the world their violence."

"And the scream they made, each May Day, which echoed through the world and was reported by Llud to Llefelys," Eileen said.

"What?" Melissa asked.

"It's in the Mabinogion," Eileen said. "An old dragon story."

Melissa shrugged and Rafferty continued. "So he told Vortigern to excavate the hill, that the masons would find a pool beneath it that was undermining the foundation. In that pond would be two large stones, and in each of those stones would be a dragon. Each night, a red dragon would emerge from one stone and a white dragon from the other, and they would fight until the dawn. This battle destroyed the tower each night. Each day, they retreated to their stones and healed, in order to fight again. Each day, the men rebuilt the tower, only to find it destroyed the subsequent morning.

"My uncle said more though, his foresight giving him a clearer view of the situation. Vortigern had usurped the power of his king, who had been one of three sons of a deceased king. My uncle compared the white dragon to one of the king's surviving two sons and Vortigern to the red one. He prophesied that they would fight until only the white dragon survived."

"So what happened?" Melissa asked.

"Vortigern commanded the hill to be excavated. They found the pond, they found the stones, and that night, they saw the dragons fight. It was a vicious battle, but at dawn, the dragons crawled back into their stones to heal. The men rolled the stones away while the dragons slept, drained the pond, and built the foundation. It held this time." Rafferty smiled. "But Vortigern was burned to death within it when the king's sons came to take their vengeance upon him for his treachery."

"What happened to your uncle?" Melissa asked.

"One of the king's sons heard the story and took my uncle as his adviser. My uncle repeated his warning that only one brother would survive, and he was ignored. The third brother killed my uncle's patron, seized the crown that was no longer contested, and then he took my uncle as his adviser."

"And his name was Uther Pendragon," Eileen said with a smile.

Melissa looked between the two of them. "Wait a minute. Isn't that part of the Arthurian legend?"

"All old stories have their toes in a truth," Rafferty said, and Eileen chuckled, toasting him with her empty mug.

"What was your uncle's name?" Melissa asked.

"Myrddin." Rafferty let his smile broaden. "And yes, it was modified to 'Merlin' in the old French stories. Can you guess why?"

She shook her head.

Eileen laughed out loud. "Because otherwise it would have been *Merdinus* in Latin, which has an unfortunate connotation in French."

Melissa laughed in her turn. "*Merde* means 'shit' in French. I remember the French crews swearing in Baghdad."

"And so it does," Rafferty confirmed.

He loved how she looked when she smiled, as if a

flame had lit within her. She seemed younger and softer, more approachable.

He sobered then, thinking of the toll life could take on an individual and remembering his grandfather's stories. "My grandfather believed his son had been found only because he had remained in human society. He believed that interaction had led to Myrddin's downfall, and to his comparatively short life. He took Owen away then, to teach him, even though Owen never had Myrddin's natural gifts."

"Which was why he'd warned Owen that he would do as much for Owen's son, and how your mother knew to expect him," Melissa concluded.

Rafferty nodded. He watched her review her notes, looking for loose ends in his story.

"What happened to your father?" she asked.

"He was killed, within days of my conception. I never knew him, save through Pwyll's tales." Rafferty looked at the fire again. "Those were dark times for us, when the hunting began."

The silence stretched between them.

But this time, it was Melissa who placed her hand on Rafferty's. "I know what it's like to have something else running your show," she said softly. There was compassion in her eyes and, seeing it, he knew he had made the right choice.

He also believed they could make a partnership for the duration.

Even if Melissa wasn't yet persuaded.

Chapter 13

It was tempting to confide in Rafferty, to share her own story with this intense and romantic man, but Melissa knew better.

It didn't help that she couldn't think straight with the darkfire dancing over her skin and through her body. Could she ever get enough of him?

Melissa had to focus on the facts, on her main objective, and not get distracted by emotional dreams that couldn't come true. She frowned as she reviewed her notes, sensing that she was missing something.

She found it, just as Eileen yawned again.

"Wait a minute," Melissa said to Rafferty. "You said that you can't do the spontaneous manifestation thing that Montmorency can do."

"That's right." Rafferty's tone was grim.

"What about the newt bit?"

Eileen froze in the act of leaving the kitchen. "Salamander," she corrected as she watched them.

Melissa nodded. "Okay. Montmorency became a salamander in the helicopter. At least I think it was him. The salamander was the same jade green color."

"It *was* Magnus." Rafferty spoke with resolve.

"And the other one ..." She fanned her notes, looking for the name of the topaz *Slayer*, but Rafferty answered her first.

"Jorge."

"He was a salamander when he first appeared. Can you take lots of different forms?"

Rafferty leaned closer. "All of us can take two forms, man and dragon. Traditionally, the Wyvern has had some ability to assume different forms, but no others among us. That seems to have been changing."

"How so?" One thing Melissa was good at was asking questions. It was wonderful that Rafferty was answering her.

What had changed in his view?

His attention was certainly fixed on her, leaving her all warm and tingly, even if she didn't look at him. And that voice ... "Some *Slayers* who have drunk the Elixir appear to have the ability to take the salamander form."

"Because of the Elixir?"

Rafferty shrugged. "Apparently so." He hesitated, flicking a glance at a watchful Eileen. "I have told you too much already." Was he personally reluctant to confide in her, or was he afraid of Erik's reaction?

Melissa didn't really care. It made sense to her that they work together. "The way I see it, we have a mutual problem named Magnus Montmorency. If we pool our information and work together, we could nail him."

Rafferty glanced again at Eileen. "You must recognize that I have an obligation to my kind and must not further jeopardize their security."

"And I've already spilled the beans." Melissa nodded in understanding. "Okay, let's make a deal. I won't tell anyone else anything about the *Pyr* without your explicit approval."

Rafferty arched a brow, but she sensed that he wasn't truly surprised. "I thought the story—and that job—was tantamount."

"I think nailing Montmorency is more important." Melissa shrugged. "And I suspect you're the only one who can really do it." She stuck out her hand. "Deal?"

Rafferty smiled. The curve claimed his lips slowly, pleasure lighting his eyes. The transformation made Melissa's heart pound.

And it made the darkfire flames burn more intensely green.

He leaned forward, all muscled power, and extended his hand. Melissa's fingers were lost in his grip, the heat of his touch making her as dizzy as the approval in his eyes. She could have fallen into his lap; she could have twined herself around him, but he gave her hand a single pump, then released it.

She saw the effect of that contact upon him when he sat back, took a deep breath, and pushed a hand through his hair.

She liked that the firestorm tormented them both.

She sat back in her chair and curled her feet beneath her, smiling at the way he watched her legs. There was hunger in his expression, a desire that she liked to believe wasn't purely because of the firestorm's heat.

She shivered in anticipation of sating it.

Would that mean his departure? The notion burst Melissa's bubble, no doubt about it.

Rafferty pursed his lips, choosing his words. "There is another *Slayer*, one who only recently revealed himself. His name is Chen, and it appears that he can take six forms."

"Six?"

Rafferty counted off on his fingers. "I have seen him as a dragon, as a salamander, as a snake, as a beautiful woman, as a young man, and as an elderly man."

"Wow." Because the concept obviously troubled Rafferty, Melissa made a joke. "That seems excessive."

Rafferty's smile was fleeting.

"So, this Chen must have had a lot of that Elixir, then."

"I'm not sure," he acknowledged. "Magnus restricts himself to three forms, and he drank most of it. By far. It was created by him, and its source was under his control."

"So, is that because it isn't possible for him to take more forms, or because he chooses not to?"

Rafferty shrugged. "I don't know."

"So, maybe there's another factor than the Elixir." Melissa smelled an answer close at hand. She flipped through her notes again, seeking it.

There it was, right in front of her.

"How did your grandfather get into the convent?" she asked, barely able to hide her excitement. "And how did he visit your grandmother in her village, without being seen even once? My experience of small towns is that everyone knows everyone else's business."

Eileen sat down heavily then, her eyes round. "Merlin is said to have been a shape shifter," she murmured.

"What form did he take?" Rafferty demanded.

"A stag," Eileen said, then began to sound like a teacher. "That's assumed by some scholars to be an example of a pagan story revised to a Christian one. Shamans often dressed as stags for specific rituals in nature religions. We even have images of them in such disguise on the walls of Lascaux. And Merlin is often considered as a shaman figure in the Arthurian cycle."

"Could your grandfather become a salamander?" Melissa asked. "Or spontaneously manifest in other places?" She leaned forward, sure she was right. "Was that how he did it?"

Rafferty's eyes brightened. "Maybe. Maybe!"

"What if those powers have nothing to do with the Elixir?" Eileen asked.

Rafferty was clearly deep in thought. "Magnus always collected old lore," he mused.

"What if he discovered a lost truth?" Eileen asked.

"More importantly, what if you can do it, too?" Melissa asked.

"What if reclaiming this old power is another legacy of the darkfire? What if knowing something is possible is the key to doing it?" Rafferty whispered, then smiled.

He laughed out loud and scooped Melissa up into his arms, swinging her around as her pencil slid across the table. He kissed her, then held her in his embrace. "What a gift you bring me," he murmured, his gaze so warm that Melissa blushed. "My grandfather always said the richest treasure in his hoard was his mate."

He then glanced pointedly at Eileen.

Melissa meanwhile caught her breath. It had been a long time since anyone had thought of her as being key to anything, and she savored the satisfaction of making a contribution.

Of making a difference.

It was good stuff.

Eileen stood up. "I feel a strange compulsion to get some sleep, right this minute," she said, winking at Melissa. She hefted Zoë higher with a grunt, then left the pair together.

Rafferty smiled down at Melissa. "I am feeling celebratory."

"Sounds as if that word has a specific connotation."

His smile broadened. "The dragon celebrates with physical pleasures of all kinds." He kissed her knuckles, sending a torrent of desire through Melissa's body. Her mouth went dry. The firestorm turned Melissa's thoughts in the same direction, but she fought its appeal.

Sex wasn't good enough—even though this was the best she'd ever had. She had to prove to Rafferty that she was worth having around, even though she couldn't give him a son.

She had to help him destroy Montmorency.

She had to help him extinguish the darkfire, before everything he cared about was lost. The firestorm's allure would wait—and even if it didn't, she knew she'd be wanting Rafferty for a long time.

Maybe there *could* be a future for the two of them. The trick would be securing it.

Donovan stood on the wharf and eyed the island on the other side of the choppy stretch of water.

"No ferry today, sir—that much is for certain."

"No. I can see that." Donovan checked his watch for the hundredth time. He was tired and frustrated, and that went double for Alex and Nick. The wind was violent, tossing dark clouds across the sky and making the water churn into dangerous waves.

Keeping him from the Sleeper.

He'd made a mistake, revealing himself here on the dock. He'd assumed they'd be able to cross on the ferry quickly, saving him from any explanation about how they had arrived. Islands with small populations were tricky in that, and he was determined to blend in as much as possible. This far out of the tourist season, it wouldn't be easy.

Bardsey Island might be home to ten thousand saints, but they were all dead. The living counted only two dozen or so, particularly in winter, so three Americans couldn't arrive without being noticed. Still, as he watched the water, he wished he'd just flown them all there under cover of night.

What would he find when he arrived?

"In a hurry are you, then?" the burly man asked.

"Impatient, yes," Donovan agreed, trying to keep his toe from tapping. "And it has been a long day of travel, as well."

"Almost off the edge of the world here," the man agreed amiably.

"It's always good to reach the destination and be able to relax," Donovan said.

The man's gaze sharpened as he surveyed Donovan, then Alex and Nick. Alex had remained in their rental car and was reading to Nick from a book they had brought. The boy leaned against her, sleepy but not wanting to miss anything. He could see the exhaustion in both of their faces.

"We don't see many visitors this time of year."

"Not so much of a visitor, as one returned," Donovan said.

The man's interest sharpened. "How so?"

"I came to Bardsey Island as a young man, although it's been a long time." It had been longer even than this man anticipated, but Donovan didn't say that. "My distant cousin owned a house on the island."

"And who would that be?"

"Donovan Shea."

"Oh, he's been gone a long while." The man's manner warmed at the mention of the name. "Seems I heard he had passed away."

"Yes." Donovan shook his head, as if to marvel. In fact, he had started the rumor, as he did every sixty or seventy years, concurrent with another round of legalities to pass his own property to himself. It had gotten more difficult in the last century, and he wondered absently how rich the *Pyr* were making lawyers everywhere. "I guess it amused him that we had the same name, for he left the house to me. Quite a surprise, after all this time."

"That would be the old white house, then."

"It would." Donovan wasn't surprised the man knew it. "I'm eager to see it again, and to show my own son the island. I'm sure it's as magical as I recall."

The man nodded. "It's a place you don't shake out of your bones; that's for certain." He eyed the sky. "I might have taken you alone, but I'll not take your boy before the sea is more favorable."

"That's fair. Any idea when it might be?"

The man inhaled and scanned the horizon, his gaze dancing over the clouds. Donovan trusted his judgment, for he likely knew this stretch of water as well as his own hand. "Before sunset," he said.

Sunset would have to do.

The Sleeper would have to wait a little longer to be defended.

Donovan thanked the man and rejoined Alex and Nick, hoping he arrived soon enough to keep his old vow.

Rafferty was jubilant. Trusting Melissa had revealed a side of his grandfather's story that he'd never seen. He had no doubt their working together could only bear more fruit.

The Great Wyvern had been right. His firestorm was a gift, and he would build a partnership with his mate.

"We need to finish Montmorency before we celebrate anything," she said with a resolve he'd already come to associate with her.

"Why don't you believe in the future anymore?" he asked, watching the play of emotions on her face. He raised a hand before she could speak. "No platitudes. You're a logical woman, and there's a specific incident at root. I would be honored if you would trust me with that truth."

Melissa closed her mouth. She looked at him, then down to her notes and the crystal that still rested on the table. "It seems only fair," she said, her words tight. "Given how much you've confided in me."

She didn't hesitate then, just lifting her chin and holding his gaze. She didn't flinch, either. "I came home from my post, only to learn that I had cancer."

"I thought I read that you had left the Middle East to get married."

Melissa smiled. "I did. He was adamant that he wouldn't live abroad. Of course, he had an anchor post already." She sighed. "I met him when he came to do some spotlights for the network in the region, when there were treaty agreements. Love at first sight, we were in sync, everything was perfect. Moving back state-side seemed like the better plan, especially when he put in a word for me to get a transfer."

"You were giving up a lot."

"Didn't seem like it at the time. A tiny sacrifice for the greater good. And what did I need a hotshot career for? Or those journalism awards? We were going to start a family." Melissa frowned, her gaze dancing over the kitchen. Rafferty saw that the story wasn't an easy one for her to tell. "I went for my first physical exam in years, never imagining they'd find anything. I was healthy." She met Rafferty's gaze. "Who would have guessed that while I was dodging explosives, the real bomb was silently growing inside me?"

Rafferty shook his head. There were no words for such horrific news. "How did you find out?" he asked.

"I had an abnormal Pap smear, although no one was overly concerned. It was supposed to be routine. But the second showed similar results, which got people's attention. Then the biopsy—they knew even before the test results came back." She tapped her fingers on the kitchen table. "Come to think of it, it was the day those results were made official that he packed."

"He left you, in the midst of such a crisis?" Rafferty was outraged.

She eyed him. "Don't you think he was right to do so? That there was no point in staying?"

Rafferty sputtered in fury. "No! Love should run deeper than that, and vows are a commitment. He should have been beside you. He should have helped you."

Melissa swallowed and tried to speak lightly. "I wouldn't be able to give him the kids he wanted, would I? I couldn't keep the terms of the deal."

"He should have loved you better than that," Rafferty said hotly.

Melissa considered him, and he saw the spark of hope within her. He knew he had to nurture that spark and feed it, coax it to burn steadily and brightly.

He took her hand in his. "No one should endure such a test alone."

"That's not what everyone said. Well, everyone except my brother." She averted her gaze unable to completely hide her pain. Rafferty saw that she tried. "So much for the job I'd barely started—turned out I was downsized within the week. So much for my friends—the real ones were on the other side of the world, and the others just evaporated when they heard my news. So much for the fairy-tale wedding, the one for which the bills were still coming in. So much for 'forever.' So much for the dream house and the promise of 'until death us do part.'" She grimaced. "Who knew I'd get to face that bit alone?"

"He was wrong," Rafferty said with force.

"Was he? He knew what he wanted. Turned out that didn't include me."

"But Melissa . . ."

"You're the one who believes in destiny, Rafferty. My marriage was doomed from the outset, even though I had no idea at the time." She made an impatient gesture. "Someone pulled back the veil, and that was the end of everything. Like a magic show, where the conjuror makes everything disappear with a snap of his fingers."

She looked at him, her gaze steady. "I respect and understand your dream of the firestorm, but you need to recognize that I'm not the mate you've been waiting for. This relationship is just as doomed. We can have great sex, but even that's going to fade. I can't ever give you that son, and if that's what you want, maybe we should call it quits now."

With those words, Melissa convinced Rafferty of exactly the opposite. He knew that mere words wouldn't change her mind, though, or convince her to share his perspective.

No, Rafferty Powell knew exactly what he had to do to win the heart of his wounded mate. He had never believed that any treasure worth possessing would be easily gained, and in a way, he welcomed that gaining Melissa's love and trust would test him. He had to sacrifice everything to the darkfire, in order to gain the reward of the firestorm. There would be no half measures.

He was ready.

Rafferty reached out and captured her hand, tugging her toward his office. They would celebrate, but in an entirely different way than he'd first imagined.

The end result would be just as good, though. He was sure of it.

Melissa didn't know what Rafferty was up to.

He was up to *something*; that was clear. There was a determined glint in his eyes, and his lips were curved in a secretive smile. He looked sexy enough to eat. "Bring your notes," he instructed, interlacing his fingers with hers.

He pulled her into his office and urged her toward the chair behind the desk. Was it her imagination that the blue light of the darkfire flames between them were burning higher and hotter? Rafferty made no indication that he'd noticed. He moved with purpose, bent on his task. He set a laptop in front of her and booted it up, connecting the modem cable at one side.

"What are you doing?" Melissa asked, although she had an idea.

"You must remember your passwords," he said, logging on to the Internet and leaving the browser running. Melissa gaped at him. He opened a drawer and put a digital camera on the desk, then connected it to the computer with a USB cable. He produced Montmorency's blue leather-bound book with a flourish, then set it on the desk before her.

He stood back and smiled. "Do what you do," he invited. "Expose Magnus's truth to the world."

Melissa's heart began to thunder. "You're serious."

He nodded, no doubt in his posture. "Your brother said the world was waiting for your update. Why don't you give it to them?"

Melissa scanned the tools he'd given her, glancing at her notes and the book even as she formulated a plan. She needed to present the story in a coherent manner, with facts that could be verified.

But Montmorency could turn up at any moment.

Literally in front of her.

"Why are you doing this? I thought you didn't want to betray your kind?"

Rafferty smiled. "But if the choice lies in revealing my kind further, or refusing to trust in the firestorm, then my decision is an easy one. I believe we have a firestorm for a reason. I believe we can be a team together. I believe there is another point than the conception of a child. There must be. And so I choose the firestorm. I choose you."

Melissa was astounded. This man was becoming more irresistible by the moment.

"What can I do to help?" Rafferty asked.

"Will you photograph the entire contents of the date

book?" she asked. "We'll upload the images to a secure server; then, even if we lose the book, we'll have backup."

"Got it," Rafferty said. "I'll do the documenting while you compose your story." He quickly set up the book so that it was braced open, and put the camera on a tripod. "How's this?" he asked as the first image appeared in a file on the laptop.

Melissa set up the receiving file to one side, then logged in to her blog, opening a new post. She checked the image. It was in focus and legible. "Perfect." She scanned the handwritten text. "Lots of names and dates to cross-check here. It'll be a lot of work."

"You'll pull it together," Rafferty said with welcome confidence.

Melissa fought against her excitement—both in the book's contents and Rafferty's support. She knew she had to focus. She had to do a perfect job so that Daphne's sacrifice wasn't wasted.

They worked together steadily until Rafferty cleared his throat. She realized he was reading her account over her shoulder.

"Maybe you should phone your friend Doug," he suggested.

"No need," Melissa said with a smile. "He'll be calling me."

She glanced up at Rafferty, loving that they were working together toward the same goal, and this time she knew it wasn't her imagination.

The darkfire burned brighter, not just between the two of them but in all the mineral samples on the bookshelves. Its impish light flickered blue-green, painting the room with erratic and surreal color.

Daring Melissa Smith to believe all over again.

*   *   *

Unbeknownst to either Melissa or Rafferty, a green
salamander materialized in the dark cellar of Rafferty's
Hampstead Heath home as the pair worked together in
Rafferty's office.

The salamander was panting, bleeding from numer-
ous wounds and unsteady on its four feet. It staggered
across the stone floor, desperate to hide itself before it
collapsed. It climbed the wall weakly, falling twice before managing to secrete itself in a crack between the
stones. It closed its eyes, its heart racing.

Then it groaned quietly, as salamanders so seldom do.

The cellar was chilly and damp, a small puddle having gathered on the far corner of the floor. It was a
hospitable space for spiders, but not so welcoming for
salamanders.

But the jade green salamander stretched out one foot
toward the ceiling. It closed its eyes and basked in the heat
of a firestorm, one in close proximity. It let the heat of that
firestorm slide through its veins, invigorate it, and coax
some modicum of healing. The firestorm blazed brighter
and hotter, almost as if it responded to the salamander's
need, although that was not the case. It wasn't as good as
the Elixir, but it was the closest alternative available.

It would have to do.

The salamander had feared the firestorm might be
sated too soon, that it burned too hot and would be
extinguished before he had even arrived to drink of its
feast.

Lit with mercury's eerie blue-green light, it burned
hotter than anticipated, infusing him with new strength.
The salamander that was Magnus Montmorency smiled
in the shadows.

Trust Rafferty to inadvertently give his old enemy exactly what was needed. Darkfire would suit him very well. His scent was disguised, and his arrival had gone unobserved.

That was far better than Magnus had anticipated.

That Jorge was alive and determined to kill him was less good news. Fortunately, Jorge was still stupid enough to believe a lie.

Or greedy enough. The details were unimportant. Without his own quick thinking, by this point, Magnus would have been Jorge's lunch.

It had been harder to follow the heat of the firestorm, so wounded was Magnus, and he had had to move closer in incremental jumps. Each shift had cost him dearly, and he was uncertain how long it would take to restore his strength.

He strained his ears to listen, his eyes widening as he heard what Rafferty and his mate did with his own book. Magnus wanted to roar in frustration. He wanted to halt this abomination before it went too far.

But he was weak, and he knew it.

And Jorge was afoot.

Magnus would never survive against both Rafferty and Jorge.

So he gritted his teeth and bided his time, seething at the injustice of it all and his thirst for vengeance growing with every word he heard.

He would triumph.

He simply had to choose his moment with care.

Chapter 14

When Eileen woke up, the room was falling into darkness. She saw Erik standing by the window of the bedroom, a shadow against the shadows. She wondered whether he had slept at all. He looked haggard, his expression drawn, his skin pale. He was staring down into the street below, but she knew he wasn't looking at the view.

Eileen watched him, waiting for him to confide in her. She knew he would be aware of the change in her breathing and pulse. She knew that he knew she was awake. But he didn't turn. She was used to Erik being grim, being driven, being uncommunicative, being utterly focused on the good of the *Pyr* he led.

This was different. He seemed to be in despair.

She got up and checked Zoë, who was still sleeping deeply in the cot that Rafferty always had ready for them. When Erik still didn't speak, she turned on her partner. He hadn't even moved.

"You heard Rafferty's story?"

"I heard it." He didn't even look at her.

"And the other bits we talked about?" Erik nodded, but Eileen had learned a long time ago to not be deterred by his silence. "So, what aren't you telling me?"

"A great deal." He grimaced. "As usual." He turned to face her, his thoughts hidden. Eileen had a bad feeling about that. "I haven't been the best partner to you. Not last time and scarcely better this time."

"Oh, I wouldn't be such a tough judge," Eileen said lightly, and moved to his side. "You have some good qualities. Lucky for you, I have a thing for serious men."

Erik didn't appear to have heard her, but he stared out the window again. His manner frightened her as little else could have done.

Eileen sat on the end of the bed opposite him, folded her arms across her chest, and leaned forward. "Erik. Talk to me. What do you see?" She referred to his ability to foresee the future, suspecting that some glimmer had soured his mood.

"Little good." He frowned.

"Sloane's verse about darkfire mentioned it changing everything."

Erik nodded, still keeping his gaze averted.

"What will it change? Why are you afraid?"

He looked at her, his eyes blazing. "I am *not* afraid. I am resigned to what must be, even though it is not easy." He sighed. "Last time, you left me. This time, I will leave you, though not by my own choice."

"What?" Eileen was on her feet, but Erik raised a hand.

"All has gone wrong. There is nothing to be gained in fighting the changes that will be."

Eileen stood, her arms wrapped around herself. Her partner's words sent a chill through her, but she wanted to know the worst of it. "What changes lie in store for you? For us?"

Erik's lips tightened. "I will no longer lead the *Pyr*."

"But you have led them for centuries! I thought it was your birthright. . . ."

He interrupted her crisply, recounting a list of his failures. "I have been beguiled. I have revealed the existence of a *Pyr* I pledged to hide. The *Pyr* are scattered and revealed to humankind. It is only a matter of moments until we are hunted once again. I have failed, in every conceivable way, and if the *Pyr* are to continue, another must lead them into their future."

Eileen's heart was in her throat. "Don't you think you should ask them about that? Have a vote or something?"

Erik shook his head and looked out the window once more. "There won't be time. I saw myself walking among the dead. The only way that can occur is if I am one of them."

"No! You talked to Sigmund before, when I was pregnant. You told me. You said it must be part of your gift of foresight, maybe a new dimension of it."

He shook his head. "I think this is different."

Eileen took his arm then, terror making her heart pound. "What do you mean?"

He enfolded her hand within his, his expression rueful as he studied her fingers. "My gift of foresight has been compromised lately. I don't believe it would develop new strength when it seems to be in flight."

"But . . ."

"You will remember that I sent Sloane to Brandt, to warn him that I had erred."

"And Sloane didn't want to go, because he had sworn a blood oath to Brandt. What does that mean?"

"A blood oath is a promise, sealed with blood." Erik glanced up. "If one *Pyr* breaks the vow, the other has not just the right but the obligation to kill the oath breaker. It is a matter of honor."

"You sent Sloane to his death?"

Erik shook his head. "No. He and Brandt have old ties. They are cousins, and there is great fondness between them. Plus, Brandt needs the Apothecary's skill. I knew they would fight, and that Brandt would be ascendant, but he would not strike the killing blow. I did see this." He glanced at her, as if insulted that she could imagine he would willingly put one of the *Pyr* in danger. "I looked for it, before deciding to send Sloane."

Eileen waited, but Erik said no more.

"So, what's the problem?" she prompted.

"I swore the same blood oath to Brandt," Erik said. "He will have no such compunction against killing me. In fact, he will deem it just to avenge himself upon me for my part in sending Sloane."

"Where?"

"Wherever I am." He nodded to the world beyond the window. "He comes, even now. He is mere hours away."

"And you're just going to sit here and wait? Let's go!" Eileen hurried across the room, making a mental list of what she had to pack. "Let's hide. Let's take a trip. . . ."

"I cannot evade him, Eileen," Erik said with force. "It is his right. I will not stand in the way of justice."

"This is not justice!" Eileen cried, not caring who heard her. Zoë, incredibly, did not stir, which maybe said something about her exhaustion.

Erik shook his head. "It is the justice of our kind. I know no other." He regarded her, a slight smile curving his lips. "Don't you see? There is no evading the reckoning of darkfire. I cannot outrun it or hide from it. I had thought there was little risk. I am much older than Brandt. I am a better fighter, although he will have passion on his side."

"But?" Eileen said, folding her arms across her chest. She felt as if she had to do so to keep herself from exploding. She couldn't match Erik's calm demeanor, not in a thousand years.

Not if they were talking about Erik's death.

"The Sleeper awakens. That changes everything."

"Okay, what don't I know about the Sleeper?"

"There are a hundred old stories that have their toes in this one, Eileen. There's only one that matters." He turned a glittering look upon her, and she saw that he shimmered slightly around his perimeter. She heard the dragon in his challenge. "What do you know of sleeping heroes who awaken after centuries? What happens then?"

"Well, Rip van Winkle lost everything." Eileen frowned, rolling through all the stories she knew. "And Thomas of Erceldoune did the same thing, while beguiled in the realm of the faerie queen. Thomas the Rhymer they called him. Ditto for the lover of Jenny . . ."

"Men, Eileen," Erik interrupted with impatience. "Those are *men*. What of those who are more than men?"

"Kings," she whispered, raising her hands to her mouth in realization. What stories had Rafferty been talking about in the kitchen? "Arthur, the once and future king. He will awaken, when his realm has need of him or when the challenge is too great, and lead his people into a bright future, one of prosperity and goodness."

"Provoking change." Erik smiled, but there was no humor in his expression. "Just like darkfire. The Sleeper and the darkfire are hand in glove. Everything must change."

"No!" Eileen protested.

"Yes," Erik replied. "Who can stand in the way of change for the sake of good? How can I obstruct a change that will improve the situation for the earth and its treasures?"

"But . . ."

"But *nothing*! There will be another leader of the *Pyr*, and the only way that can occur is if I am no longer alive."

"There *has* to be another way," Eileen said, hating how he had made his peace with his fate. "You could just quit, cede the role to another. . . ."

Erik frowned. "Lorenzo said the *Pyr* would destroy one another, if there was no natural opponent for us. I see now that he was right. Brandt comes for me, and I no longer believe that I will triumph over him." He shrugged. "Or even that I should. Sigmund said there are three crystals, and I know nothing of them. He told me the third one must be found."

"But you could find it. . . ."

"I know nothing of this, Eileen. It is a test, and one that I fail in my ignorance."

"No! It doesn't have to be that way," Eileen argued, stepping toward him. Erik stopped her with a look.

His eyes narrowed, the first sign of his dismay. He was keeping her away, and she knew it. He didn't want to do this any more than she wanted him to.

But she knew Erik. He would follow tradition. He would do his duty. He would follow the ways of the *Pyr*.

Even if it killed him.

"I would like for you to remain here with Zoë," he said, his words coming thick with emotion. "Brandt is not malicious, but he is passionate, and he can forget himself in anger. The darkfire may exacerbate that tendency." He met her gaze, and she saw his regret. "Remain here under Rafferty's protection, Eileen, so that I do not have to fear for your survival."

Eileen could barely speak, her throat was so tight. "Won't he hunt us? Won't he hunt the Wyvern?"

A great sadness came into Erik's voice, and she saw the fullness of his disappointment in himself only then. His gaze fell on their sleeping child, and she knew she saw his tears. "I fear that Zoë is not the Wyvern," he said quietly. "She is just a little girl, exactly as you wished."

"But . . ."

"I have failed my kind in every way. Do not let it be said that I failed my mate and my child, as well." His voice broke, and the last word he uttered was no more than a croak. "Stay here. I will meet Brandt elsewhere so that you two are safe."

"I love you," Eileen said.

"And I love you." A tear slipped from Erik's eye then, and his voice dropped to a whisper. His torment nearly destroyed her. "But it is not enough, Eileen. I must go." He evaded her embrace, striding from the room.

Eileen heard Erik climb the stairs to the attic. When she heard the creak of the roof access open, her tears began to fall in earnest.

Eileen picked up her daughter and lay on the bed, rocking the sleeping toddler's warmth against herself. She was as stung by Erik's lack of belief in the power of love as by his decision to leave them behind.

But Eileen Grosvenor wasn't giving up that easily on Erik Sorensson. She wasn't at all convinced that the only way forward for the *Pyr* was for Erik to die. Even if he wasn't going to be leader, he could still survive. She would find a way. It had taken her long enough to find Erik that she wasn't going to lose him after just a couple of years together.

Love wasn't strong enough to fight darkfire?

Eileen would see about that.

On the Trail of the Truth

posted 12:23:10 05:00 EST on MelsNewsBlog

Sometimes stories come together immediately. Sometimes stories are exactly where you expect them to be. Other times, the trail is tangled and takes years to unravel. There are times when the truth is never known—or can never be proved. A long time ago, I started to follow a story that led me on a more twisted path than anyone could have expected. I had come to believe that this might be one of those stories that never fully emerge, but this week, I was proved wrong. Let me take you on its trail, right from the beginning.

This story started in Baghdad, in 2005. When I first arrived there to be embedded with the troops, I met a street urchin, an orphan named Daphne. I never knew her surname. Maybe she didn't know it, either. She was pretty and she was clever. She had a charm about her, but our whole crew was aware that she made her way by petty theft. It was hard to hold that against her—there was really no other way for those kids to survive. I liked Daphne, and I tried to give her a chance. I asked her for help with different stories, and when she came through— which wasn't every time—I rewarded her. I hoped she would learn that the world didn't have to be a place where every person fended alone for himself or herself.

The first gift I gave her was a bright red T-shirt, the one I'd been wearing the day we met. She'd obviously coveted it, so when she brought us advance news of a potential hit on the troops, I gave it to her. She was thrilled. Can you remember ever having such joy from a single T-shirt? These kids had nothing. . . .

One day, I asked her to find out more about a man we suspected of being an arms dealer. She was good at finding out things she shouldn't know, and I thought she might bring us a good clue. I never would have done it if I'd imagined that question would lead to her death. . . .

Melissa was excited. It was wonderful to see this story finally coming together. She decided to write it as a diary of her following Magnus's trail. She sent a message to the cameraman, Bill, who was now stationed in Asia, and he sent her a couple of jpegs of Daphne almost immediately.

Along with a greeting: *A warm welcome back to the land of the living.*

As always, Bill made Melissa smile. It felt good to be doing what she believed she was best at doing.

She was aware of Rafferty reading over her shoulder, of the glimmer of darkfire at her back. She felt safe in his library, in his company, by his side. She liked that he went through Magnus's book as she worked, compiling a list of the ways the entries might be cross-checked.

He even found an entry that appeared to refer to Jorge killing that man in the market in Baghdad. The timing was roughly right, and Jorge was to meet this man.

She not only had his name, but she recognized it. Interpol had a huge file on the dead man, who was in the same dirty business as Montmorency.

Melissa decided to give that incident its own post. As before, she queued them up to appear hourly and was gratified to see the first one gathering hits and links even as she wrote the subsequent ones.

On the Trail of the Truth—4

posted 12:23:10 08:00 EST on MelsNewsBlog

After the shock of seeing Daphne at that fund-raising function in DC last September, I hadn't caught another glimpse of her. I wasn't sure whether she was in town or not, much less still in the company of the man in question.

Until this note was delivered to me on December 19.

Melissa—If you're reading this, I'm dead, and we both know who is responsible. I'm trying to get the truth, just like you asked me to a long time ago. I refused you then, but not now.
Now I know too much.
If everything works as planned, I'll call you first and we can make a deal. If not, you'll get this note.
And then, it'll be up to you to make it right.

Daphne

There was a key with the note, one to a storage locker. I spent all day trying to find the locker that fit the key and finally did. In it was a packed suitcase. At the bottom of the bag was a diary. In the diary were documented the means of gaining the evidence I'd asked her for so long ago.

Remember that this was a girl who had survived by her wits. I wasn't positive she was telling the truth, and I knew better than to assume as much.

I went to the morgue. I thought actually that I'd be proved wrong. I asked whether they had any Jane Does.

There were two. I was welcome to have a look.

The first was a woman with a black eye, maybe sixty years old. The tip of her nose had been frostbitten, which made me wonder where and how she had died.

For a minute, I was relieved.

Then they showed me the second Jane Doe. It was Daphne. There was a bloody wound on her temple, and one side of her face was burned beyond recognition. I knew her all the same.

And she was wearing that red T-shirt, that one I'd given her. It had faded and it was a bit worn, but it was a message.

Even dead, Daphne had something to say to me.

I knew that I owed her better than this anonymous death. I knew that I owed her justice and dignity. I knew that I was in some way answerable for her demise. She had died trying to get the evidence against the suspected arms dealer that I wanted.

And she'd left me the information to finish the job.

I did something I've never done before. I broke the law. I used the security codes documented in Daphne's diary, and I entered the home of the man in question. I went to get the book that documented his deeds.

I did it for Daphne.

And she didn't let me down. Here's the book and here's what it has to say.

Melissa uploaded a trio of images—one of the book itself and two of the pages showing dates and times of meetings. She was in the midst of compiling another post explaining those meetings and names when a comment appeared on her blog in caps.

It was Doug, demanding that she call him.

Rafferty handed her the phone.

"But it has your name on the call display," Melissa protested, well aware of her promise to him.

"I have no issues with your producer knowing my name," Rafferty said easily. "I doubt he's in the habit of telling all he knows, and what is there to tell? That I'm your host here?"

Melissa smiled and took the phone. She called Doug's cell phone, and he answered immediately.

"Whose book is it?" he demanded by way of greeting.

"His name is Magnus Montmorency. . . ."

"And where is he now? In custody?"

"No. Possibly somewhere in England."

Doug swore. "Melissa, you're taking too much of a risk!"

Before he could launch into a tirade—and really, he couldn't begin to imagine how much of a danger Montmorency posed—Melissa interrupted him. "No, Doug,

I'm giving this story the attention it needs. And I'm not stupid. I can send the full album of the images of the book's contents to your e-mail account right now."

He hesitated for a moment. "Not even negotiating for a job in exchange?"

Melissa glanced at Rafferty, well aware that he was listening. She smiled at him, noting the intensity of his gaze. "Whatever will be, will be. What's most important to me is the truth, Doug."

And the whole truth was a thousand times stranger than Doug imagined. Melissa knew the story wouldn't be complete without mention of Montmorency's role as a *Slayer*, but she had promised not to mention the *Pyr*. Without a job, she had no commitment to the news team and wouldn't have a conflict of interest.

"All right." Doug gave her an e-mail address. "And you're in England, right? Can I reach you at this number?"

Rafferty handed Melissa his cell phone, its number displayed. She met his gaze and he nodded once; then she read the number to Doug as an alternate.

Then she sent him the album of images.

"Insurance," Rafferty said softly as the file loaded.

"Such as it is," Melissa agreed, and he took her hand in his.

She breathed a sigh of relief when the transmission was done.

The file had just been dispatched when they heard footsteps running on the stairs. Eileen charged into the library, her hair loose and her expression concerned. Her black skirt was rumpled and she looked as if she had been crying. She braced her hands on the doorframe and fixed a stern glance on Rafferty. "Okay, that's it. You have to tell me the story of the Sleeper and you have to tell me now. What's this about crystals?"

Rafferty straightened, caution in every line of his body. "Why?" Melissa heard the wariness in his tone.

"Erik thinks he has to die. He thinks he's going to fight Brandt and lose, and he thinks it's because the Sleeper is awakening." She exhaled shakily and spoke with ferocity. "He has to be wrong, but I need to know the story to figure it out."

Rafferty moved to her side. "Let me talk to him."

"He's gone," Eileen said, her tone savage. "Didn't you hear him leave?"

Rafferty looked startled. He glanced back at Melissa, and she knew that either her quest or her presence had distracted him. She stood up, not wanting him to blame himself for whatever happened. They needed to focus on the facts and on what they could do to help. "I don't understand. Who's Brandt and why would he kill Erik?"

Eileen sighed. "He's another *Pyr*, one who evidently Sloane and Erik promised to leave alone. They took a blood oath with him. . . ."

"I remember this," Rafferty said softly. "It was perhaps fifteen years ago."

"You know Brandt, too?" Eileen asked. "Do you know where he is? Can you talk to him?"

Rafferty shook his head and urged her toward a chair. "He is Sloane's cousin. A most passionate *Pyr*. Impetuous, and never more so than when his firestorm went awry. It was against Erik's inclination to leave him alone, but Sloane knew him best and felt that only solitude would allow Brandt to heal. He had a son to raise, as well."

"What happened to his mate?" Melissa asked.

Rafferty winced. "She spurned him, once she knew

the truth of what he was. It was a bitter parting. I have wondered often about the son." He looked careworn.

"But why would Brandt target Erik?" Melissa asked.

"Because Erik compelled Sloane to break his blood oath," Eileen said. "He sent Sloane to warn Brandt and is convinced that Brandt will take vengeance upon Erik." She frowned. "He had a vision of his own death. No, of himself walking among the dead."

Rafferty inhaled sharply.

"But why did Erik do that?" Melissa asked. "You guys are all about tradition and protocol. He must have guessed the repercussions."

"He thought he would win, at least until he had his vision," Rafferty guessed, turning to pace.

"He had to warn Brandt, because Lorenzo had persuaded Erik to reveal Brandt. Erik didn't know what Lorenzo would do with that information."

Rafferty glanced up. "Because Lorenzo has beguiled Erik."

Eileen nodded. "He sees that he has failed in every way. I've never seen him so defeatist."

Silence fell in the library, a silence abruptly broken by a wail from upstairs. "Mamamamamamama-maaaaaaaaaaaaaaaaaaaaaaa," Zoë cried.

"The stairs!" Eileen cried, and ran for her daughter.

It said something about her state of mind that she had left the toddler sleeping unsupervised. She returned a moment later, carrying the dark-haired girl, who smiled sunnily at them all.

Then Zoë extended her arms to Melissa in silent demand.

Melissa hesitated. She didn't hold children as a rule. She didn't need the reminder of what she'd never have.

Her brother and his wife respected that. Melissa did better with older children, ones she could talk to.

"She won't bite," Eileen said with a smile. "At least she doesn't very often."

Well aware of Rafferty's watchful gaze, Melissa accepted the weight of the toddler. She took a deep breath, reminding herself that this wasn't a gesture fraught with meaning. Rafferty knew of her medical history and still hadn't stepped away from her. She was simply holding a child. No more than that.

She could do this.

Zoë nestled against Melissa immediately, clearly right where she wanted to be. She smelled of baby shampoo and baby powder, soft clean smells, and she was warm. She took a fascination with Melissa's earrings, reaching up to poke one with a chubby finger. "Pretty," she pronounced, then smiled. Her eyes shone.

And something thawed within Melissa. She held Eileen's child, the product of a firestorm, and let herself *feel* the reactions she'd locked safely away. She hadn't allowed herself to weep for what she had lost. She had been so focused on remaining strong, on becoming better, on surviving and getting back into the rhythm of life, that she had never mourned her loss.

Maybe she'd never thought she'd miss it.

But now, now she stood with a child in her arms, and she wished with all her heart that she could have been the one to give Rafferty the child he so desired.

She wished she could be the destined mate he wanted her to be.

Instead of the human who was wreaking havoc in his world.

A tear slipped from her lashes, and Zoë sobered as

she watched. Melissa would have wiped it away, but her arms were full of the toddler she didn't want to drop.

It was Rafferty who came to her side and eased that tear away with his thumb. It was Rafferty who kissed her temple and slid his arm around her shoulders. It was Rafferty who brought those blue flames to leap and dance against her skin. Zoë laughed with delight, trying to catch the darkfire with her fingers.

Melissa glanced up and lost herself in Rafferty's eyes. His gaze locked on her, and she could see the rim of gold in the deep chocolate of his eyes.

"Let me tell you a story," he said softly, his voice low and rich, and Melissa was utterly seduced.

Erik soared into the sky, Brandt's scent on the wind drawing him directly to his opponent. He was high above the clouds when he saw the brilliant orange of the younger *Pyr*. Brandt was just as vividly hued as Erik recalled. All the shades of orange and yellow were echoed in Brandt's scales, as if he had stepped right out of the fire. Even the sunlight seemed to caress his scales in admiration.

It was a good indication of Brandt's nature, for he was fiery, passionate, and quick to anger. He could be vengeful and hold a grudge for longer than might be expected.

That was the root of the dissent between the two of them.

Erik hovered and waited, seeing no point to rush to his demise. He gathered his strength, intent upon giving Brandt a good fight.

Sloane flew behind Brandt, his scales the color of tourmaline. He shaded from green to purple and back again over his length, his scales accented with gold. Erik could sense the Apothecary's disapproval, even from a distance, and guessed that Sloane had argued with his cousin over this choice.

Brandt roared as he came closer, exhaling a plume of dragonfire in Erik's direction. *"You have broken your word to me again!"* he said in old-speak. *"There will not be a third time."*

"I have done what had to be done, for your own welfare," Erik retorted, convinced of his own choice.

"And how exactly is that served by fighting?" Sloane demanded, although the pair of adversaries ignored him. They locked talons, the force of their collision sending them rolling through the sky, and the fight began in earnest.

Erik Sorensson fought with all his might. He was determined that he would not leave this world quietly.

If he left it at all.

Chapter 15

Rafferty looked at his destined mate, respected her resilience, humor, and curiosity, and believed that all could come right. He felt that she had locked away her emotions in order to deal with her illness and recovery, and in order to not be drawn down by the weight of betrayal. But she was a giving person, one filled with compassion, and he sensed the importance of that first tear.

She was healing, under the effect of the darkfire. He made the effort to meet her halfway. He chose the firestorm over the safety of the Sleeper.

It was clear that Melissa was someone who craved information. It was also apparent that no one could become fond of another in ignorance—she had to know what and who he was, just as he had to learn about her.

He liked her conviction that they could defeat Magnus together. That dovetailed perfectly with his own notion that a firestorm made a new whole of two halves. Plus, Melissa had promised to keep her silence about the *Pyr*. Rafferty believed her—and he believed that pledge to be indicative of her desire to see Magnus destroyed.

They had a goal in common, and she was prepared to take risks. Rafferty would figure out some way for Melissa to have her heart's desire, as well. It was only fair.

But first things first.

"Let me tell you a story," he said, leaning closer. The darkfire's flames leapt and danced as the distance between them was diminished. "Once upon a time, there was a young *Pyr* who had been taught all he needed to know by his grandfather," he said. "And that young *Pyr*, like so many young men, left the home he had known to seek his fortune."

"Would we know this *Pyr*?" Eileen asked.

Rafferty smiled. "You might. He traveled steadily south, crossing large bodies of water and scaling mountains. Every experience was an adventure to him, and he savored the sights and sounds of the world. Over time, though, he realized that he was seeking something, something he hadn't realized he wanted to find. He was seeking more of his and his grandfather's kind, more *Pyr*, although he didn't recognize as much until he found one. The *Pyr* stranger appeared to be a successful merchant, perhaps in his forties, but the young *Pyr* knew better. He was excited and fascinated by his discovery."

"How did he know?" Melissa asked. "How do you recognize one another?"

"By scent," Rafferty said. "He knew the stranger was of his own kind by his scent, familiar and yet exotic. Our senses are sharper than human senses: we can recognize not only our own kind by scent but often can identify specific individuals that way."

"Okay." Melissa reached for her book and made a note."

"But it cuts both ways," Rafferty continued. "The

strange: recognized the young *Pyr* as what he was in the same way, and befriended him. He took him into his household, taught him his business, helped him to gain financial success. They became great friends and allies and partners. They even shared hoard."

"A very close bond," Eileen murmured.

Rafferty nodded. "That stranger's name was Magnus Montmorency."

"When was this?" Melissa asked. "And where?"

He recognized that she needed the facts, the root of the story to make it real. "It was in Venice. Magnus traded in oil and wine. It would have been about a thousand years ago."

"So, he had already made the Elixir?" Eileen said.

"Yes, but I knew nothing of it. He traveled frequently, often leaving me in charge of his home and business. He confessed to distrusting his brother, and I took him at his word. I was young, and too ready to believe. He was good to me, and it never occurred to me that he might have his own agenda. I had never known anyone who was deceitful. It also never occurred to me that his wealth wasn't commensurate with his official business. It turned out that Magnus also traded in mercenaries, slaves, and information."

"Started that arms trader stuff early," Melissa murmured. "No wonder he's so good at it."

"More than that," Rafferty said. "I learned inadvertently during one of his absences that he did a brisk trade in medicinal supplies." Eileen caught her breath, and Rafferty knew she anticipated his next words. "A customer came into the shop asking after his order for ground dragon hide."

"But it wasn't . . . ," Melissa began to protest.

"It *was*." Rafferty was firm. "Magnus brought it with him on his return. I knew from the scent in the vial that it was precisely what the customer had requested."

"So, it was Magnus who started that," Eileen said, her disapproval clear.

"I asked him about it, one night when he had been drinking of the wine stock," Rafferty admitted. "He was quite proud of himself, and informed me that it was not only a profitable trade in itself but an excellent way to be rid of one's enemies. That Magnus had enough enemies to have built a business in their body parts told me there was much I did not know about him."

"He was a *Slayer*, though, right?" Melissa asked.

"No," Rafferty said. "The distinction was not clear at that point. It came later when those who turned against the Great Wyvern found their blood black instead of red."

"But there was always evil within the *Pyr*," Eileen supplied. "As there is in all kinds." Melissa nodded in agreement.

"And there appears to have been a gradual progression," Rafferty said. "Although Magnus's blood did not run black at that time, and he was not technically a *Slayer*, he had lived for centuries and had never had a firestorm. He was undeniably self-motivated, and his brother, Maximilian, repeatedly warned him that his choices were the reason he was without a firestorm. His brother wanted Magnus to change."

"Montmorency will never change," Melissa said, her tone grim.

"But he has a charm about him. On dark nights, in solitude, I feared for my own future. What if Magnus decided I knew too much? Or that he took a dislike to me, like the one he had to his own brother—a *Pyr* I found quite pleasant company and above any criticism. In daylight, though, I was well aware of the benefits of my situation and dismissed my fears. I reasoned that it was the brother who was deceptive—neither of them had had a firestorm, after all, despite their ages, and both were charming when they so chose."

"I'll guess that you learned your mistake," Melissa said.

Rafferty smiled at her perceptiveness. "Magnus's true nature was revealed when his brother had his firestorm. Both Magnus and I felt the firestorm, of course, for it was potent and close at hand. His brother was exultant at his good fortune, and apparently the woman was amenable to his attentions. He came to the shop to share his good news. Magnus said Maximilian had come to gloat, and he brooded that night, then declared he had to go to Spain." Rafferty paused. "I never saw Maximilian again. But a fortnight after his visit, Magnus returned early from Spain with a fresh vial of dragon bone powder."

"It wasn't," Melissa protested.

Rafferty nodded. "It *was*. I smelled Maximilian's scent within it."

The women looked as sickened by this as Rafferty felt.

"Did he know that you guessed its source?" Melissa asked.

Rafferty shook his head. "No. He was jubilant and in a celebratory mood. I pretended to drink with him, to welcome him home. Then, when he was besotted, I sought Maximilian's mate."

"Did you find her?" Eileen asked, leaning forward.

Rafferty nodded and saw Melissa's relief. Was it

his imagination that the darkfire flames were leaping higher? He was keenly aware of the charms of his mate, sitting so close beside him, and recalling Maximilian's demise made him feel fiercely protective of Melissa.

"How did you find her?" Melissa asked.

"I went to Maximilian's home, but there was no trail to follow. Much had been destroyed, burned, and broken. But I recalled that he had a faithful manservant. Magnus had never been much interested in servants, but I had spoken several times to this man—while the brothers were cloistered with their business. It took me days to find him, for his scent had been well disguised, but when I found him and persuaded him of my goodwill, he took me to her."

Rafferty frowned. "She had just realized that she was pregnant and was fighting her family's conclusion that her lover had abandoned her," he said. "I told her the truth and vowed to defend her. She was devastated by the loss of Maximilian, and I realized that she had loved him truly. It was the first time I had witnessed the feelings of any mate, and I wondered then what might have happened if Maximilian had survived."

"Your grandmother must have loved your grandfather," Melissa pointed out.

Rafferty smiled, appreciating her observation. "Indeed. You are right." He took her free hand in his, savoring the feminine softness of her skin, thinking of challenging the firestorm's flames once again.

Then he continued. "At any rate, her safety had to be assured. I hid her in a secure location while I made my plans, and the manservant kept vigil over her. I asked Magnus once about his brother and the firestorm, as if I had no idea what had happened, and he said his brother had abandoned his mate. He said she was incapable of conceiving a son, that the firestorm was a lie, and that his brother had been so distraught that he had left the city. I knew then that Maximilian's last act had been to protect his lover and unborn son by refusing to reveal her name or location."

"And you assumed that role," Melissa said, her approval clear.

"I also knew Magnus had a hoard in England and that it had been left undefended for centuries. He had accumulated it during the Roman domination of London and had been forced to abandon it. He was intent upon reclaiming what he declared was his own, but he had as yet not managed to do so. After several months, I commented that I wanted to visit my grandfather, and I offered to fetch it for him. Magnus, complacent in what he perceived to be a complete victory over his brother, agreed."

"And you took the mate with you," Eileen guessed.

"I did. And I entrusted her to my grandfather's care, in his remote cave in Wales. He was delighted by the company, for she was a new audience for all his tales. She was less happy, for she mourned the loss of Maximilian, but she was safe there, especially with Maximilian's manservant. I returned to Venice, knowing that Magnus would be counting the days, and took part of his English hoard to him."

"Was he fooled?" Melissa asked.

"Not entirely. He suspected something, although he didn't know what. He had never asked after the identity of Maximilian's mate, and without the heat of the firestorm, he couldn't find her. Perhaps deception has a scent to one who traffics in it so regularly, for by the time I returned, he was certain I had betrayed him. He counted the silver from the English hoard obsessively, accusing me of taking some for myself. He became increasingly volatile, and I truly feared for my life."

"Why didn't you leave?" Eileen demanded.

"I didn't want him to find the mate and the child."

"He had to stay undercover until the story was in the can," Melissa said.

Rafferty nodded. "I wanted her pregnancy to proceed normally, and I feared that if I returned to Wales, he would follow me and destroy them both, just as he had destroyed his brother. I didn't count upon our refined senses."

"What do you mean?" Melissa asked.

"We feel when another of our kind is born, like hearing a distant cry in the night. We don't smell the child or hear it, per se, but we are aware of its arrival. I heard Maximilian's son in the same instant that Magnus did. He came to me in a rage, in dragon form. He said he would have my hide for my deception, and we fought fiercely that night. Only when he was wounded and fallen, only when I thought him dead, did I dare to go to her."

"He tricked you," Eileen guessed.

Rafferty nodded. "He was fast on my tail, so much more wily than I could ever have been."

Melissa put her hand on his arm. "It's liars who know instinctively how to deceive. It's a learned skill for the rest of us." She smiled at him, but Rafferty still dreaded telling the rest of the story. He was ashamed of his own role in it.

"Of course, I led him to my grandfather's cave, unwittingly, but still I did it. My grandfather sat by his peat fire, breathing smoke rings into the night. The woman had died, her corpse was still there, and she looked more at rest than she had when I had met her earlier."

"And the child?" Eileen asked.

"There was a dead baby in her arms. Magnus arrived and slaughtered the manservant 'for his deception.' I was horrified that my grandfather acted as if he were more ancient than he was; that he offered the dead child to Magnus, as if that old dragon had come to honorably claim his kin. I protested, but my grandfather put me in my place."

Melissa watched Rafferty with obvious horror, but he continued.

"Pwyll spoke more harshly to me than ever he had, and Magnus, Magnus was sated by the offering. He was even magnanimous, reminding me only of my inability to deceive him as his price from me. He surrendered me to my grandfather for discipline, and they acted like old allies. Magnus then incinerated the child and claimed the ashes, abandoned the woman there, and returned to Venice." Rafferty fell silent, remembering the darkness of that night and his own disappointment at the time.

"But I don't understand," Melissa said. "What does this have to do with the Sleeper?"

"The Sleeper is Maximilian's child," Rafferty said.

Melissa frowned. "But he died."

Rafferty shook his head. "It was not Maximilian's child who died that night. It was another human child, one my grandfather substituted for Maximilian's son. Marcus had already been hidden away by the time Magnus and I arrived."

*   *   *

"But how did the child die?" Melissa asked, still confused.

Rafferty drummed his fingers on the table, and she saw that this story was difficult for him to tell. "Pwyll had killed it. He had anticipated Magnus's arrival and intent. He explained that he would have preferred to have found a dead child, but it had to have the right scent of death about it. Time and location had limited his choices. We argued about his choice. He insisted it had been for the greater good, the defense of the *Pyr* and Maximilian's son, but I was outraged by his deed."

Melissa was outraged, too. She made notes, appalled by what had occurred. Were humans merely useful to the *Pyr*?

"What happened to Maximilian's son?" Eileen asked.

"My grandfather was the last Cantor of our kind. He could spin a spell with his song. He enchanted the child and disguised him from Magnus."

"He could even hide his scent?" Eileen asked.

"He could," Rafferty said. "He could enchant anything. He could turn anything to his will. His song was so powerful." He sighed. "He called it the mystery of the crystals."

"Crystals again," Eileen said.

"Did he teach you how to do that?" Melissa asked, not entirely certain she wanted to know the answer. "Did he teach you the mystery?"

Rafferty met her gaze, and she saw his resolve. "I refused to learn. I refused to have any part in his chant. He offered to mentor me again and again, but I have never had a taste for deception."

"Then I'm guessing you don't know where the third crystal is, either," Eileen said.

Rafferty shook his head. "Nor should I know about this sorcery! Things must proceed as they must, not be tricked into serving the will of another. It is not right to put one's own desires above all else."

Eileen pursed her lips. "There is the question of the greater good."

"The greater good?" Rafferty said, his voice rising in challenge. "How was that choice good for the human child? Who is to say which life was more important? Who among us should decide who lives and who dies?"

"Maybe Pwyll knew," Eileen suggested. "Erik has foresight."

"Maybe Pwyll chose *Pyr* over human, independent of the cost," Rafferty said with disgust. "Maybe Pwyll saw himself as an arbiter. I refused to learn his powers and take that legacy."

"Amen," Melissa said under her breath.

"But you could use the power of the Cantor for good," Eileen argued.

Rafferty shook his head. "I fear it is seductive to turn others to one's will. I fear that Pwyll began in goodness, but that the power was heady and turned him to his own intent."

Melissa made a note. There was something to be said for that perspective.

Rafferty sighed. "That night, I saw only wickedness in his choice and his powers. I even accused him of killing the mate for the sake of convenience. He was enraged by the suggestion, and we fought for the first and last time. It was vicious, though we battled only with words."

He picked up the crystal and turned it in his fingers. His voice dropped, as if he were speaking to himself. "He begged me to be the guardian of the Sleeper, to become heir of his crystals, but I was too angry to do anything he asked of me. I refused him. I refused his council. I refused his knowledge. I refused even this stone. He vowed to mentor another, but I didn't care about his threats. I left and I never saw him again."

Eileen grimaced. "So the knowledge of the Cantor was lost forever."

"I have principles," Rafferty said, biting out the words. "And I am not ashamed of them."

Melissa frowned at her notes. "But wait a minute. Isn't that the crystal linked to the Sleeper?" Rafferty nodded, and Melissa noted that its light was more brilliantly blue. Zoë was watching it so avidly that she didn't seem to blink. "If you refused to take it, then how did you get it?"

"He was the Cantor," Rafferty said, tears rising in his eyes. "I felt him die. I heard his last song, a hundred years later. It haunted me in his attempt to draw me back to his side, to see us reconciled. I heard his despair that his knowledge would be lost."

"You didn't go to him," Melissa guessed, her words soft.

Rafferty shook his head. "Not even at the end."

She turned their hands so that her fingers held his, then gave his hand a squeeze.

"I refused to go. I was still young and proud and angry." He paused and swallowed. "At least I was angry until I heard the last note of the song fade to nothing, until there was no more. I knew he was gone from this world. I was certain of it when I found this crystal in my hoard, as surely as if he had placed it there with his own hand."

"He did it with his song," Eileen murmured.

Rafferty nodded, looking sick. "I could have met him halfway. I could have consoled him at the last, not left him in solitude, without learning his talent. But I didn't, and now the rift between us will never be healed."

His words hung in the library for a long moment, filled with his regret.

"What a touching story," Montmorency drawled at sudden proximity. "Or is it just a rationalization for a failure?"

The three gasped and stood up as one, turning in place as they surveyed the room. Melissa held the toddler close, her heart pounding in fear. Rafferty shimmered blue around his perimeter, his gaze sharp as he sought the intruder.

Where was Montmorency? What would he do? He was injured, so Melissa guessed he would make a daring play.

Zoë pointed one finger at the ceiling. "Orge," she said matter-of-factly.

But the salamander perched on the light fixture was jade green, not orange. Its eyes glinted like beads and its tongue flicked, the sway of its tail setting the pendulum light to swinging.

"So many choices," Magnus murmured. "The mate, the new Wyvern, or that old blood duel. How shall I choose?"

"The duel," Rafferty said flatly. "Finish what has begun." He put himself between Melissa and the salamander, and Melissa felt as if sparks were flying from his flesh. She put her free hand on his shoulder, making the darkfire crackle and leap.

Magnus sighed with satisfaction. "How kind you are to feed my strength." And he laughed.

Melissa retreated, holding Zoë with both hands and leaving a space between herself and Rafferty. Eileen came to her side. Rafferty snatched for the salamander, but it disappeared suddenly.

"Where did he go?" Melissa asked.

"There!" Eileen cried just as Montmorency manifested right in front of Rafferty. The jade salamander latched on to Rafferty's throat and bit deeply.

Right in the jugular.

Rafferty cried out in pain as red blood seeped from the wound. He shifted shape in a heartbeat, filling the library with his powerful presence, and roared. He slashed at the salamander, his talons gleaming against the carpets. For an instant, he held Montmorency in his grip. He began to squeeze, and the green salamander disappeared again. The blood flowed more vigorously from Rafferty's throat, brilliant red against the opal splendor of his scales, as he scanned the room.

"You're hurt!" Melissa cried, and stepped toward him.

"Oh no, darling," Montmorency murmured in her ear. The salamander appeared on her shoulder, his tail sliding back and forth with apparent glee. "You're coming with me."

"No!" Melissa tried to brush off the salamander, but it dug its nails into her flesh. She cried out in pain, shoving at it in desperation and revulsion. Eileen snatched Zoë from Melissa's arms and the toddler screamed. Rafferty roared and lunged toward Melissa, his teeth bared and his eyes flashing.

This time, when Montmorency disappeared, Melissa disappeared with him. She was suddenly surrounded by swirling mist, caught in a kind of limbo.

"Bye-bye," Zoë said from some distant point, then started to cry.

"Something of mine for something of yours," Montmorency taunted Rafferty. "Tell me the location of the Sleeper and I'll return your mate. Seems a fair trade, don't you think?"

"You can't ask him to betray the Sleeper!" Melissa protested. She feared that Rafferty would pay the ransom and she'd still be sacrificed. There was nothing to be gained in negotiating with mercenaries like Montmorency, but she feared Rafferty might have too much faith.

"No? I'm feeling rather persuasive." Montmorency laughed. "And if there is some collateral damage, well, justice may be served."

The mists swirled whiter, abruptly clearing to reveal a storage room made of concrete blocks. It had a steel door, which was clearly secured. There was no window and no other opening, and the floor was fitted stones. Melissa could tell by the damp smell that she was trapped somewhere in the earth, and she sensed weight over them. There were wooden boxes stacked in the corner and several coils of jute rope. It looked like a forgotten space.

She guessed that no one would answer her pounding on the door, but she moved to try, anyway.

Rafferty was shaken.

One instant, Magnus had appeared. The next he was

gone, Melissa with him. Eileen made a small noise and clutched Zoë close as the toddler cried.

Rafferty knew immediately what he had to do. His first responsibility was to his mate, independent of his injuries. It was the firestorm, after all, that had put her in peril.

He had to follow Magnus, wherever his foe might go.

He would have happily traded the Sleeper's location for Melissa's safety, but he knew Magnus wasn't trustworthy. He had to save Melissa himself first, then destroy Magnus, once and for all.

It was the only way.

There was no trail to follow from his library, in contrast to the incident at Melissa's home. Magnus had simply vanished, and Melissa with him. The only way to pursue his enemy was to use Magnus's own technique. Rafferty had to learn to spontaneously manifest in other locations, under his own power.

And he had to master it immediately.

He could only hope that Melissa had been right; that the ability had been known in the past by those who had not drunk the Elixir. It had been long believed to be one of the feats in the arsenal of the Wyvern alone, but even Sophie hadn't consistently been able to perform it. Rafferty chose to believe it was a talent lost.

He chose to believe that his grandfather had done it.

Rafferty stretched out his hand, seeing the faint flicker of those blue flames erupting from his fingertips. He focused on them, concentrating on Melissa and recalling her many charms. His desire grew and the flames burned brighter, their roots turning green as they licked at the air.

Could the darkfire guide him to his mate? The flame slid around the ring that he always wore. The white in the ring seemed to glow in the darkfire's light, taking on a blue pearlescence.

Rafferty bent his attention on the ring, concentrating upon it, thinking of Melissa; to his amazement, it seemed to swirl on his hand. He recalled that Sophie and Nikolas had died together, united in their purpose to destroy Magnus's hidden academy.

He had already chosen to work with Melissa to destroy Magnus. Now he would risk everything to see the deed done.

Rafferty could feel the ring moving, sliding around his finger. He could feel the blue flame of the darkfire winding beneath it, making the skin on his finger prickle.

He heard Magnus begin to sing the song of the earth and feared the worst. Hearing the earth reply in kind, he knew he didn't dare add his voice to the song.

Humans would be injured in a busy city like this one. He'd made that mistake before, in DC, acting on the darkfire's impulse. He would not make it again.

He would simply move through space, to his mate's side.

The ring spun, burning his hand, the white and the black blending together in a blurred spiral. Rafferty recalled his last sight of Sophie and Nikolas, and he saw the darkfire flames take the same insistent beat as had echoed through Magnus's hidden academy in that same moment.

The ring pulsed, but it pulsed with greenish blue light now.

Darkfire.

Rafferty sang a song he had heard his grandfather hum. Eileen murmured something, but he was focused. The blue light of the darkfire radiated so brightly from the ring that he had to narrow his eyes.

But Rafferty didn't look away from the ring. He dared not break the spell now, not when he didn't fully understand what had awakened it.

He concentrated and he yearned and he thought about what Magnus could do. He thought of his grandfather, of Pwyll's ability as the Cantor, and wished he had learned more when he'd had such a teacher available.

He dared to believe Melissa's suggestion that such power could have been used for good.

He recalled his grandfather's cadence, his posture, and his tone. He remembered how Pwyll's voice had risen and fallen when he told his stories. He remembered how romantic Pwyll had been, how idealistic and powerful. Rafferty dared to miss the man he had loved so well.

A tear slid from his eye at his own folly.

The ring responded. He felt his skin prickle; he felt the shimmer of the change dancing through his body. It wasn't the usual change, though; it wasn't the shift to dragon form. He felt on the cusp of something unfamiliar; something terrifying.

All Rafferty could see was pulsing blue-green light, and the spinning ring at the middle of it all.

He didn't care about the details. He had to get to Melissa.

He had to reach her immediately.

In the very moment Rafferty believed he could spontaneously manifest beside Melissa—that it was a reality, not a possibility—he felt the air move abruptly around him.

He also felt a nausea so profound that he closed his eyes and fell to his knees.

Had Rafferty done it?

Or had Magnus summoned him again?

Chapter 16

Before Melissa reached the door, a flash of green appeared on the floor.

Montmorency! Melissa moved to stamp on his tail and managed to catch the end of it under her foot. Montmorency wriggled and the tail broke, squishing beneath her heel even as he scampered away. Melissa went after him.

"Bitch!" he hissed, his small bright eyes filled with malice. "You think you can destroy me? Let's see which of us survives this day."

Melissa was willing to take the dare, but he slipped through one of the cracks in the floor. She could see the beady shine of his eyes in the shadows.

She wasn't going to let him see her sweat.

"So, you're afraid of me now," she taunted. "A powerful dragon shape shifter and an international arms dealer, but you're hiding from *me*."

The salamander hissed; then Montmorency appeared on the other side of the chamber. He was holding his gut with one arm and looked pale; he was also favoring one leg. His eyes, though, shone with anger. "You, mere human. You think you can destroy me, but I will finish you instead."

"Looks like Rafferty's winning," Melissa observed.

Montmorency scoffed. "Let me tell you something. Once upon a time, there was a young *Pyr* who traveled south from his homeland in search of his fortune and adventure. He was so stupid that he didn't know that he had left the greatest opportunity of all behind him in Wales. He was too stupid to recognize that he didn't have to go anywhere to learn everything he could possibly want to know."

Melissa folded her arms across her chest. "Rafferty isn't stupid."

Montmorency laughed. "Well, then it's a special kind of intellect that had him decline to learn the ancient wisdom of the Cantor. Twice. Any individual with a passing intelligence would have leapt at the opportunity to learn how to control everything and everyone with a spell, never mind the legacy of those crystals. I certainly aspired to learn the Cantor's skill."

"But you didn't."

"Pwyll would never teach me. He was determined to teach only those of his blood lineage, but that was an excuse. He was snotty about mentoring others, always judging character first, always finding everyone wanting. But when I sensed the grandson of Pwyll heading south, I ensured that I crossed his path. Several times. I made it look like an accident that we met. I let him befriend me."

"You intended to use him."

Montmorency grimaced. "Except that he knew nothing! Do you know how many chances I have had to destroy Rafferty Powell, yet have chosen not to do so? Do you know how many opportunities I have given him to come into his grandfather's powers, to show some glimmer of those capabilities?"

"So you could steal them."

Montmorency shrugged. "Such skill might as well be wielded by someone who intends to use it. I knew that Pwyll wouldn't want his knowledge simply to fade into obscurity. I knew he had to leave a legacy somehow for Rafferty. And he did." He leaned closer, his manner intent. "Consider now that the Sleeper stirs. Bewitched by the Cantor, my own nephew has slumbered for a thousand years. I'll bet he doesn't look his age." Montmorency's voice dropped to a hiss. "That's awfully close to immortality, isn't it?"

Melissa backed away. "It's not quite the same. More like a coma, from the sound of it."

"I'm not in a position to be overly picky," Montmorency said easily. "I'll bet he learned something from Pwyll, coming from such superior genetic stock as he does. And now the legacy of those crystals is more or less in the family."

"Not the way I see it."

Montmorency scoffed. "Imagine what I could do with a thousand-year extension? I might be able to brew a new source of the Dragon's Blood Elixir. I might be able to find a substitute." Montmorency smiled. "I might be able to turn the Cantor's spell to my own use, if I could find the Sleeper in time."

"I don't know where he is."

Montmorency laughed. "Oh, I know that. You are useless, but irritating. You have revealed me and ensured that I am exiled from my principal lair."

"Then why are you telling me all of this?"

"So you'll know how the story ends, of course. Seeing that you won't be around to witness it yourself." Montmorency smiled, shimmered, and caught his breath. Then he became a large jade green dragon, one that nearly filled the space. "The only unfortunate part is that I don't have the time to savor your death, to make you truly pay for your transgressions. Perhaps the fire will be punishment enough."

Without delay, he began to breathe fire. He filled the small room with orange flames, flames that burned hot and vivid. Melissa's sleeve and the hem of her jeans caught fire, and she could feel her skin beginning to singe.

Montmorency laughed, which only made the fire burn brighter. The wooden crates ignited and so did the rope, the room filling with dark, oily smoke. Melissa coughed and pounded on the door; then she ran her hands over the walls, seeking a point of weakness.

She didn't find one. Desperation rose within her, even as Montmorency disappeared abruptly from view. She spun, alone and surrounded by hungry flames. She heard him laugh as he abandoned her to her fate.

Montmorency's voice rose in a song that Melissa didn't know. Seeming to have no words, it was more like a chant, but was oddly rousing. It made her heart pound faster, her pulse matching the rhythm of the chant.

What did it mean?

Melissa wasn't the only one stirred by Montmorency's song. The earth vibrated and shifted underfoot, matching its tremors to a persistent yet unfamiliar chant. Even as she stared at the ground, she felt it shift and vibrate. She remembered Rafferty's claim that he had created an earthquake in DC and eyed the trembling stone ceiling over her head.

She'd be buried alive!

It had only been two nights since she'd reasoned that she had nothing left to sacrifice. In this moment, though, it was clear to Melissa that she had a great deal to lose.

Rafferty took a deep breath and opened his eyes.

In the exact same moment, he heard Melissa's voice.

"Rafferty!" she said with astonishment. Her fingertips landed on his shoulder, a flash of darkfire accompanying her touch. The heat of the firestorm slid through Rafferty, reassuring and arousing him all at once.

And there was no sign of Magnus. He'd done it!

Rafferty's heart leapt with joy, a joy he saw echoed in Melissa's smile. He stood up, catching her close, restoring his strength with the firestorm's heat even as he scanned their prison. It was thick with smoke, and the earth was shifting beneath them.

He heard Magnus's old-speak at a distance, and the words made his heart clench.

"*Find the Sleeper*," Magnus declared, "*and I'll deliver on our deal.*"

Then he heard Jorge's assent.

So, they were still allied and still alive.

"You did it," Melissa said, smiling back at him.

No, they'd done it together. Rafferty's heart glowed that Melissa had shown him the other side of the story he knew so well and had helped him to find a solution.

All the same, he wasn't entirely confident that he could move through space again so soon after the first time. He felt weakened by the exercise and didn't want to risk Melissa to his own inexperience.

They would escape this prison the old-fashioned way.

"Let's get out of here," he said, coaxing her to one side of the room. Rafferty shifted shape, nearly filling the small chamber with his dragon form. He bellowed and thrashed at the steel door, then struck it with his tail. Magnus's song grew in volume, and pieces of stone began to fall from the ceiling.

"Hurry!" Melissa said.

The door bent from the hinges, offering a gap that he could grasp. Rafferty drove his talons into the space and tore away the door, discarding it on the floor of the chamber.

"You did it!" she said, peering past him into the space beyond. She was so fearless that he smiled in admiration.

"You have to kill him and finish the duel," Melissa said with resolve. "No negotiation and no ransom."

Rafferty wasn't surprised that their thoughts were as one.

She frowned at him. "And you're still bleeding." She touched the wound on his throat. Blue darkfire danced from her fingertips, slid across his skin, cauterized the cut.

They truly were a potent pair.

No sooner had Rafferty had the realization that it was his mate who had brought him the strength to recover the past, no sooner had his heart filled with gratitude, than he felt something slip. He knew what it was even before he looked down at his chest.

He'd lost a scale. It fell into the dust on the floor, glimmering like a gem lost in ashes. He knew the import of that.

He'd fallen in love with his mate.

But their union was far from secure, and the Smith

had chosen not to come to Rafferty's firestorm. He'd have to defend his mate with his armor flawed. He'd have to kill Magnus, despite his vulnerability.

He shifted shape, his victorious mood shattered. He bent and picked up the large opalescent scale, knowing he couldn't abandon the path of the firestorm and the trust it required.

"What's that?" Melissa asked.

Rafferty handed her the scale. "Something I would ask you to keep for me."

Melissa's eyes widened, and he thought she realized what the scale was as soon as she held it in her hands. She turned it over and over, studying it. "Won't you need it put back?" she asked.

"Yes. But the time has not yet come."

Melissa glanced away. "But this means that part of you isn't protected."

Rafferty nodded in agreement but didn't have time to elaborate. The earth rumbled again, responding to Magnus's song, and he feared for Melissa's safety. "Let's get to the surface again."

He had a sense of foreboding, but he refused to indulge it. He wouldn't consider that he had too many obligations and could be in only one place at a time.

He chose instead to trust that the way would become clear.

And it did.

Once they were out of the chamber, Melissa realized they were in a storage space. It smelled cold and musty, and she couldn't see much. She held on to Rafferty's hand, letting him lead her onward.

"Aha!" he murmured, and she guessed that he recognized either the space or its scent. He moved more quickly then, which suited her just fine.

The earth rumbled underfoot, and stone was falling all around them. The blue flames of the darkfire danced between them, illuminating cut stone walls with square blocks, making the space look eerie.

Melissa realized belatedly that it *was* eerie. The blocks were actually hinged doorways, and each one bore both a name and a date.

They were in a mausoleum.

"It's beneath Highgate," Rafferty said, as if that was supposed to mean something to Melissa. "A lower chamber, no longer in use or safely accessible to visitors. I remember when it was built." Melissa just hung on to him and tried to ignore the moldy smell.

He led her to a metal staircase that climbed in a spiral. It looked rusted and entirely unreliable. It was also ornate, rich with Victorian filigree. Melissa assumed that the dead descended to this space by some other means. Rafferty leapt up the stairs, clearly convinced of where it headed.

Melissa hesitated, seeing only darkness above, then followed Rafferty's lead. She hoped it wasn't far to the top. He halted ahead of her suddenly, then grunted as he shoved against a trapdoor overhead. Dust fell all around her, and Melissa closed her eyes against the debris, her fingers locked on the handrail.

Magnus's song grew suddenly stronger. She felt the earth ripple and the staircase topple. Her eyes flew open as the entire space rocked with force and the stone ceiling began to fall in earnest. Rafferty shoved and grunted again, then shifted shape with a roar. He pummeled the trapdoor, and Melissa heard it shift.

In the same moment, she heard the staircase pull free of its mooring. It swayed as the earth rumbled and danced below. Stone panels fell in the mausoleum and crashed to the floor, dust rising in a dark cloud.

Then gray light pierced the scene. The staircase swayed as he leapt ahead, shifting shape to land in human form on the solid earth above. Rafferty pivoted and reached back to grab Melissa's hand, his firm grip closing over her hand in the nick of time.

He held fast and hauled her up to the surface. Melissa barely caught her breath before the earth shook with vigor again. They were in a cemetery all right, one thick with moss and lavish memorials. The sky was solid gray and the rain was pattering down.

And the earth was heaving in answer to Magnus's song. Crevices emerged in the ground and memorials toppled. Rafferty and Melissa ran, trying to avoid the gaping pits that opened on every side.

"You have to kill him," Melissa said, even as she slipped on wet stone. "You have to stop this."

"I'm not worried about the dead here," Rafferty muttered. "It's the living who concern me."

"What do you mean?"

"The subway tunnel has collapsed in four places on the Northern line," he said, clearly torn between his responsibilities. "Humans have been put in peril."

"Just as he threatened." Melissa eyed Rafferty, knowing he was worried about her, too. She had an idea how she could solve his problem of wanting to be in two places at once. "Do you have your cell phone?"

He blinked, then tugged it from the pocket of his jeans. He handed it to her, clearly trusting her instinct, whatever it was. "What are you going to do?"

"No one ever dies on the air," she informed him with a smile, using Bill's favorite logic for getting on with the broadcast, whatever current conditions might be. "Too many witnesses. Sometimes the safest place to be is reporting live from the scene."

"Call Doug," Rafferty said, understanding immediately. "You can be the reporter on the scene for the earthquake."

"Exactly," Melissa agreed as she punched in the familiar number. She continued before he asked. "And don't worry. I'll make no mention of the *Pyr*. We have a deal." She met his gaze. "Although I can't be responsible for whatever anyone else records."

"I can't ask for more," Rafferty said, then caught her close. The darkfire burned with new vigor as he kissed her, and Melissa closed her eyes against its vivid sapphire radiance. Rafferty kissed her as if they had all the time in the world, but he still left her yearning for what they might do afterward.

Melissa hoped they would have the chance.

"You are healing," he said, his words both gruff and cautious. "That may be the point of the firestorm."

Melissa wanted so much to give him his desire. "We could adopt. It wouldn't be the same, but . . ." she began, but he put one finger over her lips to silence her.

"You must trust in the goodness of the universe," he murmured, his words low and melodic. "You must believe there is a purpose, even if you cannot see it from where you stand. You must recognize that everything that came before has brought us here, and that what follows will be right." He smiled. "That's one lesson I did take from Pwyll."

Melissa smiled beneath his fingertips. "And you must

know that sometimes we have to choose. Sometimes we have to make our choices and shape our futures, instead of waiting passively for whatever comes along. The future belongs to those who claim it."

"Spoken like a true survivor," Rafferty mused, his eyes glowing. "Note how our views complement and complete each other. We could be a powerful pair."

She caught her breath, hearing his uncertainty. What if Rafferty didn't come back?

What if Magnus won?

Melissa couldn't imagine her life without this man with his penetrating gaze, his patience, and his romantic perspective. She didn't want to tell him to be careful; she didn't want to sound worried or lacking confidence in him.

Even though she *was* worried.

"Kick his ass," she whispered. "For both of us."

Rafferty nodded. He shimmered for a heartbeat, then shifted shape. He stretched a talon to her, his dragon eyes glittering with resolve. "Let's go." Melissa nodded and Rafferty scooped her up, leaping into the sky.

She would never get tired of this.

Melissa got through to Doug immediately. She explained quickly that she was in London and that there was an earthquake. Just as she anticipated, he was quick to agree to her impromptu reporting. She heard the familiar scurry of the newsroom in the background as they discussed the setup. Doug put her on hold for a minute, and Melissa scanned the damage as Rafferty flew closer. People were too busy with the emergency on the ground to notice a dragon overhead.

For the moment.

Rafferty chose a spot to land, near the subway station entrance.

The entrance had crumbled in on itself.

"Do what you do," Rafferty murmured, "and I'll do what I must."

It was the only way to go forward. Melissa hoped it was enough. "Where will he be?"

"At the epicenter."

And then he was gone, disappearing into thin air. Melissa's heart skipped a beat as the line clicked and she heard the familiar music that preceded a special report.

"I'm trying to get you a camera crew, but do what you can in the interim," Doug said crisply. "You're on in fifteen."

"Right. Thanks." Melissa checked the second hand sweep on her watch. She scanned the area, noting details she could use in her report. She heard the anchor introduce her, took a deep breath, and began.

"Thank you, Juliane. This is Melissa Smith, on the scene in London. The city is being shaken by an earthquake, one that continues even now. I'm in Hampstead, where massive fissures have appeared in the ground. The cemetery on the other side of the heath has been badly affected, but it's the living who are of greater concern."

Melissa took a breath. She loved doing this, and the rhythm came back to her as if she'd never been away. "There is dust everywhere, and the earth continues to rumble as screams rise from beneath the street. The Northern subway line runs beneath this area, and there are fears that tunnels have collapsed, trapping unknown numbers of victims within the earth."

"Are there any damage reports, Melissa?" the anchor asked.

"It's too early for any official response, Juliane, but I can see there has been considerable damage already.

I'm standing at the entrance to the Highgate station of the Underground or the Tube, as the subway is called here. The entire entrance has fallen in on itself. Whoa! There's another big shake. I can hear people screaming far below, and smoke is emanating from what used to be the stairs to the subway. Emergency vehicles are arriving on the scene, as you can probably hear."

"I understand that you have only a cell phone, Melissa," the anchor said, her tone urgent, "but can you send us some images?"

Melissa remembered Doug's e-mail address. "Absolutely, Juliane."

"We'll give Melissa a second to send those images. We're live on the scene in London, where an earthquake is occurring, with a special report from Melissa Smith."

The anchor moved to another report, giving Melissa an interval of time to send the shots. Melissa was used to this rhythm and knew she had only seconds to give the anchor the tools she needed to build a compelling dialogue.

"We have a short video from a bystander to show you while Melissa sends us some images, as we bring you more on-the-spot news from the earthquake currently hitting London," Juliane said. Melissa could envision her turning in her chair and the camera moving to another screen. "This was the scene in Highgate Cemetery, less than two miles from Melissa's location, just moments ago. . . ."

Melissa had just snapped the last shot and sent it to Doug's e-mail account when the mobile camera unit from the affiliate station came rocketing around the corner. She waved them down and introduced herself, then pointed up the street.

"I think there must be an emergency exit up there, for the subway. There are people coming out, and the ambulances have gone straight there."

"Hop in," the tech said. "I'll get you wired up by the time we're there, so you'll be able to hear them at the desk."

"Perfect! Thanks." Melissa was excited to be back at work, but she was worried about Rafferty all the same.

She realized suddenly that she could still feel the tingle of the darkfire. There weren't any blue flames; she supposed Rafferty was too far away from her for that.

But she could feel that sparkle of desire, that seductive heat that made her mouth go dry.

It was reassuring in several ways. Melissa figured she could feel the firestorm only because Rafferty was alive. And she knew she'd be able to find him, no matter what happened, by following that alluring heat.

She wasn't going to lose him on a technicality.

Rafferty raced after Magnus. He couldn't smell the old *Slayer*, so he headed directly for the epicenter of the damage. He followed the vibrations to the heart of the damage.

He found himself deep in the earth, in a subway train that was almost broken in half. The debris had fallen on top of the car, crushing it beneath the weight of brick and stone and concrete. A live wire hissed and sparked to one side, outside the car.

Inside the train, there was no power. There were bodies strewn through the car, and blood flowing where the car had been crushed. He heard a woman saying her prayers softly, and several people were crying.

A man was hammering on the end door of the car

with his fists in desperation, a small crowd of perhaps twenty people gathered behind him. Most were quietly panicking, their gazes flicking to the bodies broken beneath the collapsed debris.

There were more people trapped in the next car.

"Where did you come from?" the man demanded, staring at Rafferty.

The earth shuddered again, and the trapped passengers screamed as one.

Rafferty chose for the moment to help humans and spoke with authority. As was so often the case, his calm manner soothed those around him.

"We have to go out through the cars," he instructed. "We must avoid the live electrical wires."

"But they're locked!" the man said, his voice rising. "Only the ones to the tracks are opening."

Rafferty broke the door open with his fist, kicking it into the space between the cars. The man stepped back with awe. Rafferty did the same with the entrance to the next car, then led the group there. "Hurry!" he said. He kicked out the door at the end of this car, which was the last, and stared into the darkness. "Stay away from the tracks. There's an emergency exit just ahead on the right, and you can climb to the street."

People began to file past him, moving quickly now that they had been given a plan. They supported one another and stayed on the side of the tunnel as Rafferty had instructed.

"How'd you do that?" the man asked, his gaze assessing.

Rafferty chose not to answer, confirming instead that all who had been left behind were dead. He realized that the woman he had heard praying was still doing so, her voice rising and falling softly as she recited her prayer. One of her legs was trapped under the wreckage, and there was blood on her skin from her efforts to free herself. She was pale and her eyes were closed, only her lips moving.

At the sound of his tread on the floor, her eyes flew open. "Don't leave me!" she begged, stretching out a hand to him. The earth shook once more, vibrating with such enthusiasm that Rafferty feared they would both be trapped.

He bent down and spoke to her as he looked at the damage. He supposed the leg would be broken and perhaps beyond repair no matter what he did.

"We should be able to do it together," said the man who had tried to open the door. Rafferty was surprised that he had lingered behind.

"I will do it, but you must look away."

"Why? I already saw you bust down those doors." The man smiled a little. "Afraid I'll find out you're Superman in disguise?"

"Avert your gaze, now!" Rafferty roared, and the man stepped away, even as he did as he was told. "Both of you!" No sooner had their eyes closed than Rafferty shifted shape.

In his dragon form, Rafferty easily tore away the stone and metal that were trapping the woman. After shifting back, he pulled her from the wreckage with care, then eyed the man. "Can you help her?"

The man's eyes were round. Rafferty feared he had looked instead of keeping his eyes closed, but there was nothing to be done about it for the moment.

"You bet," he said, putting his arm around the woman's waist and urging her toward the exit. She winced as she limped, her one leg obviously broken.

But she gritted her teeth and held on to the man. "I can do it," she said. "Just please don't let go."

"I won't," he vowed. Rafferty watched as the pair made steady progress toward the next car. The man glanced back at the end of the car. "Aren't you coming?" he asked Rafferty.

"I have another quest to pursue," Rafferty said.

"*And here I thought you'd forgotten about me,*" Magnus taunted in old-speak. Rafferty caught a glimpse of jade green, that salamander diving into the rubble.

He lunged after it, snatching at the salamander. He had Magnus in his grip long enough to see that his tail was gone and that he was oozing black blood from the broken stump; then Magnus disappeared.

It took him longer, and his scent was no longer disguised. It might be a feint, but Rafferty believed his opponent was fading.

He followed him immediately, just barely hearing the man's muttered oath of wonder as he disappeared.

"We're back with Melissa Smith, live from London," Juliane said. "Melissa, can you give us any kind of an update?"

Melissa gripped her microphone and nodded to the cameraman. One man had led the others out of the exit, his clothes covered in dust and his expression revealing that he was shaken. He'd helped a woman with a damaged leg to the ambulance but didn't appear to be otherwise injured himself. Melissa knew a hero when she saw one, and the cameraman had caught video of the man leading the others to safety.

"Hello, Juliane," she said. "Survivors are emerging from an emergency exit to the subway system, and we have several who are willing to talk to us. Sir, can you tell us what happened down there?"

"There was an earthquake, and the tunnel started to fall in," the man explained. He shook his head. "It was terrifying. We could hear the concrete and bricks of the tunnel falling on top of the car. It happened so quickly. The train stopped and the lights went out. I guess that was when the power failed." He shoved a hand through his hair and licked his lips, disturbed even by the memory. "Then this avalanche of rock fell, crushing the car in the middle."

"It was broken in half, then, sir?"

"We couldn't see the other end of the car. Most people managed to get out of the way, but some . . ." His throat worked, and Melissa put a hand on his shoulder, hoping to comfort him.

"But I understand you organized the others and led them out. These people now getting help from the emergency crews have you to thank." She heard Doug giving instruction to run the video they'd already fed to the station.

"Not just me," the man said, his tone firm. "There was another guy who helped."

"And who was that?" Melissa said, scanning those being given assistance.

"He's not here anymore. He just appeared there, right after the worst of it. He kind of took charge, helped us regain our senses, and reminded us what to do."

"And he's not with you anymore? Is he still down there?"

The man's lips set. "You'll say I'm mad, but he just

disappeared. He appeared and helped, and then he disappeared."

"Like a guardian angel, then?"

"Not quite," the man said with a smile. "He turned into a dragon. He moved the rubble in the middle of the car, to get that lady's leg free, and when I looked back to thank him, he was gone."

"He saved my life, that dragon!" the woman shouted from the end of the ambulance. "He can be my guardian angel anytime."

"Here we go again," Doug murmured in Melissa's ear.

"Can you tell me anything about this dragon?" Melissa asked the man. "What did he look like?"

"He was huge, but beautiful. Like one of those reliquaries you see at the museum, made of jewels and gold. Just the way you'd imagine a dragon to look, really, powerful and beautiful." The man shrugged even as Melissa's mouth went dry. "His scales looked like opals, with gold edging on them, you know?"

"Yes," Melissa said quietly. "Yes, I know."

"As some of you may know," Juliane said, "Melissa Smith was the reporter to first bring us pictures of dragons in action. We're going to split the screen here to show you some of those images, in case you haven't seen them yet, as well as a YouTube video that has been enormously popular in recent days. . . ."

"You got a story for me?" Doug said in Melissa's ear.

She thanked the man for his time, shook his hand, and turned away from the camera. "I'm not at liberty to talk about that," she said to Doug, and heard his dissatisfaction.

"You could get scooped," he warned.

"I made a promise," Melissa said. "Keeping my word is the most important thing of all."

There was nothing Doug could say to that. Melissa knew that she and he lived by the same code. She knew he recognized it, as well.

Because she heard him as he swore softly under his breath.

Chapter 17

Jorge halted behind a shed, eying a cottage. He was utterly still, except for his nostrils. Donovan's scent led to this cottage on this remote island, and went no farther.

He was in there.

Was the Sleeper there, too?

Jorge didn't know. He had followed Donovan on impulse, his attention caught by the Warrior's sudden departure from Minneapolis. Donovan seemed to be on a mission, and a *Pyr* on a mission could be an interesting source of information.

Now Magnus wanted someone called the Sleeper, undoubtedly connected to Rafferty and the blood duel. Jorge believed he might once again be in the right place at the right time. Everyone knew that Donovan and Rafferty had an old bond. The story he'd heard from the locals, that Donovan had inherited this cottage, was suspect, as well. Jorge sensed a fabricated explanation.

But was the Sleeper here? He stood and he sniffed and he knew there was only one way to be sure.

Behind the house and to the left, the land rose. The spine of the island was slightly elevated, more like hills than mountains, but the land was rocky.

Could there be a cave there?

Jorge considered the house again, his eyes narrowing.

Then he moved suddenly and silently. He stopped about six feet from the door to the cottage and raised his right talon. He slashed downward, slicing through the dragonsmoke barrier woven by Donovan. The mate and child were with the Warrior, but Jorge had no interest in them.

Unless they proved to be useful.

Jorge flattened himself against the wall to one side of the cottage door. He touched the doorknob. Of course, it wasn't locked.

A trap? Or naive human trust?

Jorge wasn't even certain the cottages had locks on this island. He was over the threshold as silently as a shadow, closing the door without a sound.

He heard the mate, sleeping. He heard the child, also sleeping.

Donovan's scent emanated from the small kitchen.

Jorge eased toward the kitchen, which was hidden around a corner. There was a trapdoor in the kitchen floor.

Open.

Exuding darkness and the scent of wet earth.

And the trail of the Warrior himself.

Jorge moved with haste. He went through the hatch and slipped down the ladder. The darkness was so complete that it took his eyes a moment to adjust.

There was a tunnel, snaking back toward that hill behind the house. He had to crawl through it, which would put him at a temporary disadvantage at the other end. Jorge considered the reward and took the risk.

The tunnel was no more than three feet in diameter, and water ran on its floor. Several passages branched off on either side at intervals, but Jorge wasn't distracted from his goal. Donovan's scent was clear and fresh.

He reached the end, hesitating only a moment. He sensed a yawning cavern of darkness, then leapt into the chamber. It wasn't far to the ground, maybe two feet, but the floor of the cave was wet.

"*Nothing like unexpected guests,*" Donovan said, his old-speak deep and slow.

"*Maybe not that unexpected,*" Jorge replied.

"*Maybe not,*" Donovan agreed. Then he breathed a radiant plume of dragonfire, revealing the scene to Jorge in one flash of light.

He saw that the cavern was cut from the stone. There was a platform in the center of the chamber, like a funeral bier. A young man with long dark hair and a beard lay there, his eyes closed and his breathing slow.

And the dragon that was Donovan the Warrior, powerful with lapis lazuli and silver scales, was coiled around the platform that supported the Sleeper. His tail curled between Jorge and the sleeping man.

Jorge saw all of that in the blink of an eye.

"*The Sleeper!*" he guessed.

"*The very same,*" Donovan agreed. "*And the small complication of his defender.*"

"*For the Sleeper, then,*" Jorge hissed, then shifted shape to a topaz and gold dragon.

"*For the Sleeper,*" Donovan agreed. The pair breathed fire and leapt toward each other, their talons locking as they collided beside the platform. The ground shook with the force of their impact.

Neither of them noticed that the Sleeper stretched.

Rafferty was dizzy when he manifested in a workroom. He closed his eyes against his body's reaction to the move through space, then forced them open again.

There was no time for weakness. Magnus's scent was strong.

He could smell water and hear engines, as well as hear their vibrations. Monitors beeped, and he saw men in an adjacent room quietly conferring. There was a sign declaring this to be the control room of the Thames Barrier.

Rafferty had a dreadful idea of what Magnus would do. With the seas so high, if the barrier was opened, the city would be flooded. Who knew how many people would die?

"*Looks so peaceful, doesn't it?*" Magnus murmured in old-speak. "*Let's play.*" Rafferty pivoted to find his opponent leaning against the wall in human form, eyes shining with malice.

Magnus strolled into the room, startling the men who were working there. "What does this do?" he asked, and punched a button on a console. A mechanism began to move, rumbling ominously.

"Don't!" one man shouted, lunging toward him.

Before the man could reach Magnus, that *Slayer* shimmered and shifted shape. He struck the man who fell hard on the floor, attracting the attention of the others.

Their eyes rounded. Magnus reared back before them, his jade scales sparkling. Rafferty thought he looked less vigorous than he had, and a bit paler.

Magnus turned to Rafferty, his gaze filled with menace. *"Care to tell me where my brother's son is sleeping?"*

Several of the men glanced upward, evidently thinking they heard thunder.

"What do you want with him?"

"He's slept a thousand years. I doubt he looks it. You could transfer the spell to me, grandson of the Cantor, and save the city."

"Never!"

Magnus smiled. *"Oh look, I'm feeling persuasive again."*

Rafferty shifted shape in turn and bounded after the *Slayer*, intent on stopping him before he did more damage.

Rafferty struck Magnus hard, and the *Slayer* recoiled. Rafferty reopened the wounds on Magnus's chest, and the *Slayer* screamed in agony, his blood pooling on the floor. Rafferty heard the relentless rumble of something moving but didn't know what it was. The men evidently were distracted by the fight.

"Those two were on television," one of the men said. "The opal one was trying to kill the green one then, too."

"We should help him!"

Someone broke a chair over Rafferty's back as Magnus chuckled. Another man used a fire extinguisher, shooting the foam into Rafferty's eyes. Rafferty roared in frustration and tore at Magnus, determined to finish what he had begun. Magnus pivoted, breathing a long plume of dragonfire at his opponent.

Rafferty didn't think it was a coincidence that the flame licked a control panel on one console. Sparks flew as the board shorted out, and the men began to shout. Magnus lit another and another, shorting out the controls in the room. Black smoke rose from the console to fill the room.

"All you have to do is reunite me with my brother's son," Magnus whispered. *"That will make it stop."*

"Liar," Rafferty declared. *"You're enjoying yourself."*

"I should have tried the direct approach years ago," Magnus murmured. *"Nothing rivals a big finish."*

Magnus began to sing. The earth rumbled in response to his chant, the floor vibrating with increasing rhythm. Rafferty thought about singing a competing tune but was leery of making matters worse. Gaia had been volatile lately, and he didn't want to endanger more humans.

One man swore, bracing his hands on the last console as he adjusted the controls with desperate gestures. "The green one opened the gates!" he cried, his voice rising in fear. "The barrier is opening, and the controls are shorted out. The city will be flooded, and there's nothing we can do about it!"

"There's one thing we can do." The man with the fire extinguisher turned it on Magnus. Magnus screamed and stumbled as the foam went into his eyes. Rafferty fell on his old foe, taking advantage of the moment, and slammed his head into the concrete wall. He did it over and over again. Black blood ran down the *Slayer*'s temple as he went limp.

If he was unconscious, he couldn't move through space.

"Get out!" Rafferty shouted to the men, holding fast to Magnus. "Get out while you can." He sensed the flash of a camera or a cell phone, but ignored it. Every vestige of strength he had was used to eliminate Magnus and the evil this *Slayer* had created.

Rafferty thought of the creation of the Elixir, the

sacrifice of Sahir to the making of that vile potion. He thought of the shadow dragons, raised from the dead against their will and shackled to Magnus's command. He thought of Delaney, tormented by Magnus's desire to experiment with a newly dead *Pyr* and his Elixir. He thought of the Sleeper, hidden from Magnus for so long, and all the *Pyr* who had been sacrificed to dragon hide powder for Magnus to sell to humans as a cure. He heard the water rushing through the barrier and the torrent of water descending on the city, but he held fast.

Rafferty seized his old foe's throat and closed his talons around it. He squeezed the life out of Magnus, knowing that he was giving his kind a new future. Magnus began to struggle as he fought for air. He thrashed violently, but Rafferty held on.

Magnus flailed at Rafferty, his talons digging into Rafferty's hide. He begged. He cajoled. He struggled longer than Rafferty could have believed possible, and Rafferty decided it must be the residue of the Elixir in Magnus's veins. Magnus shimmered, evidently trying to shift or move, but failed.

His eyes opened to narrowed slits, glinting like cut gems. He grinned then, surprising Rafferty with that expression.

Then he breathed a stream of dragonsmoke. It wound toward Rafferty, burning every scale it touched. Rafferty hung on, knowing that Magnus must be close to death. He tightened his grip but couldn't stop the dragonsmoke. It wound closer. It coiled around him.

And it struck like a spear into the space where he had just lost a scale. The skin was soft and vulnerable, undefended, and the smoke's strike made Rafferty scream in agony.

The old-speak came just as Rafferty's grip loosened slightly.

"*Come get your Sleeper, Magnus,*" Jorge purred. "*I've saved him just for you.*"

Magnus shifted shape, becoming a salamander once again. Rafferty closed his grip but missed the small slithering creature. Then Magnus was gone, disappearing in the blink of an eye.

"No!" Rafferty roared, then followed suit.

To Erik's dismay, Brandt was strong, both as agile and as elusive as a flame. Erik was reluctant to use all of his strength, hoping that Brandt would vent his anger before much damage was done.

But Brandt was fighting full out. He slashed at Erik with his talons extended and drew blood immediately. "*Oath breaker,*" Brandt seethed. "*I suppose you will argue that this was for the sake of truth, as well.*" He swung to strike Erik with his tail, then breathed brilliant fire.

"*I erred,*" Erik replied, dodging both blow and fire. "*I admit it, but I tried to fix the error by warning you of my mistake.*"

"*You broke your word. Why should I trust anything you say?*" Brandt launched himself at Erik. Erik swerved suddenly, but Brandt changed direction at the last second. He sank his talons into Erik's shoulder, spinning him around and tearing at his wings.

Erik had enough of being kind. He struck the younger *Pyr* with his tail, then launched a torrent of dragonfire at his back as he tumbled through the air. Brandt changed course and charged back, his eyes blazing. Erik slashed him across the snout, drawing blood.

"*First, you condemned my firestorm; now you break your word,*" Brandt sneered. "*What kind of leader are you?*"

"*The best you have,*" Sloane argued.

"*You condemned your own firestorm,*" Erik retorted, ignoring the Apothecary. "*You were the one who lied to your mate.*"

"*So says the* Pyr *whose mate killed herself rather than face his truth,*" Brandt scoffed. "*Kay didn't want to know about my truth, and I would have hidden it from her until the day she died.*" Brandt's eyes narrowed. "*It would have worked, except for you.*"

"*It would never have worked,*" Erik retorted. "*Deception never does.*"

"*She couldn't have accepted the truth.*"

"*She couldn't accept that you lied to her.*"

"*You bastard!*" Brandt fell on Erik in a flurry of anger, all talons and teeth. Erik let the younger *Pyr* do his worst, now that he understood the root of his fury. He retaliated enough to keep himself from being seriously injured, but he respected that Brandt was driven by the hurt of his loss.

"*This is stupid,*" Sloane protested in old-speak, but the other pair ignored him.

"*You still love Kay,*" Erik said softly. "*How will killing me fix that?*"

"*You showed her what I am! You ruined everything!*" Brandt struck Erik again and again, and Erik tasted his own blood.

"*And what exactly will this deed teach your son?*" Erik asked.

Brandt paused then, panting as he hovered beside Erik. Erik could feel his consternation and concern.

"What have you told him? Is it your fault that he's turned against me?"

"I only sense his mood. I am not responsible for it."

"Liar!" Brandt would have launched himself again at Erik, but Sloane caught at his tail. Brandt flailed at his cousin, but Sloane was stern.

"You solve nothing with this. Your anger stands in the way of a solution."

Brandt's eyes blazed. *"There can be no solution, when we are led so poorly that we are all revealed."*

"That can't be changed," Sloane interjected. *"But perhaps it can be used to further our mission."*

"What do you mean?" Both Brandt and Erik turned to the Apothecary, who was looking down. Erik saw the clouds parting far below and became aware of great turmoil in the city beneath them.

"Aren't we supposed to safeguard humans as one of the treasures of the earth?" Sloane asked. *"Listen. There are greater issues here than our broken oaths."*

The sound of screams rose clearly to the *Pyr*, whose hearing ensured that they were aware of all the humans in pain.

"You were wrong," Brandt said, his gaze still simmering.

"I believed it necessary to break my word in order to warn you." Erik extended his talon to Brandt. *"We can argue, or we can make a difference."*

"We can achieve more together than apart," Sloane said, and Brandt exhaled a stream of smoke.

He was still angry, but his frustration was tempered. The younger *Pyr* glanced downward. *"Will you help me with my son?"*

Erik smiled. *"You had only to ask."* They grasped claws, in tentative accord once again.

Then the trio dove down toward the city. Erik was shocked by the sight of the gates of the Thames Barrier opening. It couldn't have been the choice of anyone running it, because the river was so high. It took only a glimpse to realize that the water would flood the city.

Erik heard the song of Magnus and knew that the *Slayer* had caused this somehow. "We have to force it back!" he shouted as he pointed. The three *Pyr* dove toward the Thames Barrier, descending out of the sky like three plumed arrows.

One was black and pewter, like the moon's light; one was as orange and gold as the sun; and the third was the magical, changeable hue of tourmalines.

Together, they would halt the tide.

"Dragons, dragons, all the world is wild for dragons today," Juliane said. "Here's a report from a bystander, with video shot from a cell phone. It shows three dragons, forcing shut the Thames Barrier. The barrier had been closed against high water, keeping London from flooding, but an apparent malfunction caused it to open just moments ago. As you can see in this footage, these dragons appeared out of nowhere to save the city from flooding. This is incredible."

"I have a remote link to some staff from the barrier control," Doug said into Melissa's ear. "You can't get there fast enough, but I want you to do the interview. Okay?"

Melissa wondered why Doug had made such a choice. Usually the anchor did these kinds of interviews, but she wasn't going to argue about more airtime. She heard Doug tell the cameraman to get the smoke billowing from the subway station behind her for the shot, and she listened to the anchor filling the gap.

"We have with us a gentleman, whom we're going to call Larry, who is speaking with us in confidence about incidents inside the Thames Barrier control room," Juliane said. "Melissa Smith will be talking to Larry. Melissa?"

"Thanks, Juliane. Larry, can you tell us why you're speaking anonymously?"

"It's on account of what I saw," he said, his voice sounding odd as it went through a mixer to disguise his identity. "I don't want anyone saying I'm crazy. I could lose my job."

"And what did you see, Larry?"

"Two dragons. They were there in the control room. One of the guys noticed that it was those same two, the two that were fighting in that YouTube video. The opal one and the green one. We thought that opal one was trying to kill the green one, and we tried to help." Larry gave a self-deprecating laugh. "But we had it backward. The green one opened the barrier. He was trying to kill all of us, everyone in the city, and the opal one was trying to kill him instead. Nearly did it, too. Then the green one, well . . ."

"What did the green one do, Larry?"

"He, uh, turned into a salamander and disappeared. The opal one wasn't very happy, but he kind of shimmered blue, and then he was gone, too. If it weren't for everything smashed, we might have thought we were seeing things. As it was, the barrier was open, putting the whole city at risk."

So Rafferty was still alive, still fighting Magnus, and the fight had moved to another venue. Melissa wondered where, but she kept on the track of the interview.

"But bystanders say that three dragons closed the barrier," she said to Larry.

"Yeah. Three different ones. One was black, one was orange, and the other was kind of purple and green. We saw them, too." Larry exhaled. "I tell you, it's like something out of a movie."

"And the barrier is closed again? The city is safe?"

"Yes. It's designed to stay put if there's a power failure, but that green dragon opened it before shorting it out. That meant we couldn't close it again. Anyway, all's well that ends well, right?" Larry exhaled heavily. "I think I need a pint."

Melissa laughed. "I think you deserve one, Larry. Thank you so much for sharing your experience with us." She turned to the camera again. "It appears, Juliane, that the aftershocks of the earthquake have stopped here in Hampstead and things are returning to normal. Although emergency crews are still extinguishing fires and providing care to the injured, it seems that we are over the worst of it. The river has been restrained again, and we hope that this is the end of traumatic events in London today. Melissa Smith, reporting from London."

"Thank you, Melissa," Juliane said crisply. "May I say it's good to have you back on the team again."

The warm words took Melissa by surprise, and she hoped she hid her sudden tears. "Thank you, Juliane. It's good to be back."

"We take you now to another story we've been following, again at the impetus of Melissa Smith. Yesterday we told you about allegations regarding Magnus Montmorency and his possible link to illegal arms dealing. We showed you some of the evidence gathered by Melissa against Mr. Montmorency, and our crime reporter, Trevor Mulholland, has been following this story. Trevor, I understand that police have searched the Washington, DC–area home of Mr. Montmorency, with a warrant."

"That's true, Juliane, although they're not saying what evidence has been found. They have issued an All Points Bulletin for Mr. Montmorency, who is considered armed and dangerous, and my contact within the police noted that Interpol was involved. This indicates that they have some reason to believe that Mr. Montmorency has left the country. Certainly no one in his neighborhood is admitting to having seen him recently. . . ."

Rafferty found himself in a cave he knew well. Again, the nausea nearly overwhelmed him, but he had no time to indulge his weakness. Donovan was fighting with Jorge on the far side of the cave, although he appeared to be losing against the *Slayer*'s violent assault. The Sleeper yawned on his stone platform in the middle. He stretched, sighed, and closed his eyes again.

A green salamander was scampering toward the Sleeper.

Rafferty wasn't certain of Magnus's plan, but he couldn't let the old *Slayer* touch his nephew. Magnus was unsteady on his feet, bleeding openly from several wounds, and his tail was broken off. He staggered, but he made a definite course toward the Sleeper.

Rafferty himself was in human form and weakened, as well. He wasn't sure he had the power to shift form again, much less to move through space. He had to solve this immediately. He couldn't afford to be tricked by Magnus again. He seized a stone and lunged after the salamander, then smashed the rock down on the small reptile.

Magnus screamed so vehemently that Jorge and Donovan froze to stare. Jorge's eyes glittered with anticipation, but Rafferty didn't look away from the broken salamander. Magnus writhed, his bones broken so that he couldn't scurry away.

"So close," he whispered, his voice no more than a hissing whisper. "So close."

Rafferty smashed his body again, and this time when he lifted the stone, Magnus didn't move.

"Four elements," Donovan said, reminding Rafferty of the ritual required to ensure that any *Pyr* stayed dead. Magnus had to be exposed to all four elements within a half day of his demise. There was water on the stone floor of the cave, and his guts were sufficiently mingled with both that exposure was certain. There was air in the chamber. Rafferty raised a finger, uncertain he could supply the last element. Donovan decked Jorge, then turned to breathe fire in a long unbroken stream. The flames blackened the green of the small salamander.

Jorge grinned, watching Donovan. Rafferty didn't have time to wonder why.

He had to be sure that his old foe was dead.

When the flames faded, Magnus began to cycle between forms. He was a dead salamander one second, then a broken and bleeding man, then a shattered dragon. He cycled more and more rapidly, switching so quickly that he blurred before Rafferty's eyes. In all forms, he was faded and broken, his blood running black.

The dragon form was his last, stretched limply across the cavern. Lifeless, finally. Rafferty held his breath and waited for some trickery.

Instead, his own challenge coin rolled across the floor of the cave. It spun before him, then fell on its side with a clatter, the gold shining in the darkness.

Rafferty bent down and picked up the coin, running his thumb across the face that had been turned up. His challenge coin was a gold English coin from the mid-fifteenth century, known as an "angel." On one side was the image of the sun with rays and a cross. The side that had been facing upward showed St. George spearing the dragon.

Rafferty kissed the coin, knowing his challenge was over, knowing the demon had been slain.

"Lunch is on," Jorge said with satisfaction, and fell on Magnus's corpse. Before Rafferty could speak or intervene, Jorge ripped out the throat of the fallen *Slayer* and began to eat.

He cast a glittering glance at Rafferty and then at Donovan. "Don't even think of disturbing me or I'll add to the meal."

"But why?" Donovan asked in horror.

"Magnus is the last source of the Elixir," Jorge declared, then sucked the innards from Magnus's chest. He ate with gusto, the black blood flowing over his chin, and Rafferty couldn't stand to watch.

If Jorge had more Elixir, he'd be more powerful. What they had to do was escape from the cave with the Sleeper, while they could. Rafferty was so tired that he could hardly think straight. How could he carry the Sleeper to safety?

The Sleeper, in that moment, sat up and rubbed his

eyes, casting a disinterested glance at Jorge. When he glanced toward Rafferty, he smiled sleepily. Rafferty took his hand, urging him on, but the Sleeper had trouble standing on his own feet.

"*Use your powers*," Rafferty said to Donovan in old-speak.

Donovan nodded agreement, then held Rafferty's gaze. Rafferty understood that Donovan expected him to use his own powers.

To distract Jorge.

Donovan came and lifted the Sleeper from Rafferty's side. That *Pyr* smiled, his expression dreamy, and collapsed on Donovan's shoulder. He dozed again, clearly reluctant to awaken after so long.

Donovan carried the Sleeper into the tunnel that led to the cottage Rafferty had given him centuries before. Jorge ate greedily, glancing after Donovan with one eye. Rafferty held his ground, as if content to watch the *Slayer*.

Rafferty knew Donovan would defend Alex and Nick and the Sleeper, as well as ensure his own survival.

Rafferty would wait to ensure that Jorge didn't pursue them.

There was a brilliant shimmer of blue as Donovan shifted shape; then he was gone. Jorge snarled, hauling his kill so that he blocked the exit. "You're not going anywhere," Jorge said.

Rafferty smiled and leaned on the stone slab, apparently at ease.

Jorge paused, uncertain. He chewed. He looked around. He seemed to sense a trick but couldn't figure it out.

Then he returned to his meal, his eyes glittering.

Rafferty heard Donovan flee toward the cottage. Then he heard Donovan begin to sing to the elements he could command as Warrior.

Just as Rafferty had instructed him. Those elements responded so quickly, that they might have anticipated the summons. Rafferty felt the earth begin to jump in time to Donovan's song. He saw the water on the floor of the cavern dance with the rhythm.

Jorge halted his feast to look around.

Rafferty smiled as if all were well. "Go ahead. Eat."

Jorge took another mouthful, then straightened in sudden alarm at the sound of stone grinding on stone. Rafferty watched as the earth moved to close the opening to the tunnel, reacting to Donovan's call.

The aperture was sealed, as surely as if it had never been. Jorge cried out and ran for the place where the opening had been. He ran his claws over the smooth stone walls in a panic.

"He's sealing us in!" Jorge roared.

Then he turned on Rafferty with a growl. Malice glinted in his eyes and Rafferty could read the *Slayer*'s thoughts clearly.

"May the better dragon win," Jorge muttered and raised his claws.

"I think I already have." Rafferty mustered his strength, closed his eyes, and forced his will upon the universe. The black and white ring spun on his hand, burning his skin, but nothing changed.

He knew the moment that a livid Jorge lunged at him.

His talons were extended, and he was breathing fire, his eyes revealing that he meant to shred Rafferty alive. "We'll die together!" he roared.

"No. You'll die alone." Rafferty wished with all his

heart to be with Melissa, and the world swirled around him.

His gut churned as he managed the feat once again.

And he heard Jorge scream as his claws closed on empty air.

It was done.

Chapter 18

The soul of Sophie, the former Wyvern, was stymied. She sought to be reborn on the earthly sphere. She wanted to have her chance to be with Nikolas again, the chance she'd earned, the opportunity to live with her beloved. She wanted to return to the *Pyr*, not as a *Pyr* but as a human who could help them in their battle against evil. She wanted the *Pyr* to win, and she wanted to be part of that victory.

But forces seemed arrayed against her.

She halfway suspected it was *Slayers* at work.

For each time Sophie found a newly conceived baby in its mother's womb, it had already been promised as a vehicle to another soul. The one time she had found a possibility, and her hopes had been high, the child had not come to term. Its demise had destroyed her hope.

Sophie was well aware of the passing of time and feared she was losing whatever opportunity she had for happiness. All she wanted was to be with Nikolas. He had returned to the world quickly, son of the next *Pyr* to conceive, and was growing up in Donovan's household even as she struggled against these constraints.

Was it possible that they weren't destined to be reunited?

The challenge tried Sophie's faith. Shouldn't darkfire change something to the good? Shouldn't darkfire create the chance she was waiting for?

She had no sooner had the thought than Sophie heard a child crying in the wreckage of the city.

A child who didn't want to live any longer. There was nothing wrong with her body, but her soul despaired.

And Sophie dared to hope that they could find a solution that suited each best. She followed the sound, straight into a destroyed apartment in London.

The Sleeper was dimly aware that he was being half dragged and half carried through a tunnel. It was like a dream. His body was weak, and still his thoughts were fogged.

How much time had passed?

How long had he slept?

When would he see Pwyll again?

He was being carried by a *Pyr*, the one he did not know. More disconcerting, he could feel the wild ripple of darkfire set loose in the world. It sparked at the edge of his consciousness, its heat emanating from a point far to the east.

How could this be? The Cantor and his line commanded and guarded the darkfire. They would not leave it uncontained. That would be irresponsible.

No. It was untethered because they had lost control of it.

The Sleeper had to go to its source. Though he was

not yet himself, he summoned that old shimmer. Pwyll
had taught him this feat, and he would use it to finish
what Pwyll had been compelled to leave undone.

He focused on the blue shimmer, willing himself to be
at the locus of the darkfire's flame. He sensed a house,
the home of Pwyll's descendant, and saw the stones with
their flickering blue hearts that were secured there. The
Sleeper knew he would find himself welcomed in that
place. He let the darkfire illuminate him, guide him, and
carry him to his chosen destination. The tunnel disappeared in a brilliant flash of light.

He knew there would be only a shimmer of blue-green
dust on the ground behind him, a mark of his own link
to the darkfire. He vaguely heard the other *Pyr*'s gasp of
surprise.

Then he was in a bed of welcome softness. The
Sleeper sighed and yawned, exhausted again.

He dreamed, quite naturally, of darkfire.

Rafferty opened his eyes slowly.

For a moment, he thought he had gone blind—all he
could see was white. Then shapes emerged, and he realized he was surrounded by swirling dust. The dust of collapsed buildings. There was rubble all around him, some
of it piled on his legs. He worked himself free, brushing
off the dust and shaking off the chunks of plaster as well
as he could. He was sore, more sore than he had ever
been, but he couldn't see any blood. His hand throbbed
where the ring had spun off the outer layer of his skin.
At least he still had the ring. There was no sign of the
Sleeper or of Donovan.

He wondered what had happened to Melissa.

He glanced around and realized he was in the ruins

of a church that had been near his home. The altar was behind him, the stained glass of the window that had been above it shattered all around like colorful confetti. The roof had fallen in, and the altar window now framed clouds and dust. The pews had fallen every which way, and the double doors to the street were open, one hanging crookedly on its hinges. There was a large crack in the floor, if not in the foundation, and Rafferty smelled the crypt beneath. The wet scent of the earth was an undertone to that smell, and he thought he heard running water in the distance.

From the street, he heard sirens and people wailing. He pushed to his feet with a wince, determined to find Melissa. He'd expected to appear directly at her side, as that had been his intent. Was he near her? Or had he simply been too tired for accuracy? He hoped she was in the vicinity.

Melissa was probably in the thick of things, helping others as well as making her reports.

No. She was close. He could feel the blue-green tingle of the darkfire. It must have been his exhaustion that had affected his accuracy.

Rafferty was brushing himself off, feeling every month of his twelve hundred years, when he saw the little girl. She had slipped through the gaping doorway to the street and watched him solemnly, her small figure silhouetted there. Her face was white, either from pallor or dust, and her eyes seemed too large for her face. She was covered in dirt, as he was, and there was a streak of blood on her temple.

"Hello again," she said.

"Hello," Rafferty answered quietly. He didn't want to frighten her. He was certain he'd never seen her before and wondered at her greeting. "Are you hurt?"

She shook her head, emphatic in her certainty. "I was looking for you, Rafferty."

Rafferty was confused by that. Who had known he would be here? He hadn't even realized he'd end up in this precise place. Had she confused him with someone else? But then, how had she known his name?

Or was she simply confused because of the trauma?

Deciding that was it, he smiled at her. "Where are your parents?" he asked.

She turned and pointed, back into the street. "Isabelle's parents are over there."

How odd that she referred to herself in the third person.

Or was she talking about another child's parents?

Rafferty reached her side and crouched down beside her. She watched him, wary but not distrustful. "Does your head hurt?"

"Where?"

"Where the cut is." Rafferty touched his own forehead. She reached up and touched her own, grimaced, then eyed the blood on her hand.

"Not really," she said. "You have to come and see Isabelle's parents. So you'll know for sure."

Rafferty assumed it was harmless to humor her. He nodded, and she left the church, skipping down the building's broken steps. The darkfire sparked a little more brightly, though the child didn't appear to notice it.

She was in shock, then.

To his relief, Rafferty saw Melissa, out in the street. She was helping an older woman, holding her elbow as they made their way toward an ambulance with an open door and a growing line. Parked nearby was a van, outfitted for broadcast and marked with the logo of a local television station. A cameraman tracked Melissa's moves.

She'd been right that she'd be safe on camera.

Still, he was very relieved.

"This way!" the little girl insisted, catching at Rafferty's hand. She tugged him toward a house that had collapsed even more completely than the church, climbed a pile of rubble, and peered through a broken window. "They're in there. See?"

Rafferty bent down beside her and looked. He saw two pairs of feet in a bed that had a ceiling dropped on it. He frowned, smelling that both people were dead. Then, realizing that the child was watching him, he nodded with purpose. "We had better get some help."

"No," the little girl said. "Isabelle's parents are dead." She fixed a clear gaze upon him. "Isabelle wanted to die, too. She wanted to go with them. She didn't want to stay."

Rafferty thought that perhaps her strange way of expressing herself had to do with the trauma, and he made to reassure her.

"It is how it must be," she said with conviction. "Isabelle is gone, too. I wanted to stay." She held Rafferty's gaze steadily. "So I traded with Isabelle."

"I don't understand what you mean. Aren't you Isabelle?"

"I am now. I look like Isabelle outside."

"Not inside?" Rafferty asked.

She shook her head. She smiled up at him, and her confidence caught at his heart. "I remember you, Rafferty. You used to call me Sophie, but you should call me Isabelle now."

Rafferty gasped. He stared. Was she truly telling him

that the soul of Sophie had taken the body of this Isabelle? That they had traded to each get their desire? It was incredible, but the little girl watched him with knowing eyes.

"Isabelle's parents are dead," she said, as if she were the one explaining something simple to a child. "I want to live with you now, Rafferty."

"It's not that simple," Rafferty said, his words falling quickly. "There are authorities and procedures and . . ."

He fell silent when she reached out and almost touched the white and black ring on his finger. Did she know what it was? Could she know what it was?

She looked up, and he was sure she did know. She smiled a mysterious smile, one that reminded him very clearly of Sophie.

"I want to live with you," she insisted, then dropped her voice to a conspiratorial whisper. "But you will have to call me Isabelle now."

Rafferty didn't know what to say, much less what to do. He looked around and saw emergency crews trying to make sense of the disaster—a city in ruins, a couple dead in their own bed, and a little girl with a curious surety. His mind doubted what she was telling him, questioned whether it was possible, warned him not to be credulous.

His heart, though, was convinced.

She had recognized him on sight and knew his name. Sophie.

"There are procedures," he told the intent little girl, "and there are people who must agree to this, but I will try. You must remember everything and answer all the questions."

"You can't leave me, not now."

"I will do my best." Rafferty offered his hand to her,

and she put her small hand trustingly into his. They climbed down the pile of rubble together, and she turned to look back at the shattered apartment.

"Good-bye," she said, waving at the window. "Good-bye and thank you, Isabelle." She smiled up at him. "She's happy now. She wanted to go with her parents."

Rafferty wasn't sure what to say. His thoughts swirling, he led the little girl toward the ambulance where Melissa was helping the injured. He watched Melissa's care and compassion, watched how she made every person feel so special, and knew she had done the same for him. He was honored to have her as his mate, and he knew their partnership would stand the test of time.

"That's the television lady," Isabelle said, awe in her voice. "I saw her on the television today."

"That's my lady," Rafferty said. "I'm hoping she'll be my wife."

"She's the television lady," Isabelle said sternly. "You can't make up stories about people, not ones that aren't true."

Rafferty smiled, enjoying that the child thought he was lying. "I'll ask her. You'll see." He extended his hand and she gripped his fingers, her trust tearing at his heart.

Could this truly be Sophie, in a new skin?

Could he manage to adopt her? Rafferty wouldn't beguile anyone. He wouldn't use his powers to manipulate others, even to get what he wanted. He'd follow the official protocol and hope that all would come right.

He had to believe he wasn't the only one who wanted Sophie to have another chance at love.

Melissa was both exhausted and invigorated by the time the crew called it a day. The damage reports had slowed, and the victims seemed to be mostly under care. She thanked the anchor and removed her wiring, thanking the crew for their help. The cameraman gave her a thumbs-up as they packed everything away. When they drove away, her shoulders sagged.

But she felt the shimmer of the darkfire, the heat of the firestorm growing at her back. Knowing exactly who was there, she turned to find Rafferty standing about twenty feet away. He looked tired and dusty, that wound scabbed on his throat. But his eyes glowed, and his smile gave her new strength.

The darkfire had been a gift on this day, telling her that he was alive even when they were apart. She realized it had been her real anchor in the earthquake that had consumed London; Rafferty's presence in her life was not something she wanted to lose.

She noticed then that a little girl stood beside him. She was solemn, her chestnut hair long and wavy, her eyes as dark as Rafferty's. She must have been about five years old, and she was dusty, as well.

"This is Isabelle," Rafferty said. "She has suggested that we adopt her."

Melissa's heart skipped at the implications in that sentence. Isabelle would never be a son, much less a dragon shape shifter. Would her presence in their lives satisfy the firestorm, though? Would it satisfy Rafferty's desire for a child? Melissa dared to hope that adoption could be a solution for her and Rafferty, just as it was for so many people.

Plus the notion of raising a child with Rafferty and making a life with him was very, very appealing. She liked that he was prepared to compromise. He wanted her enough to accommodate her reality.

And she was more than ready to accommodate his.

Melissa cleared her throat. "We should talk about this later.".

"You're on," Rafferty said with a smile, and extended his hand to her. Melissa went to his side, more than glad to feel his hand close protectively over hers. He kissed her fingertips, his eyes shining.

"You do know the television lady!" Isabelle said, then considered Melissa. "He says you're his lady."

Melissa smiled at Rafferty, then at Isabelle. Her heart was pounding. "I'd like to be." Rafferty's grip tightened, and she hoped he never would let her go. He felt good—strong and loyal and reliable. "Did you find the Sleeper? Is he awake?"

Rafferty frowned. "Not quite."

"What about Magnus?"

"Dead," Rafferty said with a satisfaction that echoed Melissa's. The darkfire flames leapt between them, turning her thoughts in a predictable direction. She was so relieved that Rafferty had survived his challenge. She wanted to celebrate that fact, and she smiled as the heat of desire slid through her body. Her gaze met his, and she knew their thoughts were as one.

"Not yet," he whispered, pressing a hard kiss to her temple. Melissa closed her eyes as his touch weakened her knees. "We'll talk shortly, but not yet."

"I'll wait," Melissa whispered, and her reward was the flash of his smile. He held fast to her hand and to Isabelle's as they headed toward his house.

Something was wrong.

It wasn't just that the darkfire hadn't been as divisive as Chen had planned. It wasn't that he hadn't been aware of the Sleeper, or that the *Pyr* had added that lost member to their ranks.

Something else—someone—had been awakened by the darkfire.

A woman.

And Chen didn't know who she was.

Chen didn't like surprises. He didn't like the sense that he had missed something, or that there was anything he didn't know. The woman's presence troubled him.

He sensed her come closer. He heard her come all the way from North America, moving steadily. He heard her footsteps on the mountainside; he heard her seeking his refuge.

He knew she tracked him.

This could only mean that she could feel the power of his spell casting. How? Chen was intrigued, even as he worried about her steady approach. She crossed his dragonsmoke. She evaded his traps. She came steadily onward, no small scent of sorcery about her.

He heard her trudge through the tunnel that led to his cave, smelled her human form, and felt his lip curl in disdain.

He might have slaughtered her, if not for his curiosity.

He might have captured her, if not for his surprise.

For it was not a human who ultimately entered his cave. He was ready for that, guarding the portal in dragon form, dragonfire ready to be loosed.

It was a snake of vibrant green that slithered over the threshold. No natural creature, it was a serpent with poisonous fangs and glittering eyes. It exuded malice and gave Chen the sense that it was not what it appeared to be.

How could she take this form?

He was so shocked that he remained still as she slithered close, coiled, and reared back to strike.

Then she shifted shape, becoming a slender young woman with short red hair. Her lip curled in similar disdain as she surveyed him, and her eyes glittered as coldly as the serpent's had.

"I'm Viv Jason. You're the one who loosed the darkfire."

Chen ceded nothing. He shifted to his shape of an old man, noting how she straightened. He chose to let her believe in her superiority—at least until he knew the fullness of her powers. "What do you want?"

She smiled a mercenary smile that Chen could respect. "To destroy the *Pyr*, one dragon at a time."

"I have no need of a traitor at my door. You have come to betray me, to steal from me."

"Wrong. I've come to ally with you." Viv didn't flinch from his hard look. "I owe you a debt for loosing the darkfire."

"I have no need of your aid."

"Think again," she said. She muttered a word Chen could not hear clearly, and all the flames burning in the cavern leapt high simultaneously. She spread her hands, and they were extinguished.

The cavern smelled of smoke, but Chen could still see her. So, she had mastery over fire.

Interesting.

What else could she do?

Could he humor her to learn her skills?

He used his own command of the element of fire to relight the lantern flames in his sanctuary, one wick at a time. When the cavern glowed with their light, she inclined her head slightly, acknowledging his skill.

"Why would you eliminate the *Pyr*?" he asked softly.

Her eyes narrowed, her old-speak resonating in his thoughts like a toxin. *"Because they owe me."*

Chen considered the intruder. She was attractive. She was mercenary. She wanted something he also desired.

And he wondered whether she could be the one to bring him the *Pyr* with the affinity for air.

Chen smiled, prepared to consider an alliance.

Whatever she was.

Eileen was holding Zoë close, uncertain what to expect. The earth finally stilled, and she heard sirens. She turned on the news, only to find Melissa providing special reports. She listened and watched, sighing with relief at the eyewitness report of an ebony dragon being among the three that had closed the Thames Barrier.

Did she dare to hope that Erik had been wrong?

Zoë squirmed as the news became less dire. "Dada," she insisted, and Eileen decided to trust her daughter. Whether this was a Wyvern instinct or simply sharp *Pyr* hearing, Zoë might know better. Eileen put the toddler down, and Zoë scampered toward the stairs. She began to climb them on her hands and knees, heading with determination toward the summit.

Eileen scooped up Zoë and carried her upstairs, her heart pounding with anticipation. On the upper landing, Zoë gestured to one of the bedrooms, her fingers outstretched. Eileen went to the closed door and listened.

Her eyes widened as she heard someone breathing inside. She'd been sure they were alone in the house.

She turned the knob silently and eased the door open. The room was in half darkness, the blinds closed.

The house had been shaken by the earthquake but not damaged, and a few books had fallen onto the floor.

But what snared Eileen's attention was the man sleeping there on the daybed. He looked to be young, but with long hair and a long flowing dark beard. He was naked and pale, and he slept deeply, his lashes dark on his cheeks.

And she had no idea who he was.

How had he gotten into the house? What kind of intruder would break into a house, only to go to sleep? Nude? What should she do? Where was Rafferty?

Zoë pointed to the roof with one chubby finger. "Dada," she said, and sure enough Eileen heard the sound of dragon talons on the roof one instant after her daughter spoke. Knowledge or a guess? Eileen didn't know.

She also heard the kitchen door opening downstairs and the low rumble of Rafferty's voice. She sagged against the doorframe in relief. The *Pyr* were back.

Was Erik truly with them?

Alive?

The access to the attic opened, and Eileen caught her breath. Sloane came down the stairs first, giving her a tight smile that did nothing to reassure her. A tanned man with auburn hair descended next, and she assumed that this must be the Brandt who had vowed to kill her partner.

Eileen didn't smile at him.

She gasped when Erik descended. He looked tired and not appreciably less grim than he had when he'd left. Zoë crowed for him, and he caught her up. He met Eileen's gaze, and she saw that he was still uncertain.

Then his gaze slid past her, and his eyes lit with surprise.

"Pwyll!" he murmured, then frowned. "But how can this be?"

Eileen assumed the intruder had woken up and that Erik knew him, but when she turned, there was no one behind her. And the angle dictated that Erik couldn't see the man who still slept on the daybed.

"Who's Pwyll?" she asked.

"My dead grandfather," Rafferty said, appearing on the stairs.

"Dead?" Erik echoed. "But he's standing here before us, as alive as can be."

Pyr and Eileen all looked to the place Erik indicated. There was no one visible there. Eileen saw doubt in the expressions of Brandt and Sloane, and guessed what they were thinking. She took a deep breath and dared to make a suggestion.

It was a far more appealing notion than that her partner was either losing his marbles or going to die.

"Maybe your vision of walking among the dead just means that you'll be able to see them," she suggested. "Not that you're destined to join them anytime soon."

Erik blinked, then looked back at the specter only he could see. He seemed to listen, then nodded slowly. "Pwyll agrees with you. He says it's a new facet to my abilities." Erik smiled at her, his relief clear. "Pwyll also says that it takes the clear vision of a mate to show a *Pyr* the truth."

Eileen almost collapsed in her relief. "But there's still one last question," she said, indicating the sleeping intruder. "Who's this guy?"

And the *Pyr* crowded into the doorway to see.

* * *

Melissa followed Rafferty to the upstairs bedroom, the doorway already crowded with the other *Pyr*. She heard the rumble of their discussion and wondered what they were talking about.

Then she peered into the room and knew.

So this was the Sleeper.

He certainly was soundly asleep. The *Pyr* gathered around him, staring down at his relaxed form. Zoë even touched him, but he didn't move. Isabelle hung back, holding fast to Rafferty's hand. Melissa noticed that she had a fascination with that black and white ring on Rafferty's hand—unlike Zoë, Isabelle didn't touch the ring.

Melissa had called the authorities en route to Rafferty's house, and—given the situation and her visibility—had been granted permission to keep the child with them until the morning.

Rafferty made quick introductions in the spare bedroom, keeping his voice low. Melissa was awed to be standing among the dragons she'd been reporting on all day, the ones that had worked to save the city. They, however, were intent upon the Sleeper.

They certainly took their prophecies seriously. Melissa pulled out her notebook and read the verse again.

"Shouldn't he be waking up?" Sloane asked. "That's what's foretold, after all."

"But the darkfire still burns," Rafferty said, reaching for Melissa to show the truth. Those flames leapt and danced. If anything, they were burning brighter and hotter.

They made it hard for Melissa to think about anything other than getting Rafferty naked.

"Was he here all along?" Sloane asked.

Eileen and Melissa shook their heads, along with Rafferty. "He was in a sanctuary, in Wales, until less than an hour ago," Rafferty said. "He was stirring there, and I left him with Donovan."

"Then how did he get here?" Erik asked.

No one answered.

"Same way you got here?" Melissa asked Rafferty, and he shrugged. She flipped back through her notes, sensing that she was missing something.

"What happened to Magnus?" Erik asked.

"Dead," Rafferty confirmed. "Donovan is fine. We left Jorge with Magnus, sealed into the Sleeper's former sanctuary." He grimaced. "He was intent upon eating Magnus, to get the last of the Elixir."

Sloane grimaced.

"Magnus was in dragon form," Rafferty said. "That feast will take a while."

"Then he'll have to get free," Erik said with satisfaction. "Good work."

"Excellent work," Sloane agreed, nodding at the Sleeper. "Which leaves us with the sleepyhead."

"And the darkfire," Eileen added.

"Wait a minute," Melissa said, noticing something in the verse. Maybe she had the solution. She indicated Erik. "You're seeing Pwyll, Rafferty's grandfather, right?"

Erik nodded.

"And Pwyll's the one who enchanted the Sleeper in the first place, right?"

Rafferty nodded. "He could enchant anyone or anything. The Cantor's song was potent."

"And you refused to learn it. And Pwyll refused to teach anyone else, because he was determined to teach only a *Pyr* with a pure heart about his skill, so it wouldn't be used for ill."

The *Pyr* looked at her in amazement.

Melissa nodded. "Magnus told me that he tried to learn Pwyll's gift. He said he befriended Rafferty in the first place to try to learn the Cantor's song." She saw that they hadn't guessed this.

"Could he have targeted you?" Erik asked.

Rafferty nodded thoughtfully. "I was not that suspicious in those days. And he always collected arcane knowledge."

"*Until the Sleeper wakes to his fate; until the Cantor's legacy is claimed*," Melissa said, repeating the verse.

"Someone has to learn Pwyll's skill to end the darkfire," Eileen guessed.

"I'll bet that you have to use what you know of Pwyll's abilities, in order to awaken the Sleeper," Melissa said to Rafferty.

Rafferty frowned. "But it is a complicated art, and I never learned much of it from him. It is not something with which one would err. . . ."

"I'll bet you remember more than you think you do," Melissa insisted, sensing that she was right. "Who watched Pwyll sing the most? Who saw him at work most often? Who heard the most of his stories?"

Rafferty looked shocked by the notion, but he rubbed his chin. "I always believed it to be wrong to use enchantment. . . ."

"What if you chose to use it for good? To end the darkfire?" Melissa demanded. He eyed her, and she saw that he was becoming convinced.

"Pwyll says his craft wasn't his sole legacy," Erik said.

"He left you the stone!" Melissa said with sudden realization.

"Sigmund said there were three stones; that the Cantor and his kind were the custodians of them," Erik said.

"And of the Sleeper," Sloane said. "My father was fascinated by the potential power of darkfire. He spent his whole life wanting to see it for himself." He sighed and shook his head. "You have no idea how many crystals he collected, or how many expeditions we took, in search of one with darkfire locked within it."

"Pwyll knows," Erik said softly.

Melissa didn't need any more assurance than that. She bolted down the stairs and retrieved the crystal. It was still lit with the darkfire's blue light, and the spark inside it became brighter when she picked it up. Melissa raced back up the stairs, even as she heard the rumble of thunder overhead. She skidded into the room and smiled at Rafferty.

"I'm sure I'm right," she said with her old confidence. She took the crystal and put it into Rafferty's hand. "You're Pwyll's grandson and the closest thing he has to an heir. You need to try."

Erik cleared his throat. "Pwyll says he'll help."

Eileen's eyes went round, and she moved closer to Erik, her hand slipping into his. Their fingers interlaced and locked, and Melissa realized they had some fear about awakening the Sleeper.

But she shared Rafferty's trust in the goodness of fate. She smiled at him, and saw the spark of hope deep in his gaze. "Maybe he sent some of that expertise to you, along with this. Maybe that's one of the things darkfire can awaken—not just the Sleeper himself, but your memories of the Cantor." And she handed the stone back to him, expectation bright in her eyes. "You should try."

Rafferty's lips took on a set of resolve, and his eyes glinted with purpose. He took the stone from Melissa, its blue light burning even brighter and painting his palms with that sapphire hue. He closed his hands around it. Melissa saw his determination grow. She saw it eclipse his exhaustion.

And then Rafferty began to sing.

Chapter 19

Rafferty was astounded. For centuries, he had mourned his failure to make amends with his grandfather, and that grief had hidden the possibility of his inheriting Pwyll's gifts from his own view. Pwyll had never used his powers for ill purposes. He was reassured by Melissa's confession that Magnus had tried to persuade Pwyll to teach him, but Pwyll had declined.

It would have been entirely consistent with Pwyll's nature to choose deliberately among apprentices.

Yet Rafferty had chosen to ignore that his grandfather had selected him and that he had been invited to learn the Cantor's gift. He had recalled only his own reasons for declining.

But the stone felt right in his hand. It always had. And he had been profoundly relieved when it had turned up in his home after Pwyll's death. Rafferty summoned the image of his grandfather and mimicked his pose as well as he was able. He could still see the old *Pyr* holding this crystal just so. He could hear his grandfather's voice and recall the resonance of his words. He knew the tune; he knew it even better than he realized once he began the chant.

He remembered how Pwyll's voice had risen and fallen when he cast his charms. Although it had been centuries, Rafferty mimicked that intonation as well as he could.

The stone responded. The flame danced bright and hot, burning his fingers and sending a charge through his body. He felt the hair on the back of his neck stand up. He felt the crackle of energy, far beyond anything he'd felt before. He saw the brilliant blue emanating from the stone. Rafferty was on the cusp of something unfamiliar.

Magical.

"Another verse," Erik murmured, and Rafferty knew he was channeling Pwyll's counsel. He didn't question the advice but simply did as Erik had bidden him.

And the power grew. It bucked and rippled beneath the influence of his song. It snapped and crackled, the stone feeling almost fluid in his grip. Rafferty realized he could shape this energy, that he could direct it with his song. He dared to believe that Sloane's father had been right, that there was good to be found with darkfire.

Hadn't he found Melissa?

He wished fervently for the darkfire to be satisfied, for the ordeals visited upon the *Pyr* by its power to be completed. He wished as he built the power; then he turned the point of the crystal toward the Sleeper.

He barely had time to brace himself.

There was a crack in the room, followed by a blinding flash of light. Rafferty thought lightning had struck within the space; yet that was impossible.

But still . . . A blue spark had shot from the stone and struck the Sleeper right in the heart. The Sleeper jumped; then the room fell into darkness. The stone was cold in his hand and Rafferty was shaking.

What had he done?

"Power's out," Sloane said softly. Rafferty heard someone flick the light switch, but the lights didn't come on.

"Flashlight," he said weakly, certain his body couldn't take any more. Melissa held fast to his hand, stroking his arm, her presence giving him strength. "Hall table drawer."

Brandt left the room, returning with a flashlight. He turned it on, and the beam of light slid around the room, landing on the Sleeper.

Who was sitting up and rubbing his eyes.

"Pwyll?" the Sleeper asked, speaking with the cadence of Welsh.

"No," Rafferty replied in Welsh. "Pwyll is dead. I am Rafferty, his grandson."

The Sleeper smiled. "He told me of you, always with great admiration. I am honored." After they shook hands, he pointed to the crystal in Rafferty's hand. "I believe that stone is mine."

Rafferty glanced down at the stone, surprised by the brightness of the spark in it. He was reluctant to let it go. "This was used to enchant you."

The Sleeper nodded. "It is but one of three stones that contain the darkfire."

"Do you know the location of the others?" Erik asked.

The Sleeper shook his head when the question was translated. "Pwyll warned me that it would be my task to hunt them. One, I know, is already lost."

"How can that be?" Rafferty asked. He felt Sloane crowding closer, intent upon hearing every word.

The Sleeper smiled. "Did you not feel the darkfire? It can only be loosed on the world when the stone that holds it is shattered. Someone set it free, someone with malicious intent."

Rafferty translated this, and the *Pyr* exchanged glances. "Magnus?" Sloane suggested.

Rafferty shook his head. "If he'd ever had the crystal, he would have kept it, bargained with it. He would never have destroyed it."

"Chen," Eileen said softly, and the *Pyr* fell silent at the likelihood of that.

But where was Chen?

The Sleeper continued, again indicating the crystal. "You have contained that measure of darkfire in this stone, adding it to the darkfire already there."

The stone did burn with a brighter flame.

"It is the legacy of the Cantor to contain the darkfire," he continued. "To command it and to ensure that it is controlled. It is a responsibility, passed through your line."

Rafferty frowned. "I do not know how to do this. . . ."

"You do not have to," the Sleeper said with resolve. "You have defended me and fulfilled the prophecy." He stood with purpose. "The quest now is mine. Pwyll trained me for this."

"The son he never had," Rafferty said softly, regret in his heart.

"No." The Sleeper held his gaze steadily, with no censure. "He said his line had paid dearly for the burden of darkfire. He loved you. He respected you. He wanted you to have the gifts of darkfire—and this is one of them."

Then he plucked the stone from Rafferty's hand,

claiming it for his own. The flame in the crystal responded immediately, burning brilliantly and then settling to a blue-green glow.

The Sleeper smiled. "It is done, just as foretold."

Before Rafferty could ask, the Sleeper looked around the room, his eyes bright with curiosity as he surveyed the others gathered there. "You must tell me of each member of this company."

Rafferty gestured to the leader of the *Pyr*. "This is Erik Sorensson, the leader of the *Pyr*."

"I welcome you to our ranks," Erik said. "We can use every talon, and Pwyll has told me your guidance will be invaluable."

Rafferty translated Erik's words into Welsh.

The Sleeper smiled. "I am Marcus Maximus. You knew Pwyll, as well?"

"Only in passing," Erik acknowledged, after translations had been made. "But he speaks to me now. Darkfire has brought me the gift of conversing with the dead, and so I greet you in his stead, Cysgwr."

Marcus's eyes widened. "Only Pwyll called me that. There is proof that you do converse with him."

"He bids me to remind you of this." Then Erik spoke carefully in Welsh. Rafferty blinked, for he knew Erik did not know Welsh and had often complained that it was too difficult a language to learn. *"Y ddraig du ddyry cychwyn."*

Rafferty and Marcus laughed aloud in unison.

"What did I say?" Erik asked, looking between them.

"One of Pwyll's favorite sayings, with a small modification," Rafferty said, recognizing yet more proof of his grandfather's presence. "'The black dragon leads the way.' Usually he spoke about the red dragon, meaning the Welsh *Pyr,* but he has changed the color on this day."

"Amen," Eileen said with approval.

Rafferty knew that his grandfather was present.

And Pwyll had released Rafferty from the burden of the legacy Rafferty did not want, finding another heir and leaving Rafferty to savor the firestorm he had wanted more than anything else. He reached to take Melissa's hand, overcome by Pwyll's generosity.

And he felt fingertips slide over his hair, just as his grandfather had touched him so many times. Tears rose to his eyes, gratitude making his heart swell. Melissa smiled up at him, her eyes shining.

No doubt about it, Rafferty Powell was a lucky *Pyr*.

"You must be starving," Sloane said to Marcus. "Come have a cup of tea. I know I could use one."

"Tea," Marcus echoed, trying the word on his tongue.

Rafferty, though, had a more celebratory intent. He studied Melissa, astounded by the gifts she had given him, and her smile broadened. When he bent and brushed his lips across hers, she stretched to meet him halfway, her hand sliding around the back of his neck. Desire rolled through Rafferty, making him yearn for privacy.

The *Pyr* were smart enough to disappear, taking both little girls, and leaving him alone with his mate.

"All's well that ends well?" she whispered, and he grinned.

"The legacy continues, through Marcus."

"I've missed you."

"Even though you were busy?" he asked, looking into the light of her eyes.

"Even so." Her smile turned impish.

Rafferty could still smell that delicious perfume of

hers and assumed Melissa used it so routinely that it clung to her skin. Her sweater sleeve was charred and her eyes shone, her lips soft and full and inviting. "That might be cause for a celebration," he murmured.

She laughed, the best sound he'd heard in a long time. "Celebrating dragon-style?" she asked, and ran one hand up his chest.

"The very same. Although I should ensure that you're feeling celebratory, as well."

"What makes you think I'm not?" She flirted with him, looking coy and luscious, and Rafferty loved her confidence in her own charms.

Another welcome change wrought by the darkfire.

"I think I should ask you a question, to ensure that we have something to celebrate," Rafferty said, pulling her into his embrace.

"Any particular question?" Melissa asked, then kissed the corner of his mouth. Rafferty caught his breath, before he kissed her soundly, sliding his hand up her back as he pulled her tightly against him. Her tongue dueled with his, her fingers slid into his hair, and he felt her stretch to her toes to kiss him more deeply. He could have lost himself in her kiss but forced himself to stop.

For a moment.

He wanted her to be sure of his intent.

"Marry me," he asked, looking down into her eyes. "Be my wife."

Her eyes flashed with delight; then she flushed a little. "Even though . . ."

"It's not important. We'll try to adopt Isabelle, and if that's meant to be, it will be. Otherwise, we'll have each other, and that sounds good to me."

"But *it* could come back," she said quietly.

He understood that this was her deep fear—and that her even deeper one was that she would again be left alone to face the challenge. "And you'll be stuck with me, every step of the way, whether it does or not," Rafferty said with resolve.

"Deal," Melissa said, her smile lighting her face. "Deal!"

Rafferty laughed and swung her into his arms, then headed for his own bedroom. He kicked the door shut behind him and rolled onto the bed with Melissa in his arms. They kissed so passionately that they might have been apart for years, and tugged at each other's clothes in their impatience to have no barriers between them.

It was when Melissa touched the wound on his throat with a tender fingertip that her eyes widened in surprise. "Wait a minute," she said softly. "There's no darkfire."

Rafferty hadn't expected anything else, not after Marcus claimed the stone.

"Does that mean there's no spark between us anymore?" he asked, smiling at the very idea.

Melissa laughed. "Not a chance," she said, and fell into his arms, her eyes dancing. "You're stuck with me, too, Rafferty Powell."

As Rafferty kissed his lady and his mate, he knew there could be no better solution than that.

The *Pyr* gathered for New Year's Eve at Quinn's home in Michigan. Sara stood in the snowy field outside the house as twilight fell, sandwiched between Garrett and Quinn. She wasn't cold anymore, which had told her the darkfire had been satisfied even before Quinn spoke to her of it. Instead, she felt a bubbling optimism for the future.

Erik and Eileen were the first to arrive, both of them more exuberant than usual. Zoë squealed with delight at the snow, and she and Garrett immediately set to making angels. Erik and Eileen had brought four bottles of vintage champagne and two of a sparkling nonalcoholic drink. "I don't have to be the Seer to know there are babies on the way," Eileen said with a smile.

Donovan and Alex came next, Nick proving to be just as eager to play in the snow. The men shook hands, as Alex gave Sara a book she'd found at a bookstore in Wales. It was an old book about tarot cards and their meanings.

"It's not very logical stuff," Alex said with her usual pragmatism, "but it's kind of interesting."

"Very interesting," Sara agreed, thanking her for the book.

Sloane came next, Marcus alongside him. Sara was intrigued to meet the newest member of the *Pyr*. Though he spoke little, he smiled a great deal, and was both handsome and charming. She sensed that he would have much to say in time. Sloane brought her a book on mystical herbalism.

"I sense a theme," Sara said with a laugh, and Quinn smiled.

Niall and Rox came with Thorolf, who seemed to be preoccupied. Rox was obviously out of her element— she was a city girl to the marrow—but gave Sara a big hug. Rox also brought a tin of organic gingerbread and another of an herbal tea. She patted her own rounded stomach. "Ginger's good for me these days, so I thought it might be for you, too."

Delaney and Ginger were just landing, Liam sleeping in Ginger's arms. "Ginger's always good for me," Delaney teased. Ginger blushed; then they all exchanged greetings.

They turned then to watch an opalescent dragon descend out of the sky. Sara watched, her excitement rising. She was looking forward to meeting Rafferty's mate, the one who had helped him quench the darkfire, and who had shaken the world of the *Pyr*.

Melissa was beautiful and charming. Sara could see that Rafferty was completely smitten with her, and that his feelings were reciprocated. They made a great couple. Just the sight of them together made Sara smile, because Rafferty had always wanted a firestorm. She was glad to see him in such a good relationship.

She was also shocked to see the little girl from her dream in the company of Rafferty and Melissa. Rafferty introduced the girl as Isabelle. Sara had heard the story of their proposed adoption but hadn't seen the girl yet.

Rafferty had said she was Sophie reborn, but Sara hadn't believed it until this moment.

Sara scanned the sky in vain for a sign of Drake and the Dragon's Tooth Warriors. She knew that the *Pyr* intended to seek them out immediately after this ceremony, and that all were concerned that those ancient warriors had seemed to disappear from the face of the earth. On the other hand, they were different and mysterious, disinclined to share their secrets. Sara had hoped that Drake and his fellows would simply arrive here. No luck there.

She'd also wanted to meet Brandt, that passionate *Pyr* with a tragic history, for she was intrigued. Sara believed that all rifts could be healed, and had specifically invited Brandt. That *Pyr*, though, had insisted at the last minute that he had to check on his son.

The son who no longer spoke with his father. The idea of a *Pyr* losing touch with both his mate and his son troubled Sara deeply, but she knew that Erik was resolved to help Brandt. That was no small thing, given Erik's determination. Sara wished she could have helped as well.

Quinn took her hand and gave her fingers a squeeze, letting her know that he guessed her concern. And that he knew the others wouldn't be coming. She knew better than to distrust his keen senses.

Melissa was direct, which amused Sara. After good wishes had been exchanged, Melissa turned to Quinn, pulling an opalescent scale out of her purse. "You're going to need this," she said to the Smith. "Do you mind if we do the repair sooner rather than later? I'll feel more festive when it's done."

Quinn smiled slowly and Sara knew he liked Melissa's concern for Rafferty's welfare. It could only bode well for their partnership. "Let's do it now," Quinn said. "The forge is ready."

Melissa couldn't believe she was in a company of dragons, but she soon had adequate proof. Rafferty murmured to her to close her eyes once they all were gathered in Quinn's studio, but she kept them wide-open.

"I think our concern has proved unfounded," Erik said quietly.

"What concern is that?" Melissa asked.

"It's always been said among our kind that humans could not bear to witness the shift in our bodies; that the sight of the change would drive humans insane," Rafferty said. He gestured to the group. "But we stand in the company of six human women who have not been driven insane by the sight."

"I should think not," Eileen said.

"Not even close," Ginger maintained.

"Maybe we're just made of sterner stuff than the princesses and damsels in distress of old," Melissa suggested.

"Maybe the problem is with virgins," Alex suggested, her tone wicked. They laughed, but then Sara indicated the two small girls, Zoë and Isabelle.

"Maybe not," she said. "Maybe times change."

"Darkfire," Marcus said softly, surety in his tone. The *Pyr* exchanged glances, and Melissa saw they didn't entirely share Marcus's confidence.

"Maybe we should get to work," Quinn said. "The forge is hot."

The air filled with a blue shimmer, one that Melissa recognized. It touched the silhouette of Quinn first, gleaming in the darkness. He shifted shape then, becoming a sapphire and steel dragon. He was large and powerful in dragon form, his musculature reflecting his human strength. He reared back and in his talons held the scale she'd brought, his eyes shining as he held it to the forge's heat.

Donovan changed next, resplendent in lapis lazuli and silver. Erik followed suit, black as obsidian, his scales edged with pewter. Three dragons already, and more to come.

Thorolf was massive, moonstone and silver, as magnificent as a jewel. Delaney had scales of emerald, each edged in copper, and he gleamed in the fire's light. Sloane's dragon form was all the hues of tourmaline, shading from green to violet and back again, his scales edged in gold. Niall was amethyst and silver, glittering and powerful.

Melissa was amazed. The mates stood alongside the *Pyr*, proud and smart women, each and every one. Melissa could sense that, and looked forward to getting to know them better. She guessed that she'd find some very good friends in this group.

The *Pyr* waited then, and Melissa saw their manner was expectant.

"What am I supposed to do?" she asked.

Sara cleared her throat. "The mate, traditionally, aids in the repair of the scale."

"How so? Should I hold it or something?"

"It can't be repaired without a talisman to make it whole again," Alex said.

"The token must be provided of free will," Eileen said.

Melissa considered Rafferty, knowing that her heart was in her eyes. "I have nothing to give to you, nothing except myself. I am all yours, for better or worse."

Rafferty smiled and extended his hand. "Shed a tear for me," he said. "Let yourself weep for all you have endured, as you have never yet allowed yourself to do. That will be the only gift I need."

Melissa caught her breath. She stared into the dark splendor of his eyes and realized he had seen her deepest secret; he had known how to heal her all along. This man, this incredible, tender, and romantic man, loved her. She felt blessed and knew that every day of their partnership would be an adventure.

Her tears gathered, and, once she decided not to blink them back, they fell with greater speed. She caught her breath, but Rafferty gathered her into his arms and kissed her hair.

"You're stuck with me," he whispered, and she nodded, her tears falling faster in recognition of that truth.

It was all she had ever wanted, and so much more.

Quinn held out the scale, and Melissa's tears slid over it. As she watched, they dried on the hot scale, seeming to form a coating over it. The scale shimmered with new light.

Then Rafferty shifted shape with a roar. He reared back, so splendid in his opal and gold scales that Melissa couldn't believe her luck. He reached down to her and lifted her in his embrace, holding her tenderly against his chest. He turned then to Quinn, who heated the scale until it was white-hot. Melissa could see the spot on his chest where the scale had been and didn't like the sight of the vulnerability.

"Air," Quinn said, as if recounting a ritual.

"That's Melissa and her gift for communication," Rafferty said. He and Melissa blew together on the scale, their breath making it burn even hotter.

"Earth," Quinn said.

"That's Rafferty's ability to sing the songs of the earth," Melissa said, smiling at him. They both gripped the edges of the scale.

"Fire," Quinn said, and both he and Rafferty breathed fire on the scale. That element was obvious to Melissa. Quinn lifted the shining scale and pressed it into place. Melissa heard the skin sizzle. She smelled the flesh sear. And she felt the shudder of pain that rolled through Rafferty. It wasn't fair that he had to suffer so. She bent and kissed the scale, her tears landing on it as it sizzled.

"Water," Quinn said with satisfaction. "From Melissa's empathy."

Rafferty shifted shape then, shimmering that vivid blue and becoming the man she loved. He held her close as he smiled down at her. "And so the four elements combine to heal the scale, just as mate and *Pyr* join to become a union greater than the sum of the parts."

"A destined partnership," Melissa said.

"As long as you believe in the future," Rafferty murmured.

"I didn't," she admitted, "but a wonderful man showed me how much I was wrong." She heard the *Pyr* cheer as Rafferty bent and kissed her. She felt the fire in the forge leap high. She felt warm and loved and full of desire.

Exactly as if the firestorm still burned.

Melissa guessed that an ember of it always would.

Epilogue

A month after the Sleeper awakened, Melissa stood once again in the Middle East. She was with a camera crew, just like old times, but she had a new story to tell.

With the full permission of the subjects.

Daphne had had a proper funeral, once Melissa's identification of her body had been confirmed, and many people had come to the service. There had been familiar faces from Melissa's years overseas, as well as strangers who had followed Melissa's news story and felt compelled to honor the murdered girl. The service had been moving, the unexpected and the traditional in precisely the right balance to suit Daphne's character. Melissa had ensured that she was buried with that stuffed puppy.

Then Melissa had gone back to work.

Marcus was being mentored by each of the *Pyr* in turn. Fortunately, he was a quick study, for he'd missed a lot over the past thousand years and had never gained much mastery of his abilities. He spoke some Welsh, but his language skills were limited. Marcus was currently with Sloane in California. He seemed to have an understanding of plants and their rhythms, and was helping Sloane with his herb nursery while Sloane mentored him. He was also strikingly handsome, and Melissa knew he attracted the attention of many women.

Melissa and Rafferty had exchanged vows in the garden of Melissa's brother's home in California. It had been a perfect day; one she would remember forever. She had treasured the gift of having those she loved around her, sharing in her joy.

And Rafferty, well, Rafferty's companionship became more addictive every day. Even without the firestorm or the darkfire, the man stirred her very soul.

The paperwork had come through in record time for Isabelle to be formally adopted by Rafferty and Melissa, so the little girl had joined their household. She never spoke about Sophie anymore, and she seemed confused when asked about her encounter with Rafferty at the church. Rafferty was certain she'd forgotten, but Melissa wasn't convinced. Sometimes she found Isabelle staring into space, lost in another time and place. The rest of the time, though, she was a normal, affectionate, busy five-year-old.

Isabelle had had a blast with Melissa's niece and nephews in California, and they were planning some family vacations together. Her brother was still hot to see inside Rafferty's warehouses in London, so Melissa anticipated they'd have company at Rafferty's London house soon.

For the moment, though, she had carte blanche with Doug. She'd negotiated to tell this story her way, and was excited about the result. She'd also negotiated with

Erik, who had decided that the *Pyr* could tell their story, so long as none of them were named or revealed in their human form.

It was sunset, Melissa's favorite time of day, and the ground hovered between the gold of the last rays of the sun and deep blue shadows. The sky was indigo in the east and filled with stars. The western sky was painted with lighter shades of blue, a swath of green, and a brilliant orange smudge that surrounded the glowing orb of the setting sun. The light was a great, rich gold, one that contrasted with strong shadows.

Melissa was wearing a white linen dress, the mic hidden inside her bra. She walked the sand-covered stones of an ancient fort, knowing the camera was following her. She reviewed the script she'd memorized as she heard Doug through the earpiece mounted behind her ear. She knew she was doing what she'd been born to do. She counted off the seconds, knowing the camera would pan the sky and the horizon.

"And on you," Doug murmured.

Melissa straightened to scan the distance herself.

"Perfect, perfect," Doug murmured. "Closing in, and turn to us." Melissa did as she was told. "And you're on."

"Hello. I'm Melissa Smith, and I'm here to tell you a surprising story." Melissa spoke with confidence and verve. "It's a story that began here, centuries ago, in the fertile crescent between the Euphrates and the Tigris rivers. It's a story of another kind of creature, one with a history entwined with our own.

"We humans have always told stories of dragons— these tales exist in every culture of the world—and the reason for that is simple. There are dragons among us. We have known them before. We hunted them almost to extinction, so they hid themselves from us. But the time has come for us to join forces and work together, to combine our skills and energy to save the earth. The time has come to meet the dragons in our midst."

Melissa turned and climbed a trio of worn steps, knowing the camera was following her perfectly. "Just as we tell stories about dragons, they also tell stories to one another. It's not the only thing we have in common. Let's start at the beginning, with the story they tell of their own creation. It's a story that has some elements you'll find familiar. This is the dragons' story."

She held her position, and Doug murmured that the camera was closing in. Melissa looked straight into the lens, as if looking straight into the eyes of every viewer.

"In the beginning, there was the fire, and the fire burned hot because it was cradled by the earth. The fire burned bright because it was nurtured by the air. The fire burned lower only when it was quenched by the water. And these were the four elements of divine design, of which all would be built and with which all would be destroyed. And the elements were placed at the cornerstones of the material world, and it was good."

Melissa heard Doug's instruction to the cameraman to pan back a bit. She raised her hands as she continued.

"But the elements were alone and undefended, incapable of communicating with one another, snared within the matter that was theirs to control. And so, out of the endless void was created a race of guardians whose appointed task was to protect and defend the integrity of the four sacred elements. They were given powers, the better to fulfill their responsibilities; they were given strength and cunning and longevity to safeguard the treasures surrendered to their stewardship. To them alone would the elements respond.

"These guardians were—and are—the *Pyr*."

Melissa stood back and turned to look at the horizon. Her heart leapt at the sight of Rafferty in his dragon form, flying toward her. His wings beat lazily, his opal scales glinting in the light of the setting sun. He was magnificent, powerful, and beautiful, like a jeweled treasure come to life.

And he was her mate.

"God, the camera loves this guy," Doug breathed, and Melissa fought a smile. The camera wasn't alone in that.

Rafferty turned with easy grace, then spiraled down to land elegantly beside Melissa. He flapped his wings; he coiled his tail; he looked into the camera with those glinting eyes; and he exhaled a small stream of dragonfire.

The Covenant, Erik's new decree and part of the compromise with Melissa, insisted that Rafferty could reveal himself only in dragon form, and he could not speak to humans while in that form.

Melissa turned to the camera again. "The *Pyr*, ancient dragons, reveal themselves with a message for our kind. As guardians of the earth, they count humans among the earth's treasures that they are committed to protecting. But we have put the earth in peril, just as we once imperiled the *Pyr*. We need to change our ways, to help defend the gift of this earth instead of destroying it. Come with me as we visit the elements, each in its turn. Come with me to learn how we can join forces with the *Pyr* and make our world a better place."

Melissa turned to Rafferty. He reared back, arching his neck and displaying the scaled beauty of his chest. His tail slid across the earth, stirring the dust. He reached out a glittering talon to Melissa, and she put her hand on his claw. She smiled at the camera with complete confidence, then stepped into his embrace.

He caught her close, roared, then soared into the darkening sky with her in his grasp. Melissa laughed as the wind danced around them, flicking her skirt and running through her hair. She felt alive and powerful as she never had before. She was optimistic in a way she'd never imagined she'd be again.

It was because of Rafferty and the gift he brought to her, the gift of his faith in the future. They soared into the sky together, and she saw stars appear far overhead.

"Cut!" Doug said in her ear, and she could imagine his nod of satisfaction. "Now *that's* television."

For the moment, Melissa didn't care. She was with Rafferty, facing a future she'd never dared to dream about, and that was all that mattered.

She had a future to believe in, all over again.

A future with Rafferty.

She couldn't imagine a better one.

Can't get enough of dragons?
Take a peek at the first book in
Deborah Cooke's new series about
the next generation of the *Pyr*

The Dragon Diaries: Flying Blind

Coming in trade paperback from
New American Library in June 2011.

Thursday April 4, 2024—Chicago

There was a guy in my bedroom.

It was six in the morning and I didn't know him.

I'm not much of a morning person, but that woke me up fast. I sat up and stared, my back pressed against the wall, sure my eyes had to be deceiving me. No matter how much I blinked, though, he was still there.

He seemed to think my reaction was funny.

He had dark hair and dark eyes, and he wasn't wearing a shirt. Just jeans—and he had one heck of a six-pack. His arms were folded across his chest and a smile tugged at the corner of his mouth.

But he seemed insubstantial. I could see through him, right to the crowded bulletin board behind him.

Was he real?

I was going to try asking him but he abruptly faded, faded and disappeared right before my eyes.

As if he'd just been an illusion. I jumped from the bed, then reached into that corner. My fingers passed through a chill, one cold enough to give me goose bumps. Then my hand touched a pushpin holding a wad of drawings, and everything was perfectly normal.

Except for the hair standing up on the back of my neck.

I took a deep breath and looked around. My room was the pit it usually is. There were some snuffed candles on my desk and bookshelves, a whiff of incense lingering in the air, and the usual mess of discarded sweaters and books all over the floor.

No sign of that guy. If I hadn't seen him, if I'd woken up two minutes later, I wouldn't have thought anything was wrong at all.

I shuddered one last time and headed for the shower. Halfway there, I wondered, Had Meagan's plan worked?

The visioning session had been my best friend's idea. Her mom calls herself a holistic therapist, which makes my mom roll her eyes. I was skeptical too, but didn't have any better ideas. And Meagan, being the best friend ever, had really pulled out all the stops. She'd brought candles and mantras and incense for my room, and even though I'd felt silly, I'd followed her earnest instructions.

When the candles had burned down and she'd left— and my mom had shouted that I should open a window—I'd been pretty sure it hadn't worked. Nothing seemed to have happened.

But now I didn't know what to think. Who had that guy been? Where had he come from? And where had he gone?

Or had I just imagined him? I think if I was going to imagine a guy in my bedroom, it wouldn't be one who thought I was funny when I wasn't trying to be, never mind one that didn't kind of creep me out.

I'd have imagined Nick there.

In fact, I frequently did.

I heard my mom in the kitchen and my dad getting the newspaper, and knew I had to get moving. I did my daily check in the bathroom, but nada. No boobs. No blood.

Four more zits.

At its core, then, the visioning session had failed.

I'm probably not the only fifteen-and-a-half-year-old girl who'd like to get the Puberty Show on the road. Even Meagan had gotten her period last year, which was why she was trying to help. But my best friend didn't know the half of it.

That was because of the Covenant. I couldn't confide in Meagan because I'd had to swear to abide by the Covenant of our kind. I come from a long line of dragon shape shifters—*Pyr*, we call ourselves—and we pledge not to reveal ourselves in dragon form to humans.

That would include Meagan.

And we teenage *Pyr* had to pledge to the Covenant after Nick tried to impress the twin girls living next door, and his dad caught him.

I still thought it was funny that they hadn't been impressed.

I, in contrast, was awed by Nick in dragon form.

The trick is that the dragon business is all theoretical when it comes to me. I'm the daughter of a dragon shapeshifter, so I should also be a dragon shape shifter. Sounds simple, doesn't it? Except it's not happening. Nothing special has happened to me. I can't do it and I don't know why—much less what I can do to hurry things along.

Dragons are by nature patient. That's what my dad

says. He should know, seeing as he is about twelve hundred years old. That's supposed to reassure me, but it doesn't.

Because dragons are also passionate and inclined to anger. I know that from spending my life around all those dragon shape shifters who are my extended family. And the fact that my dragon abilities were AWOL—despite my patience—was seriously pissing me off.

The *Pyr* are all guys—men and their sons—except for me. The story is that there's only one female dragon at a time, that she's the Wyvern and has special powers.

Yours truly—I'm supposed to be the Wyvern.

The issue with there only being one female dragon shape shifter at a time is that the last one died before I was born. And it's not like anyone has her diary. Zero references for me. Zero advice.

Zero anything.

Just an expectation from my family and friends that I'll become the font of all dragonesque knowledge and lead the next generation to wherever the heck we're going.

Sooner would be better.

No pressure, right?

My dad says that I was a prodigy, that I was already showing special powers before I could walk. Then I started to talk and all the Wyvern goodness went away. *Poof.* Instead of being special and a prodigy, I was just a normal kid.

It's been fourteen years, and I'm still waiting for the good stuff to come back.

No sign of it yet.

Some incremental progress would be encouraging. It's one thing to be a disappointment to everyone you care about, and quite another to just sit back and accept that inadequacy. In fact, I was starting to think that those dragons who believed I wasn't really the Wyvern might have it right.

Thus Meagan's session.

An act of desperation.

Because the one thing I did know was that the other dragon teenagers like Nick had come into their powers with puberty. Their voices cracked and bingo, they were shifting shape like old pros. So, being a late bloomer has bigger repercussions for me. Meagan thought we were doing the ritual for my period to start. She didn't need to know I was after a little bit more than that.

Instead I got a guy mocking me in my own bedroom at the crack of dawn.

Like I said, it wasn't the best way to start the day.

The dissolving guy was at my school.

Still shirtless.

Still mightily amused by me.

He was leaning against the brick wall, away from groups of other kids, gaze locked on me as I walked up to the school. I could still almost see through him. I felt a blush rising from my toes. Would he talk to me here? Would he tell me what the deal was?

What exactly would be the best opening question to get him talking?

Meagan caught my shoulder and I jumped. "Well?" She pushed her new glasses up her nose, almost bouncing in excitement. "Did it work?"

I glanced over at the smug, half-naked dude. "Who is that? Do you know?"

"Who? Mark Smith?" Meagan rolled her eyes. "Be serious, Zoë."

"No, the other guy. The one leaning on the wall."

She gave me a stern look. "There is no other guy, Zoë." She nudged me. "Come on, tell me. Any *results*?"

"Nothing."

The guy waved at me, smirked for a minute, then sauntered away. He had to be freezing without a shirt on. It was even starting to snow lightly. I watched Meagan follow my gaze, scanning the school yard.

She couldn't see him.

Neither apparently could anyone else.

Bonus. I was delusional as well as a failure and a disappointment. I'd lost my powers at the ripe age of two and, some fourteen years later, was losing my mind.

"Nothing?" She wrinkled her nose. "No change?"

"None."

She exhaled heavily and fell into step beside me. "Not even a cramp?"

"New pimples. Does that count?"

"It could." Meagan bumped my arm and whispered, "Did you have any dreams, at least?"

It was on the tip of my tongue. I wanted to tell her about the guy, and I would have, if she hadn't been unable to see him. When you're going crazy, I think it's better to keep the news to yourself for as long as possible.

"Nope." I shrugged and smiled.

I felt like seven kinds of a rat for lying to my best friend.

"I really thought it would work," Meagan said, so disappointed that the whole session might have been for her benefit. "Maybe we should try again."

I could do without more strangers showing up in my bedroom while I was asleep. "Maybe it just takes time." I smiled. "See you in gym?"

Meagan groaned. "Highlight of my day." She rummaged in her backpack and nearly spilled textbooks all over the floor. "Hey, draw me a dragon on my new notebook?"

Now she was trying to cheer *me* up. "Sure. Any preferences?"

"Whatever you want. Surprise me."

I took the book and tucked it in with mine. "Don't scare them with your brilliance in math class."

Meagan laughed, flashing a mouthful of hardware. She was good at math. Truly genius. Meagan's destiny was in the realm of the brainiacs.

Mine? Apparently in the land of liars and losers.

I was thinking that my day couldn't get any worse.

About the Author

Deborah Cooke has always been fascinated by dragons, although she has never understood why they have to be the bad guys. She has an honors degree in history with a focus on medieval studies, and is an avid reader of medieval vernacular literature, fairy tales, and fantasy novels. Since 1992, Deborah has written more than thirty romance novels under the names Claire Cross and Claire Delacroix.

Deborah makes her home in Canada with her husband. When she isn't writing, she can be found knitting, sewing, or hunting for vintage patterns. To learn more about the Dragonfire series and Deborah, please visit her Web site at www.deborahcooke.com and her blog, Alive & Knitting, at www.delacroix.net/blog.

WHISPER KISS
A Dragonfire Novel

by DEBORAH COOKE

The national bestselling Dragonfire series
continues to heat up...

For millennia, the shape-shifting dragon warriors known as the
Pyr have commanded the four elements and guarded the earth's
treasures. But now the final reckoning between the Pyr and the
dreaded Slayers is about to begin...

Niall Talbot has volunteered to hunt down and destroy all the
remaining shadow dragons before they can wreak more havoc.
But fate has placed him in the hands of Rox, an unconventional
tattoo artist who doesn't even flinch when a shape-shifting
dragon warrior suddenly appears on her doorstep. And as a
woman who follows her heart in matters of passion, she makes
the perfect mate for a firestorm with Niall...

Available wherever books are sold or
at penguin.com

S0181

WINTER KISS
A Dragonfire Novel

by DEBORAH COOKE

The mysterious Dragon's Blood Elixir gives immortality to Magnus, the Pyr's greatest enemy, and his minions—so it must be destroyed. Outcast from the Pyr because of his own dangerous impulses, Delaney will do anything to vanquish Magnus—and vows to complete a mission which will either redeem him or end his suffering.

But his plans don't take into account his sudden firestorm— or the hot-tempered Ginger Sinclair. The firestorm reforms Delaney closer to his old self. And when Ginger learns about Delaney's scheme, she cannot resist a strong man with a noble agenda.

Available wherever books are sold or
at penguin.com

S0182

KISS OF FATE
A Dragonfire Novel

by DEBORAH COOKE

Haunted by dreams of a lover who takes the form of a dragon,
Eileen Grosvenor searches for the truth. She never expects to
find a real dragon shape shifter, let alone one who awakens her
passion and ignites memories of a forgotten past.

Erik Sorensson is focused on leading the Pyr against the Slayers
when a powerful ancient relic reveals itself. Erik tries to retrieve
it from Eileen's possession—and is shocked by an incredible
passion. Her presence touches him in unexpected ways,
reminding him of mistakes he's determined not to make again,
and Erik is forced to make a choice—duty or love.

<u>Also available in the series</u>
Kiss of Fire
Kiss of Fury

Available wherever books are sold or
at penguin.com